The Saxon Seal

Tony Diamond

Published 27th December 2017
ISBN: 9781976743757

Acknowledgements-
Thanks to- Pauline the Wauleen, Katie, Stuart, Samuel, James, Amy & Josh, All The Family, Alan, Andrea, Bob, Brian, Carol, Charles, Colin, Dave, Dave, Dave, Euan, Eva, Jan, Janet, Julia, Judith, JJ, Jeremy, Lowel, Marie, Michael, Mick, Nigel, Pete A, Peter S, Pete W, Daisy and the Continentals.
A very special thank you to Gina, Patrick, and Ned, for garret & goodness.

Book Three- Consolation

Lincoln On The Train
Addressing Gettysburg
Lucifer And Rhode
What Is Truth
Banking The Loot
Gold In The Ground
Birdy Breaks
Seyton Calls
Birdy At The Grave
The Moose
Postscript

Contents

Book One- The First Day

Sleepin' In Time
The Moose
Lou and Piggie
The Saxon Seal
A Letter Despatched
Arnold Eats A Muffin
Birdy's Birthday
Babies Breath- Born In A Field
Babies Breath- A Queen's Confinement
Earthly Powers
The Soilman Wakes
The Stoneyard

Book Two- Edification

Maggie's End
Pegleg Joe
Snake
The Shack
Power Of The Dog
Arnold Reports
A Man On A Boat
Finding Jesus
Breakfast Enjoyed
After The Battle
To Egypt Farm
A Notice To All Citizens
Bloody Ground
The Fields Of The Dead
Business Is Business
A Correspondence
Coins And Biscuits

BOOK ONE
THE FIRST DAY

SLEEPIN' IN TIME

The Town of Gettysburg was sleepin' in time. Elsewhere, various persons also was sleepin' in different places and at different times of the day on this first of July 1863. Mrs Robinson, a sad widow, was sleepin' in a house in Ontario, Canada. She would rise soon, in about twenty minutes or so, at six in the morning. Grievin' for her dead husband and her absent child, her dreams burst out in a strange bittersweet picture, much like to a play. Right now, she was sleepin'.

Queen Victoria, much exercised with being in the right place at all times, was in a fine bed in her Palace at Osborne, on the British Isle of Wight. She thought that she was asleep in bed, it being fairly late, or early, o' the clock. She was dreaming that she was awake. This was confusing for her. In her dream she stared at the clock. She could not tell the time, and she could not command the clock. In consequence she would be tired and exhausted when she awoke, or dreamed that she had awakened, the time of day or night being utterly irrelevant to the reality. Most of the time, time is meaningless to her. Except for the fact that time crushes her into the ground. Albert is dead and in the ground. His grave gapes for her, and her burial is only a matter of time.

Birdy, a crippled darky slave makin' his run to freedom with some others, sleeps bountifully on the ground in morning sunlight under a tattered bush providin' no cover; But The Most High God bathes Birdy in light and peaceful holiness and Divine Protection, so he's okay. If'n he could point at a map, he might know that he's in the State of Virginia, not many spits away from Harpers Ferry. But it doesn't matter where or when he is. "Where" don't mean much at all until he and his friends all get to Canada, makin' their run. "When" means even less to him than his friends, essentially four in number, because Birdy is here and now, aloof from all "whens". Curiously, he is removed from time, and so are those with him. Even the angry foragin' parties of Rebel (Confederate) Cavalry could and did pass within inches of Birdy and his associates, and they couldn't even see him, then or later in time, or in any of the future time to be which is arrivin' at a precise rate of sixty seconds to the minute, jes' so far as they're concerned. To Birdy, it don't make no nevermind. He sleeps the sleep of nourishment and love, in the light of The Lord, and cain't nuthin' touch him, nohow.

Abraham Lincoln, President of these yere United States of America, had nodded off at dawn in his armchair. His head was bowed as if in sorrow but actually he was dreamin' about the time he taigled with Sally Perkins at the cornroast, wheresomever, whensomever. Oh yes, that was a fine day, a fine day.
Now, like Birdy and Queen Victoria and Mrs Robinson, he sleeps. Shallow of breath and sallow of complexion, his limited rest is nonetheless fufillin' and enrichin'. Honest Abe never did snore, and he ain't gonna start now.

Elsewhere, four or five Armies (some Reb, some Union), all in all some nearly one hundred thousand men, were ridin' or marchin' or musterin', none of them sleepin'- all of 'em aimed and conglomerated toward a town, jes' an ordinary, outta-the-way town that WAS sleepin', in Pennsylvania USA. It was called Gettysburg.

THE MOOSE
July 1st 1863

Gettysburg was just a town like any other.
Well, up to a point.
That point is defined in change.
Change is the only evidence of life.
God is alive, change is afoot.
Gettysburg hadn't had a big, big, change for a while.
In fact, for a good long spell.
But when God came flamin' thru the clouds all full of smoke and fire and thunder and lightnin', He pointed downward at the town and flashed a huge deposit of spiritual resonance into and onto and above and all over the town, reverberatin' even unto the umpteenth generation.
Gettysburg got changed right smart and instantaneous, in an instant, in the blink of an eye. A short work did the Lord make upon the land, and the earth, and the soil.
Change hit Gettysburg from the inside; and lo, it was gaspin' out change with every fevered breath.
The date, time, and provenance of this Divine doin's is largely and mostly irrelevant to the point, which is that afterwards, Gettysburg was not just a town in Pennsylvania.
Previous, it was jes' a town.
Now, it's a confluence of the waters, all commingled to change in man, woman, and beast, mainly 'cause lots of 'em aren't gonna be alive in the mornin'.
Already, on this day of days, God has infected and infested just about everybody alive and dead in His mysterious way, and now he personally spirits Himself into the mind and heart and thoughts of many in Gettysburg.
He also sends His dreams, at one and the same time, to a worried lady tossin' and turnin' some distance off of this most significant town, far away up in Canada.

Not only are His thoughts higher than hers, they ARE hers, insofar as He determines.
Gettysburg is gonna hit everybody harder than a steam train when the whistle turns into a scream and Mrs Robinson, is standin' on that track, right this sleepin' second-in time.
God flavours her dreams.
Gettysburg flavours her dreams.
Gettysburg screams gently up from the ground on this day of days, and the battle, due to commence ere long, hasn't even really got under way as yet.
It is the beginnin'.
Mrs Robinson was sleepin'.
She was on her own, and had been for some time.
Time, at such times, is pretty much intangible.
It don't seem to matter much.
Time just flys right on by.
Since bein' left alone, dear George her husband gone to the grave with the cancer, and her boy Wilfred gone south into America to New York State to fight in the big war down there, she would sleep, as now, when she could.
It was her only time of peaceful rest.
In dreams, she prayed, as always, for the safety of her son, Wilfred, which had run off from Canada to join up in the big War down there in America, somewhere, somewhere.
He was but sixteen years old, darling, dearest child.
Her boy.
Her only joy in this life.
Gone, gone to the war, as boys might and will do and is he safe and alive?
Gettysburg flavours her dreams, and Wilfred is amongst the mix.
Unbeknownst in her dreams, she is actually dreaming forward and her dreaming is real and true.
She is not observing things that happened yesterday or last week, or years ago.

No, she is actually seeing things before they happen, in this case by a margin of maybe nine hours or so.
This can only happen in dreams.
Dreamin' can be confusin'.
Dreams can be like that.
So she dreamed, not knowin' that prayers can be answered in dreams.
Oh Dear Lord keep my boy safe.
She dreamed and she saw Wilfred runnin' busy over a bright field, and approved of the fact that he had Daddy's shirt on with the Moose tucked up in his sleeve.
The Moose was a tiny golden casement containing a scripture on parchment.
It was called a metzusah, but Wilfred called it The Moose.
The scripture, George her dead husband had said, is written in Hebrew.
It says this- "Hear, O Israel, the Lord our God is one Lord".
She's pretty certain that George had said it was from the Bible.
George her husband had always said that the Moose would protect them goin' out and comin' in, and she knew it would always keep Wilfred safe no matter what.
She knew that it was so and she was right.
And she could see that he had the Moose, right there.
He had the Moose, she knew.
This was in her dream.
She could see it.
And her boy, well, he was runnin' with a shovel.
Rolling over in her bed, dreaming joyfully, she saw Wilfred runnin' with the shovel and commencin' to diggin' a trench by a railway line in bright sunshine.
He was with another boy with a soft felt hat and they both had shovels and they were diggin' a hole in the ground for a latrine, a trench six foot long and six foot wide and would presently be about six foot deep.

One boy laughed to the other.
Amazin' how like to a grave is a shithole.
Wilfred moved away from the trench, pausin' fer' breath. He moved over to and leaned upon a great rock of three stones, twisting up out of the drygulch earth like a giant tooth.
Far away in her dreamin' gunfire and cannonfire sounded, and Wilfred leaned into the big giant's stones tooth to tell his mama that he was just Jim Dandy and safe and well and okay.
The Moose was tucked up here into his sleeve, safe and well, and so was he.
Wilfred smiled at his mother, in just that way he and he alone had, which comforted her greatly, to know he was safe and well and not killed in the war.
As he bent forward into the silence of the trio of big stone teeth, a bird squawked alarmingly under the lowering clouds.
Wilfred heard it and looked up at the sky.
The other boy who was with him diggin' the latrine trench, comin' up behind, took and hit Wilfred over the top and back of the head with a shovel.
All of Wilfred's colours turned to grey, and he fell before the big stone onto the drygulch earth.
The shovel hit him with a "whump" on the top and back of the head and he lost the light in about one second in real time, it was that fast.
Several hundred miles to the northernward and away up in Canada, Mrs Robinson saw it all most clearly. She saw it. In dreamin'.
Mrs Robinson didn't feel the pain of the shovel hittin' him like that on the top and back of the head, but she did wonder why the boy might do such a thing?
The other boy wrestled briefly with Wilfred's pockets but found nothin'.
He then remembered what Wilfred had said and so he rummaged at the sleeve of Wilfred's shirt.

He found the tiny folded pocket and drew forth a thin
sliver of gold and held it up to the light.
Mrs Robinson observed accurately in her dream that
it was the Moose.
The other boy moved back over to the trench away
from the big giant tooth.
He looked every which way hither and yon.
Nobody could see nothin'.
Wilfred was laid out cold on the ground, likely dead.
The boy commenced to thinkin' that when he threw
Wilfred down into the hole and covered him up,
nobody was going to know where the body was.
A shithole is most serviceable for a grave, at need.
Clasping the little sliver of gold in his hand, he
glanced back at Wilfred lying on the ground.
It was providin' most satisfactory cover between just
the two of them.
And it would flummox anybody else who might come
lookin' for them out here diggin' a latrine as
directed.
Anybody else would see nothin'.
In one more minute he would have Wilfred dead and
buried safe in the ground and anybody else could go
and whistle.
The gold thing was his and that's what he done it for
and nobody could stop him now and it was his.
Something, he knew not what, caused him to hesitate.
For one second of time, he paused.
He noticed his hesitation enough ter' remark on it to
himself and fleetingly ponder the likely cause.
Might it be the tiny gold thing?
He wondered for a brief second as to what the hell it
actually was or might be, but now it was his anyway.
Will had called it his Moose, more fool him.
It WAS gold!
Prob'ly worth of up'ards of a thousand dollars!
That's what he done it for and what blame fool
wouldn't have done it, given half a chance?
He looked around and about.

Nobody here, the coast is clear.
Wilfred was on the ground behind him yonder not far off and there was maybe twenty or so foot to drag him over by the feet and legs and throw him down into the trench.
The boy looked down into the trench and reckoned that it was commodious enough deep as it was to throw Wilfred into once he dragged him over.
The Army would be short one third of a shithole but he didn't reckon that anybody would notice, especially with all them shots and bangs and cannonfire getting' pretty hot not too far off.
By the time he had flung Wifred down into the hole, in just about a few seconds of time more, and shovelled some soil over him, time itself would soon put that shortage right.
Warn't nobody this side of Judgement Day gonna go pokin' into a shithole fer' a grave.
Wilfred was a stupid bastard to fool around like that.
God only knows what he was thinkin' hangin' onto a goddamned bit of gold like that?
Heh, heh.
He dug the pit and now he's gonna go right into it!
He's the first squit in the shithole!
What in the name of God did he think he was doin?
Damned if I know!
His head come up as he heard a shell comin' in fast and he looked up at the whinin' noise, toward what he thought was the sound of a howitzer or somesuch and he couldn't see a thing.
Unbeknownst to anybody in general it was in fact a shell bomb from a flung mortar and it landed five foot away from him and went off as such weapons of destructive power can and will do when projected forcefully.

14

The explosion sorta bouncin' off the hardpacked ground burst fully onto more or less all of him and blew his body all to flinders except for his legs and arms with one hand still graspin' onto and upon the little sliver of gold.

His fingers and his hand closed on the gold thing, hard pressed into his palm, even as all of the physical human mechanism of lines or nerves of communication stopped once and fer' all now and forever, severed off with the explosion.

His whole arm intact and complete from the shoulder right on down to his tight graspin' hand and fist and white-knuckled fingers didn't bleed as the cut away limb spun off.

It flew neatly over and down into the hole cut for a latrine and right into it and outta sight, some soil comin' after.

The remaining pieces of his body was blown all to flinders.

Gouts and gouts of bloody bones and bits flipped down and on top of and alongside the rest of him.

As much of him as was left landed in the trench, neat as a newdug grave, him filleted like a wellcut horse steak on a butchers slab.

There was some residue of blood, but not too much to speak of, and it would be erased by the rain fairly quickly.

All his colours turned to nothin' in the blink of an eye.

Meanwhile, almost near and alongside, and silent as the grave, Wilfred lay unmolested by the explosion but looked dead.

In fact this was not so.

He was not injured in the least by the exploding flung mortar bomb behind the three stones tooth. Rather he was protected by it to some extent and degree, but he lay very quietly and open to the sunshine on the drygulch earth of Gettysburg.

Somewhere, a bird was singin' real nice, in spite of the growin' thunder of the guns.
Mrs Robinson, observin' dreamfully, watched with interest as clouds overshadowed the sky.
She pulled the blankets up and dreamed again of Wilfred when he was a small child and a baby boy in earlier and happier days.
Her dreamin' moved on consolably, as dreams do and will.
Outside her house, in the Ontario warm breath, the little stream continued to flow over the stonecold rocks.
Morning commenced to breakin' away up off Georgian Bay, up and beyond Owen Sound where the boats come in off the Great Lakes all the way down from Illinois.
She slept.
Below the eaves of her home, the wind moaned just a bit, it not bein' durin' a cold spell that particular summer, and surely not on this first day of July.

Five or six or so hundred mile or more due south and west of where she lay sleepin' and dreamin', the Battle of Gettysburg had now fundamentally broke out, or was commencin' to break out and start, anyways, in earnest.
It would not be fer' some hours as yet before Wilfred would get his orders, but the battle had begun.
As yet, like to Mrs Robinson's dreamin' it was all most confusin' and unsure of provenance.
Dreamin' can be confusin'.
Time is confusin'.
Battle is confusin'.
Bullets were flyin' and men were dyin' goin to the grave.
Time is relative in these situations.
Time unfolds unlike any clock in a parlour.

Mrs Robinson looked out from her dream onto her back garden, sunshine and shadow mingled with snow, even on a hot July mornin'.
Such is the way in dreams.
She seemed to remember that Wilfred liked to eat Johnnycake, with butter on it and sugar.
He was such a beautiful child, back then, when they were all so happy, and before her poor husband went to the grave, long gone in time.
She slept fitfully, discontinuing all visions and dreams of anything includin' Wilfred and the Moose and the other peculiar boy which had hit him on the top and back of the head with a shovel.
She rolled over in sleep and remembered no more and forgot all of it several hours before it happened to her child and she murmured a prayer as always and did not dream any more.
Meantime, time is rollin' onward, as it does and will. She did not dream again in that dream, and did not remember dreamin', for such is the way with sleep.
Such is the spirit of dreams.
Such is time, and the times in which we live.
The day had begun.

LOU AND PIGGY

ENGLAND
Osborne House
1st July 1863

Tormented with grief, Queen Victoria was now exploring the bodily movements of the domestic chicken as she stomped the corridors.
Three hours of time had passed since she woke up from her regular nightmare.
Darling Albert died again, yes, died again, for the thousandth time, just as he did every morning as she fought her way up from sleep.
Albert had choked and coughed out his final breath with an elongated burp.
He had never previously performed that action in her presence.
She was quite sure of the fact.
It had come as something of a shock.
Unheralded, unprecedented!
Now he did it all the time.
The nightmare is constant.
He's going, going, gone.
But he burped as he died.
It was an eructation, beyond question.
Frankly, she would not have thought him capable of such an indiscretion.
However, that very first lapse into improper behaviour was his final pronouncement, and no mistake.
No goodbye, no fare thee well, no woe is me, no lack-a-day, no sad adieu, just an ugly burp that went on and on.
Most distressing!
The nightmare is constant.
It never stops.
The nightmare, like the burp, goes on and on.
Every night, every day.

But now there was a new, however brief sequence, playing out at the far side of her minds eye as Albert gargled his way to the grave; yes, just as he burped, and this was a new development.
Somehow, in her nightmare, she now looked down at her hands and she was holding an old German Bible, a Saxon Seal.
And she threw it out of the window.
And there was a chicken clucking out the name of Jesus.
A chicken, forsooth!
Cluck cluck cluck.
Jesa, Jesa, Jesa.
And she was awake.
No chicken.
No old German Bible.
No Albert.
Now, raging with loss, she shall ponder the quirks and imperious cluckings of that new and unexpected chicken.
She darts her head to and fro, her body swaying, her gait mechanical and protracted.
Thus and thus, methinks, doth the chicken proceed.
She treads where she will, here in the palace of the contented barnyard fowl; cluck cluck cluck, Jesa, Jesa, Jesa, (didn't the chicken say that?)
Her numerous attendants observe her mania and say nothing.
For how shall one address Her Gracious Majesty, when she is raving mad, insane as a demented beggar wailing in Bethlehem Hospital?
Nobody is going to poke her with a sharp stick, nor is such intervention needful- she shall scream her sorrows to the skies as she so chooses, and no-one is amused, least of all Her Majesty.
Cluck, cluck, cluck.
Jesa, Jesa, Jesa.
Look on my works, ye mighty, and despair!

On other days, she had wept helplessly, and buried her face in a large silken rag, torn across.
On this day, she is stomping indignantly!
To her immediate servants and Doctors, her mood and moves are impossible and unpredictable.
Time in the palace yaws, a rudderless ship in a hurricane.
Time will not be commanded.
Nor will she.
Cluck cluck cluck.
Now she is wriggling about, like Caliban in a hot sweat.
Or a chicken in a barnyard.
HER barnyard!
Her mental attitudes swing wildly.
Here, bereft and disconsolate.
There, fiery and angry.
And now, demanding!
Well?
Well?
The Queen was demanding an answer!
Will the Baroness die today?
Hmmmph!
Well?
Yes or no?
The Royal Surgeons hovered, lips pressed shut.
How does one address the matter?
The Baroness might die today, might well die today.
Her beloved Lou was unwell, seriously unwell!
She might, heavens preserve us, expire!
The possibility was clear, although unspoken.
Naturally, nobody would dare to open their mouths to voice such a prospect, so of course the possibility was unspoken.
Nobody was going to speak, not if you had half a brain!
Least said, soonest mended!
Keep a stiff upper lip!
The better part of valour is discretion!

Now the doctors were cornered.
Every avenue to avoid a meaningful reply had been traversed, every stratagem employed. Caution dictated more caution, and more caution yet again. However, Her Majesty was scattering all of these cautions to the four winds, like ninepins tumbling.
Now, she wanted a firm voice.
No caution.
No more caution.
No shilly-shallying.
No stiff upper lips.
No CASUISTRY!
Such nonsense was for the unlearned, the unwise, and certainly not for HER!
And your opinions, learned Doctors? Dr Blake? Dr Bates?
The lady issuing commands was looking for total and immediate obedience.
And yet, they swithered.
Both Doctors were tightlipped and, yes, cautious, and permitted only empty silences to fill these emphatic enquiries, each glancing askance at the other- oh that this present cup might pass me by?
Now, Victoria raised her chin, pushed out her lower lip, and gave a tiny shake of her imperious mouth- a clear signal that enough was enough; she wanted a straight answer.
Sufficient unto the moment is the stupidity and the dithering thereof.
She speaks.
Doctor Bates? Will the Baroness die today? Yes or no?
She is gravely ill, Ma'am.
The reply was tremulous and fraught with danger. Even as he spoke, the Court Physician saw the royal lip shoot out even further, and the tiny shake of the mouth intensified.
Yes or no?

Doctor Bates felt the cliff's edge behind him, and decided that he might as well be hung for a sheep as a lamb.
Any more testing of the wind or prevarication would result, he knew, in his dismissal from this lofty position, here on the Isle of Wight.
So he took his future firmly into his hands and spoke up with sound confidence, even if it was pretence.
No, Ma'm. I pray, as we all do, for her sure recovery.
But she is quite unwell.
The Royal mouth twitched, once.
Doctor Bates saw it, and hastened to make good any appearance of further hesitation.
However, I am convinced that she will prevail. The continued health of the Baroness is now in the hands of The Lord. My hope is in Him, Ma'am. No. She will not die today.
Victoria's countenance brightened.
Thank you, Doctor.
We are persuaded that your judgement is correct.
Thank you.
Cluck, cluck, cluck.
Aaawwwkkk!
We shall see Baroness Lehzen at once.
Doctor Bates medically forbidding nature screamed out "no" to him; no, no, no!
The Royal "we" must in no circumstances go near the bedside of a dying woman!
It might mean Death!
But he was too old a hand to know that if he objected, he would be contradicting his earlier statement, the one that had got him back from the brink.
Whilst discretion was one thing, professional suicide was quite another.
Enough, he thought.
Least said, soonest mended.
Hold your hour and have another.

Queen Victoria lifted her chin, faced leftward, and cleared her throat abruptly, thus signalling her determination to proceed unaccompanied.
Cluck, cluck, cluck!
Jesa, Jesa, Jesa!
Thus doth the chicken proceed!
Her ladies stepped together behind her, and lowered their heads in perfect unison, rooted to the spot.
Doctor Bates and Doctor Blake froze themselves into the background, and were at once, to all intent and purpose, invisible.
They were getting to be quite good at this; they were getting lots of practice.
Victoria Regina snapped her chin back to centrality, the chicken clucking alarmingly.
We're off, her body language announced.
She hunched her regal shoulders and leaned forward and down.
Awk, awk, awk!
Jesa, Jesa, Jesa.
Thus doth the chicken proceed, practised in her movements.
Queen Victoria set off on the brisk walking that occupied so many hours of her day.
But the time….
The time…..
Fiddlesticks!
Thus doth the chicken proceed.
Observe, oh ye of little faith, of the majestic movements of this most delightful fowl, oh ho, ho, ho.
She marched on, clucking and shrieking "Jesa" aloud, and she stifled the overwhelming impulse to squawk.
On she marched, head clucking, feet bobbing.
This progress would take her toward the extremity of Osborne House, where her darling nurse, Baroness Louise Lehzen of Hanover, lay in seclusion.
Now she was stomping, in a fine fury.

The imperious chicken progressed down the corridors, head clicking to and fro in short jerks, ordering all and sundry from her path. Out of Our way!
Begone!
Go to the depths of wherever you want, go!
Just so long as the very shadows do not encroach.
Cluck, cluck, cluck.
Jesa, Jesa, Jesa.
A few minutes forced march brought her to The Freihaus, the private den of her childhood nurse. Here, on entering, the Royal chicken evaporated into forgetfulness.
The room was dim and bare; deliberately so. Baroness Louise Lehzen, in her seventies, hated (and had long hated) ostentation and the trappings of wealth.
In fact, there were only three items of furniture to be seen; the simple bed in which the beloved darling, Lou, reclined, propped up by many pillows; a lone chair hard beside, and a convenient table upon which rested a large Lutheran Bible, open to reveal the Teutonic text.
No clock.
Time is silent.
But not Lou.
There were no tearful and heartrending formalities exchanged.
The Queen bobbed a courtesy and the Baroness snorted at her and pointed a rude and accusing finger.
She sat up abruptly.
Huh!
Drina!
Huh!
Now you are here!
Aha!
Little Drina.
You are here.

Drina, sit here by me.
Shut it!
Do not speak.
You are well, I can see.
Sit down.
I knew you would not leave me for very long. Come, Little Piggie, sit down at once, here, close to me.
Sit.
Sit.
Shut it, Drina.
The Queen did as she was told.
Only her "Lou" could speak to her like this.
Only Lou called her Drina, or Little Piggie, and told her to shut it, and ordered her about, and totally monopolized every conversation.
But the Baroness was all the more beloved for that.
Now, Little Drina, my Piggie, you must listen to me.
Victoria bobbed her head, and pursed her lips, and wanted to weep a little, but she knew that her nurse would scold her, which she promptly did anyway, even though no crying ensued.
Enough. Shut it little Drina! No tears. Enough. Now listen to me.
Victoria had not said a single word, but the commands coming from her dearest servant, bedridden or not, had to be obeyed.
Besides, Baroness Lehzen had not the slightest intention of dying, even if this was her deathbed.
Death would have to jolly well take up a proper place in the queue.
Nothing was going to cause moderation of her opinions, Death included.
And no other agency, human or divine, might sway her.
Certainly not mortality of any kind!
Speak she would, speak she must, and death was unimportant.
Drina must shut up and listen.
Little Piggie had to be told!

Little Piggie would be told!
She must open her ears and listen.
Speech from her royal lips was needless.
No, Piggie must not speak.
Shut it, Drina, and listen to me, while I speak!
And of course Baroness Lehzen of Hanover was dramatically more than capable of discharging both sides of this conversation, as with all the conversations they had enjoyed during the forty-four years of little Drina's life.
Lou would dogmatically outline her purpose and just as dogmatically declaim any of little Drina's objections before they were uttered.
As a result, they never needed to be uttered, and this was most satisfactory to both parties involved.
Victoria confined herself, as always, to bobbing her head in Royal acquiescence.
This was happiness.
Lou knew.
And Lou was always right.
Now, commencing her tirade, Lou would repeat her motto.
This signalled the fact that she must not be interrupted, not that she ever had been, or would be, this side of the grave.
We are beggars!
Little Drina!
Do you know who said that?
Do you?
Of course you do.
We are beggars!
Queen Victoria, ruler of the wealthiest nation on Earth, bobbed her head in agreement.
Of course she knew, but she also knew that the question was rhetorical.
We are beggars, she concurred miserably.
We are beggars.
Yes, Drina! Before God, we are nothing but dirt and filth and ordure! We are the scum of the world!

Yes, We are, thought the Queen.
Scum and dirt and filth and ordure.
She wondered, not for the first time, what ordure might be?
But she was in no doubt that she qualified if Lou said so.
Filth, Piggie!
And now we are brought to this!
Supplication!
Supplication in the Palace!
A helpless cry for mercy!
We kneel before the Throne of the Lamb and we cry out- Mercy! Mercy! Mercy!
Exactly so, thought Piggie.
Mercy, we cry.
Mercy!
Oh, we cry endlessly.
We beg endlessly.
We are beggars.
The fact that she had never in her life cried "mercy" mattered not a jot.
And the fact that she had never begged for anything did not occur to her.
It was the excellent, self-pitying drama of the moment which appealed; and in the world of Queen Victoria, to think was to be.
Everything she had ever wanted need only be voiced to become reality- a good, solid, practical living fact if ever there was one.
The REAL fact was that any and every one of her voiced wishes would become reality in a very short period of time.
Baroness Lehzen burst in on this never to be recognized epiphany.
Now, Piggie, listen to me. Do not speak. Shut it!
Drina! Shut it! And no tears! Be silent! Attend!
Queen Victoria, comforted no end by this onslaught, closed her trembling lips, nodded her head, and leaned forward, greatly relieved.

Lou would not die today.
Doctor Bates was correct.
This invalid was much too opinionated to expire.
Excellent.
Lou raised a finger, pointed skyward.
I must beg of you! I must beg of you!
Lou was now expressing amazement to Drina. That it should come to this? That a lowly, begging Baroness should have to ask a favor of her Queen?
Drina nodded in ecstatic agreement. Shocking, truly shocking. That it should come to this? SHE must beg of ME? Astonishing!
Clearly, Lou had a request. Good! Now, Drina would be permitted to actually do something for her darling Lou! Such wonderful kindness! So unexpected! Wonder of wonders!
And now, I must confess my miserable heart.
The penitent slumped forward; the suitably surprised confessor brightened.
Baroness Louise grimaced impatiently.
I lie here before God and I must humble these bones and confess. Hmmmph! I confess to you!
To you only, my little Piggie! To you alone! I confess! Hmmmph!
Only a good child, only a Queen, only my sweet beloved Drina may listen to this litany of wickedness and wrongdoing. Such sin and misery! Oh Lord, according to Thy Word, I beg your mercy and your lovingkindness.
Ah, yes, thought little Drina. Psalm fifty-one. The Psalm of the penitent. Most appropriate. Well done.
The penitent sinner paused for breath, and then continued, reinvigorated.
I have sinned in the sight of God and man. You will help me to atone, my darling. You will do this for me and I will absolve you of all further kindness to me in my life.
Queen Victoria nodded sympathetically.

I will get up from this bed and go, for my Piggie will help her Lou!
I will go naked into the cold byways.
I will accept banishment and disgrace. I will!
I will leave your gates henceforth and wander the muddy roads in hunger and misery until my death; this I deserve! But my heart will sing like a contented bird, for you will do this thing for me!
Yea, though I bow my head at the last beneath the rain and snows of the rocky crevasses, I will absolve my little Drina.
I will absolve her of all, for she has paid all debts!
All debts!
All of my wickedness and sin!
By her sweet and gentle lovingkindness to her only Louise, useless, slothful servant, unmannerly.
Unworthy though that piteous sinner may be, undeserving of her most Royal bounty, Drina will absolve me!
The Monarch of the United Kingdom and Ireland pursed her lips and possessed her soul in patience, excitedly wondering what the wickedness and sin might be.
This was turning out to be a most impressive day.
Humility fostered such exquisite benefits!
The Baroness leaned forward until her chin was nuzzling Victoria's cheek.
Now, little Drina my Piggie. Shut it. Listen to me!
Little Piggie shut it, and listened.

THE SAXON SEAL

Piggie, I am old. Soon, I must die.
Victoria, perfectly on cue, opened her mouth to sob appropriately, thought better of it, and sat back equably.
Shut it, Piggie. I am not dead yet. Now, listen carefully to me.
The Queen leaned forward again.
I am old, as I said. Soon, I will be gathered to the arms of the Good Shepherd.
But I do not regret and you do not mourn, no! Why? Because my salvation is sure!
Piggie nodded at this comfortable doctrine. Yes, salvation is sure.
But I must repent of my sins. I must confess with my mouth and believe in my heart.
I must atone for my sins, as much as I am able.
I now choose to confess to you, my Piggie, my Drina, my darling.
And to whomever else in this vale of tears should I turn?
Huh?
Tell me that?
Piggie nodded sympathetically, knowing better than to say anything at this crucial juncture.
So, my darling, hear me now. We are beggars. We are beggars. Do not speak. Do not interrupt a foul beggar crying out for mercy. Now into thy hands I commit my spirit. Shut it.
The Queen opened one eye quizzically.
This was getting rather closer to the scriptural mark than was called for.
Lou was pious, good; but there were times when she veered alarmingly close to blasphemy in her zeal.
Many years ago, I was young and beautiful. Now I am old and wasted away with the sinfulness of men.

Oh yes, I have been a scoundrel and a wastrel. My only joy has been my service to you, my Piggie. But it was not always so.

I have loved. Yes, I have loved. I wanted, I desired, I was desperate for love, oh, so long ago. There. It is out. My sin is naked before your gaze. I am full with shame, Piggie. I must beg mercy of you. Will you forgive me?

Piggie maintained her silence, trembling with the anticipation of God knows what debaucheries coming her way.

Thank you, thank you, my own Queen! Thank you!

Victoria had not moved a muscle. Such forgiveness, she knew, was best taken for granted, like the air we breathe.

Bad, wicked, foul thing that I am! I never told my love.

He never knew. He did not so much as guess!

Oh, I am the greatest of sinners. Yes, Piggie, I am worse than the evil one. Pity me? Pray for me? I know that you will weep when I am gone.

Here, Victoria gasped appropriately, and seemed to stifle a choking swallow, much like a mournful wail strangled at birth. This was perfection, neither sobbing nor weeping, and yet not quite maintaining silence. Lou was impressed, and did not miss a heartbeat in resuming her soulful outpourings.

He was a young man!

Now it was Victoria's turn to be impressed. A young man? Who'd 'a thought it? Even though the fact had been hinted at and obliquely alluded to some minutes before, the bald statement was devastating.

A young man?

Good heavens!

Would wonders never cease?

Louise had built up a good head of steam in her confessing.

Now, with her compliant audience reacting magnificently to every nuance, she forged onward.

He was a Minister in Wittemburg, in Saxony! And the son of a Minister.
He was serving at the great Castle Church, where dear sweet Brother Luther lies.
Yes, there I saw my man, my only lover in this life.
My darling, my dove, my dear.
I looked at him.
I adored him.
Oh, it was so sinful in me!
Be sure thy sin shall thee find, oh be sure!
His name was Doctor Martin von Leben.
He was extolling the Gospel of Johannes, chapter four, the woman at the well.
I was there with my Gunhilde, who loved me more than her life.
As soon as I saw him, I knew that he would be my only darling.
I knew, with all of my heart.
I was sixteen years old.
My Martin was twenty-three. Yes, he was much older than I.
Piggie, my darling, I completely lost my head.
I would have given myself to him there, in the Church, before God and man, before all the world.
Such is my sinfulness.
But he did not even see me.
After the service, he left the congregation, as is only proper.
I saw him go into a little room at the side.
I ordered Gunhilde to stay at the door, to stop any interlopers or interruptions. She did so.
I went in to my beloved.
He was not there.
A doorway led to another chamber, then a corridor.
There were two doors.
I entered.
There were robes and vestments and a very old, very beautiful carved cabinet.
My darling was nowhere to be seen.

However, on the cabinet there was an engraved book,
a little Testament.
What we call a Seal.
A Saxon Seal.
It had a Cross with pretty flowers, and the initials
"M L" on the top.
Martin von Leben.
I looked at this treasure.
His hands had touched this box.
It contained the pure essence of his very being.
I was in love.
Hopelessly in love.
What could I do?
What was I to do?
There was only one thing to do!
I stole it.
Victoria gulped at the enormity of this disclosure,
truly flabbergasted.
The Baroness did not falter, merely chucking her
chin a bit in weary agreement.
Yes, Piggie.
I know.
I am a thief and a vagabond.
I am a robber and a malefactor.
I have destroyed the lovely commandment of God,
"Thou shalt not steal".
I have sinned before God and in your sight!
But all is delicious in love and war!
I must win him.
I could see no other way.
So I stole the box.
I stole the Saxon Seal.
Off, off I flew.
My Gunhilde met me with joy, as though I were
returned from the grave.
Off, off we went.
My beloved to preach the Word to the miserable, me
to worship him from afar, but soon to return to get
him and hold him fast.

So, there it was.
When I returned to my home, I hid the box very carefully.
I knew how it would be.
I would again attend the church.
I would meet him and be formally introduced, as good Christians will be in all the accounts of love such as ours.
We would stand, talking joyfully of this and that.
Perhaps his servants cultivated roses, or cabbages?
Who knew?
Certainly not I.
I know nothing of such things, Gunhilde all!
But it would be holy, and modest, and magical, this I did know.
He would mention, in the course of casual conversation, that he had lost, misplaced, no longer had, his engraved box, his Seal.
I would at once search for it in the pews with my Gunhilde and very quickly, with God our help, we would find it.
Yes, Gunhilde would find it.
This was sure.
And my darling would be grateful.
How better to reward than at once proposing marriage to me?
Of course! Only God must be praised for this happy outcome, for is it not written, marriages are made in Heaven? Ah. But this was not to be.
As my Gunhilde often said, man does often propose and The Lord does always dispose.
Yes. She was very wise to say so. That is great wisdom. She was very wise.
I was very foolish.
No, my determination, my wickedness, would not prevail.
My stealing would not be blessed by The Lord.
For He is just and righteous.
I am vile and smelling.

When I returned, it was only to find that my Martin
was gone.
Was gone, alas, away!
We visited the church.
Some Minister greeted us.
Not an attractive man.
I could never have liked him.
Huge and round, not delicate fingers, no.
He was wiping the sausage grease from his mouth,
ein hundt!
Oh, a sausage!
He ate a sausage!
My Gunhilde enquired as to my Martin.
No, this great fat butcher said, Martin was gone.
Gone to America to win souls for Christ in that
heathen wilderness so far away.
He was gone.
Am I to accept such a bleak message?
No, I must have more!
This is mine own beloved one we bespeak, huh?
Shut up, Piggie.
Be silent.
Listen to me.
I was not going to take this.
This is not enough.
So I sent Gunhilde to the marketplace.
The marketplace!
There, everything is known, everything is spoken of
among the lower classes.
There are no secrets from such as Gunhilde.
Good girl. Yes. She went at my command, to the
muck and filth. To the lowest dregs.
To the scum of the streets. Yes, she reported back to
me.
She learned all. She told all. May the good God shine
perpetual light upon her sweet soul. But shut it,
Piggie. Do not speak.
The young meister had been sent away.
It was the talk of the town.

It was scandal. Sin in the cloisters. Well, not really
sin. Nothing could be proved.
Anything might have happened.
Best to look not upon thy father's nakedness.
Thou shalt not discover thy brothers skirt!
Something, it was whispered, had gone missing from
the church whilst in his charge.
An engraved box. A great treasure.
No, nothing was known as to what was in the box.
But my darling Martin was held accountable.
And so they sent him away. To America. They sent
him to America.
I went home.
Myself and my Gunhilde looked at what I had stolen,
the Saxon Seal.
It was not too heavy for so small a thing.
It had a clasp in the shape of a pretty flower.
Gunhilde pressed on the beautiful letters "M" and
"L", my Martin Von Leben.
The casing opened with a snap.
Inside was a Bible, very small, very neat, very old.
But it was not the Bible of Martin von Leben.
It was the Bible of Martin Luther.
Piggie, it was the Bible of Martin Luther.
Yes. Signed. In his own hand. Martin Luther.
Fifteen Forty!
Now was my shame revealed to me.
I had stolen Brother Luther's personal Testament.
The very Bible which Martin Luther held in his
hands as he received the Word from The Lord. The
Saxon Seal! This is my great sin, Piggy.
I stole the personal Bible of Martin Luther!
You must help me to atone for that sin.
I must return it to him.
Piggy, please help me?
A clock chimed ten to one in Little Piggie's head.
Botheration, she muttered aside.
Time will NOT be commanded!

A LETTER DESPATCHED

Sir Charles Grey, Private Secretary to the Queen, was thinking three or four steps ahead of the game as he approached Her Majesty's Office.
He had already sent for Arnold.
The sloop was being readied, even before he spoke with the Presence.
Her body language and her absence of discretion would tell him the rest.
And, as so often before, he was correct in every particular.
She was seated at <u>his</u> desk, where Prince Albert had so often managed the mountain of Royal correspondence. So it was a personal letter. Her quill was upright in the inkwell, so, as yet unsigned.
Therefore, he might, very possibly, be given it to read, if fortune served. No need for pesky interceptions, seal-copying, and tomfoolery of the kind.
Her hands clasped before her rigidly- there was work for him to do. He approached.
He advanced to the perfect distance, his quick eye marking the very spot, and made an elegant bow, knowing that her unseen Royal head was bobbing briefly at him.
Sir Charles.
(The Presence always speaks first; her words a plethora of information- this time a flat statement, not a question or assertion. So, she is in a tolerant mood, and she wants something very important. Good.) Ma'am.
His answer echoed hers, a neutral acknowledgement.
A fine day. (She IS in a good mood)
Very fine, Ma'am.
A pause.
(She doesn't know how to put this. She really does need my help. Good.)
You are well?

(So, it's family business. Probably the Baroness. No urgent summons to an impending funeral, not with that bright aspect. King of Prussia?)
Very well, Ma'am.
· That is good. Sir Charles, there is a matter….
Queen Victoria pursed her lips and stopped dead in the water. She had said enough for enough to be said. Sir Charles would have to take it from here. She had arrived at the Rubicon of her moderation. Now it was up to him to pull her out of the swither she got into when she needed something but didn't know how to ask for it.
Asking for help was never her stongest suit.
So he would be bending all of his diplomatic skills into arranging things so that the words he would manufacture must seem to emanate from the severely closed lips of the Presence herself.
He must demonstrate his acutely sensitive, almost psychic abilities.
His anticipation must be unerring.
Like a first-class gundog hearing the flapping wings of a falling pheasant, he was off.
Happily, the Presence was just his size, and he had this business well in hand.
He could swim and fly and dive in this environment.
The ball, so to speak, was directly at his feet.
The phraseology was vital to the success of his endeavours, but he was on good ground of his own choosing now- his future very much in his own hands.
He glanced at her, weighing the conviction in her countenance, and he saw the little girl begging for approval, and hoping that someone other than herself would frame the compliment.
Ma'am, he began with a confident flourish of enquiry, perhaps someone has spoken?.
(A comfortable gambit, risk averse. Someone had always spoken, so he couldn't go far wrong with this line. But Victoria brightened perceptibly. He had hit the mark. Good. And they were off and away!)

Indeed, Sir Charles.
And the gracious compassion for which Your Majesty is known, yearns, ever and always, to benefit those most in need?
Exactly so, Sir Charles. Exactly so. Your perceptions are uncannily accurate.
Ma'am.
This was easy, plain sailing on a calm sea with a following wind and an amenable current.
She was openly approving.
Even better, smiling.
He had not seen her smile quite so fulsomely for many months.
At times, she was very easily handled.
Now for the "frank challenge". Lord, how she loves the "frank challemge".
Ma'am, may I tell my mind? Please do, Sir Charles.
Ma'am, forgive my zeal. I have little skill in speech. My only desire is to serve. I know, here in my heart, that Your Majesty shall yet again give and give of Her very being. Now Your Majesty may have need of a footsoldier to bear your will to the world. I beg to be that footsoldier. I believe that Your Majesty is proceeding in righteousness to bring forth mercy and justice. To quote the scripture- 'the only thing that counts is faith expressing itself in love', and this is so. Let this be the hand that bears the sword of wisdom for my great Queen. I shall expedite this kindness to the uttermost of my being, if Your Majesty will but grant my most fond wish. Command me in all things.
Queen Victoria positively beamed at him.
Sir Charles, how is it that you know Our mind so perfectly?
Ma'am, one need only venture onto the pathways of truth. In doing so, this poor fellow will always find his Sovereign awaiting his arrival patiently. T'is not so very hard, Ma'm.'
Another nod, another smile.

Sir Charles, you please Us. Yes, We are most
heartened with your offer to serve.
But to the business. Pray, Sir Charles, look upon this
communication, drawn up in Our own hand.
So, he would read the letter. Good.

FROM THE HAND OF VICTORIA
TO OUR DEAR FRIEND
PRIME MINISTER OTTO VON BISMARCK
1st July 1863
MY BROTHER IN PIETY,
In Piety, We are beggars.
In Piety We approach.
In Piety We beg..
Please extend your kindness in Piety.
Our Friend would gaze again upon the joy of her
youth- juventutem meum.
We earnestly entreat Our dear brother to speed this
treasure, in earthen vessel, to your Friend.
Our Apostle conveys Our trust, only in Piety.
We are beggars.
From Piety to Piety, in Piety

VICTORIA REGINA

Sir Charles Grey winced inwardly, his mind racing.
Dash it! What on earth was this all about? He faced
his Queen with a knowing smile, all the more
dissembling for the ignorance it concealed.
She beamed at him, her face full of confidence,
inclined her chin briefly, and positively wheeled away
with a spring in her step.
He bowed, but he was full of worries, and his
thoughts were very dark.

ARNOLD EATS A MUFFIN

On the following afternoon, Peter Arnold recited the strange contents of the Queen's letter to two men in a boat anchored near to Portsmouth.

It was a small, but comfortable, sloop; perfect for this urgent meeting. Tea had been served, but remained as yet untouched while Arnold spoke across the buttered muffins.

The Prime Minister, Lord Palmerston, cocked an eye askance at Sir John Mitson, Head of Intelligence.

Hell d'you make of that letter, Jack? asked Palmerston.

Rum, Sir, rum. Lot of piety going on there, d'ye think?

It would seem so, M'Lord. It would seem so.

Palmerston glared at his colleague accusingly.

Damn rum, as you say. Don't know what to imagine. Strange woman, what? Secretive, capable. Wouldn't matter a damn but that she's Queen of England. Feckless. Determined. Mind of her own. Take no denial. Won't be ruled. Hmmmph. I suppose that's as it should be. Arnold, what do you think?

Peter Arnold had been a professional spy for all of his adult life, and he knew better than to tell anybody what he thought.

His instinctive reaction was to answer a question with a question.

He reached for his tea and sipped at it before looking up.

Do you think that this is coded language, Sir?

Hmmm. Good point. Not sure. Jack?

Mitson stirred uneasily.

Everywhere there was danger.

Danger in this corner, in that corner!

Danger might lurk in every corner, every nuance of every action.

Except for the fact that most of the time there was no danger.

Misgivings abounded.

'Well, Sir. Well. Yes indeed. If that is so, that they are speaking in code, we must consider the implications, all of the implications, in all of their fullness.
Permit me to make a little speech; to think out loud, as it were, while I ruminate.
Is it code? Ah, it very well might be code. Code indeed!
But what do we infer from that supposition? Thing about code- every encoding is a decoding. Bit like the chicken and the egg. Can't have one without the other. And which comes first?
Bear with me while I ramble for a bit. Is it code? Question. What, I ask, does that mean? Another question. Well, sir! I answer my own question, any one of 'em. Egg hatches.
That means that we are asking yet another question. What other question?
This one- are they speaking to each other in a private language? Chicken lays egg.
Is Her Majesty the Queen speaking to the Prime Minister of Prussia in words which only they two comprehend?
That is what we are asking when we enquire as to whether or not it's code.
Let us not be naïve. It could be real. The letter is real.
But what does it mean, the fact that this is, or might be a coded message?
Is this an intimate conversation?
Majesty and Monarchy are not at issue here.
Gender and human nature jolly well are.
The facts remain obscure.
Is this a coded signal of some kind?
And this is a man and a woman, remember?
We know what men and women get up to in private. Let us not permit loyalty and veneration to blind us to the possibilities of reality. The letter is real, as I said. This is, at root, a transaction between a man and a woman.

More perfectly considered, this is a woman writing to a man. Again I put the question.
Is it code?
I'm under no illusions as to the obvious inference, because she's female and he's male; but it's too much of a mountain to climb.
If it is code, then where is the origin? Every encoding is a decoding.
What has she encoded for him to decode? Or vice versa.
Is this the chicken or the egg? If it IS code, it's one or other.
No question. If it IS code, a private language, then there is a game, with defined rules.
When did they agree those rules? Where does it start?
When was it hammered out between them?
Do we presuppose a prior understanding amounting to a confidential affiliation between our Sovereign, Victoria of the United Kingdom, and Otto von Bismarck, the Prime Minister of Prussia? That's a horse that won't run.
She hasn't laid eyes on Bismarck for twenty years, to our certain knowledge.
He didn't see her when he came over in '62, no he didn't.
Not Otto Von bloody Bismarck, no he didn't. We know that.
Nobody did, not after Prince Albert died.
Her mouth's been fastened shut since he expired of a sudden.
Speaking of whom, she has nine children to that worthy gentleman, her recently deceased and totally faithful husband.
Apropos which, he worshipped the ground she walked on and she, incidentally, enjoyed and demonstrated complete reciprocation in that regard.
Palmerston leaned forward, listening.

No, I don't believe it. It is not code. Has to be something else.
Fact.
No question.
Palmerston nodded grimly.
Mr Arnold. Pray repeat that sentence about the Apostle?
Arnold folded his hands.

"Our Apostle conveys Our trust only in Piety. We are beggars. From piety to piety, in Piety"

Palmerston bridled, spluttering.
Which damned Apostle's she on about? Hell's that mean?
Ah, I think that this would be myself, Sir, said Arnold.
To be more exact, myself as the furthering agent of Sir Charles Grey. He is charged with delivering the message from Her Majesty to Bismarck. He instructed me. He sent me. An Apostle is one who is "sent". That's Bible-speak. Perhaps that's the origin, nay, the fabric of their private language? Bible-speak? Furthermore, now that I think on, it actually sits up and works as a possibility.
Especially in this case.
The evidence is here.
I think we've cracked it.
I am the Apostle.
That fact is borne out by this fact.
I have a personal word to deliver into the private ear of Bismarck himself, from HMQ via Grey's lips to von B alone, pain of death and infamy to repeat to anyone other.
Do you, Sir? Do you indeed? Well, out with it, man?
Arnold did not hesitate.
Pains of death and infamy did not trouble him in the slightest.

'In Piety. Baroness Lehzen is quite unwell, sustained only by her faith. Her Bible is at Schloss Lehven, Saxony, in a holy casement, a Seal. Please forward the Testament at once, affording all good speed to the bearer.
Apart, wherever is Brother Martin von Leben, of Erfurt?
All prayers. In Piety.'

Palmerston stared at Arnold as if he had just spat at him across the carpet.
That it? Hell's that mean? More mystery! Who can tell her mind? Blast this nonsense, speaking figuratively, of course. Call a spade a shovel! Hmmm. Jack?
Mitson nodded mildly, his voice a soft counterpoint to Palmerston's arch bray.
That would be Baroness Louise Lehzen, of Hanover, Sir.
Lehzen, you say?
Hmmmm, yes. I recall. Baroness Lehzen is the old hag she brought with her out of Germany. Pleasant enough when young, fine looking girl, 'til she opened her mouth, and then she'd put you off your mutton chops in a hurry. Mad as a hatter. Swivel eyed loon.
Thought she was long dead. Seems she's "quite unwell". Bible in a case, makes it a Seal, fair enough.
Wants her Bible, d'ye think?
Dying, falling off the perch, calling for the Lord, that what she's about?
Hmmm.
Schloss Lehven? What do we know about that? Who gets up to what in that vicinity?
And just who is this "Brother Martin von Leben, of Erfurt", eh? Hell's he up to?'
Erfurt is a town in Saxony, Sir, Mitson volunteered pleasantly.

Birthplace of Martin Luther. I rather think that Schloss Lehven is the childhood home of the Baroness.

Arnold now spoke.

As to von Leben, I took the liberty of enquiring, Sir, before I left Osborne House.

Did you, bigod? And?

The von Lebens of Erfurt are a well known family of Lutheran Ministers, sir. Money and Rank count for nothing in Erfurt. If you're religious, you're a millionaire, though you haven't a farthing. They used to breed Lutheran clergy. Six or so generations, every boy a Minister, going back three hundred years. The eldest son was always named Martin, after Luther. The second son always Philip. If you're Peter or John you're of no account. Daughters strive to wed a neighbouring Martin or Philip.'

Why Philip? interjected Palmerston.

Another Apostle chappy? Baptised a eunuch somewhere or other?

No, Sir, answered Arnold. It's in honour of Philip Melancthon, co-founder of Lutheranism.

Never heard of him, snapped Palmerston. You were saying?

Ah, yes, Sir. There are still von Lebens in Erfurt. But no Ministers. Not any more. All farmers, to a man. The Ministering lot didn't procreate sufficient to trouble the wedding banns anywhere in late eighteenth or early nineteenth Century Germany. Childbirth outside wedlock simply does not occur. Pious lot, indeed! Well, as far as I could ascertain from my fairly reliable source, the last Minister named Philip, second son, died childless, ten or so years ago, aged seventy-odd.

The last Minister <u>Martin</u> von Leben, eldest son, brother of the above fore-mentioned, did not marry, held onto his piety and all that goes with it with both hands, and emigrated as a Missionary about eighteen-oh-five. Fifty-eight odd years ago.

Present whereabouts unknown, Sir. He would have been an almost exact contemporary of the Baroness, and is probably the fellow after whom she enquires. Interesting, that. She calls him "Brother Martin". That means that he's a Clergyman, Sir. He would answer, right enough. If he's still alive, he would be in his late seventies or eighties. If he's the chap, old and grey, then it does all appear to tally up in a bowl of soup where very little else does!
Right-oh.
Good show. Thanks. Good man.
Jack, hell are we here? Is this just a meaningless lot of drivel between two or three German imbeciles (saving HMQ, pardon me), or is Bismarck up to something?
Or is this just a mares nest we've concocted in our cups?
Are we just seeing shadows?
Hell d'ye make of it, man?

Well, Sir. There, indeed, is the rub, isn't it? That is the question, to quote the Bard.
My cursory examination of the facts, at least those of which we're aware, leads me to conclude that our venerable Queen Victoria is not about to elope with Otto von Bismarck. Nor is she divulging state secrets to a foreign power.
Also that her true purpose is possibly, indeed I might say quite reasonably, the requesting of a Bible in a box; a Saxon Seal!
That, you see, is to comfort her dying nurse; yes, that scenario seems to hold water, insofar as we can imagine. Oh, and by the by, is the chap who baptised her granny still flourishing?
This is all fine and well, except for the fact that the request is made to Otto von Bismarck, currently Prime Minister of Prussia.

Now, Sir. I don't scare easily. Fear does not rule in my house. Never has. But it is my business, your business, our business, to make an accurate judgement as to who or what I should fear, just in case.

And, if I may say so, Herr Bismarck scares me all the way down to my very comfortable leathern shoes, made for me by a little fellow in Whitechapel remarkable cheap.

I say that we are failing in our duty if we ignore this…., what shall we say…, this transaction, Sir. As our dear colleague Disraeli said, in my view enigmatically, watch out for Bismarck- he means what he says!

Palmerston nodded in agreement- 'Quite so, Jack. Nail on the head, I think. Nail on the head.

Mr Arnold? You're going to be the donkey on this business, traipsing off to Hanover or wherever. You'll be the chap actually sipping tea with the Bismarck. Penny for your thoughts, Sir?

I agree with Sir John. I'd watch Bismarck like a hawk. As we say in Taunton, keep a good eye on your friends, and you'll never have to worry about your enemies.'

Palmerston laughed. Hmmph! Taunton, eh? Good show. Common sense lot down there. We say that in Whitehall as well, or we should if we don't. Nail on the head, Arnold. Nail on the head. Jolly good show. Well, we've done a thimble-full of thinking ourselves along exactly similar lines. Damned similar, not to overstate the case.

Let's keep a hawk eye on our German friend. And let's make sure that he's our friend, for good and all. You pop along to Berlin and get this Bible in a box, this Saxon Seal. Straight back to HMQ with it. While you share a muffin with Bismarck you will give him a nice little present. First of several, if not many. Very nice, if I do say so myself. We'll be bearing lots of these over to Germany shortly. Jolly good.

Let's stay hugger mugger with him, let him know we love him dearly. Oh, yes, Otto. We would like you to be firmly onside, and onside on OUR side, my dear German chum! You're going to be in Bismarck's company as quick as we can get you there. Off you go, Arnold. Jack will fill you in en route. Nothing written, of course. We'll send that on later. Just musing a trifle, I think we'll give Bismarck all of the latest French spy reports on Prussian defence capability in the Ardennes. Yes, that should do the trick. We'll kick off with the Prusso-German defences in the Ardennes. As envisaged by Boney's grandson or whatever he is. Yes. Should make the fur fly, eh?

Forgive me, Sir, asked Arnold. Why would Prussia have any defences at all in the Ardennes? Hundreds of miles from Prussia? Different country? That's Belgium and Luxembourg, ain't it? And those fellows have no armies to speak of, or I'm a Walloon?

Just the point, retorted Palmerston. And you're not! Just as you're alarmed and Bismark's not until we light his fuse! No armies to speak of! Neutral territory. Not a soul in sight. March a French Army through those woods and you're in Cologne before anybody reads about it in the papers. Bismarck should find that possibility interesting.

Let's bring it to his notice, among other things. Nail on the head, old chap. Nail on the head.

BIRDY'S BIRTHDAY

Nobody workin' the soil counted the War in years.
Nobody in the fields pickin' cotton spoke up an' said that this was the second full year of this damn War Between the States.
Time flies in the seasons.
Soil births crops and swallows living flesh when it stutters.
Time is alive unseen.
Two years gone.
Certain sure, it went un-noticed and unspoken.
In distant Plantations, far from the theatres of battle, and down among the pupping hutches and the cottonfields, the only important thing about the War was that most of the white folks were uppity about the whole thing, whatever it was, and lots of them were gone, anyways.
But the Slater Plantation, so titled because of the granpappy and pappy of the present Mr Slater, owner of the whole Plantation, was pretty much self-sufficient, out here in East Virginia.
It was cut off, back of beyond, ass end of nowhere, and that suited everybody jes' fine.
Tobacco was the main crop, cotton well to the fore and most profitable; lotsa hogs, and some vegetables, mostly for food and variation, and of course the sale of darkie slaves of a time but only now and again. Not often, nohow.
In the main Mr Slater warn't much interested in tradin' in darkies- it upset them too much and a contented and well-fed darkie is a happy and a hardworkin' darkie.
Some of his fieldhands were prize stock, and he looked after them.
But chief of all, and most valuable by the sun and moon and stars in a landslide, was Birdy.
Birdy was amazin'. For one thing, he had lived nigh on eighteen years as a slave, if a very special one.

Not that being a slave in Virginia was particularly onerous on it's own, dependin' on where yer' lookin' from, but bein' a darkie chile born with but one use-able leg and but one use-able eye and a terrible look of hangdog suffering and a boiling mass of fat black flesh at his throat under his chin certainly set him apart, and it was amazin' that nobody had killed him yet, if only for the look of him.

Nobody ever took the trouble. Nobody wanted to kill him.

Nobody above ground, anyways. Yes, Birdy was amazin'. Not only had nobody killed him but folk positively liked him. He had been born in a cornfield.

He was conspicuously marked as deficient, disabled, crippled, probably poxed, disfigured like that.

And never mind him bein' probably a chile of the Devil hisself anyway with that twisted leg and the evil eye and weepin' tears copiously down his face.

Anyways he was always singin' "Jesa, Jesa, Jesa", which he done considerable.

Fact is, he done it more 'er less always, give 'er take, mos' all the time.

People liked him, notwithstandin'. They felt good and holy around him.

It was a mystery, and so was he. He quieted people, even when he didn't say nothin'.

People got quieted.

The Hossman had went out into the cornfield and had found the little darkie woman, a girl really if the truth be told, lyin' dead in her own birthin' blood and somethin' got him to hesitate.

He knew her, in every sense of the word, and didn't give a lick and never would, now that she was dead as a useless darkie bitch lyin' in her own birthin' blood. He looked down at her, careful to assess the residual value of this stock, if any.

This was his job and his responsibility and he was damn good at it!

He always gave Mr Slater the owner of the whole
plantation good value fer' money, yes sir!
Business is business. Don't you never fergit it! This
was his agenda.
He observed at a glance that the whelp was a cripple
and warn't no account.
He didn't normally hesitate, bein' a man of certain
convictions.
But anyways he took out his knife to cut the little
darkies throat, cull the sumbitch, as he normally
would.
But somethin' made him stop and, mebbe for
practice or I dunno, Joe, he didn't cull him.
Instead, he cut the umbilical cord that was wound
around the throat of the tiny sumbitch, gaspin' and
chokin' blood and soil out of his tiny lips.
Let the li'l basser' keep his luck, anyways.
The Hossman made his decision.
He put his stamp on the matter, and felt better right
away.
He got quieted.
He saw the pouch of flesh under the chin, mistakin' it
fer' bloody flesh as might result from a birthin' in a
field, noted it, but never thought once of goin' back
on not killin' the little basser.
He had made up his mind.
He sorta scooped up the whelp and took him home
for reasons that he did not understand.
Maggie, his hardworkin' woman, woulda' jes' threw
the lil' basser' in ter' feed the pigs.
Why she didn't was a whole 'nother story but
somethin' got her to hesitate.
She looked at the chile and she stopped.
She got quieted on the spot, all passion spent, all
anger cooled.
As a rule, she woulda' give The Hossman what fer'
fer' bringin' in a useless darkie slung from the womb,
but she didn't on this occasion.
For some reason she kept her mouth shut.

That was amazin' in it's own right, never mind a useless darkie.
She got quieted.
Instead, she washed the twisted wreckage of a birth, his head all bruised and bloody.
She washed him, his ankle danglin' uselessly awry, and his tiny black lips turned down in sorrow as he fought fer' breath.
Maggie carefully cleaned the mud and caked earth and grass-seeds outa his poor mouth, and noticed that mebbe he had but one eye.
It was difficult to tell, there was so much blood coagulatin'.
She wiped and washed it onto the ground.
The blood dripped out with the water and she noticed that the two seemed to clean each other up of dirt and dead flesh in the sunshine at the window or comin' in the door. It was like pus runnin' out of a wound.
Inside herself, Maggie was as dead as a cold stone propped up in a graveyard.
All of her tenderness and innocence and gentle femininity had long ago been beaten out of her, long, long time ago.
She had no time, no time for kindness.
No time for consideration.
Such things was strange, remote and far off as the North Star or Texas or Kentucky.
Not that she ever thought about it.
All of that truck had been beaten out of her by time and necessity.
But now somethin' made her hesitate, and that was amazin' too.
She bossed her tiny shack like her man bossed the darkies with a will and she took no truck from nobody.
Nobody woulda dared speak back at her.
Least of all The Hossman.

He had the good sense to keep his mouth shut for the most part and say nothin'.
Maggie was more than capable of doin' enough talkin' for them both, not that she often did.
But now, things were different.
She hesitated, took an inward breath, and shut her mouth without sayin' a word, which was rare in itself.
She cleaned up the blood and the mess, holding onto the baby the while, ignoring the Hossman.
This suited all concerned.
He commenced to keepin' his mouth tight shut.
She turned her back away from him and left her sorry basser' of a husban' ter' see to his own dinner fer' once, serve him right.
The Hossman was in a kind of hushed awe.
After a minute or so he went out again and lef' her to it.
He would never normally interfere with Maggie's runnin' of the shack, but he did on this occasion.
She kept mum, even if he meant well.
But then on the other side of the knife, he shouldn't have brung the baby back unless it was dead, to feed the pigs.
She kept mum.
Somehow, Maggie took the child into her life, from that very moment.
Iron-hard in her own will and practice, the baby softened her determination, and cried out timelessly into her deepest heart.
The little child fed her.
The little child fed her, and that was amazin'.
The Hossman come back to the shack in a while.
He had fetched a darkie woman, Mama Bear, ter' give assistance.
Mama Bear was a good darkie.
That warn't the point.
This was not only goddam downright trespassin', it was takin' another goddam liberty.

He oughta knowed way better, but Maggie said nothin'.
Maggie didn't even hesitate, didn't hesitate fer one second, even though she could have done by right but she didn't anyway.
She just took it by right and not a word 'a bitchin' never mind cussin' the basser ter' hell n' gone.
No, she didn't even hesitate at this outrageous encroachment and she took this right on board without umbrage.
Wordlessly, she communicated her high judgements from the mountain to Mama Bear regarding this sweet darling child and that it be fed and nourished according to her orders and commandments.
That was amazin', too.
The darkies in the field hutches might wonder, but Maggie would raise this darling child as her own.
Mama Bear took note, and didn't speak, knowin' better.
She as well knew the wisdom of shuttin' your mouth tight and settin' your jaw just so.
Yes, Birdy was amazin'.
People who encountered him went sorta quiet, on the whole, and generally set down ter' think about nothin' in general fer' a spell.
He had that effect.
Somethin' made people hesitate, and not just black folk.
Indeed, the first revelation had been and was granted to The Hossman.
He got quieted.
Maggie was the same.
As a consequence, she figgered she would feed Birdy.
Birdy commenced feedin' her.
After more than a year or so, Maggie heard him say his first word- "Jesa".
Birdy had talked before he could have walked, if'n he had two workin' legs.
And he said "Jesa".

She knew the word.
Him speakin' it like that was like to a bullet from a carbine rifle that hit her smack in the top and back of the head and blew her ignorance all to flinders.
This was a revelation and she took it as such.
In fact she took it as a mighty sign and there and then asked God to come into her heart and set up store and guide her, just like her own Momma had told her to do that but she never done it, previous.
Birdy was the cause.
His first spoken word, "Jesa" shocked Maggie.
It blew away her darkness, let in the light.
Words formed in her mind, concepts of kindness and consideration.
Birdy said "Jesa".
And he spoke the word, as if tryin' it on for size.
In time to come he spoke it constantly.
After a long while he commenced singin' and made a song out of it, hummin' soft, "Jesa, Jesa, Jesa".
Hearin' the word, the healin' had begun.
Maggie found her stomach pains vanished when the child sung to her.
She was convinced.
She was convicted.
She believed, now.
Her back and neck pain diminished and then vanished all because of his singin'.
The pains in her knees and hips softened and faded into nothingness and nonexistence and she commenced to getting' healed in her body and in her mind, and it was him that done it.
Birdy sang on and on, chanting in the candle light, singin' him and her to sleep.
He never did sing or say nothin' different.
But change started.
Personal shakeup might or might not be genuine.
Outward signs and wonders can't be faked.
Much was to follow.

Mama Bear, now firmly in place lookin' after Birdy, was joined by the additional and necessary company of Mama Caliba, a worthy darkie woman if ever there was one, who'd given her breast to many, many new babies, black and white.
Maggie nodded her consent, that these two darkie women would look after the child.
Usually, Maggie would have give a nigger a damn good larrupin' to learn them God fearin' ways.
But now all that viciousness had drained away with her bodily pains.
It was all because of Birdy, and there was nothin' of hatred left in her mind, so she never would and never did again take a switch or a stick to nobody never.
The darkie women came aboard.
Maggie did not speak, takin' it all as her due. Mama Bear and Mama Caliba nodded, like they knew that this was the way it was meant to be.
They fed him with milk and cornbread and kindness.
He fed everybody with his strange appearance and his fulsome song.
People liked him.
That fact was amazin'.
More was to follow, and they both saw the next instalment of genuine revelation when the child was about three years old.
His bad leg would dangle uselessly behind him as he crawled. From time to time he stood upright, awkwardly, propped like a stork.
But come the day when Birdy commenced to bein' revealed.
The women knew, just knew, that Birdy was very special.
And then they saw it.
And everybody saw it, certain sure.
Mama Bear and Mama Caliba knew it.
An' they made sure that everybody on the whole Plantation, black and white, knew about it, and before long they had all seen it for themselves.

It was a sign, certain sure.
As a rule, Birdy crawled here and there, draggin' his poor leg behind him, stumblin' and totterin' as he hobbled.
Mama Bear and Mama Caliba would trundle him out to a quiet spot and put down a blanket on the ground beside him for the child, and sometimes he would roll over onto it and sleep.
Nobody and nothin' would disturb him.
Mostly, he just played in the dust, pokin' at the drygulch earth, sometimes tappin' with his finger, sometimes with a little stick or wisp of straw.
He would sing "Jesa, Jesa, Jesa".
This changed right quick.
One day a vicious cottonmouth come out of the trees and the dry field and the bushes and was right on top of them before anybody could holler Jesus to the skies. Birdy didn't even have the time to whisper or speak or even sing "Jesa", it was so fast.
The snake twisted out of nowhere and aimed straight for Birdy, playing in the dust with a wisp of straw in his hand, pokin' at the hardpacked ground and the drygulch earth. Birdy didn't so much as whimper, not that he woulda knowed.
An' he knew nothin' about a deadly snake six foot long that can get all fired up and kill you in seconds with one strike.
Such attacks are very rare and almost unknown, but this one was for real and no mistake.
Mama Caliba nearly fainted with the fear, and then looked up and saw that Mama Bear was far away as herself from the child.
Both of them could do nothin' and both of them looked on helpless to do anything as the serpent moved up to the little boy, and nothin' was gonna stop that vile thing from biting the beautiful darling and his death throes would be agonisin' and pronounced in the extreme.
But Birdy was amazin'.

Without ever looking at the snake, and sorta not even noticing it at all, he sorta got up and stood up.
Of a sudden he was tall and comely for all of his three years breathin'.
Without noticing anything in the slightest, and whilst giving no sign of alarm or fright, he glided sideways most gracefully as the snake struck viciously at him but only hit mid-air with his fangs strainin', because Birdy warn't there anymore.
Birdy had shifted ground without movin' his feet, not even his useless leg.
And with hands that were slow-movin' and strong and sure to a degree unknown in any baby boy, Birdy grabbed the snake by the back of its neck.
He grabbed and held the thing as it flashed by, missin' him wonderfully. He held it with a strong and tight grip in his baby fingers.
The women saw it.
Birdy flicked once with tiny hands in a mighty whipping arc and broke the snake's supple spine in one smooth movement, killin' it deader'n hell for all to see.
The women were stunned and frightened and shaken and relieved and disbelievin' and overwhelmed.
Birdy was smilin' contentedly, calm and happy, like he had just emptied the breast of Mama Caliba.
The reptile was right there, full the size of a good sized fieldhand, just as long anyways, and virtually ready for the pot.
But first everybody must be told, and the dead still corpse of the cold snake was right there, not even twitchin', and incontrovertible evidence that nobody was dreamin'. The toddler, this toddler, had killed a snake, a redhead diamondback cottonmouth.
Killed it with his hands, him but three y'ar, and with a useless leg and mebbe but one eye.
Two good workin' darkie women seen it, and give testimony that it was so, and they sure as hell never killed no snake, nor woulda said so.

But the snake was right there, deader 'n hell fer all to see, and no tall story out of a canebrake.
Word travels fast, and the word spoken was that this beautiful little darkie with but one leg had the power over snakes.
The Hossman heard about it.
He accepted it, swallowed it whole, and knew it to be true.
Stories like that don't get invented and there was the damned snake to prove it.
He felt a deserved pride, like he knew he was right all along not to cull the little basser.
But somethin' had made him hesitate, and now his deeper wisdom was there to be astonished at.
He give himself a chuck under the chin, a little punch of approval on his own arm, and figgered there was more to him than met the eye. Henceforth he cultivated a deliberate long slow pause in his speech, like to what he imagined great men do.
Maggie wept when she heard it, great tears of joy and relief and happiness, but she yelped out in pain with the fear and then it subsided in her breast.
He was safe and alright.
Maggie wept.
Shoutin' out aloud to God for his mercy, she hugged Birdy, cryin'.
The tears cleaned out her darkness inside her like no broom had ever swept out a bats cave high up in the hollers.
Birdy was safe from a deadly snake attack.
Now he was everybody's focus point.
Birdy was observed to move that way again, on several if not many occasions.
This was sorta' glidin' most graceful, almost flying gently, but in about one second, and all smooth in the motion and never movin' his legs.
He would sorta float instead of limpin'.
No snake in the field ever come near him again, let alone the one that he killed, and everybody seen it.

The damn snake was real.
This thing truly was the king of the cottonmouths.
Everybody seen it.
Everybody said they'd never even heard of a snake as big, or as riled.
And they'd never heard of a baby not even walkin' strangling one with his bare hands, never mind a crippled darkie.
And how in hell do ya strangle a snake anyways?
Damned if it warn't possible?
Ain't never seen nothin' like to this!
Lord have mercy!
But they'd seen this one.
There it was, taiglin' down from over the rain barrel.
Deader 'n hell and twice as ugly.
Even a strong fieldhand couldn't have done that, and none had the horse sense or the strength or even the gumption to do it nohows.
How in hell do ya break a snake's back anyways?
Not but that any one of big strong darkie fieldhands couldn't of done that!
Of all of 'em!
They were all terrified of snakes, and rightly so.
All the fieldhands came to look at the dead snake and the little boy and the word spread.
The cottonmouth was over six foot length, big as a fieldhand writhin' in the pupping hutch.
When split open, it had a whole coney part digested down in it's craw.
Mama Caliba pointed at it and remarked, and they threw it away deliberate.
Pigs gotta eat too.
Mama Bear cooked the snake deliciously and Birdy ate the choicepiece head well boiled.
It was all soft with just a tiny pinch of pepper and salt crushed under a hot rock.
It fed all the fieldhands, 'cause everybody got a bite.
Mama Bear made sure, and Maggie nodded, wordless in certainty.

It was so, and no mistake.
A white man from the hollers came along with The Hossman one day.
He, havin' heard, come to look at Birdy and, unbeknownst, to test him for the Devil Seed.
Such are the ways of folk who live on the land, and in the drygulch mountains and the parched eviscerate soil.
Birdy was playing with a straw, pokin' in the hardpacked dirt.
The Hossman came up quiet.
And the white man held a tiny, poisonous snake in his hand and he called it a Holy Krait.
He knew what he was mebbe up against in the spirit and the truth, so he didn't even let go with a flicker of doubt, never mind pause for consideration.
He walked right on in and knew the child even before The Hossman pointed at him and said it's that darkie there, not but that there was only one small darkie anyways.
The white man went right on in and up, certain sure and determined and he raised his hands holdin' the Holy Krait and put forward his fingers flickin' and his eyes never faltered.
Before anybody could stop him, he cast the snake at Birdy and it landed on his neck.
Birdy never so much as flinched, and the snake wound itself around the growing mass of curdled flesh just below his chin.
Birdy looked up, bright-eyed and smilin'.
He sung out "Jesa, Jesa, Jesa"!
The white man started, startled, hit hard, shocked.
He'd never heard or seen nothin' like to this before.
His mouth opened, and he wet his lips gone to dryness and he thought of his own tongue movin'.
Never in his born days, not seen because not looked for, yearnin' and strivin' he stared amazed at signs and wonders by which ye shall know them.

The snake licked his tiny pink tongue at Birdy's birthmark lump, but obstinately did not bite him.
The white man held his own right hand out, palm upward, as if stoppin' a wayward horse or testifyin' in church, which was his own peculiar way of pronouncin' on the veracity of the child.
This little baby is of salvation. Cain't no demon seed withstand the Holy Krait. Signs n' wonders. Signs n' wonders. He is kin to Jesus. Power over the evil of the field is giv' him. I declare my witness. Thank you Lord. Thank you, brother.
I have seen the glory of the Lord, and so have you, did you but know it. Now lemme go in peace afore thy sight. Amen. Glory hallelujah. Amen.
And he reached out and took the Krait into his palm and secreted it out of view and went out as quick as he had come.
The Hossman positively glowed, and hurried to tell Maggie, and Mr Slater, the owner of the whole Plantation, and word spread.
Maggie was scared that the Holy Krait had been flung at Birdy, when she was told, but glad to know that he was not bit, and was safe.
And yes, she concurred.
Birdy was kin to Jesus.
It was a sign, and the story spread.
Birdy was taken out to the miles of cottonfield on the plantation and he chanted his soft song, "Jesa, Jesa, Jesa" and the fieldhands come up to look at him and say that it was so and they worked happily and protected as never before.
The women hummed and sung their joyfulness.
The little boys and girls reached out and touched him fer' luck.
Big men, fieldhands all, hardened in the hot sun came to just look at him.
This was the child, certain sure.
Mr Slater, the owner of the whole Plantation heard of these doins' and nodded his consent.

A blessed darkie is a happy darkie, and you cain't buy that fer' nothin' from any feedstore.
Birdy was a cherished treasure fer' Mama Bear and Mama Caliba and they didn't work no more other than lookin' out fer' Birdy.
Everybody from bottom to top knew that he was blessed, and them with him.
Not long after, Sister Phelps, a white woman of the Church of Holy Fire, decent white folk all that went there, come to look at Birdy. He was playin' on the hardpacked ground with a soft straw, and she knelt in awe and wonder cause she could clearly see the dove ascendin' and descendin' over his head.
She had the sight, and testified that it was so.
And she called fer' Sister Tomalin from the same fellowship, and she came runnin' and she could see the dove ascendin' and descendin' over Birdy.
Yes, it was so and they knelt there on the hardpacked dirt, white folk both, gazin' dumbfounded in the very Presence of the Lord.
And Birdy chanted, not even lookin' at them, "Jesa, Jesa, Jesa".
The women wondered.
They whooped their glory be to Jesus that it was so.
It was a sign.
Another sign.
Certain sure.
And the word spread.

BABIES BREATH- BORN IN A FIELD

When a child is born, women usually, and to a degree remarkable, rejoice.
This might conceivably be accounted for by the fact that what is really going on is their Biblical deliverance from the curse of Eve, mother of all mothers, which might indeed be cause for celebration, and they generally know of it as a rule and custom.
The inherent paradox is that it is the actual process of childbearin' and actual child birth that frees the woman from the curse of childbearin' and childbirth.
That means that only women who have actually done it actually understand it in reality.
Of course they always tell the other women all about it so that they'll understand it too.
This means that these innocents should know all there is to know and as well as them but they don't really know until it gets to happen to them.
By and by, and in time, that generally comes to pass.
Mostly, women are very happy that babies are born into the world.
This is not necessarily because they're now in the know about themselves bein' delivered from the curse of Eve, mother of all mothers, certainly not!
First up, this is not always the case if it ain't the first birth. Deliverance from the curse of Eve, mother of all mothers, has already kicked in.
It's more to do with the fact that they're just sorta happy about the new life aboundin' and that the numbers of folk in general are bein' kept up considerable.
The Good Lord is breathin' in the Spirit, and the blessed business of the continuation of populatin' the world is getting' on at a steady rate, and that thar' woman thar' is doin' a fulsome job and pullin' allocated weight as directed, like somebody shovelin' sixteen tons of number nine coal.

With menfolk, it's different.
Come a new sucker, some men are in-different, to a greater or lesser degree, dependin' on their level of commitment and involvement, and sorta up a stump. They're mainly left wonderin' about all the fuss, with no particular opinion pushin' ter' get out. They wind up feelin' kinda' guilty as if nobody got around ter' pointin' the finger at them just yet, but if they're gonna, they might.
The way they see it is that it was really them in particular that got the ball rollin' in the first place, that night after the cornroast.
Not that they ever told nobody at the time.
Why would they wanta' advertise the fact ter' nobody anyways?
Taiglin' resultin' in puppin' ain't fer discussin', no sir!
And not at this late juncture anyways, and they sorta would admit to liability if requested (an' who in hell is gonna request?) but would rather hope not to, all things looked at.
But now all the womenfolk are lettin' on that it's the fourth of July come early.
Eee-hah!
Everybody should be settin' off fireworks or somethin' equivalent.
All fer a taigle in a corner, or wheresomever.
Ain't nobody's goddam business, nohow.
Why in the Sam Hill would ya open yer mouth?
The dog got off the porch.
That's all there is to it.
Waddya gonna do?
Women think different.
Women smile, noddin'.
This is ter' show approval of what was a very complicated and perhaps even dubious activity at the time.
Heads get scratched considerable.

Other men, possibly more Church-inclined, or who might have got religion, take an alternative path. They see the whole thing as a blessin' and a gift. No dog getting' off the porch, no bitch getting' pupped. No, the Good Lord is pourin' out his munificent bounty, and grace overflows.

This is especially so if they hankered after somebody, necessarily a boy as a rule, ter' leave the feedstore to, or help out with the farm in years ter' come, and they reckon they can take the credit but they won't because the ladies are gonna hold all the megaphones and why would anybody with any horse sense want to say anything anyway? Everthin' in it's place an' a place fer' everthin'!

Still others break out with cigars, handin' them 'round promiscuous and accept congratulations from wise and shrewd uncles an' Granpappys.

These veterans are votin' exactly the same ticket and in agreement all the way. They've commenced ter' keepin' their mouths shut on several if not many occasions, before, durin' or after a cornroast, or wheresomever.

They know the monetary and fiscal value of a new child right down to the nickels and cents, and pour out a good three fingers of red-eye, or corn liquor, and don't contaminate it with water, neither.

These folk are certain sure, an' their portion, fer' the mos' part, is certain sure. Darkies in the fields ain't got that element of tenure an' security. Gen'rally, an' to a degree, they don't know where the next bite's comin' from. Birdy's mother didn't get much of a show, before, durin' or after the actual three-part business of givin' birth to Birdy.

Unbeknownst to all concerned, it was The Hossman who sired Birdy, very much as a casual afterthought, with very little commitment or decision or even physical effort on his part even in that brief transaction.

Just doin' his job, he was gonna give value for money in all situations.
Bein' at all times attentive to the wellbein' and good condition of the stock on the plantation, the maintenance wherof was his main concern, he reckoned that a pupped darkie was more valuable than a fallow one, and that it was his business to make sure that if he could just get on and mind his own business with a willin' hand, then that was the line to take.
Sirin' Birdy didn't take more than a minute or two of his time and energy.
To some degree, he even enjoyed doin' it, not that he was particular one way or the other.
Business was business, after all.
He certainly didn't experience much doubt, or regret, or guilt, or very much of anything at all at the time.
An' anyways he never knew about it later on or subsequent.
He never did find out, and wouldn't have cared about it if he did.
It was out of time and out of mind.
It was not seen because not looked for.
Birdy's mother was called Calpurnia.
She was just a young girl, but she was big hipped, ripe for pluckin' and risin' fifteen y'ar when The Hossman told her to get her black ass in the hutch until she was pupped.
But then he calculated that possibly no darkie fieldhand had covered her as yet, there was just a good chance, and so he told her to shuck down there and then and made sure he did it himself on the grass of the field, her weepin' considerable, as bitches do when bein' broke in, so he was satisfied that he was right in his discreet judgement.
Business was business, and no mistake neither.

The way he saw it, first come, first served, and this was very much his own business anyway as a rule, and he thought no more of it, everthin' in it's place and a place fer' everthin'.

Calpurnia didn't moan overlong. She crawled on into the hutch to get pupped, and said nothin', which was at least a good start.

That's about as good as it gets in the circumstances prevailin', them not entirely fav'rable.

As The Hossman might have said if he ever would of but never did anyway, she'd bes' keep her goddam legs open and her goddam mouth shut, and so Calpurnia got off to a damn good beginnin' insofar as keepin' her mouth shut went anyways.

Takin' things all 'round, she mighta squawked and bitched and cried and generally upset the applecart, not that such a determination woulda' done no good anyways, but she never did.

She set her jaw and shut her mouth and made do the bes' she could in the circumstances, which warn't too bright, considerin', startin' at the outset with the calculated urgencies of The Hossman.

This was jes' as well, not that anybody never give much of a damn anyways as to what she mighta' said in any event, much less getting' pupped.

Mr Slater the owner of the whole Plantation took stock in the notion that a happy darkie is a hardworkin' darkie, and that a Plantation full of hardworkin' and happy darkies is a damn profitable enterprise. If a darkie put in a good day's work in the cornfield or the cottonfield, then that there darkie should be rewarded with the additional incentive of getting' into the hutch and puppin' the bitch inside and welcome.

And everybody was subsequently grateful all the way around, and that's the way it ought to be. The Hossman did a damn good job of keepin' up the stock regular, hardworkin' darkies puppin' willin' bitches, and everthin' in it's place and a place for everthin'.

Subsequently, after fifteen or twenty sweatin' fieldhands had received their due reward fer' a damn good hard days work done, Calpurnia was found ter' be with child. She come out of the hutch and was put on light work in the fields pendin' the arrival of the new sucker. And of course nobody was to lay a hand on her, or lay anything else, including their sweatin' selves, on her, fer' that matter.

She might lose the sucker and throw the whelp if they did, and then that there would be Plantation business and that there'd be hell ter' pay, and no mistake and everybody knew it. That didn't stop considerable of the fieldhands from revisiting that particular honeypot when possible, which was in fact often, and any time they happened on her in the field, light workin' or not, they done it, whether she would or no.

Most of them deemed themselves as sufficient and capable judges of what jes' regular Plantation business is or was or might be anyways. They were a damn sight more involved in the day to day welfare and prosperity pertainin', and who the hell was gonna say different, never mind coverin' a pupped bitch when so inclined?

But Calpurnia was damn good stock, and she didn't throw the whelp.

To his credit, The Hossman personally refrained from such additional and subsequent misbehaviour and diversion, because he invariable chose not ter' interfere with the stock, once messed with by darkies, on principle, and because it was his tried and tested custom. Business is business when you look at it, all things considered.

The other darkies, the female darkies, the women slaves of course, made sure that Calpurnia got considerable vittles and milk, now that she was pupped.

Their voices were raised in righteous anger and they warned the fieldhands off of coverin' her when she started swellin', threatenin' them with the terrible revenge of The Hossman if she should throw the whelp because of their messin' with her.

This was no idle mouthin', no empty threat nohow, because The Hossman would give out a damn good whippin' if he felt inclined and some uppity darkie was gittin' above hisself. Business is business and The Hossman wouldn't even hesitate to lash a darkie that deserved it. If necessary, he'd kill the basser', whip him to death, an' no mistake, 'cos a goddam nigger is gonna' learn, or else! And nobody would say nothin' an' damn right too! Negro slaves have their standards and social conventions which are as contractually and ethically binding as the domestic practices of the aristocracy of Schleswig-Holstein.

Business IS business. Everybody knows it.

Recognition of this fact resulted in Calpurnia making it through to her seventh or eighth month, virtually unmolested thereto, or ar least not for a while, five or six weeks, give or take.

This was only to be expected lookin' at matters with a shrewd eye, because the secretive urgings of fieldhands will not be thwarted, any more than the commands of a Queen.

All things considered, she done pretty well up to then, certainly as well as some, or most.

However, the birthing process, the delivery itself, did not go well.

Perhaps this was only to be expected, because she done pretty good up to then.

But it warn't gonna last. Her luck run out. She didn't get much of a show, start, middle or finish, but Cassie jes' done her best first, last, and end. Not that she got much choice nohow. Returning with a large bucket of water from a distant pond, this bein' light work,

Calpurnia was approached in a lonely meadow by a particularly recalcitrant fieldhand, unconcerned with the niceties of propriety, or even domestic priorities, and who insisted on covering her there and then, at once, whether she would or no, her views to the contrary.
Despite her impassioned pleas for clemency or mercy or just not ter' do it anyways or somesuch, and her feeble attempts at resisting, he prevailed in his determinations.
The consequences were both grave and immediate, even as he snuck off before nobody could point a finger at him and say that thirsty basser done it.
His urgencies provoked the birth of a sudden.
This was not "throwing the whelp".
Labour had been most forcibly induced.
To some extent the timin' was precipitate, but jes' about up 'ter scratch as things go.
The upshot was that Birdy was born without the aid of a nurse as Calpurnia, abandoning the water bucket, struggled to get closer to the fields where other slaves laboured, before blackness descended, as it was doin', a factor unrelated to the time of day, but rather more to do with her own personal health and deportment.
She got as far as under a tree in a cornfield, and then time run out fast.
Her luck, such as it was, had long departed.
Her bein' but yet a child her own self, givin' birth to another child, and with no help to hand, was both difficult and painful.
She was on her own, and the process of deliverance from the curse of Eve, mother of all mothers, was the most painful thing that had ever happened to her in her short time of life, which warn't too long extended thereafter.
Reaching down, she drew the child forth, with much attendant discomfort to herself.

She was bleeding profusely, as some women will when childbirth is literally forced upon them and the baby arrives unseasonally, as Birdy did.

She managed to partially loosen the cord that was strangling him from about his neck, but her strength was faint, and fading, and sleep or unconsciousness and what was really the business of dyin' in her own birthin' blood eventually claimed her.

All of her colours became as one with the blue of the sky, and she rested, delivered of her manchild, delivered from the coils of the serpent, subtlest beast of all of the field, yielding fruit in the midst of the tiny buds of ears of corn.

Some hours afterward, The Hossman found the body of Calpurnia and the baby, and made an unusual and variant decision not to cull the little black basser', as he normally would have done, good humour or somethin' prevailin' at the time.

Instead, he took the child home to Maggie, and that most variant determination resulted in her remarkable adjustment to circumstances. This of itself was most erratic and unusual, and she hesitated at first and then kept her mouth shut, both of which was amazin'.

More was to follow.

The Hossman went outside, leavin' her with the blood soaked little basser'.

Abruptly, he ordered two fieldhands to find and bury Calpurnia, both to keep down the rats and to learn the darkies God-fearin' ways.

BABIES BREATH-

A QUEEN'S CONFINEMENT

In something of direct contrast to these practices and events, Queen Victoria's ninth pregnancy proceeded in a much more orderly, a more genteel manner.

This was several years earlier, when Festivals abounded, and Princess Beatrice joined the human race, the business unfolding in three distinct stages.

The first was the act of reproduction itself, long heralded as the most sacred duty of every single monarch in all of history- to procreate with a will. As the Bible instructed- "be fruitful and multiply". Queen Victoria and Prince Albert were most prolific advocates of this determination.

By the time of her final pregnancy, the Queen and her darling had added each of their own one to the other's one and then mingled three times three, so one plus one multiplied by fruitfulness equals eleven thereby showing a fine example to the entire nation and the world.

The coupling was almost incidental, unnoticed by either participant in the early hours of a moderately warm summer night in Braemar, after several generous infusions of hot whiskey, presented in fine crystal glasses, to assist the processes of Royal digestion and healing sleep.

Congress was casual, memory flickering.

The involvement of both parties to the transaction might best be described as routine, pleasant, and relaxing, unfolding as it did in the veriest lap of luxury. Neither even remotely remembered the activity, but both were unsurprised when resultant possibility became Royal certainty.

However, although this gradual epiphany was hardly earth-shaking, it heralded much approbation amidst tight smiles and wise nods among many thousands of others.

Privacy, intimacy, and holy discretion were eased delightfully into the wealthy vessels of subsequent joy and surprise, as though Her Majesty had achieved something wonderful and unusual, with great skill and ability displayed in the production thereof.

That a woman should find herself "with child"? Yea, verily, wonders might never cease!

And all accomplished in privacy, secrecy, Royal Intimacy, and the best possible taste!

The second stage in this holiest of holy processes, that of pregnancy and confinement, unfolded, paradoxically, in both public and marked gaze.

The next nine months and ten days were total Hell and agony for everybody except the happiest of happy couples.

Her Majesty's royal wrath was unleashed.

Ne'er to be crossed in wish or whim, new heights of intolerance abounded on all sides.

An army of servants and public officials and royal personages fled and fell, cut down as chaff before the sickle consequent to and from the wraths and rages of Her Majesty.

Only Prince Albert remained aloof from the fray, lips pursed in contented approbation, his duty done, his posterity extended.

He suffered not a jot or tittle of pain, doubt, guilt, or embarrassment.

Nothing was said, but everything was understood in complete perfection as to exactly how the happy state of the grateful spouse had come to pass.

Nobody was in any doubt as to exactly who had impregnated the lady; as to who had done what.

Nor was there the least blink of disapproval.

Prince Albert was the man.

He was proud and blessed, above all trouble and inconvenience, his portion sure. Not for him the obscurity of swift flight after an urgent fumble in a cornfield.

All was peace, perfection, and painlessness under Heaven.
His lady joined him in this attitude for the birth itself.
She was the one person who was determined not to endure even a second's worth of discomfort at or prior to or even during the birth.
Queen Victoria, having been delivered eight times from the curse of Eve, mother of all mothers, was well satisfied that she had done her bit, and this was number nine and all curses could go hang, and good riddance to them.
Fiddlesticks!
Laudanum had proven to be ineffective, several times and again.
Massage and cordial did nothing.
The Queen had experienced PAIN!
This would NOT be repeated.
A new medicine, chloroform, was mentioned. Might this wonder-drug be helpful?
Although the Royal Physicians hummed and hawed and prevaricated and even hinted most obliquely, in fact almost invisibly at "another way", nobody had the gumption to actually speak to the Queen.
Nobody was going to say that chloroform might really just be very dangerous for both mother and child!
Nobody would ever say that this semi-poisonous chemical was life-threateningly dangerous!
But Her Majesty remained unpersuaded of the existence of any difficulty, not least because not concerned with the possibilities of persuasion at all, and she remained stoically convinced that chloroform would be quite delightful.
So she resolved that she would have plenty of it.
This to perform, the Royal Surgeons conferred, and they applied the most modern thinking to the matter- to wit:

A mare in foal, immediately prior to delivery, weighs approximately twelve hundred pounds in weight.
The Veterinary Surgeon, in his office as Anaesthetist, places exactly one pint of chloroform into a leathern pouch and covers the mouth and nostrils of the distressed animal.
This soothes and tranquilises the pain.
The mare sometimes lapses into deep sleep.
VERY deep sleep!
On occasion, it never wakes up.
But the foal emerges in fine fettle.
Most of the time.
Chloroform works for horses.
Therefore, mathematically speaking, twelve hundred pounds of mare demands one pint of chloroform for efficacious delivery.
A pregnant Monarch, yea though she be a woman, and not a horse, weighs approximately one hundred pounds.
Ipso facto, the application of one twelfth of a pint of chloroform must be the correct and appropriate dosage.
Quad erat demonstrandum.
But there is more, for the learned Surgeons are not envisaging the birth of a horse, but of a Prince or Princess of the Blood!
The proper study of mankind is man, or women, in this case.
So all avenues must be explored.
And here indeed was the rub!
A female human experiences contractions, yea, even though she be a Queen!
These contractions, although painful, are a vital and necessary element in the process of childbirth.
They mark time.
They signal process.
Chloroform will diminish or eliminate contractions.

So Doctor John James of Norfolk has prescribed a tincture of Refined Ergot to be mixed with the chloroform.
Great care will be taken.
Refined Ergot is the base constituent of a most unusual tincture- that of lysergic acid, but little is known as yet about all of the benefits inherent.
Refined Ergot will facilitate contractions, acting both with and against the non-discerning Chloroform.
The size of the dosage must be determined by common sense, since Refined Ergot is not used on horses.
A small spoonful should be sufficient!
Mingled well with the chloroform, of course.
Shaken, and not stirred!
Most efficacious!
And since the office of "anaesthetist" does not yet exist for female humans, let alone Monarchs, who better than Prince Albert himself to apply the dosage? Doctor John James has devised a most ingenious apparatus, whereby the sedative compound is dripped onto the breathing vessels of the sleeping patient. There will be no pain at all! None!
Nor shall there be waking consciousness!
And lo, there were none of these, none at all.
No pain, no consciousness.
As a result, therefore, Queen Victoria was the only person of many centrally present at the birth of Princess Beatrice who knew and experienced and recalled nothing.
No detail at all under Heaven assailed her, and the new baby's opinions remained unsought and unspoken.
Subsequently, however, inspired no doubt by previous confinements, the Queen nagged and bullied everybody she met about the dreadful agonies which had assailed her in those darkest of dark hours, the veritable Hell she had suffered and endured.

Her chin went down and her eyes came up and she glowered accusingly and spared none, laying stress on every word.
Her objections drilled out staccato, spewed like bullets at the abused ears of the innocent.
Prince Albert took no notice, and gave out glasses of spirits and champagne to many.
His lower lip probed forward proudly, gracious handshakes abounding.
Cigars he despised, and so they did not feature in his festival of celebrations.
Not for him either guilt or avoidance.
He gladly and gleefully accepted congratulations from all comers.
He was fully in control, totally aware that he was the true originator of all the fuss; the architect of his luck; the captain of his right little, tight little, ship.

EARTHLY POWERS

It was Maggie who got the next amazing revelation about Birdy.
It happened when he was risin' five year old, and she told The Hossman right quick, and The Hossman came runnin' and just took one long look.
That was enough to convince him there and then.
He saw that it was so and he went straight up to the Big House where Mr Slater sat in glory and commanded the whole Plantation, him bein' the owner thereof.
He was entitled to be told this news sooner and quicker than anybody, because Birdy was his darkie.
Also, he insisted on hearin' ALL news, good or bad, in right quick time, and no mistake.
And so he did.
This was good news.
Birdy had been playing with a soft straw in the hardpacked dirt outside the back door of the cabin, like to as he often did.
Maggie had eased her sorrow to the extent that she now took a warm interest in Birdy's doin's, and felt good just lookin' at him playin' in the dirt and singin' "Jesa", as he did.
So it was Maggie who saw first, and to whom the fact was given, and the revelation.
Maggie was lookin' at him, belovin' him greatly.
To some extent this was quite fittin', her bein' all kindly and motherly to Birdy, which definitely benefited him, but probably benefited her more.
Anyway she was alert to the possibility and the fact, and it was so, certain sure.
Maggie saw him pick up a straw, just an ordinary straw from a bit of dried grass, and sorta poked it into a dried crack in the hardpacked soil, dry as a bone in summer heat and no rain.
She watched, at first just a little bit amused and thinkin' "oh shucks what's he doin' now?".

But then she got right curious and she saw what she saw and she could not believe it.

Birdy worked the wispy straw ever so gently down into the crack in the hardpacked ground, and then he wiggled at it and touched it on into the tiny rift so gentle and at the same time he tapped the ground with his little finger on his other hand.

He tapped and wiggled and a big piece of drygulch soil literally popped up outta the ground, and split into dust right in front of him and right in front of Maggie's astonished eyes. The piece of earth was as big as Maggie's fist, but now lay demolished and in bits.

This was impossible.

If the child had a crowbar he would have had difficulty doin' that.

If Maggie had wielded a crowbar, she couldn't have done it.

But Birdy didn't have a crowbar or even a storebought shovel or pitchfork, he had a tiny piece of straw.

Maggie watched in awe and wonder as he poked the straw into the ground again, this time deep into the considerable hole opened to inspection.

An equivalent sized piece of hardpacked ground came flying up and out, breaking into cloudy dust with some small stones in it. The child proceeded to excavate the growing excavation in the ground.

And ever and anon the soft straw poked deep into the hard ground and splintered it up into bits, with just a wiggle and a tap.

Maggie went fer' The Hossman and told him what she saw and he didn't stop to discuss the likelihood or not of her evaluations.

The Hossman came runnin' and he took one look at Birdy, and looked at the ground, and that convinced him.

He saw that it was so, that she was right.

Off he went to the Big House.

Mr Slater came runnin' right quick and saw that it was so.
He patted The Hossman on the shoulder for a good job well done in not cullin' this little darkie who had power over serpents and reptiles.
Yessir, he has power over the evil of the field.
This is the child and the word had spread.
This was the child himself and was the very same one which Sister Phelps had seen the dove arisin' and descendin' upon, and now there was no doubt.
Sister Tomalin had confirmed it.
And there warn't no doubt at all.
Not that there never was, but now everybody would know, as plain as can be.
Maggie was right.
The Hossman was right.
Mr Slater was right.
The truth was right here.
And the truth, as everybody knew, is the foundation of all excellence.
Birdy was a Soilman.

THE SOILMAN AWAKES

Perhaps once in a hundred years a Soilman is recognised.
He can be blessed from the womb, as Birdy seemed to have been, or he can suddenly feel the call in his teens or early twenties. Because the skill and the craft and the ability is so special, the Soilman will not remain unrecognised for long.
The Soilman has knowledge of the Earth.
He knows what is in and of the soil.
He can tell how the ground lies, in what folds and twists and rivulets it is constituted, and how to easily uncover anything underneath or in or on the grass or the trees, or the drygulch earth.
Using only a soft straw, a Soilman, even a little child like Birdy, could penetrate and excavate and dig up the hardpacked soil. He could make rock clusters explode and blow up into helpless dust fragments.
The Soilman can tell, just by looking, if a field is rich in promise or barren as the desert acres.
He can point to the source of a spring. Other, physically stronger hands shall labour under that instruction, and a good overflow of purest water will gush forth as in the sparkling of wellwet grounds of green pasture.
The Soilman knows.
He can ease great rocks out of their lordly tenure, and even an army of them, and make a jagged stoneyard into a fruitful meadow.
Mr Slater immediately gave to The Hossman and Maggie a better house, nearer to the Big House, a good cottage with its own well from which to draw abundance and even a porch.
Maggie had never had her own well, in her own garden, in her whole life.

She wanted to cry but reckoned that since she didn't have nothin' ter cry about, it would be a waste of time and consideration.

There was an outhouse and a shack nearby, and Mama Bear and Mama Caliba came with the property, livin' in the hutches, and all to care for Birdy. Only Mama Bear knew that Birdy's mother, Calpurnia, had been her own sweet child, her own little baby. Birdy, she was certain sure, was her Grandson. This was fittin'. But Mama Bear kept her mouth shut, as sensible darkies do and will. So now she would care for her daughter's son.

Birdy was a precious asset, and recognised as such.

The Hossman was given charge of the boy.

Mr Slater brought The Hossman right into the Big House, and sat him right down in a fine chair in the room with many books lining the walls and Mr Slater instructed The Hossman on rearing Birdy as a Soilman.

Mr Slater impressed on The Hossman that there was no more important task on the whole Plantation than the development of Birdy.

From now on, he said, your money's doubled.

Don't you never let nobody lay a hand on him, and he's to have the best of good food.

That goes fer' you and Maggie too and don't you never stint at nothin' and give up the plenty to Mama Bear and Mama Caliba, because they are going to earn their keep in spades.

Also, Big Neg is to fetch and carry Birdy if he can't walk and whatsomever and that which you declare to be in his interest.

But the priority is Birdy. These three darkies live here in the shacks now. I'm pullin' them off the field.

Here on in, they just look after the boy.

They do not go to the field with the other darkies.

They care for Birdy.

If you choose to bring in another man to do your work, under you, that shall be okay by me.

This boy is the true priority.
You and Maggie have the running.
I shall never interfere.
If you can bring me a Soilman aged twenty or so years, then it will be more than well worth the trouble.
You will have done your job and that fact shall not be forgotten.
You and Maggie have charge.
The cost is not a factor.
Money ain't no object.
Lissen' good.
Listen well.
Keep him safe.
Keep him well.
Maggie shall get and provide good britches for him, good shirts and shoes for the winter.
Yes, just for him.
He is very precious.
One other thing.
Brother Josiah Phelps says that Birdy has power over the evil of the field.
I do not know in what manner of wise this will manifest itself.
You must be alert.
Should it transpire that we have a Soilman in our midst, then we shall truly know the plenty in many avenues of prosperity.
You shall see.
Nurture Birdy.
Treat him like to a precious colt, never to be broken.
This good fortune has come about because you gave trust to your inner knowledge, to your own especial instincts.
I reckon that you were, in those precious moments, guided by the hand of the Lord.
This is part of the whole deal.
Business IS business!

You're in this, even if you don't know why or how or what.
You're in this.
That's a fact.
I am aware that I am right about this in acknowledging your part, and therefore you shall prosper as Birdy prospers.
Never forget that.
I know he is a darkie.
That really doesn't matter in this instance.
I want you and Maggie to treat this baby boy as if he was not a darkie.
Why?
Because he is a Soilman.
That is the only thing that matters now.
Nurture him.
Bring him to fruition.
We shall reap the harvest.

THE STONEYARD
Reap the harvest they did.
When Birdy was five years old, The Hossman walked and part carried him with Big Neg up to the Stoneyard, a rocky outcrop of ground far up on the Plantation, flattened out into a field of about ten acres.
There were big stones everywhere, fast rooted in the drygulch earth, sharp and jagged.
They was twistin' both up and out to cut into intruders flesh and down yonder into the eviscerate soil preventin' extrusion.
As Mr Slater said, it wasn't called the Stoneyard for nothing. A man couldn't walk over the length of it without tearing up his good leathern boots.
A darkie or a fieldhand in bare feet with no boots couldn't walk over it. Nor would they wish to do so.
Weren't no point. A horse or colt run off would pause and pick a bit at the outset, and then just loiter at the commencin' of the Stoneyard, and wait fer' collectin'.
No grass, no trees, grew on the Stoneyard.
Largely it served as an impassable boundary between workable parts of the whole Plantation, but it was a real difficulty sittin' there doin' nothin' but make everybody go a long way round.
Mostly, it just got in the way.
As Mr Slater said, it toiled not neither did it spin, not that The Hossman or Maggie ever did understand that particular axiom or epithet.
The party that went up to the Stoneyard proved experimental to a degree.
This was because The Hossman soon realized that while Maggie and Mama Caliba and Mama Bear would provide good vittles fer' a picnic of sorts, and carin' hands fer' Birdy at need, they weren't at all inclined to lever on a pole and wrench rocks outta the ground.

Fer' that purpose four or five big darkies, within easy call, would fit the bill, if required, because nobody as yet knew the outcome.

The Hossman was in charge.

Just now only Big Neg, carryin' Birdy at need, was the only darkie like to lift anything out of the ground. The Hossman was damned if he was goin' ter' work himself when there was lotsa strong darkies within reasonable quick hailin'.

The Hossman determined to see what developed in this instance, business bein' business.

Birdy was set down at the commencin' of the Stoneyard.

He was set down right on the end of the edge where the grass dried out into dirt with no moss and the sharp rocks ripped up outta' the hardcut ground. He had a little blunt knife that The Hossman had honed fer' him outta an old broken off spar on a wagon that had sorta' rusted out and come adrift and nobody never threw somethin' like that away anyways. Birdy would poke into the ground with his blunt knife and sing his little song, "Jesa, Jesa, Jesa," as he trailed his useless foot behind.

Mama Bear and Mama Caliba got right down to makin' coffee and a fire. Maggie spread herself on a blanket and commenced hummin'.

Maggie sung considerable of late.

The darkie women joined in.

Birdy had sorta led the hummin', singin' "Jesa, Jesa, Jesa," which he did continually when at his ease, which was pretty much most of the time.

Big Neg glanced sideways at The Hossman, who winced a bit even as he rolled his eyes upwards in sympathy.

Not that the two men were unfamiliar with the character, content, and desirability of knowin' Jesa, or Big Jesa, as Mama Caliba called him, but Big Neg and The Hossman weren't much given to open manifestations of matters sacred and profane.

In short, they were embarrassed.
The Hossman hung back at the edges with Big Neg, both of them male animals howsomever divided by class and colour but united in gender anyways and determined and agreed to stay to Hell away from the women's doin's and keep outta trouble.
Birdy commenced to pokin' at the ground with his little knife.
Other than the word "Jesa", Birdy more or less said nothin'.
He could nod.
He could shake his head.
He could point to somethin' or other.
He did so now.
There was a big pointing rock, sharp and jagged, surgin' up outta' the earth like a disagreeable argument waitin' fer' ya in the dark, jes' so ya could break your head fallin' on it.
Birdy looked up at Big Neg and poked a bit at a groundspot about four foot away from the rock.
Birdy pointed at the rock as he poked with his little knife, and moved his tiny fingers in a pullin' gesture, singin' "Jesa, Jesa, Jesa" the while.
Big Neg looked quizzically at the sharp rock, and looked backwards askance at The Hossman, who shrugged and shook his head and then nodded as if agreein' he'd just lost an argument.
Whut the hell do I know n' you know as much as me?
Thus empowered and duly authorised insofar as delegation might or could be legally considered to have been delegated, Big Neg placed both of his hands on the rock.
He waited.
Birdy pointed at the rock and at the ground.
He tapped twice with his tiny fingers and poked again with his knife and Big Neg gave one shovin' push upwards in the direction indicated and the whole rock levered itself up outta the ground and rolled right out lengthways.

It was a good thirteen or fourteen foot long and the size of a beached whale but all dark blood soil in colour and tearing up roots and the bindings of other stones as it emerged blinkin' into the daylight.
Big Neg stared amazed.
He had hardly give a good mansized shove with his hands, but the rock had just rolled right up and over outta the ground.
It now lay on it's side and a man on his own couldn't move it.
Two men or five couldn't move it.
It would take a strong horse to pull it away.
In the fulness of time that's exactly what did happen.
A strong horse pulled it away, but that was later on in the day.
The Hossman stared amazed.
His jaw dropped and kept on droppin'.
He'd never seen anything like to that in his life.
The women hummed and hummed and nodded with love and affection at Birdy, playin' in the drypacked earth with his little knife and his bad leg trailin' in the dirt.
Another minute and another rock of equal size and weight had been ripped up right outta the earth with Birdy tappin' a bit and pokin' betimes as he sang to Jesa and pointed and indicated and this time nobody needed additional instructions and Big Neg half pulled and half pushed at a rock three times his own considerable size and weight and it rolled over on it's side awaitin' a strong horse to shift and drag it up off the Stoneyard field.
The Hossman sent Big Neg to fetch four strong fieldhands and two strong horses with rope and tackle and to fetch Mr Slater fast to see what was commencin' to occur.
The Hossman knew best to keep him well informed, an' good news always travels fast, even if ya don't understand it as yet.

Mr Slater the owner of the whole Plantation arrived in style grinnin' like he knew all along or mostly suspected that this day would come and now it had.
In two hours a more purposeful party was assembled and The Hossman and even Big Neg were givin' out orders and instructions to the four new arrived fieldhands who laboured joyfully and more effectively than they ever had in their lives.
Birdy pointed and tapped and poked and more giant rocks were torn up whole outta the drypacked earth.
Mr Slater didn't give any orders to anyone, having made that task plain to The Hossman some time before.
He stood nodding approval, mentally counting the dollar bills on a pile so high that he couldn't never get all the way up to the top.
He looked out upon his previously useless Stoneyard and knew that it wouldn't be long before it would be the finest of green pastures.
And he knew that he was right.
Not too much time elapsed and more or less half an acre was cleared for the plough that had never before felt more on it than a good pair of leathern boots bein' tore up considerable or sore feet mangled by skippin' and jumpin' over the sharp rocks.
The horses were well watered and workin' well, happy and havin' a relatively easy time.
Maggie and Mama Bear and Mama Caliba gave out food and fruit and coffee and biscuits to the fieldhands and Mr Slater nodded his approval at The Hossman.
Givin' credit where credit was due, The Hossman had more than earned his keep and then some.
He merited a darned good pat on the back and the word of approval was more than called for.
Ere long the whole Stoneyard would be forever transformed into a rich and green pasture.
There was not the smallest pebble in sight, never mind big foot-tearin' rocks.

Birdy sang Jesa, Jesa, Jesa to the skies and the women hummed and prosperity abounded as Mr Slater saw his whole investment repaid in full and with interest in that one amazin' day.
The fieldhands weren't even overworked and tired, and went off singin' and well fed and watered to tell everybody about the amazin' child that had power over the evil of the field and was a true, honest to God Soilman.
They had seen it with their eyes and it was a sign.
Yes, Mama Caliba said it was a sign.
Factual evidence, and not just wagglin' mouths, showed it clear.
About five hundred great big jagged rocks were open to inspection as never before.
These had been ripped up by human hands and towed away by strong willin' horses not even strainin' at the chompin' bit and that on it's own was more than ample testimony to the fact that they had a Soilman who had come amongst them, who was in their midst.
Maggie seemed to remember a scripture from away back, that the stone was rolled away, the stone was rolled away.
This was from the grave, she seemed to recall.
Though she didn't have all the pickin' details of the matter, she knew it to be true and more of the sign.
Birdy was a Soilman.
An honest to God Soilman.
Livin', breathin', sayin' and singin' Jesa, Jesa, Jesa for certain sure.
Birdy was the livin' proof; the substance of things hoped for, the evidence of things unseen.

BOOK TWO-

EDIFICATION

MAGGIE'S END

When Birdy was risin' eighteen years old, and widely known to be the best Soilman ever seen, his mysterious abilities had made a whole pile of plenty for Mr Slater.
Time and again Birdy had gone as directed to other plantations, held in high regard fer' a darkie. But now he mebbe limped in with Big Neg as arranged, and transformed a stoneyard or a poisoned field or a swamp into a luxuriant pasture, and that in no time at all.
Business was business, and Good Lord How The Money Flowed In.
Hired out to them that payed upfront through the nose but whooped subsequent in the pocket, Birdy was truly amazin'.
He was a Soilman, certain sure.
Mr Slater stuck to his lifelong aim- ter' get more land.
And so he bought useless bits of ground here 'n there, all full of tangled stumps or riverrats or big rocks, and bought it for a song sung by Birdy- Jesa, Jesa, Jesa.
Birdy would come in singin' and Mr Slater would reap the plenty.
In one season that useless piece of rock or swamp was sproutin' corn or cotton or tobacco, relative to the whim of Mr Slater.

And Birdy sung his song, Jesa, Jesa, Jesa into the hearts of many.
His success meant a great change for Maggie in that she begun to be convicted.
Maggie tended Birdy alongside Mama Bear and Mama Caliba, and took to prayer and religion down amongst the darkies.
Maggie took to prayer, kneelin' in the fields with Birdy sayin' Jesa, Jesa, Jesa, and her tiny Fellowship with heads bowed.
Maggie commenced to hearing the Word of the Lord.
Much to her amazement she got told once, twice and again.
The Word shocked her and surprised her.
The Word told her that The Hossman was her child in this world.
He was her Stoneyard full of jagged rocks.
Mebbe his heart was a stone.
She understood that she had to make him good soil.
Maggie got convicted that she had to pray for her husband.
In some real sense that she did not understand, her salvation depended on his salvation.
Since she didn't know nothin' about salvation anyways, to some extent she was up a stump, an' no mistake.
Maggie hadn't never borne a child, but now she knew that her husband was her child, and that it was up to her to bring him to the Lord.
Her only help in this task would be her prayers and her own common sense.
Maggie understood in finality that she had got to truly get to know her husband- what made him tick, what he truly wanted and did and desired. That was her job.
And then, and this was the most strangest part of all of it- see it from his side of the coin.
Maggie commenced to bein' quiet and respectful to The Hossman, and kind to the darkies.

She prayed considerable to Big Jesa, and things seemed to get better.
Now she shut her mouth when he talked, and she pondered his words and actions.
It didn't take too long for her to realise that The Hossman was one mean and intemperate son of a bitch.
She had her work cut out and then some if'n she was gonna clean him up and take away the stone in his heart.
But she commenced to prayin' fer' him considerable.
Birdy's association with The Hossman and Maggie and Mr Slater came to an abrupt end of a sudden, unannounced and unexpected.
The War was ragin' now, and folk were on the move.
The War was ragin' and everywhere the brave soldiers of the Southern Cause went off to join fellow patriots in fighting the Yankee scum.
The Hossman was pushin' sixty, so he stayed with Mr Slater, who was over seventy, to continue to manage the whole Plantation.
Some of the young and nearby eager beavers got themselves pistols and rifles and headed elsewhere to lick the Yankees.
Good Ole Virginny!
States Rights!
The South!
The accepted wisdom was that one good Southron was worth ten damn Yankees and it was all gonna be over before Thanksgiving.
Similar ideas, prognosticatin' swift victory, were being promulgated all over the land, for one side or the other.
But there was another, a separate group of men with a different determination.
They wanted money and food and liquor and happy tail and lots of it.

They wanted these things now, and they didn't give a damn for North or South or good ole Virginny or nowhere else, fer that matter.
Watching their worthy neighbours marching off to the battlefields, they observed that many rural properties were now effectively unprotected.
Unprotected, that is, from such as themselves.
When a War is ragin' folk get on the move.
Good folk move off.
Bad folk wake up and see things from a new perspective.
When the entire menfolk of an entire community or entire county or entire state, or several such, all fit and well for active service, and full of piss and spit with their dander up, go off to learn the Yankees not to interfere, then the only good folk remainin' to protect the weak and aged and vulnerable is pretty much nobody.
All that's left are the women and the old men and the children and the slaves, and none of them could do much protectin', as a rule.
And the bad folk, with a new perspective.
Women and old men and children are easily got around or overcome with reasonable ease by such as are or may be determined to do so, the same bein' spry, energetic, and able-bodied.
Business IS business!
Opportunities abounded.
Valuable Commodities could be seized and sold.
Demand was high.
Hogs were most saleable, and grain, and almost everything that you could eat or carry.
Slaves were a valuable commodity, and could be easily sold in New Orleans or Atlanta or anywhere.
The fact that all such goods must be legally owned to be legally sold was moot, at best.
Legal was as legal did, and be damned to the finer points.

What the Buyer don't see the Seller don't grieve over.
Business IS business!
Bills of Sale and ownership papers could be readily acquired, if needed, by pickin' them up out of a dead man's hand.
Or mebbe go to a whole passel of willin' lawyers, none of whom went off ter' kill the damn Yankees, and, for a modest fee, get them falsified.
Now and then, howsomever, the genuine documents might be very close at hand.
Very close indeed, in a raided Plantation fer example, sittin' right there in the desk up at the Big House.
IF ya had the spit an' dander to go lookin' with enthusiasm and the expectations of immediate reward, mebbe that new perspective would pay off straight away? Horses, mules, sheep, cattle, grain, dried meat, good dogs and healthy darkies would fetch admirable prices. Possession was nine points of the Law. But this only applied if the Law was takin' an interest. If the Law was misinformed or warn't gonna be informed at all, then possession was jes' all ten points of the Law.
Happily for some, the Law was quite amenable to adaptation and generous interpretation on many points.
Happily, if'n you had a free hand, the Law was whatever you damn well pleased.
Getting' hold of these valuable assets, like very saleable darkies, was less trouble fer' them as done as they damn well pleased.
They, generally, were the happy ones.
The War provided a vast traffic of resources, between owners dealin' with dealers, themselves tradin' with other owners and other traders, and the biggest dealer and owner and trader of them all was The Army.
Often few questions were asked.
Business IS business!

Sometimes the enquiries amounted to nothin'.
The only question was who was sellin' what ter' who, and how much they were gonna grease a willin' palm.
Business IS business.
But sometimes there had to be some distance between where you got yer' merchandise and where you sold it.
Folk was on the move.
That way, there warn't gonna be too many questions about who owns who.
And who owns who could be easily enforced with a rope or a chain an' a bullwhip.
Such were the times.

On a given day, Birdy kneeled to pray in The Stoneyard, now a verdant meadow of corn and pastures of plenty with a group comprisin' Big Neg, Big Mama, and Mama Caliba, Maggie, and Cassie.
Cassie was a young darkie girl risin' fifteen years old, big hipped and ripe fer' pluckin'.
The Hossman had told Big Neg to tell Cassie to get on over to Slave Row, mebbe to work in the Big House for Mr Slater.
Big Neg was to tell her nice 'n quiet, and he followed instructions and did jes' that, but Maggie was hoverin' nearby and heard him and got to wonderin'.
Maggie knew that Slave Row was a ways off from the Big House, so somethin' didn't stack up here, and her husband was at the bottom of it.
Little did she know but that The Hossman had in mind to stick Cassie in the Hutch 'til she got pupped by the deservin' fieldhands.
And he also reckoned that there was a good chance that no darkie had covered this young bitch jes' yet.
There was jes' a good chance, everything considered.
Naturally he would check to make sure the bitch hadn't been broke in as yet, like to his normal practice.
He figgered on doin' that today.

He had to admit that he was lookin' forward to breakin' her in jes' before she would crawl into the hutch ter' get pupped.
This was mostly because he hadn't broke in no bitch for quite a spell.
He didn't want nobody thinkin' he was losin' his touch, not that nobody would anyway, but he had to keep his pecker up, leastways in his own estimation.
The fieldhands would get his leavin's, an' that was okay on all sides.
Not to mention that a pupped bitch would further improve the quality and numbers of the stock, all things considered.
Business is business.
Maggie knew nothing of this, but she found herself wonderin' about the strangeness of what Big Neg had whispered ter' Cassie, so she set her jaw on goin' with Cassie over to Slave Row.
Maggie was keepin' an eye on The Hossman, in all his doin's.
Now Maggie found herself lookin' at Big Neg, leastways with a mind to knowin' about whut The Hossman was sayin' about Cassie.
Mama Bear and Mama Caliba knew that Maggie was quite right ter' have suspicions, but they never said nothin'.
They had been keepin' an eye on Cassie fer' a good spell.
Cassie, in the meanwhile, had, by notional coincidence, found her eye lightin' on Big Neg.
This warn't too strange, given his physical prowess an' ripplin' muscles.
He would be a good catch and mebbe they could jump the broom, which she'd heard about.
Apart from that, Cassie didn't know much about nothing.
Anyways, she was gonna go up to Slave Row, as directed.
But now she was gonna be accompanied by Maggie.

Maggie was goin' along, feelin' well disposed in prayer for her lawful wedded husband that mornin'. Had Maggie consulted Mama Bear and Mama Caliba they woulda told her that Mr Slater, the owner of the whole Plantation, never got any bitches to work in the Big House for him.
This was a lie put up by The Hossman.
But Maggie didn't know that.
Anyways, Maggie and Cassie hurried on over to Slave Row for to meet up with The Hossman.
Unbeknownst, he was meeting up with Mr Slater there about selling somethin' or other.
Mr Slater had a field in consideration- he always did.
But The Hossman was thinkin' about breakin' in Cassie.
Jes' before Mr Slater got to Slave Row, The Hossman got busy.
Cassie come up as directed, an' The Hossman told her ter' shuck down and get her ass in the hutch.
Cassie threw off her shift and knelt down, naked, in front of the hutch.
But Maggie had hung back jes' fer' a minute and she heard him. She came up out of the bushes.
The Hossman was shuckin' hisself down, and was gonna taigle with Cassie on the ground.
His intentions were clear ter'see, certain sure.
Ter' make things worse, Mr Slater, the owner of the whole plantation showed up earlier than expected and he heard and saw The Hossman as well.
He surmised as a rule that The Hossman would break in a darkie bitch, and why should anybody even give a damn about that?
Don't muzzle the ox that treadeth out the corn!
Business IS business!
Mr Slater was standin' there grinnin'.
Maggie was standin' with her mouth open.
The Hossman got caught between a rock and a hard piece of dirt.

He didn't give a damn about Mr Slater comin' outta the bushes like that, he knew he was jes' doin' his job anyways.
But now Maggie had come up at the same time as he opened his britches an' shucked down an' got ready ter' break in Cassie.
Maggie jes' stared at him, clear-eyed.
The Hossman figgered he'd have to forego that particular duty on this occasion.
Maggie jes' stared, shocked.
Mr Slater stood there grinnin'.
Cassie was in wonder, not ever havin' been in the middle of three white people before, never mind that she was naked.
An' all three was lookin' at each other, not her.
The Hossman was up a stump, and no mistake.
Cassie, much to her subsequent advantage, sorta resolved things by crawlin' into the black darkness of the puppin' hutch.
She lay there on the stonecold earth, shivering, but not with the cold.
She had heard a whisper tell her somewhere in her mind that this present portion was always intended for her, as for all female slaves risin' fifteen and ripe for pluckin'.
Dozens of fieldhands would now claim her as their rightful and just reward for a conspicuous hard days workin' in the cottonfields.
She warn't altogether sure what they would do, but she knew how to be apprehensive at need.
Bein' a slave tended to reinforce the fact that if you reckoned things were gencrally bad, you warn't gonna be too far wrong in consideration.
To be fair, she was afraid.
Maggie, however, had never been present at somethin' like this.
It had never occurred to her that things could be just so; indeed she had no knowledge of the normal habits of The Hossman doin' his job.

She watched, confused, as Cassie crawled off into the Hutch.
Maggie looked an' saw The Hossman lickin' his lips as he looked at the loins of the departing child, and she saw his lust from the back and the front.
She had no resources to deal with this sudden epiphany.
It had hit her out of a clear blue sky and random circumstance.
Somewhere in her mind she briefly reckoned herself a fool not to see what was plain as the nose on her face.
This had been goin' on so long that she couldn't even guess.
How long, oh Lord, how long?
She mused with growin' anxiety on the time, the time…..
Unbeknownst to Maggie, time itself was draining away out of the hourglass that was her existence.
Her spirit was pluming for flight even as her mind raced.
She cried out in her heart to Jesa even as she recognised her husbands filth.
Time ran out.
Time landed, whomp, right onto the top and back of the head with the revelation that he was a mean, rapin' bastard.
And she bowed her head in travail as the full import of her lawful wedded husband's actions and responsibilities walloped her soundly in the stomach, and she gasped and grabbed at herself.
Mr Slater just smirked, noddin' at The Hossman, damned women, what are ya gonna do?
He had comprehended in no time at all that Maggie was probably right jealous, not that he hisself gave a hot or cold damn for black flesh at any juncture.
He didn't so much pity The Hossman as reckon that maybe he could say Hell Slap It Into Ya.

So he had little or no sympathy for this predicament but he could see the joke just as clear.
Cassie had crawled, naked, into the hutch.
Maggie had watched her movin' into the dark, like a hog goin' in from wallowin'.
Maggie catched her breath.
The Hossman smiled a tight smile back at his boss, but he knew he was in big trouble with Maggie, her lookin' at him with disbelief and mountin' horror.
Different strands of different things began to come together in her mind.
The speed of her thoughts increased apace as she swallowed one fact right in front of another.
She started to grasp for the very first time in her whole life how matters stood with her husband and the darkies.
Jes' exactly what he did and who he was!
So this was the source of many a useless darkie slung from the womb?
This was not just here and now, but always.
And Birdy?
Had Birdy sprung from this filth?
And it hastened into Maggies consciousness with a speed that has no place in time that her lawful wedded husband had broke in many a darkie bitch.
She looked at The Hossman and knew him for the first time.
She saw what a mean sumbitch he was.
She saw what a lyin' basser he was.
Bought and paid for, he warn't nothin' but a white nigger.
All this time….
All this time….
And now, here he was, standin' grinnin' up at his boss, like nobody give a damn….
Her holy conviction kicked in.
She loved and respected and was responsible for her husband.
No matter what he done.

Now was the time.
Now was her salvation, in acceptin' his sinfulness.
It all made sense, all at once.
Her salvation rested on his salvation.
And his salvation depended on her forgiveness of him.
No matter what he done.
She choked a bit and muttered a prayer for The Hossman.
Jesa, Jesa, Jesa!
But her time was runnin'out fast and she didn't know.
Nor could she.
The hourglass was drainin' even with the words of prayer resonatin' in her mind for her man, child of all of her life struggles.
Lookin' back at The Hossman, she turned toward Mr Slater, who was smirkin' considerable, countin' money in his mind.
With her last thoughts in her life, she begged a blessing on both her husband and Mr Slater, on the grounds that father forgive them for they know not what they do.
And it was finished, right there, right then.
The sand run out.
The time was up.
The hourglass was emptied into a vacuum of nothing.
Mr Slater had other concerns.
He was contemplatin' sellin' or buyin' a field, a practice and habit he enjoyed as a rule.
And he wouldn't have usually and as a rule set foot in Slave Row, but for the fact that he would meet up with his overseer.
And so he had inadvertently witnessed this event- seein' good steps took to continue and improve his possessions, like the darkies, and the fields, which themselves brought forth the wealth and plenty of the good soil, which he might sell or buy as he chose.
Business is always business.

And Maggie's reaction, goddam woman, he could read her like a book.
Fact is, Maggie didn't know nothin' about bendin' yer' ass to make a buck, speculatin' ter' be accumulatin', and generally turnin' a profit by sellin' a field.
She couldn't or didn't know nothin' about sellin' a field, and had no notion about his necessary calculations!
You gotta maximise personal profit, goddammit!
Business IS business, goddammit!
The time to take a goddam profit is always NOW, goddammit!
NOW was the time!
NOW was HIS time!
His call, his decision, his business.
Warn't nobody gonna goddam interfere with HIS goddam business!
He had no TIME fer' Cassie, or Maggie.
He had no TIME fer' this foolishness.
The Hossman knew that!
But Mr Slater did not know that his Time was up, an' all done fer'.
In a short while he would know nothin'.
Like many plantations, this one was no longer well protected, as it would have been in earlier, pre-War days.
A group of four scavengers, well armed and discreetly silent in their motions, all motivated by the desire to maximise personal profit rather than do battle for their country, arrived at Slave Row.
This was at approximately the same time as Maggie looked up at The Hossman with a new prayer on her lips and sorrow in her eyes.
She prayed in her mind, and this was the very last of her thoughts before the sand run down and on out into infinity.
Mr Slater was walkin' to and fro on the lawn, contented.

He was overall satisfied with the way things was goin', and contemplatin' buyin' this and maybe sellin' that, and generally considerin' relevant business appertainin'.
Business is business, dammit.
He looked up at Maggie and The Hossman, lookin' at each other most amazed.
He harrumphed a bit to re-establish his authority pertaining and to shut Maggie up, not that she was saying nothin' anyway.
But he rightly perceived that The Hossman was jiggered with no opinions.
He moved toward them to discuss matters financial, selectin' as relevant The Hossman's thinkin' about the low meadow where the creek don't rise.
He was somewhat surprised, understandably so if only briefly, when a carbine bullet drilled him dead centre in the chest, killing him instantly.
All his colours turned to a flaccid grey, and then he knew no more.
He dropped at once to the ground, his life blowed out like a candle at dusk when turnin' in early after a hard days work buyin' and sellin'.
Business certainly was business, up to a point.
That point was here and now.
Business was done fer' good and all insofar as he was concerned or never would be now.
The Hossman spun around, jaw out, dander up, and got himself right over to Maggie to protect her.
He had not seen the gunshot, but he had heard it, an' he mebbe had gauged the direction from which the shot came.
But he was no coward, and he looked out not only for Maggie but also for the cause of such matters on instinct, actin' before thinkin', as he sometimes and often did.
He stood up tall, wonderin' whut the hell?

He got hisself square between the line of fire, in front of Maggie, her facin' back thataways, confused an' prayin', and her chin came up.

In consequence, the bullet that drilled him dead centre went clean through him and hit Maggie right in the top and back of the head, snuffing out her life in the blink of an eye, arguably painless in execution.

Both of them were killed at the same moment, that first bullet doin' the job most effectively.

That shot was rapidly followed by four others, none of which did nothin' that their immediate predecessor hadn't.

The Hossman was dead, five bullets cuttin' dead centre.

The waste of ammunition did not trouble the purveyor thereof, not for one second of time.

Business is business, even if the currency utilised is occasionally passing strange.

With no regrets, the four scavengers approached, in a guarded if leisurely manner.

They looked down at three dead white folk, musin' idly that this was a damn fine lookin' woman, heh heh heh, the killin' bullet havin' hit her on the top and back of the head .

That didn't interfere with the fact that she looked damned tasty even lyin' prone in death and what a goddam shame that was or might be heh heh heh.

Thereafter, they moved on and carefully and unconcerned commenced to riflin' the Big House for money and papers, of which they found considerable amounts.

They rounded up all of the slaves they could lay hands on, packed the stores, such as they were, onto wagons, and headed off to realize the proceeds from their attack on the Plantation.

Some of the darkies in distant fields ran for their lives when they heard the gunfire.

Some couldn't get away.

Others tarried to make enquiries, more fool them.

Some watched from concealment as their mothers, sisters, brothers and uncles and sons were shackled up and led off in an orderly gang, some in wagons, to be sold.
Cassie stayed quiet in the hutch, confused and terrified at the noise of the gunshots and the subsequent cries and screams and whoops.
When it was dark, much later, the escaped slaves that hadn't been in the vicinity or had run off pronto generally drifted back and returned to discover and much later on bury the dead bodies and try to figure out what to do.
Cassie shivered on and in the cold ground, like to a grave.
Birdy and the others looked down at the murdered corpses, wonderin' if there was anything left to eat.
After a bit, Birdy felt moved somewhat in the spirit and went over to the hutch.
He knew, bein' a soilman, that there was somethin' there in the blackness.
He leaned into the hutch and called out "Jesa, Jesa, Jesa" softly, softly, to where Cassie lay shiverin'.
Cassie crawled out and Birdy covered her up with a horse blanket.
Mama Bear and Mama Caliba come up later and give her a real dress that she found and took from the Big House.
Mebbe it would have been give by The Hossman to Maggie in days to come.
Mebbe not.
Maggie wouldn't ever need it now, not that she probably ever would have, and Mr Slater wouldn't have no opinion no more.
Frightened, they slept out on the grasses and the canebreaks, listening intently, unknowing.
The stonecold moon rose over the open roads.
It was a warm night.

PEGLEG JOE

It was sheer coincidence or howsomever that led
Pegleg Joe to the Plantation the very next day, his
views to the contrary.
He would have said that it was the work of the Lord.
Pegleg Joe was a White Man, albeit with a wooden
leg, and an Abolitionist.
Nobody here had ever seen one of them before, a
white man with an unusual opinion regarding the
ownership of human beings.
He didn't hold with it.
He took no stock in it.
Fact is, not only was he against slavery, he was totally
dedicated to the destruction of it, and he reckoned
that you gotta fight and kill the dragon until the
dragon is dead, which was not a general view in them
particular parts at the time.
Wooden legs, however, was a recognisable if not
completely common thing.
Pegleg Joe had a wooden leg himself and if he didn't
boast about it, he didn't shrink from the bare and
fulsome acknowledgement of it neither.
Abolitionists were a dern' sight different, and that
was a fact, and even much more rare in them parts, if
at all.
Still he didn't kill nobody on his approach or
subsequently and he didn't steal nothin' and he spoke
right kindly to all darkies, which was indeed unusual,
to say the least.
Nobody knew which way was up.
It was Pegleg Joe who explained that they'd have to
try to make a run for the North, to try to get to
Canada, to try to get to freedom.
They'd have ter' go clear acrost Virginny, out of the
hills, and get right around Richmond by the South,
and make for Harpers Ferry, at the confluence of the
waters.
Too many Greycoat soldiers North of Richmond.

The longest way around is the shortest way home.
The final end was to a place far away up in Canada, on the Georgian Bay, to a town called Owen Sound, where the boats come in off the Great Lakes from as far away as Chicago and Detroit. Nobody but him had never ever even heard of these places.
For them as wanted to try, for them as dared, now was the time.
Now was their chance.
He was there to not only tell them, but to help and guide and direct as required.
When he talked, he talked with certainty and conviction.
Only The Lord will feed us and protect us and sustain us.
Only The Lord will guide us in the wilderness. Who among you will put their trust in The Lord?
Birdy, seemingly crippled as he was or mighta been and Big Neg, formidable, and Mama Bear and Mama Caliba, wise and experienced, and Cassie who was young and spry and risin' fifteen were as one in their joint willingness to try.
Try they would, even if Cassie warn't too sure, she bein' more frightened of uncertainty, not least on account of her recent brush with naked fear and anticipation of worse to come in the dark.
Pegleg Joe sensed at once that respect must be accorded Birdy, although considerin' his danglin' bad leg and his but one eye and his mass of black flesh growin' out from under his chin the reasons weren't overly evident.
But bein' of Christian and Biblical persuasion Pegleg Joe judged not by the outward appearance, knowin' that the Lord ponders the heart.
And so he addressed himself to Birdy, and asked him if he was willin' to try.
Birdy closed his one eye and nodded, bowin' his head as though in reverence.

His chin came up and the strange folds of flesh shook out like the crop on a chicken, and he cried out, all softly, "Jesa, Jesa, Jesa".

The others sorta hung their heads and murmured "amen", strung out variously or in the case of Cassie not very much.

Pegleg Joe nodded and made his pronouncement- "Blessed is he who comes in the name of the Lord". As one, the gathered bodies, Birdy solely excepted nodding only, said "Amen", and they set out that minute, not lookin' back.

SNAKE

Snake was perched up high between two great stones,
well hid from pryin' eyes, and he saw the little group
of runaways comin' outta the woods, about one
hundred yards off.
That they was runaways, he had no doubt.
He'd seen as many, and from this very spot.
Hundreds of the bassers.
All the runaways come this way, ter' get ter' Harpers
Ferry off the roads n' highways.
Business was business.
They was runaways, certain sure.
Snake knowed them from the back!
Six bodies, three n' three!
One white man up front, and a big buck carryin'
another buck, mebbe hurt.
Three gals to rearward.
Quite a party.
Unusual.
Travellin' light.
Likely foragin' fer' scraps and such, mebbe squirrels
or rabbits.
Now they had come out of the woods 'n up the hill a
bit and they'd have to pass through what he called
"The Gates", an avenue of tiny rocks on one side the
line cliff pass as the way ascended.
No cover once you were into The Gates.
This was his spot.
His ground.
Overlookin'.
In command.
All of the advantage and edge was his with him up
here and them down there.
At need, he could shoot 'em all, every one, once they
was in The Gates.
No cover.
No escape.
Not that shootin' more'n one was likely!

Waste 'er damn good money!
Business is business!
No need ter' waste fine 'n valuable slave stock!
And it was a good twenty odd mile trek over hard ground ter' anywhere.
No help comin', not likely.
Not fer' them, noways!
And no interference.
But the white man, damn abolitionist, would have ter' go, would have ter' die.
Should die, by all right n' proper ways of lookin' at the situation.
Fer' an example, fer' one things, to learn him not to trade in runaway darkies, and more generally ter' show 'em, yes why, Lord, jes' show 'em goddammit who's Boss.
He'd have to die.
Couldn't sell the white sumbitch anyways!
Not in this state, anyways.
Not in no state now, the way things was fixin'.
Was that a wooden leg?
It surely looked it.
So, more trouble!
Can't sell the baser anyways!
And not with that goddam wooden leg, which irritated somewhat.
Like a brand on a horse or a cow.
Sorta marked him out.
Oh yes, the basser would have to die.
Serve him right.
He'd shoot the white man first.
Best put him down.
One shot.
No point in wastin' valuable ammunition!
Business is business.
Then he'd call out, show 'em the rifle.
Get control of the situation.
From there, it got easier.
Hogtie the bucks, both of 'em.

Make sure they's incommoded.
Safety first, and then take his time.
Heh heh.
See if any of the bitches was worth coverin' (they generally was!).
Mebbe all three, if'n he'd have the stamina!
Heh heh.
Oh yes, he'd have himself a time, taiglin' them bitches.
And then?
And then?
Well, traipse down and sell the whole passel in Harpers Ferry.
The Greycoats was there and layin' out good prices, all things considered.
Not bad fer' a days work and one bullet.
But the white man had to be put down first and foremost.
Business is business!
Time to attend to business!
Snake was a good shot at distance, mebbe two hundred yards, with the Spencer rifle, certain sure.
But this was gonna be only mebbe forty foot, barrel to breast, as soon as he figgered he could cut dead centre in that goddam peckerwood's gut.
Easy pickin's!
Aim fer' the belt buckle.
Miss high, you get the heart.
Miss low, you blow his balls off.
Don't miss wide.
That ain't no good ter' nobody!
Put yer' man down!
These calculations were moot, to Snake's way of thinkin'.
Snake had never missed wide in his whole life, not with a squirrel gun, and never with the Spencer, new got, well, stole actually, three years agone.
He warn't gonna miss now.
Oh no Joe!

He warn't gonna miss.
There'd be some commotion.
The darkies, of course, would try'n scramble back 'er forward but Snake reckoned it more likely that they'd get over'n hunker down by the sparse rocks as they would come up ahead and on the left.
No cover there.
No cover.
His ground.
His spot.
His edge.
Either way they run or hid nowheres, one warning shot, if'n needs be, oughtta tell 'em who's Boss.
As the group approached, moving faster now than Snake had anticipated (and he noted this with profound and marked approbation), it became clear most certainly that the white man up front had a wooden leg, of somewhat sturdy construction, and yet it had to be light.
He moved quick over hard ground.
That there wooden leg didn't appear to hold him back.
No way.
He was coverin' ground not just tolerably but in fact remarkably well.
Snake approved of any such aptitude, bein' very aware of the difficulties inherent in travelling over this bleak terrain.
And the faster he came, the quicker Snake would kill the basser.
He warn't gonna miss from here.
Idly, he took a bead on the man, waitin'.
As he did so, blinkin', there was a general shiftin' and movement and rearrangement.
Of a sudden the group had stopped and altered order and composition, fifty yards or so away.
Snake lowered the rifle fer' to see clearer than what was evident, even with good eyesight and an untrammelled view.

The barrel touched the ground, nestled into a tiny patch of soil between the stones.
He had 'em, cold.
All of 'em.
They warn't goin' nowheres from here.
Now what?
Astoundingly, the white man was no longer there, no longer visible.
Impossible!
Snake looked again.
Gone.
Outta sight.
Impossible, but fact.
More movement.
Now the big darkie was puttin' down the other one he'd been carryin'.
Snake noticed the twisted leg danglin' and the thick bubble of flesh growin' outta the darkie's throat.
If'n he was a cripple, which he sure was, hobblin' now in front, why was they carryin' him?
Why was they carryin' him?
Runaways carryin' a injured or lame darkie?
Didn't make sense.
Where'n hell did the white man go?
Snake looked again.
No sign, no sign of him.
Where did the white man go?
There warn't a rock or tree fer' him to taigle behind.
Gone, clean gone.
This was mysterious.
Lord have mercy.
Well, waddya know?
Five bodies.
Five darkies.
My darkies now, and will be in a minute, certain sure.
To do with as I like.
Lord have mercy, heh, heh.

Snake lifted the gun up again, the barrel as he did so scraping off and up most minutely, softly dipping into the soil.
He checked the group again.
Yes.
The white man was gone.
Still, didn't make no tangle as to which one Snake was gonna kill now.
His darkies, his choice.
Business was business.
That thar' big clean-limbed buck would fetch upwards of forty dollars, fine boy that he was, and twenty-five fer' the bitches.
He didn't reckon he'd get nothin' fer' a crippled darkie.
Snake raised the rifle and took a bead on the limpin' darkie, now lead up front.
Front and center, certain sure!
And then Snake noticed with great interest that the cripple, danglin' leg or none, warn't crippled at all, or didn't seem to be, but was movin' free and clear, simply gliding along up the path, almost strollin', unencumbered by any bad leg or evident disability.
Snake approved.
Amazin'.
Amazin'.
Wonders weren't never gonna cease.
Snake adjusted his aim.
Front and center.
Go fer'the gut.
Shoot the black basser.
They were close, closer.
Closer.
Right up almost to exactly where he wanted 'em.
Here we go.
He could hear the lead darkie calling out- "Jesa, Jesa, Jesa".
Snake smiled.
Wanted Jesa, did he?

He'd send the basser' home ter' Jesa plenty quick enough, now, certain sure.
Fifty feet.
Forty.
Perfect.
And then, just before he squeezed the trigger, Snake hesitated, only for the most brief of brief seconds.
Something, he knew not what, caused him to hesitate.
Not fer' long.
Jes' enough to note, almost in passing and with some mild interest, that he had indeed hesitated before killin' this darkie.
But business is business.
Snake had taken perfect aim ter' cut dead center and kill the darkie, shoot him in the gut.
Unknown, not known because not looked for, there was the tiniest sticking of soft soil inside the barrel of his rifle, just right inside that opening for the bullet to burst up and out of, aimed fer' the gut, certain sure, and if he missed- to blow the black bassers balls off.
His finger moved, jes' squeezed, jes' tightened.
The gun fired.
Birdy, rapidly approaching, heard the explosion ahead and did not look up and out toward the nest of rocks afore all of them.
Pegleg Joe heard it too, and he turned in the path where he walked right in front of Birdy leadin' the enterprise and he nodded in reverence, lips compressed in compassion as he prayed.
Birdy's head came up, and he sang out- "Jesa, Jesa, Jesa".
Pegleg Joe murmured a silent amen.
Big Neg took up the cry, nodding, and the women joined in song "Jesa, Jesa, Jesa", and the group toiled on up the path, never deviating to the left or the right, making surprisingly good progress.

They did not look into the nest of rocks ahead, ignorin' where the noise had come from, simply passing by and moving onward.

For Snake, death was claiming him. His time of death had come. For many, death is or may be, in time itself, instantaneous, taking but the blink of an eye or the shifting of one's gaze.

But there are times n' occasions when death might seem to deliberately take time, lots of it, by design, almost relishing the delicious seconds, extending the process, enjoying the unstoppable and relentless posturing. This was one of them.

At the all too brief instant of squeezing the trigger implicit in the active process of firing the Spencer rifle, aimed certain sure fer' the gut, cool and cold ter' kill the darkie crippled and useless li'l basser', Snake had clearly seen a flash of red and black and blue and white fire. Time itself stopped and shrugged it's imperious shoulders, in an attitude which had no place in time for time itself. Light commenced to dancin'. A great welter of pain hit him square on in his eyes, blinding him at once even as he blinked unavailing, and all his colours turned to many colours amidst a rising shock of agony.

The gun had exploded in his face.

As the charge expanded in the barrel, the little smudge of mud had stopped the bullet firing, and the heated metal, precision filed, and forced impossibly back, had split outwards, bursting all of it and all the breech and workings full into Snake's eyes and mouth and nose and head and obliterated his skull and scalp as it cut dead center.

Snake scrabbled on the ground, wrigglin' horribly, head all destroyed ter' burstin', his days of ambush and murder and extortion and sellin' off runaway darkies and taiglin' with the bitches and such filled up to the brim and overflowed and all done and dusted.

Too surprised to scream, mouth all blowed to flinders and bits anyways, he jolted awkwardly away on the rocky ground, twitchin', with nowhere ter' jolt to.
He continued to writhe about in agony for quite some time.
The time of death can be and is laborious, even unto extremes, certain sure.
His death was coming slow, crawling on and into his mind and flesh with the fading shadows of the day.
There was no help to hand. No help. The darkies had gone on ahead up the hill and through The Gates.
Snake had picked his spot, this spot, leaning heavily on privacy fer' business and the remote bearings of this little nest far away from the interferences of any kind. Now, as death surged unstoppably on at the variable speed of it's choosing, there was no interference of any kind.
Nothin' would or could or did interfere.
Snake suffered, physically and mentally.
As he gargled out his final breaths, threshing, he wrestled with two questions in his diminishing senses, a tangled puzzle which he could not untie or undo or fit together.
Where did the white man get to?
Why were they carryin' the cripple?
What fer'?
Why?
Gradually, all of his colours turned to black.
His struggles, with his questions, as yet unanswered, stopped altogether.
Night came down.
His body lay where he had fallen, between two great stones, overhanging The Gates.
The vermin and attendant animals would do their work.
Soon enough, even in this dry place, he would all of him become as one, not too far from the yew tree, with the parched and eviscerate soil.

THE SHACK

Deep down in the cold and foggy weather vacillatin' wildly with the sometimes burnin' heat and glare but now it was freezin' the little party moved carefully across the hills and forests of Virginia, aimed and set to get to Harpers Ferry, at the confluence of the waters.

Cassie cried betimes, not because of the cold, but because she had set her cap at Pegleg Joe now, and it was gradually getting' home to her that he warn't the marryin' kind and that he didn't seem ter' take no stock in the prospects of romantic persuasions anyway. In short, he had other things on his mind, her priorities as yet unconsidered.

He was in this taigle for reasons unknown and undiscerned by her but it seemed to be apparent to anybody with enough sense to come in out of the rain that he was listenin' to a different drummer.

Time and again materials come to hand like a sack of flour and a sack of sugar and a pot of oil, and the everpresent fire meant that Mama Caliba and Mama Bear had a sure enough sack of mealie biscuits, sweet and delicious, left out and open fer' everybody feelin' hungry ter' eat as many as they wanted and there was always more to come an' lots left over.

Even Cassie got to be proficient at bakin' mealie biscuits on heated rocks and improvised ovens in the ground. Provender abounded, and even if the rivers was frozen solid, Birdy would break the ice at a given correct place, and pure water would leap up like a fountain from the stream.

Another time Birdy just pointed and Big Neg kicked at an icy spur in the ground and fifteen great big 'taters just flung up out of the icy soil where they was lyin' undisturbed in the wintry earth. Underneath and behind them was seven large parsnips full growed, waitin' how long Lord only knows, but sweet and delicious roasted over an open fire with just a pinch of salt from the rocks.

Nobody was hungry at need, and pastures of plenty was in constant evidence.
Pegleg Joe said that the good Lord would provide, and it was so.
Pegleg Joe was endlessly cheerful.
One time, travelin', they had no biscuits left in the sack, none at all.
The fog was deep and all encompassing and closed off the stonecold ways but faint enough in the gloom and left cuttin' rocks concealed so much so that yer' feet coulda' got blood-opened like to a knife slicin'.
Everybody should have been freezin', even Pegleg Joe, cheerful or not.
But Mama Bear and Mama Caliba had their own and everybody's feet well wrapped in ripped blankets that they had got from an empty straw manger in a knocked down horse shed way off in the mountains.
Now, they slid easy over the ground, sharp rocks or none.
Mama Caliba knew the trick of twistin' the remnants around over the toes ter' keep the warm inside and the cold out, even with sleet and ice and snow prevailin' but it held off the twisted roots and fibres and even juttin' rocks.
Cold in consequence warn't a problem pertainin' fer' all concerned,
But hunger gnaws at the vitals, and fog blinds vision, so that the enemy of doubt and fear is only partially discerned.
Fog fog finds it's own enemies and just hangs in air over all, like a soaked horse blanket dipped in the trough, and sleet flies in yer' face and in yer' eyes and yer' lips and mouth.
Hunger makes it all worse.
Eatin' the biscuits gave everybody a lift, but the sack was not bottomless.
Fact is, it was all run out.
It was empty, certain sure.
Not far away, they could hear gunfire.

Big boomin' bangs like a dull drum in the distance.
Ragged barks like a broken lock rattlin'.
Guns.
Cannons.
Far away, the War, and the battle is ragin'.
Now the prospect of a weary night in a foggy ruin of a storm and ice-cold rain blizzard with no grub at all was loomin' up real close in the gloomy fog.
Fear showed up with discernible features of pain and sickness or injury juttin' out like an angry argument waitin' a chance to pounce.
Not only the hunger, which to be fair hadn't yet really taken hold, but the fear of starvation in this bleak grey cloud hinted at desperation and sudden menace.
Gunfire.
Cannon.
Fear.
Fear can be tasted in the air.
Fear can invade lungs and breath and bones, certain sure, and may not be banished once it gets hold.
Skirtin' a rocky carapace, doubt and misery descended like a second fog over the travellers, cloggin' up everything.
Fear itself, and the dread of fear, sucked up of a sudden, sneakin' into all of their thinkin' like cold and freezin' air gasped at on a deathbed of sorrow.
Snifflin' was common, even if it was only Cassie cryin'.
Pegleg Joe looked at Birdy, who had not stumbled once now over hard and difficult mountain and hill ground in more than twenty miles without stoppin', and he knew that Birdy was about blowed, like as to all of them were. Birdy looked up at Pegleg Joe, and he smiled in confidence. He smiled a tiny smile, lopsided but happy.
Birdy pointed ahead on the way, up to an unseen pathway at the edge of a long drop, one lonely finger extended in a slow and deliberate gesture.

Nobody could see a thing, but Birdy pointed the way certain sure, and Pegleg Joe didn't doubt fer' one second.
He knew that it was so, and his head was lifted up outta the gloom, even as Birdy's head went down.
Pegleg Joe smiled amidst the swirling fog, and caught his breath, and held it.
And then Birdy turned to Big Neg, and seemed to sort of almost whimper to him, and Big Neg folded Birdy into his arms like a loving father gathers a child up just before bedtime, and held him close as he wilted into an immediate sleep.
They stumbled on, blinded by the cough-gut cloud lowerin' everywhere, everywhere, so that nothin' was apparent and every step a God- forgotten risk.
Big Neg carried Birdy.
A quarter of a mile further on up the way through and in the rocks, there was a shack standin' proud, it's back built into the stone fer' additional shelter, like an overcoat keepin' out the howlin' rains.
There was a downward slope nearby.
Pegleg Joe knocked.
Nobody responded.
It was a stout doorway, built to last, good oak in these mountains, but it opened at once.
They crammed inside, out of the vile wind and storm, sleet cuttin' bad weather, gaspin' and stampin' and safe.
For the first time, they noticed the roar of the wind beyond the door.
They could no longer hear the guns.
There was an oil lamp in good trim, and flint near to it.
Mama Bear hastened to strike a light and the spark combusted on the dry oily wick at the first pass.
They were all outta the cold and sleet drivin'.
There was a stove, set up but not lit, and tinder for a fire.

There was a jug of corn liquor, whisky spirits, and a cord of hardwood fuel, and a leather bottle of water, all wrinkled up.
There was flintlock matches.
There was a whole side of bacon, dried and deepset, hung from the roof inward, covered with spiders webs and dust glintin' in the crackle of the flames as the stove lit.
As Pegleg Joe had said before and now said again, he prepareth a table for me in the midst of mine enemies.
There was a cot in the corner, and Big Neg laid Birdy down on it and put the mouth of the whisky bottle to his lips for a tiny sip, which he took weakly, and spluttered a bit, and subsided into rest and recuperation.
Wordlessly, Mama Bear and Mama Caliba looked to the fire and the bacon.
Cassie hovered, ditherin', tryin' ter keep out of the way.
Big Neg and Pegleg Joe set down and shut up, knowin' their place now that they were settled indoors, their job done, and done well.
In the first off, the bacon looked to be but a great hunkin mess of dead and unedible black solids, but the woman knew better.
They knew that cured and smoked meat, even if cold to the point of seemin' dead, nevertheless could be cut off in thin slices and be warmed up considerable in the skillet on the stove.
Pegleg Joe was offered food first, and, as was his way, he declined, indicatin' that Cassie, weakest of them all, should get priority.
Mama Caliba grinned at Mama Bear weren't this just like a man?
Lord have mercy but makin' Cassie, the most useless, first in line over everybody else?
What would you do with him?
No sense, none at all!

Still, he was a gentleman, not that they comprehended the vulgar definition of the word, bein' but ignorant darkies, and so was Big Neg, in his way, and so was Birdy.
Of such is grace and politeness.
They looked tenderly at Birdy, and knew that their own nourishment was met in feedin' him, which they would in time, and that Big Jesa was not only providin' and providin' well, but probably grinnin' along with them at the happy and innocent stupidness of Pegleg Joe!
This was joy.
This was comfort in chaos.
Everything appeared like it was all laid out fer them, a table prepared in the wilderness.
Freezin' sleet off the roof melted wetly in the pot, changed to clear clean water, and thirst was nonexistent.
Now they could drink, and there was a wonder all in itself.
Just a sip of the corn liquor, which Pegleg Joe eschewed, warmed them up and set off a fire in their bellies and in their hearts, banishing all fear and fog.
The bacon slices, smoked to a turn, were delicious, and there was plenty for all, and lots left over to chivvy up Birdy come mornin', or whenever he woke up, which might be short or long, but they would be waitin'.
It was a picnic, sudden, unexpected, and very welcome indeed, comin' as it did in the nick of time, avertin' disaster and dismay, banishin' fear and sorrow.
It was a feast, served up amidst the enemies of fear and death and just not knowin', doubt hangin' like a thick fog.
Now all such fickle foes was destroyed utterly and overcome.
There was no sound of the guns.

Pegleg Joe prayed and prayed thanks and thanks fer deliverance outta darkness and despair.
The bacon was delicious.
The hardpacked ground was sufficient of space for all to sleep in relative comfort, and the near proximity of other bodies warmed up everybody, the stove burnin' brightly, the cordwood fuel endurin', and addin' to the heat and shelter considerable.
Out of the darkness and cold had come pastures of plenty.
There was no more sound and noise of the guns.

POWER OF THE DOG

Pegleg Joe and Birdy and Mama Caliba and Big Neg and Mama Bear and Cassie moved on in faith.
Some time out, maybe weeks or it could have been months in that they didn't know and warn't countin' out makin' their run, a dreary fog closed in all around and there was nowhere for them to go forward or back without maybe somebody fallin' off the mountainside.
The fact was that young Cassie had set her mind to taiglin' with Big Neg, and Big Neg hisself had more or less arrived at the same conclusion by a slightly different progression.
Cassie had no experience at all in this arena, but she was feelin' certain stirrings she hadn't never felt before except for mebbe a scared tingle when The Hossman had told her to shuck down and get her black ass in the hutch 'til she was pupped.
She didn't know nothin' then, and she didn't know nothin' now, but somethin', some black shadow, had walked over her grave on that occasion and she had a lucky escape, not that luck had anythin' to do with it.
Birdy had called her out of that darkness.
Now, she warn't as certain sure.
Now, she looked at Big Neg, and he was lookin' right back at her.
Both of them had the hots for each other, Big Neg bein' the more tempted of the two.
Young Cassie didn't really understand the forces pullin' at her on the inside.
She was young and spry and ripe for pickin' but Big Neg had no excuses for hisself and knew by conviction that he was goin' the wrong direction.
Pegleg Joe comprehended the nature of the difficulty at once and told them all to stay put until they could tell the mind of the Lord.
Deliver my darling from the power of the dog.

Big Neg looked at Birdy and his twisted leg and Pegleg Joe with a wooden stump and got convicted and took it to heart.
Cassie found out that after sleepin' considerable, she cooled off. Some things looked more sorta settled, and Mama Bear and Mama Caliba looked out for her anyway.
Passion subsided, and Pegleg Joe said to stay put.
Wait on the Lord, he said, and the Lord will wait on you.
Sit tight and stay put fer' a while and it's gonna be all right, yes Lord.
They stayed put where they was and Pegleg Joe said that the Lord was tellin' him to just wait for a bit until things cleared up.
Put your trust in the Lord and he will provide.
Birdy sung out "Jesa, Jesa, Jesa".
The three women said amen and even hallelujah.
Maggie had said it was okay for them to say that when they were prayin' in the cottonfields way back before they started makin' their run.
Pegleg Joe said blessed is he who sits still and waits in the name of the Lord, paraphrasin' somewhat of joyous necessity, and he chuckled at the thought of it.
The fog persisted without stoppin' for two or more days and nobody could of gone anywhere, even though there was the sound of guns firin' in the distance, great shakings of the earth and the booming of explosions far away or nearer, nobody could tell in the fog.
Pegleg Joe said let not your heart be troubled neither let it be afraid.
Mama Bear and Mama Caliba came to Pegleg Joe on the mornin' of the second day and said they were worried about food and that there was only the biscuits and the water bottle which was full about two days ago but now it might not be enough if they was to stay in this place much longer.

Pegleg Joe said just go ahead and eat and drink what vittles we got for the good Lord will provide.
Mama Bear warn't too sure about that first off, but then she reckoned that everything to do with getting' hold of the biscuits and the water bottle she and nobody else had done nothin' about anyways, so what was she fussin' over?
Mama Bear bit at a biscuit and took a sip of water and said thank you Jesa amen and felt better straight off.
Pegleg Joe got a word from the Lord not long thereafter and he always done what God told him anyways, so he went out on his own later that night but nobody could see nothin' in the foggy dark or the night and he come back with a young darkie gal.
She was all fired up in her eyes and she was spittin' fury and confusion, like she blamed him and the five others for whatever was her trouble.
Her name was Pooter and her mouth was turned down in a pout and she hadn't got no manners.
She wouldn't say please or thank you when Mama Bear offered her the water bottle and the biscuits, just grabbed it off her like it was her due, and drank and ate as much as she damnwell pleased and be damned to everybody else.
Mama Bear said sorta sideways to Mama Caliba that she wondered where Pegleg Joe had got her from but he didn't say nothin', head bowed in prayer.
When he did look up he said now is the hour of darkness and deliver my darling from the power of the dog.
Pooter looked up easy at Big Neg and give him the eye, certain sure, lip shootin' out, head noddin' in disdain.
Big Neg looked at Pooter and shuddered, he didn't know why.
But he looked at Cassie and knew her for a good girl, and a sweet child.

Even if her clothes were dirty, her hands were clean. Somehow you couldn't say the same about Pooter. She had on what was left of a pretty dress but now the red calico of it was all cut with thorns and briars and tore up considerable and with splashes of dirty mud all down the back of it. Her hands looked like talons that wanted to scratch somebody, scratch their eyes out. Fact is, she warn't a lady. Getting no response outta Big Neg, her scorn turned swiftly to contempt. She looked at all of them and commenced to askin' what was wrong with this yere' nigger with but one eye and a trailin' leg all aslant where he layed sleepin' in the dusky ground, Big Neg hoverin'.

Why was these two bitches pamperin' him and cluckin' after him like he was special or somethin'? Why should this yere' nigger get any of the vittles goin'?

Why feed him diddley-squat when the likes of her was more entitled and they warn't gonna get nowhere with him holdin' them all up anyway, so what in hell was he there for anyways? She had got away from the big house where she was a fancy, workin' in the big house as a special, and all the other niggers knew it but she had got away when the Bluecoats come and burned it and they were all dead and she was damned hungry and they better all get outta her way or else. And anyway she reckoned nobody here knew nothin', all runnin' around like a chicken with it's head cut off in this yere' fog and prob'ly they was all gonna die out here of starvation anyways if the Yankees didn't catch them first.

An' if they goddam did they'd goddam hang the useless goddam nigger first an' then the rest an' if'n they didn't they'd goddam starve anyways.

Pegleg Joe shook his head ruefully and said that she was welcome to all she could eat and drink in the precious name of Jesus, freely give and freely take, amen.

That shut her up for a minute or so while she took him fully at his word and she commenced to concentratin' on the biscuits and the water, slurpin' and even spillin' the leather jug in her thirst and she didn't say nothin' least of all that she was obliged, which she surely warn't.

But she reckoned she was plum tuckered with all this goddam talk and she went over and then took Pegleg's blanket with not so much as a by your leave but a conspicuous air of get outta my way even if she said nothin'.

She lay down, turned her back on all of 'em, and stuck one nekkid leg out of the blanket in defiance jes' ter' show 'em she didn't give a good goddam.

And so she slept while Mama Caliba and Mama Bear led prayin' for safety and deliverance from the powers of the dog, which this time Pegleg Joe said was in the Book of Psalms chapter twenty-two.

Cassie didn't know what he meant, but she could feel the tension goin' on, and kept her mouth shut as a precaution.

Pooter just rolled over and snored considerable and didn't say amen or nothin', mebbe because she was pretty well blowed even if she had heard.

Pegleg Joe said that she had got her cross to bear like everybody else, and that the measurin' rod by which anybody judged her would be the measurin' rod by which they would be judged themselves.

The fog had sorta settled and couldn't nobody tell day from night in the haze and nobody had any clocks anyways.

From time to time Big Neg or Cassie or even Birdy would rouse up and ask for a biscuit and a drink outta the leather bottle.

Even Mama Bear and Mama Caliba who had looked anxiously worryin' about where the vittles was gonna come from once the biscuits were gone come up and drank their fill, wonderin'.

The water bottle and the biscuit store didn't seem to get no smaller and it was so.
Pegleg just said the good Lord would provide and then they all commenced to understandin' that the biscuits warn't gone and the water bottle was not dried up and they said thank you to Big Jesus for lookin' after them in the wilderness and they smiled.
Later on and nobody could have said exactly when but Pegleg Joe had presumably got more orders from the good Lord and he always done what he was told and so he went out on his own again and come back with two black men tryin' to make their run.
The newcomers, Billy Dog and Bobby Dog, were from Texas, and were all full of doubts and mistrusts and suspicions.
They were brothers, and they didn't know what to expect or think.
Their arrival made up the party to nine souls in the wilderness lost in the fog and goin' nowhere, and Pegleg Joe was the only white man.
To Billy Dog and Bobby Dog this was unusual if not outright strange dependin' on how you looked at it from their point of view at that particular moment in time.
First up, they didn't understand this.
One white man, and all of these darkies were all making their run, escaping from slavery?
The other darkies were two men, if you could include and count the half-blind, limping cripple, Birdy, as a man, and four women.
Three of the women kept themselves together, for safety and decency and counsel and protection among themselves, as women will, and for continued instruction in all manner of ways to provide for and tell the men what to do.
The other gal layed apart and didn't rouse when they come in, but she looked pretty tasty; she was a peach and no mistake and their eyes slid over her slender form considerable.

She was on a blanket which was exactly where they woulda' wanted her.
Nobody said nothin' about it, but everybody probably knew anyway jes' what they had in mind. The other two ole darkie gals warn't no account, both of 'em getting' on, pretty ole and prob'ly stupid and mainly bent on fussin' around the third one, Cassie.
She was young and big-hipped and ripe as a plum peach but she kept off from lookin' at them with her eyes down.
Anyway she didn't move away from Mama Bear and Mama Caliba and she likely couldn't tell sheep from goat, or dog from dog.
Most of all, the three women cherished Birdy, who looked like a cripple, and they prayed over him considerable when he slept.
By and by he got rousted out and the womenfolk was all fer' feedin' him up.
He was pretty chewed up lookin', and very strange, to put things moderately, on account of him havin' his bad leg danglin' out to the side and a big gout of black flesh all swollen up under his chin and with but one eye squintin' when he sung out "Jesa, Jesa, Jesa", which he did oftentimes and considerable when he was awake.
Billy Dog and Bobby Dog noted the respect accorded to him, even by the white man, and they didn't understand none of that neither.
Indeed, all of the party, male and female, apart from the sleepin' vixen, accorded Birdy deep, almost reverent respect- almost looking up to him as much as to Pegleg Joe.
Pegleg was the leader, no question.
Anybody would have expected that, given what he was, which was a white man out front of six darkies. These two bucks and four bitches by rights shouldn't have no normal opinions about what or why or who and how much.

But Birdy, with his squinting crossed eyes and halting stutter, and useless hind leg trailing behind as he hobbled here and about, or set hisself down to eat and drink, was something else entirely.
He was very strange in the sight of these additions to the endeavour.
Bobby Dog and Billy Dog were initially inclined to openly question Birdy's inclusion.
But they just listened when Pegleg had said who they all were, includin' Birdy.
Never mind that he was right there, listenin', not that they cared, but somethin' got them to hesitate, they didn't know what, and they then had the good horse sense to keep mum and keep their mouths shut.
They would of said of themselves that they was as cunnin' as a fox and twice as mean between the two of them both but they warn't gonna tip their hands nohow and why would anybody who knew to come in outta the rain do that anyway?
By and by the slender sleepin' bitch roused up and looked at them with a mean eye that didn't need no spoken invitation to go along with it.
She didn't say nothin' but then she didn't need to say nothin' with the set of her mouth and the fire in her eyes.
Also there was the way she sorta leaned sideways walkin' over to the water bottle and then she first drunk up herself without nobody's sayso and then she kinda hunkered on over to them with a big eye and handed it up to them and told them to help themselves and to eat the biscuits if they wanted, like she was the one givin' out the plenty.
Pegleg Joe said the good Lord would provide and they should eat and drink what they wanted and so they did.
But they should wait here and not wander off like sheep that has gone astray and put their trust in Him and Him alone meanin' Big Jesa which they knew he meant anyways.

Billy Dog and Bobby Dog and Pooter didn't really take no stock in that agreement, their opinions to the contrary unspoken.
With plenty of eye contact and nods and winks that everybody present saw and was aware of and that didn't fool nobody anyway they made a different agreement of their own without sayin' nothin'.
But it was most clearly understood between them if not to everybody else that Pegleg Joe could speak his goddam Word from the Lord as much as he wanted and be damned to it.
The cripple could sing out Jesa and welcome.
Big Jesa could go and climb a tree in Jericho.
These two brothers and the bitch with come and get it in her eyes was gonna light out on their own just as soon as the possibility prevailed.
The power of the dog was risin'.
The good lord and this uppity white man and all these yere niggers could all go to hell and welcome, but they'd take their chances in the fog, and be damned to them.
Cassie looked on and got hit hard in the spirit and commenced to an understandin' that the power of the dog was right there in front of them for all to see.
She was lookin' at it, certain sure.
Billy Dog and Bobby Dog positively licked their lips all out in the open at Pooter, she reciprocatin' with consensual intent an' no mistake.
Their speech, initially guarded, grew louder, all restraints busted out of an' disregarded.
Anyways, they reckoned this useless nigger Birdy wouldn't be able to keep up makin' no run with that horrible limp, they had pointedly witnessed him hobblin', not that they said nothin' at the time but they all thought similar to themselves.
So the two brothers and Pooter set themselves apart and had whispered at the first, sorta murmurin' their discontent at the way the land seemed to lie.

They grumbled about what they reckoned everybody should do, startin' with the fact that they didn't need Birdy.
Did he have the devil in him, his eyes crossed like that, ifn' he had two eyes?
Did he?
What was he, anyways?
Why'd he talk like that, all slobbering?
What was that swollen, festering mass at his neck?
Was it the mark of the devil?
Was he the devil?
What was he doin' here, anyway?
What was they all doin' here, anyway?
Like as not the Yankees would get them if the Rebs didn't, and either one or the other would hang them anyways, certain sure, especially the limpin' nigger if not the white man first in line.
That there darkie had the evil eye, and no mistake.
Their voices got louder as their desires became more open and evident.
Who was this goddam limpin' nigger?
But the three women continually clucked over him like mother hens, and Big Neg, who surely was a fieldhand, and a big one, just smiled at their fear-born misgivings, and smiled at Birdy and said amen, answerin' the prayers.
The damn prayers just kept on comin'.
The women smiled and nodded.
Cassie, the pretty little girl, youngest of the whole group, could have charmed the brothers if'n she had a mond to it.
But she didn't say nothin'.
Meantime, Pooter promised everthin' and then some without sayin' nothin' at all about what they knew was gonna happen as soon as it got dark and they lit out.
Cassie felt moved to speak out.
She smiled at them with her smile, an' begged a blessin' aloud, an' that made them mad as hell.

She smiled at Birdy most of all, and she smiled at Pegleg, and she smiled at Big Neg, and she smiled at them.
She didn't smile at Pooter, but Pooter didn't smile at nobody.
Pooter just glared at the two brothers as if daring them to come on right now and be damned to all this pussyfootin' around waitin' for it to get dark and why wait fer' the dark anyways, warn't it dark enough?
Billy Dog just pursed his lips up, puckerin', and Bobby Dog licked his mouth all around, chasin' down any crumbs that mighta' missed consumption.
Pooter nodded at them, shootin' out her lip, with a drawn out certainty that she could taste their evident thirst, and was gonna slake it for them good and proper and didn't they just know it?
And any more of these yere dogs that cared to apply, lookin' backwards over her shoulder just to let them know that she didn't give a damn how many dogs come taiglin' with their tongues out and tails floppin'.
Big Neg never looked at Pooter, didn't answer her brazen looks at him, but just kept on attendin' to Birdy.
He kept his eyes down.
Birdy with the three womenfolk, now and again sung out "Jesa, Jesa, Jesa", and they would all bow their heads and say amen.
The brothers stayed for some time, hours it seemed but nobody knew and nobody could tell.
Time was hidin' in the bushes, and in the fog.
Time was everywhere and nowhere.
The brothers was lingerin' conspicuous with Pooter, nobody able to tell how long was how long in the fog.
They was just sorta mutterin' and murmurin', waitin' for it to get dark.
They waited and waited, longing for the darkness to descend, for the blackness to come, impatient.

It didn't.
The fog seemed to encroach the more, winding around them all like a moony vapour, tasting of fear and confusion away off in the distance.
Pegleg Joe had his head bowed in prayer.
Now he rousted up and spoke out and said they was all gonna be tested, watch with me for one hour, for the time of trial is at hand.
Now is the time of evil and the power of the dog.
Deliver ye my darling from the power of the dog.
Bobby Dog smirked at his brother who smirked back, and they both looked full at Pooter, who glared at them as if daring them to damn well come on, come on, come on.
Fact was she didn't know nothin' about why they was hailed as Billy Dog and Bobby Dog, but it sure warn't for nothin'.
The six other humans seemed to recede into the distance, the fog encroaching, with only the dull murmurings of prayers and amens distinguishing them in the gathering gloom.
Suddenly, the brothers and Pooter realized that the hour was at hand; that this was their hour, and that the power of darkness was upon them and they were in good agreement with it.
Darkness was here and now and at last and they could do as they liked.
The time had come, and they didn't need to worry about this goddam white man and his fancy prayin' niggers, and they could take what they wanted and do as they damn well pleased.
They were all over there in the fog, over there, doin' nothin' about nothin', and nothin' warn't gonna stop them now lightin' out of the camp.
They were goin' away from all this rubbage about Big Jesa providin' everything and Big Jesa could jes' go and see a man about a dog.
They whispered a bit together, all three in agreement.

Then they snuck off forever into the dark, takin' all visible supplies and foodstuffs that they could get their hands on.
These amounted to the bag of mealie biscuits and clean water in the leather bottle.
From one perspective, they warn't really stealin' at all, 'cause the biscuits were left out fer' eatin' anyway.
And the water fer' drinkin'.
The women had made the biscuits some days before, they said, before the fog had come down, bakin' in the rocks of the ground with God providin', and God only knew what materials, but they were delicious.
Billy Dog silently lifted the sack of mealie biscuits as they gestured to each other.
He looked at the prayin' niggers in the fog, darin' them to come on an' stop him.
Bobby Dog smiled and licked his lips, eyes askance at Pooter.
She nodded wordlessly, very much part of the deal agreed.
Time was now.
Talk's cheap, and likker' costs money!
Time to strut yo' stuff!
Come on, boy, what's it worth?
And him as well!
Bobby Dog looked again at his brother.
He was toying with the idea of cuttin' the white man's throat, but his brother knew his mind and shook his head, lookin' at the three women in blankets next the fire and Big Neg sleepin' lightly, like as not, nearby.
He would be a handful, certain sure.
The cripple was pretty there too, not that he would have been able to put up much of a fight.
Best not for no nigger ter' kill a white man, no way.
That was horse sense, and they knowed it.
It give them pause, even while they both eyed Pooter.

She looked straight back at them and didn't need to say nothin'.
Her mind was on other things.
Whatever they wanted to do was okay with her, but let's get to hell outta here and start doin' it off from all these holy joes.
Oh yes, they were gonna have a time, but what in hell were they hangin' about fer?
Big Neg might have a knife.
Mebbe the women had knives?
Oh, yes, mebbe risk killin' the white basser' and that might be a peach, but better look out 'afore pickin' that offn' the tree.
That peach mebbe was poison?
Like a rotten apple?
Looked at coolly, the price of pickin' that peach would be havin' to murder at least three men, one a white man, and probably all the women too, for good measure.
That might turn into a fight, an' who knew?
This could all go wrong, and bad wrong, and for what? There warn't no pickin's goin' amiss, nohow.
Billy Dog just stared.
Bobby Dog pursed his lips.
Caution prevailed, weighin' it all up.
Killin' them all at need warn't gonna bring no more biscuits, and they couldn't eat these niggers and the white man, could they?
And killin' any white man, never mind the niggers, just weren't good policy, nohow!
They could get into a real bad tangle, certain sure.
Or they could just head off, quiet like, and who knew what next day might bring?
Bobby Dog nodded, silent in the fog, knowin' the common sense of it, and graspin' the fact that they could just take all of the supplies anyway.
Why not just light out?
And so that's what they did.

The fog closed in behind over Pegleg Joe and his companions.
Billy Dog and Bobby Dog and Pooter hit the road.
Easing away into the stark scrub, the three of them hurried on real fast to as far as they could get to before discovery, not that anybody was in pursuit or even followin' them.
Silently, they were off and away into the fog.
The gradual blackness fell softly, even gently all around, and nobody noticed, not then at the time.
Off they went into the fog, into the deepening blackness of night that they yearned for, and had finally arrived.
They were gone.
Gone in time, an' clean off and away from the light of heaven's grace.

For Pegleg Joe and Birdy and Big Neg and Mama Bear and Mama Caliba and Cassie the next day was different.
The fog lifted at last and sunup sorta glowered briefly in delayed alarm fer' what mighta been, but thank God wasn't and hadn't come about and been anyways.
When Pegleg told the others that Pooter and the boys had run off and were gone in the night,
Cassie was inclined to cry for fear.
Hadn't they took all the mealie biscuits, and the leather water bottle too?
And now all of us left was gonna have to go and scavenge around for something for breakfast?
There was nothin', apart from river water.
Pegleg said only that the good Lord would provide as always; let not your heart be troubled, neither let it be afraid.
Consider the lilies of the field.
They toil not, nuther do they spin?
He didn't hesitate nor be in doubt fer' even one second of real time, not that it mattered.

Cassie didn't take no stock in eatin' lilies anyways. Furthermore, Pegleg said that Pooter and Billy Dog and Bobby Dog had their part to play, and who can tell the mind of the Lord?

Big Neg kept his eyes down from lookin' at Cassie, and she kept her eyes off lookin' at him- both of them reckonin' that they had a good example of a bad conviction played out right in front of them, and they both didn't have no doubts as to who could tell the mind of the Lord. Leastways they both knew they'd come up short.

Pegleg Joe repeated the phrase- "who can tell the mind of the Lord?".

His ways are higher than our ways.

Who knows, he asked rhetorically.

Who knows?

Birdy laughed out loud, and said "Jesa, Jesa, Jesa".

He limped clumsily out of the camp, Big Neg close behind and they came back in ten minutes, just ten minutes later with seven large river trout and all of the fish as big as Birdy's head.

Big Neg was grinnin' ear to ear.

Pegleg Joe nodded.

Birdy called out "Jesa, Jesa, Jesa".

Cassie wiped away her tears, stumped, and sort of embarrassed for her bein' afraid like that and her mistook fears.

Birdy knelt before her, and Big Neg looked up at her with something like sorrow in his gaze.

He knew he'd had a close call.

So did she.

She dropped her eyes, fast, not lookin' back, not lookin' at anybody.

Mama Bear and Mama Caliba smiled at each other, and set to, tendin' to the fire, while Big Neg energetically gutted and split the fish.

There would be nobody hungry on this day of days, not in this camp anyways.

As Pegleg had said, the Lord would provide.

He had and he did provide, much to Cassie's
bemusement and confusion.
She thought about it, eatin' her fish.

Twenty miles away, in grave and present darkness
unbroken by any dawn, on a bare hillside, devoid of
shelter or weal of any kind, shivering on a stonecold
rock, the brothers from Texas looked down at the
naked and useless body of Pooter and the scattered
mealie biscuits lying dank in the foggy black.
Time had stopped somehow.
Time was gone.
Time had run off and left them.
Time was earlier on, back thataways, when they had
fled off in frantic glee.
They had run into the fog and the soil underfoot
seemed smooth and easy and they just flew along,
heads full of lust and determination.
They fairly raced, eager to get to hell away from all
them holy joes.
Screaming in unchained delight they strained at the
leash, barkin'.
Not giving a damn for the diminishment of the
terrain below, they run howlin' like dogs at the moon
up in the hollers.
Tearin' onwards they come to a dry place with no
signpost or indication of their whereabouts.
This was a sorta clearin' of the soil but with the fog
kinda crowdin' in on all sides like black bushes
bespeakin' evil.
Baby gonna eat tonight!
Mebbe it was the devil in them but give the devil his
due they warn't gonna argue the point, and now they
were gonna have a time, and be damned to waitin'
any longer.
When they stopped, panting openly, the brothers
decided to learn Pooter just how they got their names
of Billy Dog and Bobby Dog. They went straight at
her, shucked down and laughin' loud.

She responded right back with brazen lust of her own.
Pooter was damn-well determined to show these yere dogs that she could beat any dog in this activity.
She was shucked down and up and at them in no time like a bitch in heat, ready and willin' to roll in the dirt.
After pawin' and goin' at the bitch like hounds on the trail, barkin' joyfully and slakin' their hot lusts, the boys began to feel anger and a sorta male pride.
They got uppity, very much ruled by the power of the dog.
Their urgency was driving them on into a frenzy to just learn this bitch who was boss, her grindin' sassy and considerable.
Time was come to learn the bitch good manners.
So they commenced to hittin' her and slappin' her and then hurtin' her and beatin' her with their fists, kickin' out.
The bitch tried to fight back with bitin' and scratchin', but that didn't make no nevermind.
In no time at all both dogs were exhausted.
Pooter had give up after not too many kicks and punches, in fact she was deader than hell.
Her still form lay lifeless before them, all of her screams unscreamed any more and her head all bloody and bruised and broken, neck hung on the side, dead in the fog on the mountainside.
The leathern bottle was gone.
The mealie biscuits had all spilled out in the melee.
These were all rotten now with maggots, unedible even if you wanted to sick them back up in vomit fer' the satisfaction, stinking and smelling of death and menace.
Pooter was dead an' useless.
They looked at her and wondered how to get something to eat, and what they could steal next.
They pawed at her but she didn't stir.

But time had stopped even if the fog and the dark didn't.
There was no time.
There was nothin' but the naked and useless body of the dead girl, her bloodied lips all shot out and swollen like to a busted apple or peach rotten on dry soil.
There was no time for nothin' no more, and they run off, away from each other.
And then the other one of them warn't there no more anyway and there was nothin' to say and nobody to say it too neither.
Both of them ran off blindly into the blackness, runnin, runnin, they knew not where.
There was no signposts or indications of where they was and it was all smooth runnin' underfoot even on the mountainside or dry ground anyways not going upwards but only shelvin' gradually down and they ran away in separate and different directions.
When they were both exhausted and could run no more, they stopped for breath in the blackness, and found themselves alone where they had started.
The other one wasn't there.
Pooter in her blood was lying all broken on the coldstone earth, and the mealie biscuits all around maggot-ridden and stinkin'.
Fog and black darkness was considerable.
They run off again, each his own, runnin' and runnin' until breath was all gone and they didn't know nothin', no signposts evident in this present darkness, terror on every side.
Blowed and busted, they found themselves at the same spot again and again, Pooter naked and dead and useless right there in the fog.
After the second or third time it happened Bobby Dog screamed at the horror.
Nothin' came outta his mouth, even if his scream hurt his helpless ears and hearing.

Billy Dog was nowhere to be seen, unbeknownst havin' his own emerging hell and chaos.
Pooter didn't move, dead on the dry ground, blood drippin' from here and there, eyes open but glazed and startin' in to sinkin' in the black.
Everything was darkness and screams and wails and miserableness and terror on every side and nothin' in front except the busted bones 'n body of the girl, blood seepin'.
Time was out of the bag and now time was it's own master, subject to no wise man's measurement.
The hour had elapsed.
Time had stopped, and eternity had begun.
The fog and the blackness intertwined and became as one in the murk.
Over all of it, the wind began to howl.

ARNOLD REPORTS

July 20th 1863
Meanwhile, away off in the future and in the mysterious realms of England, matters proceed apace.
Peter Arnold has returned from Prussia, bearing a Bible in a Box- the Saxon Seal.
He has a secret message to convey from Otto Von Bismarck.
The boat crept into Harwich in the early dawn, and Peter Arnold vanished like a rabbit into a burrow.
In Whitehall, he handed his report to Mitson, along with the Bible in a Box.
Job done.
So much fuss over a German Bible?
Huh!
Mitson received it gratefully.
From his unerring grip, it passed to the Prime Minister, and was conveyed quickly onward to Her Majesty the Queen at Osborne.

ARNOLD TO PALMERSTON-A REPORT
Prime Minister,
This report is for your eyes alone, as per our recent agreement.
Bismarck is formidable. He was very grateful indeed for our timely intervention, and is most intent on returning the favour.
I met him on the 6th; a private interview in an office in Berlin. He gave me this information and bade me Godspeed;
Two things you must know and act on at once-
The French are about to despatch a huge consignment of BRITISH rifles to the Confederate States.
Their intention is to drive a wedge between ourselves and Washington, foment distrust, poison wells, and strengthen the Rebels.
The vessel sails from France.
It must be stopped.
Secondly, and this is very strange indeed-
Somehow, I know not how, the French have been made aware of the request by Her Majesty concerning the Saxon Seal.
The French want the Saxon Seal.
I am unaware of any avenue of intelligence whence this information might have been transmitted to them other than by Bismarck himself.
The French have connected three points- Her Majesty, the Saxon Seal, and President Abraham Lincoln.
Therefore, a Jesuit Priest has been tasked with stealing the Saxon Seal and murdering President Lincoln.
Baffling as this revelation may be, Bismarck assures us that it is genuine, and that we should endeavour to protect Lincoln and prevent the Saxon Seal from falling into alien hands.
I think that we must take him at his word.
Send somebody.

**Find the Jesuit.
Stop him.
Do this urgently.
In strict confidence,
Peter Arnold**

A MAN ON A BOAT

In consequence of that missive, Sir John Mitson
despatched Michael Anderson, sometime Latin
scholar and Cambridge Double-First, to France.

Three weeks later Anderson surfaced in his new and
most recent incarnation on a boat.
Employed as one Jean Felix, on the French steamship
La Reveille, he was part of a crew of thirty chugging
quietly out of the harbour in Le Havre, and bound
for a lonely coastline not too far away from
Savannah, Georgia, Northern States naval blockade
permitting.
But the French Flag should see them through.
The only cargo was guns.
The vessel was a mile out in the central surge of the
swell, in very deep water, where the tongue of the
Atlantic descends away down off into a sudden shelf,
plunging to blackness below.
"Jean Felix" was alone now, not for the first time, in
the squalid hell of an engine room below decks.
Being the new mush, he had the least space of all in
which to live- a hammock slung at need over his
oaken sea-chest in a smelly corner, right down here
in the heat and cold and sweat and filth, and all of the
dirtiest jobs to do.
In his case this meant more or less perpetual stoking
of the great boiler which powered the vessel.
Day and night, this was his task.
Now, yet again, the others had left him to it, and gone
aloft to catch a last glimpse of France.
He had no time to spare now if he was to live. This
was perfectly fine with him, for he had no intention
of dying.
He was on his own.
Time to act.
His sea-trunk was close to hand, and he had it opened
in seconds.

He extracted the prize within, pushing aside the threadbare shirts and curios, to reveal a crude wooden box, strapped with leather.
This was a gunpowder fuse-bomb.
There was gum sealing the flaps, and the internal contents were wrapped in cotton cloth, but the intense heat would burn through this very quickly. Seizing his moment, he crammed the device, brought on board for this very purpose, into the fire of the steamboiler. No time to waste! Go! Go now! Go, go, for your life! He hurried onto the deck.
The shoreline was still visible in the dusky light, and he marked it well, outlined in the last rays of the sun low down in the red west.
He had time enough to astound his fellow crew member One-eyed Dan by leaping, fully clothed, over the side, and striking out for the shore, a mile away. Anderson was a powerful swimmer, and cared not a damn for the ebbing tides, or the remote chance of a shark disturbing him. Besides, his work was done now, and done well. Shaking his head at the folly of mankind, and with some sorrow, "One-eyed Dan" tapped the tobacco out of his pipe before ruefully making his way below to tell the others. Oh, he had seen queer sights in his time, but this was, more than most, out of the ordinary. To think that a young man like that would choose to take his own life? As he reached the gangway, the bomb, by now well heated and expanded, exploded violently.
The ruptured boiler was transformed in a trice to a giant fireball, ringed with cast iron bursting outwards, and it gouged a hole the size of a big staging carriage from out of the entire keel of the ship.
The sea rushed in and broke the back of the boat into two large lumps of steel and splintered wood, and it seized the vessel by the flailing guts and dragged it right down into it's own whirling depths in about thirty seconds.

"One-eyed Dan" had not yet refilled his pipe, nor would he, ever, again.
Knocked out cold by the first bang, all of his colours turned to green, and he died on the ladder of the gangway.
Every man of the crew drowned, and the cargo of ten thousand rifles stored in the hold vanished in a twinkling, vomited out forever, lost to the world and to the forces of the Confederate States for which they were bound.

Anderson swam to shore, pondering the likely timing of his next meeting with Mitson, and his next job.

FINDING JESUS

To address the matter of a Jesuit assassin, Jeremy MacDonagh, former Priest, sailed in a fast packet to New York. His orders were explicit, and he carried nothing in writing. Find the Jesuit. Terminate his involvement with extreme prejudice.

Weeks later, Jeremy MacDonagh had arrived in Washington. He had been a salesman, smooth and blithe. Now his contacts, other salesmen, were out looking for the Priest. Salesmen can go anywhere. They talk a lot, and so do their customers, and if the customers always get a much better deal than they expected, well, business is business. Talk is cheap. Liquor costs money. Customers are always eager to talk, always willing to make a better deal.

So they talk even more, and they hold the hapless salesman on a string- poor sucker should gossip less if he wants to make more money! One born every minute! Now a salesman, one of many who came off worse in every deal in every case, had sent in a sales report. MacDonagh was closing the net. New York. Buffalo. Trenton. Now Baltimore. Ultimately, all roads led to Washington.

FAO MR BENNELL

Dear Sir,
There is a clothier, a Directeur, working for the **JEAN LESTRANGE COMPANY** of Montreal. He is now engaged in this sector. He is expected to arrive in Washington, there to liase with the top salesman of the region. I shall attempt to engage his good offices on behalf of London. Regards,
Jenkins

(Jean Lestrange, the Jesuit Priest, travels to Washington to murder President Lincoln. He is known and identified.)

Breakfast Enjoyed

On the day Queen Victoria despatched the Saxon
Seal to the New World, Albert returned!
The nightmares stopped.
Albert awoke from his sickness and was never sick
again.
God delivered in spades.
Peace fell on Queen Victoria, as softly as the gentle
rain.
Time stopped, like the run down hands on a clock.
The Saxon Seal is gone from the hand of Victoria to
the President of the United States.
She stood at the window, scribbled briefly therein,
signing her name.
Victoria R.
God told her to sign it.
The Testament of Martin Luther.
Queen Victoria, a little lower on the page.
Good.
Well done.
It is finished.
It is done.
The Saxon Seal is despatched via Sir Charles Grey.
It is gone, just as if Her Majesty had flung it out of
the window.
Of course We did not fling it out of the window, but
in some sense We might construe that We had done
precisely that!
Fling it out of the window?
How curious?
The image persists, even as sorrow fades.
The Saxon Seal is gone.
Prince Albert, everpresent in her mind, stopped
burping at once.
Instead, he sighed.
A soft sigh, a gentle sigh.
Drina, my love.
Drina giggled, for he was getting well.

The Saxon Seal is gone.
Albert is recovering.
No more eructations.
No burps.
Little Drina rejoiced, and promptly turned over on her side and slept for thirty glorious minutes as Albert explained, gently and patiently, that he had been, perforce, away.
Now he had returned.
Now he would never leave her.
Behold, I am with you all days.
Oh, yes, meine leibchen!
Albert smiled his happy and contented smile that only he might smile alone for his only darling.
Queen Victoria was more refreshed than she had been for months.
She need only close her eyes, and Albert was with her.
Now, not burping but smiling!
At Osborne House, all sorts of things got better, at once.
The clocks began to tick.
Time came under her control.
The food, which had been tasteless shadow fruit, now romped in as delicious.
Bread and cold milk was served first with every meal, as Albert had decreed.
Generous measures of whiskey were doled out in profusion.
Chocolate was delightful.
The heavy boxes of the new, hard chocolate, two pounds in weight, just kept on coming.
Coming from that nice Fry Family in Bristol, and that nice Cadbury Family in Birmingham.
Life was good, and Albert was a treat.
All flowed from that silly book, the Saxon Seal.
Even now she was beginning to forget it, and the chicken and that terrible burp.
The Saxon Seal was gone, and Albert had returned.

It is enough.
It is done.
Lord, let now thy servant recover in peace?
The Saxon Seal is gone to President Lincoln.
There!
I've done my bit!
Enough!
Enough is as good as a feast.
I'm ravenous.
We are ravenous!
Hey ho!
The Crown shall enjoy a small portion of bread and butter!
With cold milk!
Good!
The Saxon Seal is off my hands and I'm starving!
Flung out of a window if you will!
Huzzah!
A simple meal!
Black bread and butter!
And milk!
Yes!
Simple and delicious.
Enriching!
A meal suitable for the least of Her Majesty's subjects.
Did Jesus not walk among the poor?
Did he not?
Well?
Might He not have enjoyed just such a repast as this, with his Disciples?
Bread and butter, and milk?
(Did they have butter, one wonders?)
Well?
Albert approves in joy, nodding as Her Majesty sits to table, and she keeps up a rapidfire discussion with him even as she stuffs her mouth with bread and milk.

And he chats animatedly back at her, and she smiles and laughs and giggles and returns the compliment.
Figgy, her Maid At Table, is pleased to see her Queen so happy, so happy.
It matters not a whit that she talks to the air and laughs and giggles and consumes large portions of buttered bread, twelve slices to the plate.
Oh yes, Figgy, twelve for the twelve apostles!
And a pint of cold milk for Jesus!
Figgy serves up huge meals of bread and milk and our Gracious Queen gobbles up every crumb and drop.
Albert never leaves her.
Albert never burps again.
God's in his heaven, all's well with the world.

AFTER THE BATTLE

The fifth of July 1863 found the town of Gettysburg
in total ruins for the first time in its history.
Bodies littered the ground everywhere, homes
tumbled down.
The Union scouts rode out further and further.
There was no sign of the enemy.
As the day expanded in time with the sunshine on
and into the evening's grace, they reported back with
increasing confidence and frequency.
Yes, the Rebs were up and primed even on last
evening, but no attack had come from them.
There was no action in or out of Gettysburg.
Now the Southrons battle-lines had wilted and
vanished like snow rollin' off of a ditch in
Springtime, never mind just high water in high
summer on the Fourth of July.
But the bodies of friends and foe lay like corn cut
down before the sickle.
General Meade was exhausted from labouring at
plans and calculations all night.
He was determined in caution not to stop defendin'
his position until help came.
Never mind attack!
Help was coming, certain sure.
And now, over cold water, he had received the very
welcome revelation that the Army of Virginia had
departed during the night.
Gone.
Gone.
Most probably, Sir, back down across the river
toward the Shenandoah Valley.
Gone.
His men were all done for the moment, and so was
he.
Assured that this was so, General Meade lay down in
his tent, his Aide-de-Camp glowerin' like a bulldog at
any intruders, and slept, and did not dream.

The evening stars brought more good news.
Harpers Ferry was back in Union hands.
This called for a celebratory cup of coffee, and attention to the men.
Morale was high.
Supplies were good.
Extra grub all round.
And yes, help was arrivin', certain sure.

The following day brought the best news of all, staggering in it's enormity-
Vicksburg had fallen to Grant, and the South was cut in two, the bloodline of the Mississippi River severed for good and all.
Another Scout arrived with the same message.
An Official Troop arrived to confirm the fact.
Vicksburg had gone down.
Lincoln had sent reinforcements to Gettysburg.
However, these were advancing carefully, so as not to expose the city of Washington to Lee's Army, wherever it was.
The word was that three more big Armies was on the march, approaching from three directions, with sixty thousand men and upwards.
Somehow, those numbers didn't stack up or tally nohow, so most likely that was horseshit lettin' on to be dogshit.
Regardless, General Meade could now look at Gettysburg.

Yes, the storm was past.
But the dead were everywhere, everywhere, fer' a fact.
The houses and buildings were destroyed and levelled to the ground, piles of bricks and smoking rubble heaped like brown flour rock cakes with bodies forming the colour of sugar on top.

The smell of death and rotting flesh, horse and man, was in every nostril, and none could tell which was the worse, or the more predominant.

Plans for burying dead men were hurried and haphazard, but would mebbe work, with a willin' hand and a follerin' wind.

Money, in the form of promisary notes from the Army, would guarantee payment to drafted in labourers, grave-diggers new to the profession, four cents a grave.

Pastor Gressler of the Lutheran Seminary would call in the townsfolk and coordinate the Churches efforts.

Young Lieutenant Peter Gressler, nephew of the above, would hunker down in the shade with a great big Army rubber stamp and ten edgy soldiers. He had direct commands to shoot or hang anybody, alive or dead, that got up to any misbehavin' whatsoever, his discretionary powers exceptional in the extreme emergency circumstances, at least 'til more help got here.

Fact was that were was just about nobody to dig the actual graves, never mind lever so many thousand bodies outta the field and trees and rocks and even the flower rose gardens of the town and beyond, where they hovered promiscuous, stinkin'.

Another secondary problem was the dead horses.

These, lyin' in profusion, were nevertheless much bigger as a carcass than a man on a individual basis. They gave off a stench even more pronounced than a poor boy from Illinois shot in the gut and lyin' dead three days unburied.

Lord have mercy but the reek of foulness and shit and blood and horror was jes' perennial.

There was no escape.

People comin' into the town in buggies several miles away up to Hanover Road would vomit as a big waftin' wave of putrifying stinkin' would attack their noses and breath.

General Meade surveyed the wreckage.

He concluded that, take all things all the way 'round,
it was just about total.
But he had no time to waste.
Right quick, he had sounded out Pastor Gressler.
This was the best way to get things done.
The good Pastor, Head of the Lutheran Seminary in
the town, would take charge.
He must both gather and bury the bodies.
God and man dictated that this should be so.
He had his orders.
The Army guaranteed the money.
General Meade knew he warn't gonna lose a nickel
on the trade.
The Army were only too happy to joyfully defer to
the authority of Pastor Gressler.
In reality, right here on the ground, there warn't no
Army anyways.
Pastor Gressler and the worthy burghers of the town,
them that remained, would make up the numbers.
And he would, metaphorically speakin', put his
shoulder to the wheel, in that he would organise the
enterprise.
Thing was, getting' the wagon rollin' with no wheels
'ter put anybody's shoulder to, and no shoulders
anyways, and no horses except dead ones that stank
to high hell never mind to pull nothin', was no easy
task.
In a manner of speakin', The Army passed the buck
to Pastor Gressler.
Pastor Gressler would hold the reins and lead the
way.
Young Peter Gressler with his ten edgy troopers
would provide discipline at need, not that there was
likely to be much unrest and drunkenness from so
many corpses.
The main thing was that there was nobody to pick up
a shovel and dig.

Pastor Gressler might have the full support of the Army (and their money) and his nephew all fired up to impose martial law.
But he was up a stump, and no mistake.
He needed working men, and he needed them fast.
It was Joshua the coloured man who came up with the first and best and indeed, the most successful solution, on that very first day.
This showed a great deal of gumption, and foresight on his part, given that he was himself likewise up a stump, relatively speakin'.
Joshua had been a runaway slave that had got recaptured but made it back agin.
He had been delivered, suh, jes' plum delivered by de' han' of de' lord, suh.
He stood in the Seminary Office holdin' his hat twistin ' in nervous fingers.
Pastor Gressler said that yes by all means he appreciated Joshua's comin' all the way up here to speak.
Yes Joshua and just please go right ahead we greatly value any suggestions at this time and what is it, Joshua ?
Fact was that Joshua was sayin', well, he reckoned he knew where them Rebs as stole forty darkies before the Battle had took them, he figgered, and was pretty sure.
Fact is he'd been caught on that there same Farm a ways off but not too far, just acrost the River to Jackson County Virginney, and by points West over to beyond Harpers Ferry. He'd lit out quick, them thinkin' he had fever, and they leff him alone jes' long enough, and din't send no dawgs, neither.
It was a stud farm, suh.
Fact is that there was probably mebbe getting' on to three, mebbe four hundred slaves on that farm, bucks and bitches, suh, and he reckoned that the Rebs that stole them forty 'uns woulda took them there for a quick sale.

But mebbe if'n we can get them back, then they'd be obliged to help with the buryin' of the dead soldiers. And besides, comin' to the point, his own brother Caleb was one of them stole and he can take and handle a shovel better than nobody else can and I reckoned I'd tell ya, suh.

Joshua the coloured man chose not to emphasize the additional fact that his young child Serena Mae had also been stolen, at the same time, and in the same party as his brother who could heave a shovel.

Serena Mae couldn't heave a shovel and she was but fifteen years old, big hipped and ripe for the marriage bed.

Yessir she was a peach.

Not that any handsome beau was gonna come taiglin' fer' her hand, not with her shucked down and lyin' in the hutch ter' get pupped on a stud farm, which was most likely her current situation.

All things looked at sideways, Joshua played his cards well, and even got to go and lead the party, such as it was, because he knew the lie of the land, and because one volunteer is worth ten pressed men, never mind that they warn't many available anyways, but Joshua sure was.

Within an hour, Pastor Gressler spoke to General Meade, who jumped at the chance.

Pastor Gressler thereupon despatched his nephew to find Egypt Farm, near to Harpers Ferry across the river.

It was perhaps forty miles away or so, and Young Peter had but two objectives- free those slaves from unlawful captivity, and more importantly, bring back a good workforce to bury the bodies of those fallen in the Battle of Gettysburg.

TO EGYPT FARM

Subsequently, Lieutenant Peter Gressler presented two written versions of the rescue of four hundred and twenty-six negro slaves from Egyptian Farm, or simply "Egypt", as it was known.
Both reports were fairly similar in content- the one for his Uncle, Pastor Gressler, the other for his Commanding Officer.
Both dealt reasonably accurately with the totally successful results of the expedition.
Some of these results were quite unexpected.
Both of the Reports and all of the unexpected outcomes brought deserved credit and praise and accolades and eventually, later in time, promotion to Peter.
First up was returning with a good job done, and done well, and no mistake.
The manpower problem for the task of burying the fallen was solved, at least initially.
Four hundred and twenty-six darkies had been liberated from the coils of slavery- things were certainly looking good.
All of the freed slaves were very happy to enrol as Employees for the first time in their lives, digging holes for graves at four cents a pop, or, for the gals, feeding the menfolk who would do the digging, wages to be agreed.
Even the little children could help, spotting bodies, and they would be paid as well. Everybody was happy with the new deal.
Gettysburg now had a willing and highly motivated workforce.
It was a good start to what had looked to be a bad end.
The beaming Minister was delighted, not least because he could now and henceforth draw reasonable parallels between himself and Moses, certainly in his own closet.

The facts that he himself had not ventured down into Egypt, nor thundered at Pharaoh, and had not really done anything other than to delegate the job plan to Peter did not occur to him.
But Peter had done well.
Peter ticked all the boxes to qualify Pastor Gressler as Moses- even if some of Peter's account was short weight.
Peter had leaned heavily on some truths- the slaves freed from bondage were many and various, healthy and willin', clean-eyed and straight-limbed.
Most were, to a degree.
He had (as Commander of the expedition) unquestionably achieved this.
He had gone down into Egypt's Land and told old Pharaoh, in a manner of speakin', to let his people go, which had come about, in a manner of speakin'.
But in his Report to General Meade, Peter had been forced to acknowledge some things whilst not really mentioning others.
He was hoping that the additional duties (of the military kind) which he had performed, would get him out of the woods.
He need not have worried.
He had swotted a home run, scored a bullseye, hit the nail on the head.
In consequence, and entirely by the way, he had acquitted himself more than satisfactorily, and had even returned with additional prizes.
First off, as to the forty stolen darkies, well, they were all present and correct and he hadn't lost a single one of 'em.
Plus, there was more, much more!
Yes, there were now four hundred and twenty-six (four hundred and thirty-one, in fact; but five were of questionable provenance) darkies freed up and flexing their muscles to get down in the dirt, diggin' graves and such.
But there was more!

First, there was a large quantity of supplies- much oil, sacks and sacks (about fifty in all) of grain, a sizeable pack of hardtail chaw, and many dried sides of beef and of pork, a whole rack of turkeys, dozens of bottles of wine and a cask of low beer.

Here was God's bounty, certain sure.

All this was handed over to the Army after Peter had given orders for the freed slaves, and of course his own ten worthy soldiers, to be fed and watered there and then, this bein' well within his competence, an' no mistake.

The black women had bent to the task with gusto, and all were restored to health and vitality- in truth they had been somewhat neglected in that quarter during previous days, and they also got exercised joyfully in other matters unspecified, but Peter didn't stress those facts.

He did, however, mention the forty thousand dollars in Confederate money which he had seized from the property.

Better still, almost three thousand dollars in good Yankee money was found in company with a quantity of gold coins and some silver dollars, all of which had been confiscated and was now hereby handed over for safekeeping to General Meade.

Oh, and there were one hundred and fifteen rifles, brand new they looked, and many cartridges for same.

Dreyse models.

French, he thought, from the letterin'.

Not to mention twenty-five good horses and fifteen mules and sixteen wagons which had carried everything back, some of the darkies clingin' on for a ride.

For this treasure alone, the Lieutenant was certain of approbation from his superiors.

Peter had not suffered injury or loss to his worthy troop.

However, he did have to regretfully report that there had indeed been a certain element of armed resistance which he was forced to overcome and subdue.
As an Officer in his country's Armed Forces he had found it advisable to respond with commensurate and proportional measures in order to defend himself and his people against violence perpetrated contrary to lawful authority in a time of war.
And yes, they had fired first.
Rebs.
They missed.
His men did not.
As a consequence, a total of six armed belligerents had died.
He took full responsibility.
They had been properly buried, he himself observing the necessary order of services, and the freed slaves digging the graves at no cost to the taxpayer as a gesture of goodwill.
They had been glad to do it.
All of which effort was much appreciated in their new career prospectus.
Peter was glossing over more than he was revealing here, straining every sinew, biting his nether lip.
Again, he needn't have worried.
There were no casualties or wounded, either civilian or Military, among Union charges.
General Meade, desperately in need of a success story (any story would do!) didn't even ask for particulars of how and why and who and what had come up with and happened to contribute to this magnificent solution, never mind a ton of loot outside and a fair bit of money on his desk.
And at a cost of what?
Six dead and buried Rebs over the river in Jackson County?

There were Lord knows how many dead and lyin' unburied Rebs right here stinkin' in the sunshine all the way down to Devil's Den, and then some!

He commended Peter on the spot, shook his hand, patted him on the back, and awarded him fifty of the captured Yankee dollars for a good job well done, and gave him a week's furlough in New York when time allowed, and sat back down and wrote a glowing report to Washington.

General Meade knew the importance of rewarding success, and sharing good news at once.

So he did not stint to emphasize the dangers and difficulties surmounted in the enterprise, all of which he fabricated instantly, hinting obliquely at caution and military discretion.

He pulled Rank, claiming the right to see to it personally that justice and credit was dispensed. This was necessary to his greater purpose, especially as he did not mention the Yankee money in the official Despatch.

All of the Guns and some of the supplies and hardworking darkies and many dead enemies was more than enough! Six decently killed and buried Rebs became seventy-five with a flick of the pen and who to ask awkward questions? He would make sure that Peter would be favoured from then on, but all of the credit for everything would of course go, very rightly and properly, to himself.

That's why he was a General!

Across town, in the Lutheran Seminary, Pastor Gressler, having read Peter's much-truncated Report, commenced to re-reading The Book of Exodus.

He had a new-found vigour.

He was already seeing himself correcting and exhorting the Israelites to righteousness, wearing a long white robe, with a long white beard, and lecturing God and anybody else on the importance of maintaining dignity at all times.

He was inspired by Peter's account of events.
Peter was not.
Peter was very aware that both of his accounts were incomplete.
Had Peter chosen to trouble his Uncle or his C.O. with greater details, awkward uncertainties might have emerged, and Peter really did not feel up to that.
He had, he discovered, been sticking his nose into something that was plainly not his business.
Peter had messed it up, and he knew it.
He also knew would not have been able to do anything about it anyway.
The fact is, during this holy mission, Peter had been confronted with his own human frailties and grim confusion, and had come off worse by a long chalk.
If it wasn't for the crippled darkie with the boilin' mass of black flesh bubblin' up off of and outta his throat, he never would have found Egypt Farm in the first place.
Fact is, five miles out of Harpers Ferry ridin' due West, he became totally lost.
Nobody knew the terrain.
Fact is, they were jiggered.
Joshua was all fired up with worry for his brother and, secretly, his child, but looked about him wildly and it seemed that he hadn't never been down this yere way afore.
The path, at commencement of startin' a well travelled road, then diminished into a rough track at best, and seemed to tail off into a bare mountain with nothin' on it except drygulch earth and soured grass.
There was no sign of no slave farm in any direction and no mistake, neither.
Joshua had insufficient information and lacked any clear resolution. That was a fact, certain sure. He was stumped.

But back and on in the treelined way they had come down earlier, a number of figures had stepped out into the roadway and was wavin' at them.
In fact, these enquirin' strangers hailed them loud and long.
The soldiers turned back with grim authority that looked ridiculous in it's severity as if they were gonna just take these strangers in hand and set 'em straight when in fact it was the other way around.
Thank the good Lord for 'em and how might these strangers be hostiles in any capacity, wavin' openly down the roadway steppin' outta the trees like that?
Anyway, it turned out to be five darkies, two men and three women, who pointed them on back and down the road a ways.
The leadin' darkie was a cripple, which was unusual at best, but he seemed to sorta float off the ground a ways gesturin' with his pointed finger and sayin' "Jesa, Jesa, Jesa" with a boiled black mess of flesh bubblin' up from and out of his throat like a slug wallowin'.
The other darkies smiled and said "amen" and such, and "you'll see, you'll see" and pointed towards the same way.
Fact is, there was what looked like a growed-over woodpile a ways back, on one side of the road by a big stone, but the truth was that it was a bivouac emplacement of trees and bushes and branches lightly pulled aside by the big darkie with the muscles, surely a fieldhand. It had been put there to conceal the wagon ruts in the road and the path conspicuous spreadin' onward and even back therefrom! But the road behind was cut wide, rutted with wagon tracks, and showed every sign beyond the concealment of bein' well-travelled.
This was beyond question the ways to Egypt Farm and now Joshua was noddin' like crazy where before he had just been scratchin' his head and wallowin' in angry confusion.

Two mile off down the track now laid out with good small hard shale stones for easy access (could you but find it) there was a big spread with many farm buildings.
There was barns and such, and a long low line of woodshacks like pig wallows that made up nothin' more than the squat hutches of Slave Row.
It was a Stud Farm.
A sign on the gate said that work makes you free, with a scriptural reference that couldn't be made out but that it mighta been or was like to somethin' outta Exodus.
A mean lookin' cracker let off a rifle at the approachin' party but missed wide and one of Peters' troopers shot him down, cut him dead center with a pistol and the soldiers took up good firin' positions as his body lay there in the roadway, their dander up and ready for more of a tangle as easy as that.
Four more white men with guns come runnin' and shoutin' but Peter had the approach covered now and fired a warnin' shot.
That took all the spit and piss out of them, not that there was much and then he took good smooth command of the situation, just like he was always told to do.
Anyways they didn't have no fight left nohow once they saw it was Federals and Bluecoats and they was outnumbered.
They had thought it mighta' been scavengers lookin' fer' an unprotected stud farm to kill the men and taigle with the women and steal everything in sight afore sellin' off the stock, prob'ly in Harpers Ferry or up in the backwoods apiece.
But it wasn't, and they was up a stump, jes' fer' the minute.
Goddam Federals, a body never knew which way they was gonna jump?
Peters' men swiftly disarmed them and took good control.

Lieutenant Peter Gressler, harkin' back to his study manual in the Officers Mess, remembered that it stressed the importance of establishing and maintaining GOOD CONTROL of any developin' situation.
Peter looked at this situation, puzzling as it was, but now he saw that it was good, and not developin' overly quickly for a fact, and that was okay with him. He saw that he had firmly established control now and that was good too.
It might develop, but just now it looked pretty good, all things reckoned up and considered.
It was good in theory and in practice.
He was just goin' to exercise his powers of command when he saw a big fat white man in a cream suit with a matching top hat and a lighted cigar comin' outta the main big white Plantation House just as calm as can be.
And then nothin' wasn't any good at all in theory or in practice.
In no time at all Peter lost control of the whole dang situation.
It developed all to hell and gone and spun down into the shithouse so fast he didn't even have time to spit.

The white man waved his cigar at Peter and smiled. My name is Simon Legros, he said, owner of this establishment, and we have been awaitin' our deliverance for a good spell but we knew you would come and now you are here in triumph to set us free. We are blessed this day, he said, and welcome to you all. Totally in command, he assumed the role of father advisor, dolin' out grace and compliments with a bounteous hand. He cursed sideways at his own men cowering under arrest and spat contemptuously at the dead fool who hadn't known enough not to welcome a bright and promisin' Officer of the forces of liberation. Thanks and praise and gratitude was dealt out in spades.

He shook hands liberally and patted Peter on the back and thanked him again and yet again and one more time for the record.
Then he invited Peter up and on into the house to celebrate with a drink and a cigar.
How's about mebbe a little friendly tail?
This would likely ease the tensions arisin' from this evident, regrettable, and unfortunate misunderstandin'.
Unfamiliar as he was with this terminology and implication, Peter's head was spinning.
He was confused, and up a stump, and no mistake.
There was nothing like unto this outlined or explained or even mentioned in the Army Manual for virgin soldiers out in the field for the first time.
Simon Legros proceeded with admirable smoothness, with polished aplomb and gracious panache.
In truth, Peter could not recall a word of the gushing benefice pouring from the lips of his host on the brief stroll to the fine mansion house stretched out on the verdant lawn, aslant in the heat amongst willow trees.
All was reason and perfection.
Peter was most welcome, expected, even punctual to a fault.
Should they not express their thanks unto providence itself?
This was a Federal Establishment, Simon Legros explained, licensed, controlled, and responsible to the lawful authorities in Washington.
Let the rebel reprobates sink into iniquity down and away in their Richmond filth.
Bad cess to them all, confound their cause.
He, Simon Legros, had laboured openly for the good fight, the way of freedom and equality, truth, justice, the pursuit of happiness for all men, black or white.
Peter briefly stammered a question as to slaves and slave-trading.
Simon Legros reached easily into his desk and produced a veritable sheaf of ownership documents.

All was open and above board.
Here, suh, here was proof positive of his probity and integrity.
Legal documents, suh!
These were filed and approved by his agents in New York, Washington, Philadelphia, detailing his valuable holdings and property as constituted and directed by the Law of the Land under the good authority of the Federal Government.
No slave-trader he, no! He was a businessman, and a darned good 'un! Business IS business.
Would Peter not take a glass with him?
Would Peter and his men care to taigle with the willin' gals, many and beautiful?
Yes, young and big hipped, ripe as peaches, and just eager, suh, eager, to share their favours with him and his fine young men? Surely, said Simon Legros, we are past enmity and confusion? Are we not brothers?
Surely, we are as one?
Surely, said Simon Legros, the bitterness of death has passed away, like former things, suh?
Birdy entered the room with others, Big Neg in tow, and busted and broke the spell.
"Jesa, Jesa, Jesa" he cried, and it was as though a great hammerblow rent the air, and split the stifling atmosphere asunder,
Peter came to his senses rapidly, as one who has been drowning. His head emerged, gasping, as if breaking free from beneath the freezing waters of the cold lake in which he has been perishing. Simon Legros clutched at his ownership papers, and held them forth angily. He reached for a Derringer concealed inside his silken jacket, and drew it forth.
Joshua the coloured man stepped up toward the desk of Simon Legros, partially knocking Peter aside, and brought a shovel down and onto the skull of Simon Legros, splitting his head open like a melon at a picnic.

Joshua continued to hack at this owner of the whole Plantation.
He seemed unhurried.
He was being thorough.
Peter gaped, shocked into silence.
The shovel cut away hands, feet, burst the buttons of the silken weskit, exposed and destroyed the breast.
Simon Legros made no sound.
All his colours turned to darkest black in a trice of time, and his life was over.
Joshua turned the blade of the shovel this way and that, most inventively, as he sliced up Simon Legros.
His fury was expressed as calm determination, directly active in execution.
Big Neg patted Peter on the shoulder, nodded at him kindly, and restored Lieutenant Peter Gressler to his feet, his dignity, and his command of the situation.
Emerging from the room, now rank with the smell of blood and spilled viscera, Peter breathed afresh in the wide hall and bright doorway. Here he learned that his men had explored the farm buildings and discovered more than four hundred slaves, many bound in chains.
Little children were held in neck manacles.
Women were naked, tied to wicker cots, convenient for the pleasurable access of their abusers.
Dozens of the male darkies were hog-tied, and had been whipped.
Caleb, Joshua's kin, was one of them.
Those captured from Gettysburg some days earlier were still chained, lying in their own filth, unaccommodated.
It was Birdy who had pointed out the cold cellar concealed beneath a gate of grass and tufted mud earth.
It was in the soil and Birdy knew of it without lookin'.

The entrance lifted up right out of the ground, and Joshua's daughter Serena Mae was lyin' in there chained to a cot.
She was naked, tied up nicely for the access of Simon Legros, as his personal chattel and field whore, she bein' big hipped and ripe for pluckin'.
Mama Caliba and Mama Bear set to, rubbin' circulation back into her strained limbs, coverin' her nakedness with a horse blanket.
Birdy limpin' lightly and Big Neg and Joshua and Caleb limpin' but determined headed off to the Big House with more in tow, and a firm purpose of amendment and intention.
Simon Legros had got his, and about time, too, as Joshua just cut him up all into bits and didn't even hesitate, Peter lookin' on, amazed and astonished.
None of these matters were in his control.
Now, surveyin' the stud farm, grave evils were evident.
Birdy and the others showed him around.
Peter gazed down, horrified, at a young girl staked out, bleedin' from several places.
Other women were similarly displayed, naked as needs must be elsewhere on the Stud Farm, and the soldiers set about releasin' all of them.
No sooner were the male darkies untied but they set about the four overseers held captive by the soldiers, hittin' them with shovels.
There was a brief attempt made to protect them, leastways 'til the Lieutenant happened on the scene. But it was half-hearted and wouldn't have done no good anyways.
The angry darkies chopped them all to pieces very quickly, with shovels rainin' down considerable, and no time for discussion or opinion, neither.
Peter very politely enquired as to whether the darkies would agree to bury the murdered overseers, and also Simon Legros, and they was willin' and did, happy to be of service.

Big Neg joined in, showin' a fine technique, makin' a willin' example.
Peter commanded that food and drink be served to all, indiscriminately, and the female darkies took over, as is their way, and commenced to run things in an orderly manner, Mama Bear and Mama Caliba up front with a strong determination to set things right.
Birdy pointed out the caches of guns and money, all hidden underground, and the swelling workforce loaded up the wagons.
From time to time the ten soldiers absented themselves briefly, drawn away into privacy by the female darkies, eager to show appreciation for their deliverance from evil.
Peter ignored these incidents, questionable as they might be relatin' ter' good order and military discipline. He was learning, as it were on the hoof, that what the eye does not see the heart does not grieve over and anyway he couldn't have done anything to stop it, and he didn't want to as well.
He was slowly but surely re-establishing his lawful authority over the new military and civil situation in which he found himself.
The overall situation was developin', certain sure.
His men were very motivated.
The released darkies were well fed and rested.
Morale was good. Morale was high.
It was a happy ship and a winning team that returned to Gettysburg, crowned with success.
Peter decided that he would not trouble his Uncle and his C.O. with many of these details.
They had, no doubt, other fish to fry- people to see, work to do!
With the money, he was scrupulously honest; well, to be fair n' square, almost.
He put one hundred of the Yankee dollars in his own pocket and thought no more about it than that it was his just due.

He certainly deserved reward for a darned good job well done.
Furthermore, he reasoned, if considered from a sort of approvin' eye, he didn't steal even one cent of the Confederate money.
And then he called his troopers into the big house one by one and gave them each ten dollars, jes' fer themselves an' keep yer' mouth shut or else.
He warned them that he would hang them as thieves in a time of war if they said as much as a word to anybody about it to anybody, includin' themselves.
Never had such bloodcurdling threats fallen on more receptive ears.
From then on, the men loved Peter as a great and just and wise leader, and the word soon spread, hangin' be-damned.
In the meantime, they was off to the bushes again in ten minutes to taigle with Cassandra, or mebbe Mindy. She was most accomodatin', certain sure.
Both gals and some others were waitin' in the cool of the leafy shade and other relevant locations with a warm smile on their faces, and welcomin' arms.
Morale was high, and so was the grass.

A NOTICE TO ALL CITIZENS
Gettysburg
11th July 1863
From Pastor Martin Gressler
To- All Persons of Godly Persuasion
My dear friends,
I am charged with the task of burying the bodies of those who fell in the terrible battle that assailed our town some days ago.
Together with other good folk, we are organising this work under the authority of the United States Armed Forces.
Our need is great, and very urgent, and pressing hard.
I appeal to you to help us now and at once.
Money is not the issue.
We need labourers.
We need those who will bring bodies to the place of burial.
We need able-bodied men to dig graves and to inter our fallen in a good, Christian manner.
Clergy will be present.
We need support for all of these workers.
We need cooks and nurses and general helpers who will assist as directed.
Can you read and write, even though not fully abled?
We require many clerks and scribes.
We must make and keep good records of this job.
Are you a child, light-limbed and spry?
We need such to locate the fallen in obscure places all about our town. Also they must alert them as will more ably convey to rest the bodies of our brave soldiers.
Children are vital to this work.
Can you fetch and carry messages under instruction?
There is so much to do.
We need your help now!

Have you a wagon or a buggy or a cart, or a horse or mule or donkey that can aid in the work of bearing heavy burdens?
Please help us, now!
The United States Army will pay stipulated wages for all who assist.
I say EVERYBODY will be paid good money for their work!
Men, women, and children!
Do you want a job?
This payment will be overseen and administered by a Board of Trustees graced by representatives of all of the Churches in our town, Lutheran, Presbyterian, Congregational, Baptist, Brethren, Friends.
Make yourself known to the above, if you are minded to assist.
Everybody, man, woman, and child, has got a vital task to do.
Them as are housebound can help us also by praying for the labourers. As the Poet say- "They also serve who only stand and wait".
Please come forward at once.
Some people have already started working, but we need much, much more than them.
This was begun before anybody else was asked, and all them as did so volunteered to work long before wages was even mentioned.
Now, Praise the Lord, we can recompense all from here on in.
If the free citizens of Pennsylvania and elsewhere will join and help us, we cannot fail.
As the Word of the Lord say- "Go ye also unto my vineyard, for the harvest is plenty, but the labourers are few".

Pastor Martin Gressler
The Seminary

BLOODY GROUND

Pastor Gressler prayed as he walked, the helpless master of all he surveyed.

The bleak clouds of a miserable morning hovered like vast rooks and ravens circling in darkness above the town.

Bodies littered the ground.

The good people of Gettysburg had fled the scene as best they could, with what pack animals there were left to draw hastily covered buggies away to the north or the east, or even to the west. Nobody actually knew for certain when or whether the Rebel Army might reappear, or where, and what would be the outcome if they did. Nobody wanted to ask these imponderable questions, let alone try to answer them.

Even General Meade, somewhere ayont them thar' sentries, drinking his morning coffee, was just as uninformed as the townfolk, awaiting the return of his Scouts and Riders.

Sitting there, the Commander of the Union Army assumed that his enemies had gone south, possibly back across the river and on into Virginia.

That would make sense.

Lee knew that a good-sized force stood between them and Washington, lest they venture in that direction, so the eastern route was effectively blocked.

For the Rebs to go further West would be both pointless and stupid, with Union armies converging swiftly.

He'd like it if they'd gone West, but he was too hardened a hand to hope for it, as his mother had said of a time.

Bend your back to the spade, son, and pray for rain to get the ground soft, but don't count on it!

So he wouldn't do that, no he wouldn't, thank you Mother.

All his instincts told him that they had gone south to regroup.

This he surmised, or at least believed.

But he didn't know.
What he did know was that General Lee had taken one hell of a beating.
The evidence was everywhere.
But then, so had the boys in blue; the same evidence cut both ways.
Bodies.
Human remains.
Some young men lay in death as though they were asleep, cradled on the ground.
Others had been obliterated by bombs and shells and bullets, and grotesque conglomerations of body parts jutted out, defying description amidst the bright flowerbeds.
Here, a dirtied hand, tendons extending wetly, lay atop a rosebush.
In truth this flower of death lacked only a living, busy gardener.
He, with secaturs, would be able to prune that red bloom, likely by folding it up into a horse blanket with other bits. There was no blood evident, and only the pewter ring on a mangled finger declared the fact that this was, or rather had been, a married person, a human being, a man.
But all of this man was gone, blown to bits and probably eaten in tiny morsels by the birds, and only the hand and the be-ringed finger remained.
The casual observers were stunned, and not too casual for long.
Horrible discoveries abounded.
Over there, an indescribable fleshy mess that might have been on display in a butchers table could conceivably have been a mad twist of horses guts, or the open chest and stomach and vital organs of a young farm labourer from Tennessee.
It was impossible to tell exactly what they were, not that many were seeking to enquire.

And so General Meade pondered, and Pastor Gressler strolled among his flock, encouraging, edifying, comforting.
The four hundred odd darkies, now willin' volunteers, organised themselves into balanced work parties to cope with the task of burial.
They had towels tied across their black features to ward away the smell, which was ghastly in the extreme.
They spread out from Seminary Ridge, penetrating into the fields of dead bodies.
Each group had at least two strong men, and three able-bodied women.
Horse blankets were piled high, and near to hand.
Children, spry and energetic, were valued participants, for they could delve easily into bushes and clusters of rocks and stones to locate the dead.
At the outset, Pastor Gressler had laid out the initial strategy.
He had decided that gathering the bodies together was the priority.
Find them, find them.
In truth, they choked the earth.
Find them, he directed, for many dead were hideously concealed under bushes or even right up into tall trees, killed as they spied out or fired their weapons from advantage.
Locate them, and bring them to a central spot.
Then, when they were brought together, then let us be piling them up in numbers at a reasonable patch of ground, well guarded from predators and convenient for movement later.
This would be more important than digging graves now and putting men under the earth one at a time.
And so they proceeded.
The tough horse blankets, coarse and wiry, abandoned by the Army after countless animals were hit by flying death, proved a wondrous blessing.
And more horse blankets had come in on wagons.

These were plentiful, and excellent tools to their purpose, for they could both cover up a vile mess, or serve as a travois, and their multiusage, though subject to repeated and bloodspattered coverings, made them favourite resources.
Yessiree, horse blankets was jes' jim dandy.
When a body was tipped onto this conveyance, sometimes even a very young woman on her own could drag it hundreds of yards to where others would place it in a line or pile to lie in a row, awaiting many fellows, especially if it was a downhill trek, and the corpse light.
Naturally, the horse blankets were impervious to the blood, not that much was seeping out of the bodies now anyway.
Other secretions would burst out and pour along just everywhere, especially when a body was being dragged over rocks or jagged earth.
Wonderfully, the tough horse blankets did not rupture, although the more frail dead soldiers within did.
Unlike flesh and skin, the woven bags, made to ease saddle sores on horses and mules, would endure long and arduous wear and tear.
Therefore these improvised winding sheets were most effective and well suited for the task in hand.
For the four hundred freed darkies, the toiling few, it was going to be a long job, over many days.
But they were undaunted and undismayed.
Hard, backbreaking work had been their lot since they were very young indeed, and they were used to it.
But this work was different, and that difference was putting a spring into their collective steps that had never been there before.
They were elated, even jubilant, because they would be getting paid for this work.
For the first time in their lives, they were gaining lawful remuneration for agreed employment.

Morale was high, and so were the piles of the dead. Pastor Gressler, commencing at four cents, was now promising five cents for each body retrieved.
Ten cents for each subsequent burial.
More administrative help was to hand as good men came forward.
All monies would be paid into a pool to be distributed when the task was finished, months later and thousands of dead bodies away.
All who toiled would be paid, the labourer, young or old, being worthy of his or her hiring. Go ye also unto my vineyard. Pray ye therefore, saith the Lord!
This good man of God would hold the purse, and see fair accounting, for the labourers were indeed worthy of their hire.
More sources of cash spending had and would come to the fore, although some of the notes of hand being presented might not have been worth dogspit on a normal day.
This was not a normal day.
New people were arriving every day, eager and willing to do something, something to ease the tragedy of it all....
Pastor Gressler was glad of their involvement and most grateful to the Lord and Author of all things for the grace extended to him in organising this enterprise and providing the workers.
As of this day, they were not slaves.
Rather were they labourers in the vineyard, rising early to meet the harvest, and oh, the fields were full.
Verily, the fields were full of bitter fruit.
Although many were needed, few had applied.
Many were expected, few showed up.
Pastor Gressler was very, very grateful to them as did, considerin'.
So he had resolved to pay them well, and feed them often. Feeding Christ's lambs was his calling, giving thanks in prayer his trade.

And he would feed them, and not just with the Word, although that was comin' too, and right gladly and quick.
He had the resources, and he intended to use them, with General Meade backing his every move.
Horse stew and green vegetable and nettle soup was available, plentifully so, because horse corpses littered the ground, and the wild onions and edible grasses were to be found even under the spattered bodies.
Nothing would be wasted.
Even a three days dead horse could provide right good eatin', n' fer' a whole passel of hungry mouths!
Ya jes' gotta know how to handle 'er right.
These simple folk sure did.
Some of the women were busy at once, preparing food, working hard, with hope and reward in their hearts as never before. They would be paid for this cookin'.
Pastor Gressler had said so, with the truth of the Word in his mouth. They also served who only stood and cooked, none more valuable.
So the women hummed happily even as they sliced the meat and cut out the bones, and carried firewood and water.
And, for the first time in their lives, they tasted of that food even as they served it up to their colleagues.
Pastor Gressler passed among them, smiling, and encouraging his cooks to sample the food. Oh, they must know that it was fittin' for them to do so and feed themselves whilst hard at work! And how better, than by makin' sure yourself? Thanking God the while, he revelled in the fact that there was more than plenty to go around.
The cooks were crucial to the whole task, because food would be the only payment comin' for a spell.
They also were to be seated in the Congregation of the faithful, and he would join in serving them himself.

This was no plum cake dainty, destined but for the white masters table, darkies come not near.
It was good hot vittles on the hob, grub up all round, come and come again, and all welcome. Many had been called.
Few had showed up.
Them as did would be compensated.
Thou'll not muzzle the ox that treads the corn, nor the cook that boils the broth and readies the steaks.
The only rottenness to spoil this scene was the sickening odour of death over and above the town, in every crack and hallway and in every leafy plant and tree, befouling the sunny day.
It was rank and vile, and it was everywhere.
Pastor Gressler, General Meade, and every labourer in the vineyard of putrefaction that was Gettysburg had it right up into their noses and nostrils and even their eyes.
If it hadn't been for the smell, everything woulda' been jes' fine.
Pastor Gressler, gagging, ruminated on the great works of mercy, spoke by the Good Lord his own self.
Feed the hungry.
Heal the sick.
Bury the dead.

THE FIELDS OF THE DEAD

Mrs Robinson, I appeal to you.
I understand your upset.
Truly, I do.
I appeal to you.
In charity.
I do.
Your precious child lies slain, somewhere on this battlefield.
You want him to have a good, a decent, Christian burial.
So do I, Mrs Robinson.
So do I.
And you want him found now.
So do I.
You want him laid to rest.
Properly.
Decently.
So do I, Mrs Robinson.
So do I.
And you feel that it is improper for coloured people to be carryin' out this important work.
I appeal to you.
I have accepted the task of burying our fallen heroes, Mrs Robinson.
I have done so because I am a Christian Minister, and I cannot close my eyes to the tragedy which has engulfed this township.
I have had to accept certain things, without question.
The first thing I have had to accept is that approximately sixty thousand soldiers in two huge armies have destroyed our towns and homes in these days.
They have come upon us like a whirlwind, and we are devastated by the destruction wrought hereabouts.
Our very town is ruined, and unto us is desolation, yes Ma'am.
Perhaps mercifully, those armies have now departed.

But I also have to accept that they have left a great number of their slain brothers behind, and from both sides.
So many are they that nobody can count the fallen.
Among them, perhaps somewheres, your precious child.
I have agreed to coordinate the efforts of those willing to bury the dead.
First of all, we have to find them. And the human bodies lie everywhere, spread over ten miles of battlefield from east to west.
Gettysburg is right in the middle.
Mrs Robinson, I had assembled, at the outset, some twenty-four good people of this town and nearby to help me with this task.
Twenty-four, bein' twelve men, eight women, and four youngsters of varyin' ages.
That was my command.
The Army could not give me one single man.
Oh, they've promised help is a' comin', but that might be days or weeks.
Our difficulty is now, and I need all the help I can get.
We've gotta bury about at least eight, maybe ten or more thousand precious children of the Lord.
More than ten thousand, I say, and that is not an exaggeration.
The truth is, nobody knows how many.
Just in our town precincts.
The bodies are everywhere.
You have seen them as you made your way here.
Fathers, husbands, brothers, sons.
All perished.
All unburied beneath the heavens.
That is our task.
I had, at commencin', but two able-bodied men among my labourers, both of them over seventy years of age. The rest was crippled or wounded or both. A man can't dig a grave with but one hand.

Every other single man had either perished in the fighting or gone off after the Rebs.
I have appealed to whomever's still here to come forward to assist.
Of course, most of the people have fled the battle.
I cannot blame them, I do not accuse them.
I merely tell you true, that I needed manpower and there was none to be had.
Then come, by the goodwill of Providence and nuthin' else, Mrs Robinson, nuthin' else, some four hundred odd black folk, men and women and children.
They were delivered from unspeakable evil.
But they were not bitter.
They were willin' and eager to help.
Was I glad to see 'em, Mrs Robinson?
I tell you, I rejoiced before the Lord.
And so should you, Ma'am.
So should you.
They didn't set down to smoke or demand vittles.
They brought but their own selves.
They din't ask for no payment.
All they asked was how best they might help.
And they said, set us to work, Sir, we'se willin to do as you bid us.
And so them darkie young'uns is out on Cemetery Ridge, and up on Big Hill and L'il Hill, and over to the Devils Dyke, tryin' to help.
They're locatin' bodies, is what they're doin'.
Them black men is diggin' graves as we speak.
The women and them as can are bringin' bodies from out'n the trees and the fields and the rocks.
Draggin' them in sacks along the ground.
They use horse blankets for the job.
We ain't got long enough hours in every day before dark, when no man kin' labour, and I know that to be true.
Even so, as yet we've tried to endure, despite that truth.

We got men diggin' graves in the dark, in shifts!
But they can't work all the hours of every day.
They must be fed, and rested, and yes, they must be encouraged in their work.
Otherwise they'll break down.
And they're doin' this voluntary, Ma'am, and right willin' they are.
And Ma'am, until the Army sends me a single soldier plucked here from the wars, then I haven't got but these black people to do this precious task!
So I appeal to you.
Do you want your child to have a good, Christian burial?
Then help us, Mrs Robinson.
First up, help us find your precious child.
Go out on the big road below the Seminary Fields.
That's most likely where he fell.
If you do find him, well?
If you do find him, then ask some of them black folks to help to bring him to where we can look after him.
I tell you, you won't find any but black people amongst the dead.
Anybody that can read and write has got their hands full as we try to identify the fallen.
The darkies can't read 'n write.
Some of them poor boys has letters on them, that might tell us who they are.
And then, many have what we call their dogtag about the neck. But Mrs Robinson? We don't make no distinction here. Some of the soldiers, our boys, are black boys. They gave their very lives in this battle.
We ain't gonna separate them out, now they're dead.
Perhaps they were mebbe savin' your child in the battle as they faced their own dyin'.
Yes, they could've done that.
We've found many black boys lyin' as if protectin' their fellows, and as many as nine or ten blowed up by a howitzer, and one or two white boys in the midst.

**Death don't make no distinction.
So I appeal to you.
In charity.
For God's sake.
Help us!
Help us to help you.
You want to find your boy?
So do I, Mrs Robinson.
So do I.**

BUSINESS IS BUSINESS

The weeks went by.
Gradually, men from the Armies of the North began to be sent to Gettysburg.
Pastor Gressler's difficulties began to ease as soldiers and supplies commenced arrival in the town, first as a trickle, then as a good broad stream, and then the word got out to the other towns and cities across the mountains, and an increasing army of helpers were on hand to provide for the dead.
The Army and the Nation assumed command, and land was purchased and put aside for this main purpose, as rocks were removed and stones overturned in the search.
General Meade put out a notice, verbally and in writing- let it be known that any person discovered to be plundering from the dead, or any profiteer seeking to wring Army dollars from any dealings that have anything to do with Gettysburg will be summarily hung by a Military Court, sitting in emergency session in a time of war.
So ordered!
The population slowly returned, many to find that their homes had simply vanished in the cannonfires of the battle.
Others located a ruined shell of bricks, or a mound of rubble, detritus of a home .
Some found their dwellings intact, but now a dormitory of sleeping soldiers was installed in what had once been their living rooms.
Most of the undamaged buildings had been sequestered for the use of the troops.
There was talk that the Government in Washington would dedicate the whole municipality as a graveyard site, and do it by compulsory purchase.
The place would become a National Park, and no power would prevail in opposing the measure.

Local entrepreneurs considered the options, their normal greed somewhat tempered by the Army notice.
But, hey, business IS business, ain't it so, Joe?
Gettysburg, they felt, was gone as they once knew it, and warn't a'comin' back, nohow!
But, hang dog, Joe, Money DOES talk. N' what it sez is- let's you 'n me git t'gether n' go 'n have a good time!
Anyway, the Bank building was no more than a greasy spot, blown to Kingdom Come, and all records thoroughly destroyed thar, har har.
Oh, there'd be some leeway extended to claimants as might come forward, but for the most part, Gettysburg was done as a thrivin' community.
The war had seen to that.
Gettysburg was done.
Done 'n dusted!
Local Aldermen could go and spit- the Federal beaurocrats would run things now.
Was yer money in or out?
Opinions varied.
Nationally, the financial powers-that-be were mindful of the people's reaction- that Gettysburg had become a grave, and must be respected as such. The sheer number of dead dictated that fact.
And then there was the feeling of finality in the air- that things were coming to a close, and, if the North hadn't won, well it sure hadn't lost.
Ayeah, Joe, we might be lickin' our wounds, n' ain't no joy, Leroy, but Johnny Reb had come off worse.
So national fervour soared, and the normal practice of searchin' fer a nickel in the Churchyard and finding a dollar in the shithouse diminished, for some.
Money-making opportunities would be limited.
Building contracts would be closely scrutinized.
There would be no fast bucks, and the pork barrel was empty as regards THIS town!

The Army had it's dander up, and no fat man with a high hat and a fob watch was going to be allowed to plunder the legacy of those whose bodies littered the ground.
That was okay, George, but business IS business, ain't it?
And the talk rolled on.
Things began to take shape.

Only the Lutheran Seminary retained it's respectable prominence in consideration by Government, not only for the very real and important role which it had fulfilled in the battle itself, high tower, lookout point and HQ on the first day, but also for the urgent and largely successful activities emanating from that quarter in burying the bodies.
Pastor Gressler found grace abounding as his efforts, humble at first, drew approval of all kinds from afar.
There was disbelief and anger when others in other towns heard that the several Armies had arrived in vast numbers, devastated the town, destroying many buildings, shed thousands of dead in their wake, and left the shell-shocked civilians to clean up the mess behind them even as they moved onward to more destruction.
And a Pastor, a poor Lutheran Pastor, was granted the legacy of this terrible chaos.
His team of helpers grew as the word spread, and distant churches sent well equipped men to assist in getting the job done.
Now wagons arrived, with fresh mules and sharp new spades and strong limbs to exercise them in putting the bodies under the ground.
Goods and grub was arrivin' from back East.
Somebody was diggin' deep into their wallets, and no mistake.
Everywhere, the horse blankets arrived, were opened and distributed in never-ending supply.

Vittles came with them, meal and hardtack and dried meat and raisins and cornbread loaves, which even the smallest daughter of a home could bake and do their bit.

Them as could journey to Gettysburg, did.

Some of these volunteers were injured from the war, missing an eye or a foot, but willing to help. A small few had done their stint in battle, and because of age or sickness had been discharged.

Mothers, wives, sisters, and sweethearts of missing soldiers turned up often, looking for a loved one, searching in vain.

Mrs Robinson proved to be one of the first in a long line of these unfortunate women, searching, longing, straining their eyes to see, without hope, and without joy.

Her initial reaction to the darkies labouring among the precious dead was shared by many of those bereft of kin, for a brief time, before reality struck.

For most northerners outside the big cities, darkies were strange and odd aliens, not understood because never dealt with.

In truth, these people knew almost no negroes. They had none on their farms and none living nearby.

Their ignorant, casual racism went utterly unchallenged.

They owned no slaves, and most of them had never seen a slave in their whole lives.

Local Preachers never declaimed on the matter because it didn't pertain to folk in their community. Anyways, din' the Bible say that darkies SHOULD be slaves, by right 'n all?

There was ignorance, and there was confusion, but there was also them that din't give a damn, took no stock in it, and better jes' get on, jes' one damn thing after another, one damn thing after another.

So there was a common misunderstanding about black people.

There was a common misunderstanding about the rights and wrongs of who should bury white bodies and black bodies.

There was ignorance about the proper way to do things in a civilized society.

Here, in Gettysburg, where the only white skinned labourers were also dead ones, practical reality hit, and hit hard.

If the darkies weren't here to clean up, the sweet bodies of cherished darlings would rot on the ground, like apples on a tree that ain't picked, and so attitudes changed.

Opinions changed right quick.

When the civilized society ruled by reason and honour and God's truth has produced thousands of dead bodies in urgent need of burial, values must needs be re-examined, and fast.

Fairly soon, the usage of the term "niggers" diminished, being replaced by "darkies", and then, in almost grudging respect, "workers".

Women, old, young, and ageless gradually found each other and made common cause.

Mrs Robinson, first into the fray, took the ascendancy, as women will.

She had swiftly lost her animosity towards the black workers, very soon after speaking to the Pastor.

She was stumped, wavering.

She realized that she had never contemplated the matter before.

She imagined herself as an apple on a tree, one whose time has come, and that a change of mind and heart would plunge her to earth.

She was on the brink, teetering.

And then she went searching for Wilfred.

One look at the bodies of the soldiers on Seminary Hill did the trick, and she felt a keen judgement upon herself that she had ever spoken as she had.

With not one white face to confront, she knew not where to turn.

All of the righteous indignation in her, all of the swelling anger that she was bottling up, ready to hurl at whoever wasn't doin' their job in findin' HER boy, dissipated into repentance as she looked at a great line of human bodies lying in a row, some with trinkets or letters or pictures tucked neatly under their heads.
These were MEN!
Boys!
Children!
Dead men, boys, children.
Hundreds of them.
And away, there, there in the next field, were more hundreds and hundreds, some with faces turned to the sky, some with faces turned to the earth and grass and dirt. She could see them.
Were there other mothers like herself, wanderin' like lonely ghosts amid the dead?
Were there sisters and daughters and wives? No, not wives now, but widows?
All, all bereft?
She looked at a black woman dragging the body of a child in a horse blanket.
It had to be a child, it was so small.
So small, near to her.
They came closer, came right up to her, passing her close by.
Now she could see most clearly.
Yes, it was a small body, and surely didn't look like a full grown man.
Yes, at first glance, a child!
But the child had a full beard and whiskers, and the smallness was accounted for by the fact that the dead man had no legs or middle attached to that weskit, curiously serge in the sunshine. No, this was not her child, her precious boy. But it might have been.
The black woman struggling with the load was being both respectful and tender, in her way.

And she was right here, right now, helping to bury this poor soldier.
All the stay-at-home voices were shown up for what they were- empty barrels.
This ordinary black woman was worth a million of them.
Lord only knows where she came from or what had happened to her, but she was right here, labouring in the vineyards of the Lord.
Other women could nag and cavil.
She was doing the work.
Mrs Robinson's heart went out to her.
She suddenly heard her words, tasted her unkind thoughts again, and the gorge in her being revolted and she felt only shame.
Bursting into hot and tired tears, she spoke to the heavens-
"Forgive me, Lord," she said out loud. "I was ignorant. I'm sorry. Please forgive me. I'm sorry. I won't ever do that again. Please forgive me."

A CORRESPONDENCE WITH GENERAL MEADE

10ᵀᴴ NOVEMBER 1863
FAO Major General Meade
The Army of the Potomac
Washington DC

From-
Mr Bowes Roberts
Director
Morgan Bank
Astoria,
New York NY

Dear General Meade,
I write to you in person concerning a matter which not only touches us both, but also affects us in the negative- you in your role as custodian of United States Army affairs, myself in mine as a Director of Morgan Bank.
Many others, like you and I, are also squarely (although unfairly) tainted by this squalid Mr Septimus Ince business which has now come to light.
That it has been discovered at all is due only to the most merciful intervention of Providence.
I was personally (and professionally) involved to the utmost degree.
I have witnessed this at first hand, I tell you.
And I will subsequently testify when this matter comes to Court, as it must.
I am determined to do that.
Had it not fallen out as it has fallen out, then a most foul fraud had been perpetrated upon our dead heroes- those who have paid the ultimate price for the freedom of our country.
Among these hallowed dead is my own child.

An infamous cheat has been unmasked, and the ordinary and regular business practices of your Office and my Bank have been upended and unravelled and shown to be not worth dogspit; not worth the paper they are written on!
Both you and I have been all but undone.
But it was not random chance or mere accident which led to the apprehension of the thief, but the hand of the Almighty.
This fact is evident, as I will testify herein.
The perpetrator, soon to be formally accused- that same Mr Septimus Ince, is now in the custody of Marshall Daniel Gintner, prior to Trial.
He is being held at the Army Barracks in New York. If I have any say, he will remain there permanently, and, in the end, not above ground.
These events unfolded in the town of Gettysburg in the aftermath of the great Battle there some months ago.
The crimes which he has committed were perpetrated knowingly and deliberately in the arena of your jurisdiction and pertaining to US Army finances in a time of War.
For that reason, which I reiterate emphatically, I count this as nothing less than treason.
Treason, I say, against our nation!
This miscreant has sullied and dishonoured many worthy soldiers and willing citizens, including my own fallen child.
Hence my personal thirst for justice- but there is more, much more.
The consequences are damning, to speak mild.
Your Administration Office is tainted and befooled- your procedures suborned to theft and personal gain; the entire basis of your trust with the people of America is perverted and abused.
May I assure you that I do not charge you directly with these failings.
I can, and I do, admit to them myself.

However, you and I are the Executive Officers involved, even though we knew not of the fraud and the theft.
But in direct consequence we (you and I) must bear the responsibility.
We cannot avert our eyes and pass the blame on to subordinates.
As the wise Chairman intones (however smoothly), the buck stops here.
However, as I said, the theft and fraud was discovered.
The main damage sustained is to the reputation of my Bank and your Army.
As of now, there is only knowledge of the matter within those offices.
This is not out in the open, at least not yet.
So there are various consequences arising and resulting from that fact.
We can staunch the wound, and let us not pretend that we are not wounded, and seriously.
We can present this to the nation, not as a failure, but as a victory for law and order; but let us not diminish the magnitude of the defeat we have suffered.
At the least, not amongst ourselves!
Let us not befool ourselves.
Let us not lie to each other.
We have been brutally injured.
The transgressor looked to escape unscathed. His expectations were high. Briefly, he held the ascendancy. He would, he thought, get away with our money and disappear, scot free!
He no longer enjoys that confidence, or that possibility.
I think that you will agree with me as to the best course of action.
I communicate with you now to lay before you the complete evidence whereby this vile person can be brought to the Justice he deserves.
To my mind, that will be a rope and a scaffold, gratis.

This thief merits nothing less.
But let us work toward that end, and leave the verdict to the Jury and the sentencing decision to the Judge.
That is, if there is a Jury.

Another possiblility emerges; this crime, touching upon offences against the Armed Forces in a time of War, might be best considered "in camera".
If that transpires, then I will be heard at that Court, none louder.
You know my opinion.
I want him dead.
His end is my end, if you will.
The Lord helps them that help themselves.
I have provided herewith the administrative documents pertaining to the business.
All of these are certified within our Governments own (yours for the Army, mine for the Bank) highest standards of approbation.
All of these have passed muster.
They are recorded and and notarised and registered as competent, compliant, sound.
They are nothing of the sort.
All of these are thoroughly fraudulent.
In the vernacular, they are worth nothing.
However, they constitute unquestionable evidence of the extent to which this grubby business succeeded in pulling the wool over our eyes- yours and mine.
I will write again.
My purpose will then be to acquaint you with how I personally became involved, and I might say embroiled, in tearing the mask away to reveal the rotten edifice within.
Yours Faithfully,
Bowes Roberts

12TH NOVEMBER 1863
FAO Major General Meade
The Army of the Potomac
Washington DC

From-
Mr Bowes Roberts
Director
Morgan Bank
Astoria,
New York NY

Dear Sir,
I have received your acknowledgement and the missives from Captain Andrews.
I am grateful for your swift acceptance of my account of the falsification of the documents and I trust that we will proceed in harmony to clean up this mess and get Mr Ince into the prison graveyard where he belongs.
I have traced the sequence of events which commenced within but a few days of the terrible battle when our forces fought so magnificently. This same sequence of revelation concluded, or I could say unravelled, only some very few days ago- by my own direct and personal involvement!
It is a wonder; a wonder, I say.
I will justify that statement.
I shall begin by telling you about my son.
I have reason to believe that his name and his exploits on the field of battle may not be unknown to you.
He died at Gettysburg repelling the final Rebel Charge on the third day.
He was my eldest son, Corporal Ned Roberts, and he joined the Astoria Volunteers as soon as the War commenced.
On Day One he signed up.
He was just seventeen years old at that time.
He didn't live to see his twentieth birthday.

I admit it, I was against him joining up;
I could have spent money, and I intended to spend money, to procure some sort of deferral-but he was adamant.
More importantly, he was of age to fight.
There was no discussion, in any event.
Ned had wanted to serve his country all his short life.
His grandfather on his mother's side fought at New Orleans. My father-in-law is still alive. Ned worshipped him. Ned had an uncle, son of the same, brother to my wife, who fought and died of his wounds, got at San Jacinto. You will have heard the name of that battle.
Until fairly recently, there could be no greater boast in a family- our kin fought, our kin died in the Mexican War.
You could say that fighting and dying for his country was in his blood.
He inherited it.
I didn't.
My people started in feedstore sales and went on to Banking.
My father chose the safe and the sure way.
He passed his cautious profession to me and I wanted my eldest son to follow in that family tradition.
Ned wasn't interested.
The only thing he ever wanted to do was join the Army and fire a gun.
But firing the gun arrived first.
His grandfather gave him a squirrel rifle when he was seven. That's when Ned started firing in earnest.
He taught himself how to make the tiny balls, melting and casting them at the blacksmiths forge. He made them himself.
He would go out hunting and come back with rabbits and partridges, but that was too easy for him. He wanted bigger game, better bullets, finer ammunition charges, and better rifles. He got all of his wishes.

We had a family place up at Woodstock, all open country.
Ned progressed with regularity, remarkable in one so young.
He could kill deer.
He once got a bobcat that was killing cattle. He showed the head- one shot right between the eyes.
Remarkable!
We were very proud of him.
Everybody liked him.
Of course, he was the best shot in the school, best in town, and he progressed until he became the best in the county.
Every target shoot, every turkey shoot, he would take part.
Youngsters, of course, couldn't live with him. Older hands, farmers, soldiers, roughriders, well they could outshoot him, but they'd all extend a warm congratulations to him afterwards!
Why?
Because it takes gumption to stand up among men and compete.
These men, some of them, had been shooting guns all of their lives.
A boy, nine years old, laying down his dollar admission at the County Fair?
And then getting into the second and third round?
Maybe one hundred participants, and my son in the final twenty, on one occasion the final ten, shooting with skilled veterans, some in uniform?
This little boy, stepping up to take his turn, his name announced repeatedly as others were eliminated?
Nine years old?
I'm sure you'll agree that this was a fine achievement, and impressed many with his determination and ability.
He did exactly that, and the other competitors, well they surely appreciated the fact.

He would get commendations and honourable mentions.
The outright winners would thank him for taking part, and point him out.
The Mayor and retired soldiers would ask to shake his hand, and mine.
It was unusual, to say the least; The proud father deriving reflected glory from his young child.
This went on as he got better and better, now ten, eleven, twelve years of age.
I was most impressed.
Then, rising thirteen, he began to win competitions.
He was very gracious in victory, very magnanimous.
He had learned that.
You see, he was not only smart, but generous?
He knew that a few words spoken in victory honoured others and cost nothing; but it bought precious affirmation!
More glory to the father.
I just accepted it all as my due.
I was very proud of him.
I just couldn't see, at that stage, that he was mapping out his own future, according to his own values.
But that's what happened.
Yes, firing a gun was in his blood, and everybody approved of the activity.
He was singleminded, and dedicated to shooting his gun.
He would practice, hour upon hour.
I had always impressed on him the fact that practice makes perfect.
He took that wisdom to heart.
Ned would practice.
There is no luck, he would say.
The more I practice, the luckier I get.
He practiced by the hour.
He wanted two things- perfect accuracy in his aim, and to continually extend his range, firing from distance.

Still, as he grew older, I attempted to interest him in finance, hoping that he would find his place at the Bank.
He didn't care in the least. It didn't touch him in any way. It simply did not resonate with him.
Oh, he could do the math, none better.
He just saw no value in calculating compound interest or the evaluation of stock options in a Bear Market- he just wanted to shoot a real bear.
When I prevailed on the schoolteacher to suggest the study of higher mathematics to Ned, he opined that Ned would excel.
He always did; that was the paradox of it- straight "A"s, top of every class, never missed his homework.
Never missed any target he aimed at, whether turkeys or the multiplication tables.
Apparently, Ned took to trigonometry like a duck to water.
The teacher wrote to me in joyous commendation.
Top of the class, top of the school, outstanding, and polite and mannerly with it.
And then we found out the reason that Ned was so successful.
He was using the trigonometry to calculate range and distance when firing a rifle.
I laughed, but it was a dry laugh, tempered with just a shade of frustration.
How was I going to make a Banker of him?
Like a kind of King Midas, everything he touched turned, not to gold, but to guns!
Ned was unstoppable.
I coached him in constructing and presenting a business letter, emphasizing the importance of correct terminology, cogency, economy of effort.
Know your subject, I said.
Not only did he heed his venerable father's direction, he bettered the instruction!

He wrote a letter to the Head Engineer of the
Armoury at Springfield, Massachusetts, a Mr Henry;
approached him pertaining to methodology for
striking a stationary target at two hundred yards-
what was the optimum bore for specific ammunition
of varying calibre?
I saw it.
Mr Henry copied me the correspondence, like any
wise father and businessman would.
These were excellent inquiries.
Correct terminology?
Cogency?
Where did he get it from?
Had I taught him that?
How, he asked, did the weight of the powder charge
(specific to each shot) impact on the waste residue
within the barrel after firing?
How could this wastage be diminished or minimised?
How far could a projectile travel, in theory, with
maximum velocity achieved?
In what respect might the theory succumb to
alteration relative to varying factors?
How many bullets can be contained in a chamber
before diminution of balance?
How many of these can be fired in a sequence without
reloading?
What, in his learned opinion, was the finest weapon
currently in production to effect this determination?
And what did the gentleman think of Ned's own
documentations regarding the matter, drawings and
designs herewith enclosed?
This terminology was a mystery to me.
But not to an Engineer at the Armoury.
Designing the barrel and chamber of a rifle?
Working toward the concept of a "repeating rifle"?
This at fifteen years of age?
I could not find fault with his industry.
He was endlessly busy.
His written submission was outstanding!

He was polite and respectful, and many parents commented favourably on the fact.
The truth is, I was very proud of him.
Nobody could have known that the war, this war, was coming.
I certainly didn't.
Not in any real sense.
Not in the sense that it would affect my family, my life, and cause the death of my eldest boy.
Oh, I could see that war was coming, and would indeed come.
What businessman couldn't?
But I only recognised the joyful idea that this would bring about amazing opportunities to make money.
I could not foresee the tragedy, the struggle.
There is no struggle when you count dollars and cents.
As the poet says, there'll be time enough for counting when the dealing is done!
Ned, however, knew that war would mean that rifle bullets would thud into a man's chest or skull, blowing away his breath or his brains and his life.
I calculated the profit ratio on the production of ammunition.
He calculated the calibration of sighting methodology relative to decreasing visibility.
I would say to him- "the time to take a profit is always now".
He would say to me- "a target vanishes at five hundred yards".
Ned understood what the ammunition was there for, what it would do.
Ten bullets, ten dead enemies.
I did not think in those terms.
My outlook was very different- so many grains of black powder, such and such a weight of refined metal, so much profit in dollars and cents.
In retrospect, I can see that he was very much a man of his time.

Not my time.
No, I couldn't see that, at the time.
You will appreciate that I am grieving here.
I ask you to indulge my sorrow while I search for words to fully express the ways in which our paths divided and finally sundered.
Mine was the determined private struggle, oh yes, presented as public service, to provide ostensibly the public, but in fact myself, with personal security, and financial solidity.
What a rogue and peasant slave was I ?
Where was foresight, where was wisdom?
Drowned, I tell you, under a shower of coins!
I was a hypocrite, and the wages of my sinfulness are paid in full, and I deserve them, none moreso!
Ned was only interested in freedom.
I couldn't see that.
Freedom was something I took for granted, never had to reach for- it was just there, like my clothing.
I cannot remember a time in my life when either clothing or freedom was in question.
Ned knew better.
He was right.
I once asked him to define happiness.
What is happiness, I asked him.
Please define happiness for me?
I had just made a killing in something or other.
I was very happy, or so I thought.
And I didn't really want to hear his view of happiness.
I wanted to present my own to him.
I wanted to wipe out whatever he said, if he said anything.
I wanted to slap my great opinion on the table, and stop all argument once and for all.
I wanted to deliver the knockout blow.
I wanted to deliver a punchline, something like-
"when I realise a profit of twenty thousand dollars in one hour, then I am truly happy"!

Ned did not think in those terms.
He paused, briefly, I admit.
Probably he wanted to get his words in order. And then he looked at me and smiled, trumping my ace most eloquently before I had even played it.
He said "Happiness is the full use of all of your powers along lines of excellence".
I did not speak, because I could not.
As I think of that moment when he expounded the difference in our values, he was telling me that he loved me from the swelling depth of his being.
I see myself as only a shallow, greedy, miserly egoist, grabbing at gold.

My dear wife passed away when he was sixteen years old.
I cannot speak easily of that painful time, as you will understand, but Ned was stalwart in consideration to myself and his three brothers.
He was endlessly kind. He was a tower of strength in a time of affliction. No father could be more proud.
At about that time, or at least not long after, he decided to make his own way in life.
I don't blame him.
He was right.
I was wrong.
I wanted him safe and comfortable.
He wanted no such thing.
I have to admit that I was blind to the spirit in him, the spirit of concern for our country.
I had decided that the common herd should go and fight.
Not my children.
There was going to be a lot of money to be made in this war.
Me and mine should have our portion of that pie.
Fighting rebels was beneath us.
In my heart, I despised the common soldiers. Cannon fodder, that's what they were.

However, Ned, by his example in giving his life, has kept me from that shameful posture, then and now- and he was right to do so.

I am paid fitting wages for my falsehood, in that my child is dead.

But Ned has redeemed the family name.

I know that now.

In a very real sense, he has washed me with his blood.

I wanted Ned to go to college, perhaps study Law if he didn't take to Finance.

Ned, by this time, had a healthy correspondence on the go with not only Mr Henry, who he wrote to, but also with Mr Smith and Mr Wesson.

These men were all Partners in the enterprise.

They knew about guns.

By the time I thought it opportune to hint to Ned that he might wish to approach certain Colleges, I was too late.

Ned unfolded his own plan.

He had got himself a most excellent employment- a management position, good wages, sensible career prospects, even a pension- this at age sixteen.

In fact, he was already in situ; had been for a month.

He was going to work as an Engineer- designing and developing firearms for our armed forces. And he would test-fire them himself.

He had the know-how and the vision, and the confidence of youth.

He was one of several persons involved in the design of the Henry Rifle; yes, the breech loading repeating rifle.

Ned did that!

Indeed, the development of that weapon would be a substantial contribution to our country's welfare in itself, especially with war approaching.

But he didn't stop there.

Ned was getting on with business, except that it was not his father's business (if you'll pardon the wry and somewhat irreverent humour).

I was determined to make it his father's business.
I could only see things as a balance sheet, with profit and loss writ large in bold type, and nothing in the "loss" column.
I knew in my bones that Ned was destined to bring great profit to me; that his internal call to the worship of firearms was only a tangential foray before he rejoined the flowing stream of delicious and delightful dollars.
Now I had the Directors of a major Arms Company singing the praises of my son, and the prospect of endless profits, millions of dollars, extended unto me and mine through his juvenile efforts.
Did God not, I asked myself, work in mysterious ways, His wonders to perform?
This was in eighteen and sixty.
I made enquiries as to the fiduciary capability of the Company.
And it was remarkable!
Fiscal solidity guaranteed!
Blue chip!
Sound and safe!
There was more!
Sniffing the wind, so to speak, I soon learned that there was a very hefty Government Contract in the offing.
In consequence I went to my Board and recommended a substantial investment in the Firm.
Speculate to accumulate, I trumpeted!
Invest to succeed!
They approved.
We moved.
When a big Bank makes a big move, the Earth shakes.
That's what I thought, that's what I said.
But I was a liar, and only fooling myself.
This was no speculation.
It was a licence to print money.

Effectively, we were guaranteed to succeed, with government backing.
There was no risk, no risk at all.
If the government asks you to fund the manufacture of a million rifles, and all you do is work out the cost and add a big fat profit onto that and send the bill to Congress, where's the risk?
How could we lose?
We couldn't.
We were first onto the ground, first in the game.
When the other banks got around to wondering if the project was feasible, we had it sewn up.
By the time they laboriously sent somebody to take a look at the Factory from outside the stone walls, we were sitting inside the Offices, drinking coffee, and offering the money up front.
Forward funding!
Cost and risk eliminated!
We were going to grease the wheels.
This was my territory, and my Bank made an immediate killing.
Why?
Because the product was so good! And the terms we asked for and got were ridiculously weighted in our favour- I could say scandalously so!
Nobody cavilled.
Business IS business!
Seize the day!
The time for profits is NOW!
And how had Morgan Bank arrived at that pleasant position?
Ned gave us that advantage.
It was all down to him.
I was delighted. He had made good in Banking! Thus I contented myself. In private sales alone, advance orders, we realized a big profit. The main spinoff was yet to be harvested. Why rush to grab a ten percent profit when you can see double that in an hour?

Oh, the time to take profits is now! We cast our bread upon the waters and got it back in five minutes.
And the spinoff was beyond calculation!
We would finance the sales of these guns to all nations now and forever!
Cash on the barrel and your principle back doubled, tripled, quadrupled? With more to come? And that guaranteed by the Bank of America?
In common terminology, we were buying dollar bills for a dime.
In Banking language, a nine-hundred percent profit on a minimal outlay is commensurately acceptable.
Now came the biggest game of all.
Men of vision and clear sight knew the wisdom of preparing for war, when every fieldhand and blacksmith would need to hold a gun in his hand- the cost of which was three years of his personal wages rolled up and paid for by his fellow taxpayers.
Happily, when that occurred, we were the only team suited up and ready to play ball.
We got in on the ground floor.
We even produced, as a diversion, (and it greatly amused me at the time) an expensive Competitors Tender from one of our subsidiaries, which naturally lost out to our more economically advantageous offer.
We beat ourselves at our own game!
Everybody was happy and my Bank brought home the bacon!
We financed the production of the Springfield Rifle for the Army.
We got the contract, and it was a whale indeed.
It was an ocean full of whales, and we were the only fishermen.
This was God!
This was God!
God was walking among us, dispensing hundred dollar bills!
All of this came our way because Ned was involved.

I have always adhered to this motto- "Business is Business. Seize the Day!".
That is what I did in regard to my son's employment.
He was designing guns, and test firing them.
I was financing the whole business to make a sizeable profit therefrom.
I very much approved of the business side of his business, and I took full advantage.
I had found God, and I put my trust in God.
In God we trust, and everybody else pays cash!
And my own firstborn son heralded the New Jerusalem, sticking to business!
Come unto me, all ye that crave a repeating rifle, and I will give you a Springfield.
Or a Henry, if you can afford it!
So when his business became the serious business of him putting his life on the line to fight for our country, I didn't have a leg to stand on in opposing him.
In truth, I was the most foul, the most abject hypocrite.
I wanted the profits, but not the responsibility.
Isn't that the prerogative of the harlot?
Such was I, oh, such was I.
I found out, too late, that a balance sheet is only a balance sheet if it is IN BALANCE!
Profits- colossal.
Loss?
Did I truthfully believe in my heart that the losses would be nonexistent?
I suddenly realised, far too late, just how much out of balance the scales of justice and righteousness were tilted.
I had succeeded, magnificently, in convincing myself that what goes up won't come down.
I had fooled myself.
So when War did come, and it came, I desperately searched for an alternative to the course of action to which I was soundly committed.

Suddenly, I wanted to reverse engines.
Suddenly, I found God, the real God of truth and holiness, and I appealed to that God to deliver my children from the consequences of my entrenched progress.
God help me!
Dear God, don't let my son go to the war and die?
Please, God?
I had been saying to God, for many years, that his will would be done, God willing, but only when mine was completed.
Not before.
Oh yes, that was my watchword- "MY WILL BE DONE"!
I had been saying to God- "the basic idea of this religion and so forth is very good for keeping the plebians in line, but listen to ME, God- just shut up and sit down while I create a profit here, out of the dust of the earth"!
Now, God said to me- "There thou hast that is thine".
However, all I had was money.
Away, ye hypocrites, that strain at a gnat, and swallow a camel.
I had swallowed the camel.
As you reap, so shall ye sow.
But I didn't want that harvest.
What good was it to me, now?
I had no principles, none to speak of!
My own voice echoed in my head- "Business is Business! Seize the day!".
My own voice mocked me as I tried in vain to summon an argument to dissuade Ned from doing what he had always wanted to do.
He entertained no such doubts.
He joined up on Day One.
While I was all for counting dollar bills, Ned was fighting for the soul of our country.
May the Lord bless him; and I know that you will say "amen" to that sentiment.

Much of the rest you probably know.
Ned approached his Commanding Officer and asked to train the men in shooting their rifles.
And while he was doing this, he devised the idea of selecting a group of special marksmen, called snipers, all using Henry Rifles, and their job would be to pick off Rebel Officers.
Of course, he quickly demonstrated the practicality of the task.
He could hit the middle pip on a five of spades from two hundred yards.
After that, hitting a Rebel Colonel in a grey uniform, up on a horse, would be a cinch.
Moreover, he wanted to hold just junior rank. He was, he said, perfectly placed as a Corporal.
He didn't want promotion.
In this, he was wise beyond his years.
He realized that he could address the men with more credibility, train them in the use of their guns, if they out-ranked him.
Because they could see clearly that he had the true ability.
Not only did he know what he was talking about, he could show them that he could DO what he was talking about; and so could they!
That really mattered.
I have made close enquiries to discover Ned's progress in the Army.
The Reports are glowing, for a fact.
I have several accounts of the training speeches he made to the men.
They all agree as to the substance of his instructions.
The consensus is remarkable.
He would be introduced by a Senior Officer, a Major or a Captain, who would call him "Corporal Roberts", and would then join the men in paying close attention, showing deference.
They'd notice that, of course.
And so Ned would begin.

"You are here to kill the Rebels, and I am here to show you how."
He wanted, he would say, to show them how THEY could fire fifteen shots a minute, and he would pause to let that sink in.
Fifteen shots a minute.
From THEIR guns.
Fifteen shots in one minute.
Impossible!
Unheard of!
But he was right there!
Were they listening?
If they didn't believe that it was possible for THEM to do that, then he had a demonstration for them to make his point- he called it "Rally Round the Flag".
Fifteen men of those assembled would run, when ordered, to a flagpole, two hundred yards away. They would run in a marked lane, Ned firing over their heads. That would take them no more than a minute, timed, if they were going fast. Some might go a lot faster.
Once they started running, Ned had three targets, small clay pots, set up eight foot high on each Flagpole, at the end of every lane, to hit and demolish before any man got to their objective.
Any soldier touching the flagpole before the target on their run was destroyed was deemed to be alive.
The rest were dead with the clay pots.
Using the new Henry Rifle, with fifteen shots in the breech, Ned would hit fifteen targets again and again and again.
He would do this three times with three fresh sets of fifteen men running in groups one after another.
Not a one of all of them got even close to a flagpole.
That was a demonstration, and no mistake. They could all see it.
You could say that that was some shooting, and you'd be right.

And of course he impressed them all very much, not only with his ability, but with his humility.
More than anything, he had humility.
Where he got it from, I don't know.
Very possibly, from his mother.
It certainly wasn't from me.
I acknowledge that I had cultivated pride.
But pride is voiceless and powerless before humility.
I know that now.
Ned had humility.
He would say to the men- "I'm a Corporal. I'm not anything special. I'm just a soldier. As to shooting my rifle, I work hard to make myself good at it.
But I'm just a Corporal, and I'm nothing special. Some of you will be Sergeants, Lieutenants, Captains. My purpose is to show you that every single soldier can be better than me. Not just as good as me, but better than me. With this weapon, you can kill the enemy. I am here to prove to you that you are not only better than me, you are better than the Rebels. Now their boast is that one good Southron is worth ten damn Yankees.
You will prove them wrong.
The best they can do, all along the line, is to fire five bullets in one minute.
That's not boasting.
They can do that.
Yes, they can fire five bullets in one minute. Some of you who know how to fire a gun might think that's pretty good.
It IS pretty good, or at least it used to be.
But five bullets a minute is not pretty good.
Not now.
If you think it is, well, you're wrong, and I shall prove that fact to you. We're not only going to fire twice as fast as they can fire, at best- we're going to do it three times as fast.
Furthermore, the best of their marksmen look to hit us at one hundred yards.

I say to you that you will be able to fire fifteen bullets in the time it takes them to fire five. I say to you that you will kill a Rebel not at one hundred yards, but double that- at two hundred yards!

Yes, at fully twice the distance, you will shoot the enemy, long before he can do the same to you.

I say to you that you will shoot fifteen Rebels long before any one of those fifteen can even discharge their weapons with any chance of hitting even one of you.

And you will hit them with every shot.

You will not waste ammunition.

You will plug them dead centre and they will go down. You will shoot them in the head, shoot them in the chest.

You will do this because that's your job. That's why you are here today. You are here to kill the Rebels.

They are the enemy. You will do this for your country. And what is your country?

I tell you that it is not just the mud below your feet. I say that it is your home, though it be the meanest hovel. I say that it is your family- your father and mother, your sisters and brothers, your Granpa who got shot in the leg in the Mexican War, your Granma who cooked you cornbread and Johnny Cake. I say that your country is your wife and your children and your sweethearts, all of those that love you. You are here to defend them, and they are praying for your success right now. That's why you are here! Don't let them down! Don't let them sink into the mud."

And here he would shout like a Preacher

"We will welcome to our number….the loyal, true and brave- shouting the battle cry of freedom! And although he may be poor, not a man shall be a slave- shouting the battle cry of freedom!

Are you with me?"

Well, they would roar their approval.

He'd shout back at them- "You are here to learn how to kill the enemies of our country, and I am here to show you how. Now, who's with me?"
They would cheer. They would shout and huzzah. He would inspire them. And they couldn't wait to get their hands on those Henry Rifles and start shooting the foe, fifteen bullets at a time.
Ned was very good.
And everybody loved him.
He called everybody "Sir", even new recruits. He treated them all with great respect. He would put his chin down as if he was bowing to you, but look you right in the eye. He did that deliberately. He taught himself to do that. He could connect with Colonels from West Point. He could smile in sympathy with farmhands from Maine.
He was my boy, beloved of all.
His Officers recognised this, of course.
He had great power.
He could talk to the men, and they would listen.
That ability is given to few.

And so he, Ned, stood front and centre on the podium, while the Sergeants actually distributed the Rifles to the men, placing each gun into the hands of the individual soldier.
And when every man had his shining new Springfield Rifle in his hands, Ned would speak. He would say to all assembled-
"Our Country is putting our trust in you. Use it well. Our greatest weapons are not these fine Rifles. No. Our greatest weapons are the obedience you show to your superiors, and the discipline you develop. You uphold that sacred trust when you obey orders. May God bless you, men. And may God bless these United States of America!"
And the men, they would cheer. They would raise a huzzah!
I made enquiries when and where I could.

I tried to piece together Ned's service. I know that he was at Bull Run, although I have not gathered any of the facts of the matter. It's hard to consider that this was only two years ago. Such a short time, but it seems like an eternity.

He was commended for his actions at Shiloh. He had by this time organised his snipers, and he was developing the idea of concentrated fire in a defensive action. His Commanding Officer, Colonel Lamb, well he told me that. It would seem to appear that while attack is acknowledged by all to be the best method of defence, defensive discipline pays greater dividends.

Yes, defend by attacking!

But Colonel Lamb said that after you've attacked gloriously and lost ten thousand men going up against an entrenched position, you're basically powerless to defend yourself.

I know that Ned was at Fredericksburg. I am told that every single man in his handpicked band of brothers is dead. They all died, those which were left, at Gettysburg.

Ned himself died on the third day of the battle. There is compelling evidence that he fought well.

Apparently, when the Rebels attacked in that last great charge, they poured in and almost overwhelmed our boys.

Ned and his company came in late, at the very height of the action, and gave concentrated fire at close quarters, just what Ned had perfected.

Defensive discipline.

The best method of defence is attack, but it isn't. Not unless you have the vision to see that the power of the rifles Ned developed is in itself a method of attack from a defensive posture!

And as he said, it is not the guns that are the weapons, it is obedience and discipline.

That's what he fostered.

That's what he developed and maintained.

That's what he displayed.
It is said that Ned and his men broke the charge, or certainly helped to break the charge, by their fierce reaction.
One man, badly wounded, told me that Ned's men were getting off as many as twenty shots a minute, most of them.
This was disciplined firing, concentrated into the mass of attacking Rebels.
He said he had to keep his head down, and nobody on either side had ever seen anything like it.
Ned and his men fought well.
They did their jobs, defended their sweethearts.
And then they themselves attacked, firing at the retreating Rebels.
They were in good order, several have testified to the fact.
But every man in that squad died.
It has proved to be virtually impossible to discover what happened.
The battle was still raging.
They might have been hit by cannon fire.
Perhaps the Rebels rallied and counter-charged. We just don't know.
What I do know is two things; one, that Ned fought bravely and well for his country, did us all proud.
And though I lament his passing, my tears and my grieving are eased by the honour attending his spirit.
That's the first thing.
The second is that he died on the third of July, eighteen hundred and sixty-three.
A day of blessed memory, and thereby hangs my tale.
Just how and exactly when, at what time, he died is not known.
But he died on that day.
That much is sure.
He didn't answer Roll Call on the third of July, or subsequently.
That is a fact.

Two Officers have spoken to me, recounting his worthy service on that day.

They also, both of them, mentioned the concentrated rifle fire that Ned and his men put down on the Rebels.

They could tell me no more of his fate, and that is understandable. Such things happen in battle. Things fall apart, the centre cannot hold.

That's what General Lee believed!

People become lost in a haze of smoke and gunfire.

The Rebels aimed to smash our boys with an attack front and centre.

They believed that the centre would not hold.

They were wrong.

The centre did hold, and Ned's bravery and discipline are writ large in the annals of that terrible fight.

General, I have gone the long way around to establish a given fact, but I do not apologise for that.

My approach is totally germane to the matter at hand, as you will see.

The fact is that my son died on the third day of July.

I was informed of Ned's death some seven days later, on the tenth of July. I have Captain Lambert's letter before me as I write. He is very considerate, writing, as he did, on the seventh of July.

I wanted to travel to Pennsylvania at once, but I was asked not to do so because the shifting sands of the war could not be gauged accurately, and my presence might only add to the difficulties of our forces.

I was successful in establishing a correspondence with Pastor Gressler, the Lutheran clergyman overseeing the burials in the town.

He is a very Godly man, and I emphasise the fact.

I first wrote to him on the twelfth of July.

I will explain, in due course, why these dates are so important.

He told me that he would learn as much as he could, and welcome me to the Lutheran Seminary when the time was ripe.
In my naivety I told him that he was very kind, but no, I would stay at some convenient Hotel.
He wrote back to tell me that there was no Hotel, or indeed Hostelry of any kind, in existence.
They had all been blown to pieces by cannon fire.
Pastor Gressler told me that in fact there were very few buildings standing.
I simply did not imagine that this would be so, or that this could be so.
But of course I had no knowledge, no experience at all, of what had happened.
I had no idea of what a small town might look like after it has been systematically destroyed in a battle where over twenty thousand men (or more) had died, my son among them.
However, I determined to do as much as I could to help.
I had very significant power.
I had all of the resources of The Morgan Bank at my command.
If Gettysburg did not have a Hotel, surely the town would need the services of a Bank, with cash money to hand, to fund the re-building of the town.
I set out to explore the Banking facilities available in the town.
At that very moment, as if on cue, I met Congressman MacPherson, Proprietor of The Gettysburg Bank.
Ah, I said, we must talk, and so we did.
He told me that his building was hit by cannon fire on the first day. His employees were dead and all records were in a heap of stones and dust.
What remained in the vault was buried under twenty feet of rubble. He appealed for my help- set up a new Bank in Gettysburg!

The Army would be involved- the Army would need this new Bank, MY new Bank, to be up and running, strengthening their arm at need.
And so it proved.
Business IS business!
Seize the day!
The time to take a profit is NOW!
By the fifteenth of July I had despatched three of my best men to Gettysburg with twenty thousand dollars in cash and instructions to do their utmost to help the Army and Pastor Gressler.
Now I could help my country!
And I started to send in supplies of all kinds- food and tents and blankets and hammers and nails and timber. I despatched buyers to nearby towns; backed by cash dollars and notes of hand.
I told them- feed Gettysburg! Clothe Gettysburg! Rebuild Gettysburg!
The truth is that I was not risking anything.
The name of what I was doing was underwriting, but it wasn't really even that.
Any of the notes of hand which my Bank produced would be redeemed for cold, hard cash.
I couldn't lose.
I was just printing money, not for the first time, with only the most brief diversion away from the front door of the Mint.
I knew that the Government would repay me, and commend me for my industry and my community spirit.
But by this time, I didn't care about the money at all.
I only cared about Ned.
Finally, Ned would be my shining light in leading me to serve my country, as he had done, so faithfully.
This was my job, my business.
Now I could truthfully use my business for my country, and for our people.
I could utilise the full use of all of my powers along lines of excellence.

I would do this to honour the memory of my child.
And at the back of my mind was the fact that I would hold everybody accountable for the money.
Ned had given his life for that money.
For MY money!
My boy paid with his life!
Thereto, I also told my people that if five cents of my money went astray that I would smite down with great wrath and furious anger when I laid my vengeance upon them and they would know that my name was Bowes Roberts.
And my boy was Ned Roberts.
God would punish anybody who cheated my boy.
That was my determination when I journeyed to Gettysburg.
To see the burial place of my child.
And to follow the money.
I judge that I may seem to have become somewhat morose and unhappy in the recounting of these matters.
Nothing could be further from the truth.
No, rather I am possessed of a fierce anger born of injustice and outrage.
"Vengeance is mine", saith The Lord, and so it is.
But it is my prayer that mine will be the hand to enact that vengeance.
Let this vile thief suffer as I suffer; not because he stole money, but because he sullied the honour of my boy.
And when judgement descends on him, when that sentence of death is pronounced against him, then I will be on hand to lead the puny throng who will cry out for mercy.
I will lead them, I say!
I will put myself at their head.
And I will make damned sure that any efforts they make to pardon him will flounder into oblivion.
Oh, I will extend hope to him.
Again and again I will raise the possibility of mercy.

But there will be no mercy.
There will only be the death cell, and the last meal, and the Guard and a sad old Padre, arm in arm he'll walk at daybreak.
He will go to the gallows.
After a good long time, I admit.
Let him twitch in apprehension. Let him agonize in despair. Let him hope for mercy. But there will be no mercy.
My power and my money will see to that. I will pursue my ends with vigour.
In so doing I adopt one of the more recent European philosophies- "stone dead hath no fellow"!
I leave you, for the present, with the following facts which I have established-
Ned fought on all three days of the Battle of Gettysburg.
He distinguished himself with his bravery and discipline, contributing soundly to the success, such as it was, of our forces.
Ned Roberts died on the third day of the Battle, on the third day of July of eighteen hundred and sixty-three.
The third of July, General, of conspicuous memory!
I shall write again very soon,
I send my compliments to you.
I thank you for your patience and for your understanding.
Most sincerely,

Bowes Roberts

14TH NOVEMBER 1863
FAO Major General Meade
The Army of the Potomac
Washington DC

From-

Mr Bowes Roberts
Director
Morgan Bank
Astoria,
New York NY

Dear General,
Further to my previous letters, I submit the following for your consideration.
As I have said, my boy Ned died in battle on the third of July.
I spent much of July, August, and September in the business of restoring Gettysburg from afar.
I sent my best people. They brought with them cold hard cash and my determination to help the people of the town. More money and manpower would come in due course.
I concluded a formal merger and alliance with Gettysburg Bank to officially fund not only the re-building of the town ravaged by cannon fire, but also to provide for an Herculean task- the burial of the fallen.
As you will understand from earlier missives, I had a keen and personal interest in the matter.
Very quickly, I established direct lines of communication between the Army representatives in Washington and those working in the area around Gettysburg.
Much centred on the involvement of Pastor Gressler and those at the Lutheran Seminary.
They had the job of burying the dead.
I set out to strengthen their arms, to encourage and aid and provide for them.
I envisaged a triangular structure of cooperation. Picture a pyramid, if you will.
This was my vision with - Pastor Gressler at the topmost point, burying the dead; a most sacred duty.
Secondly, the Army dispensing money to me; yes, they are the Paymasters.

And my Bank engaged in providing supplies and maintenance, feeding the workers, paying the Tradesmen, drawing together the life force of the community to regenerate the town.
From the Reports that I received, all seemed to be going well.
I travelled to Gettysburg on November the first, arriving shortly after twelve o'clock.
I had scheduled meetings with my employees at the Bank (housed for the interim at the Lutheran Seminary) and also with the Army administrative officers.

Since they too were quartered at the Lutheran Seminary, and since my overall priority was to meet with Pastor Gressler and to view the final resting place of my beloved son, I knew that I would be spending much of my time in those precincts.
However, matters unfolded in a very different context to that which I had imagined.
Pastor Gressler met me at the train station with conveyance to the newest military cemetery.
I remember shaking his hand and thinking- "a fine man, a good man". I can tell that from a handshake.
Then we were in a carriage and we entered the town and my head began to swim.
Evidence of the battle was everywhere. That much was plain.
Four months in the past?
How was this possible?
Initially, I failed to take in the reality of the neat streets with no buildings.
I could see the jagged edges of burnt out ruination.
By this time I was, I suppose, expecting it.
But such was not the cause of my inability to comprehend.
The reason for this mental confusion was the smell.

There was a pernicious odour in the air, all pervasive. It was a dank and rotting stench that made me think of rats and decay.
Pastor Gressler apologised, and offered me a handkerchief wherewith to stop my nose. I accepted it with thanks and appreciation.
The smell, he explained, emanated mostly from the carcases of dead horses, of which there were several thousand, all over the place.
These had to be left where they laid, open to the elements- because finding and interring our boys came first.
I agreed, but the smell was overpowering, and awful.
Nor was it fully accounted for by the vileness of the dead horses.
There were human remains in the mix, a high almost sweet reminder of burned pork.
It was not the flesh of swine, but of mankind.
The Army had decided to re-bury all of those interred in the first weeks after the battle.
Land had been purchased.
I knew this.
I had arranged the finance myself.
The Bank had realised a most acceptable profit from the transaction.
I was gagging with every breath, and close to vomiting.
Pastor Gressler continued to talk at my side. I think that I caught not one word in four.
He commenced to tell me about the good work he was concerned with.
There were most competent surveyors already hard at work, planning, rearranging the graves of the fallen.
I remember his words.
I leaned forward, shocked into attention.
What was he saying?
Horse blankets.

His words poured out, tribute to his industrious application.
He spoke, a good man, a fine man, speaking carefully chosen words.
The horse blankets, the horse blankets.
We travois the bodies in horse blankets.
The importance of horse-blankets.
I recall the effect they had on me.
They jolted me into the present, that this was not a nightmare or a dream, but my lot, my portion.
The ghastly atmosphere was profane in the extreme- the putrid reek of Hell.
This town, this field of death, this arena, was where my precious child had laid down his life for his friends.
Now the good Pastor was, all unbeknownst, offering a foretaste of the truth of Ned's end.
I remember his words very well, which tailed off as he grasped the dreadful import they would have for me.
This is what he said, a fine man. A good man.
"Coffins are non-existent, and we use horse-blankets to wrap around the men, where we find them. These are very serviceable, but sadly, they don't contain the stink…."
I had authorised the purchase and distribution of the horse-blankets.
Twenty thousand of them.
Again, oh, again, a most acceptable profit had been realised.
The time to take a profit is now!
Who would have imagined so much profit in horse blankets?
There thou hast that is thine….
We proceeded down a slight hill. On all sides there were black men labouring in the fields. They were digging graves. How curious, I thought. I had never seen any black man working before. And now, so many of them!

Here, hard by the road, was a working party of six black men, attended by two black women.
As I watched, they were pulling a corpse out of the ground. And then they wrapped the body in a fine new and shining horse-blanket. They reached down into the same grave and pulled up another body, reached for a fresh horse-blanket.
Oh, trees and sky!
I pushed the handkerchief into my face, almost sucking on it.
Anything to keep out the smell.
I thought that I would faint.
But how, I wondered, could I keep out this terrible reality, this evidence of my blindness?
Now, as I looked, I could discern at first dozens and then hundreds of similar work parties. Hundreds of piles of neat horse-blankets, shining black in the sunlight!
Dozens of little parcels heaped up, every one of them exactly the size of Ned.
And the hundreds of black men working, shovelling, lifting out corpses, with a gentle dignity that was unmistakeable!
Black men, black men everywhere!
Oh, how I remonstrated with myself.
Every shovel, every square foot of displaced soil, every white handkerchief wrapped upon a black face, and most of all, every shining and durable horse-blanket that couldn't keep out the smell, represented a fine and good and acceptable profit to my Bank.
Pastor Gressler was talking at my side, and his words got through to me.
Waiting, at the site of Ned's grave, would be the men who had found his body and also buried him, and then re-interred him in a place of honour.
They were very special, very special indeed.
They had come forward at the first, and they led by example.

They were, said Pastor Gressler, his two most industrious and profitable workers, labouring here since the Armies had left the field and Washington had taken over the administration of the job.
I was, I admit, grasping at any straws of comfort in this maelstrom of agony. But I wanted to see these soldiers and shake them by the hand.
I wanted to thank them, enquire as to their experience of the battle, perhaps ask them about...but it was only a vain hope, whether they might have been there, whether they had seen Ned fall?
Had they fought with him?
Had they known him?
Oh, God, I cried out in my inmost heart of hearts, let there be one of his comrades present to speak him fair?
Oh, how I shall shower that brave soldier with bounty!
Thus I wept in my grief.
We entered a new arena, neat and ordered.
The graves rested in clear lines of white crosses- hundreds, no, thousands of them.
Here and there were bright sparklings of flowers on a heap, here and there a bonnet tied to the cross, ever and anon a coloured ribbon blowing in the breeze.
The smell had abated somewhat.
The wind was contrary, for one thing.
Blessedly so.
All looked peaceful and clean.
A fine spot.
A fine spot.
This was the new Army Cemetery.
And now Pastor Gressler was pointing ahead, up higher, go higher to a place of greater honour, he seemed to say- go higher!
And so we proceeded onward, up to where the very first rows of sturdy white crosses were disported, first fruits of the battlefield of death.

I looked for the soldiers, looked for the Military
Guard, looked for the Flag draped and Honour
Party, fronted, doubtless, by a General.
Nothing would be good enough for my boy.
But there was no Honour Party, no respectful Guard,
no Flag draped sadly o'er a humble grave.
There were two negroes waiting by the plot- one of
them leaning on a shovel.
Not soldiers, spruced up and best foot forward, but
barefoot negroes!
And what a contrast?
While the one was all muscles and teeth and great
rippling strength (surely a fieldhand?), the other was
only a twisted wreck of a cripple.
And from the look of him, one eye all askance and the
other shaded, he was a congenital idiot.
His hand and leg were all awry and he looked like a
small hunchback, chin up to confront me, lips turned
down.
The other, the taller of the two, was hanging back, in
clear deference to his fellow.
Pastor Gressler was advancing, down from the
carriage, and extending his hand to the cripple.
The poor man had twisted fingers, like to the afflicted
in our sanatoriums, and could only thrust his fingers
forward.
I take great note of handshakes. I think that a
handshake denotes character.
This wretch could not summon a firm grip,
wrenching strongly from the shoulder to show his
strength in the sinewy recognition of equals.
That's what I demand of a handshake.
If I don't see that strength, then I say that the weak
purveyor of a limp wrist is not a true man.
This hopeless gimp (for that's what he was) could
only put up his fingers ends to the Pastor, and it
seemed to me that the good Minister was giving
honour where it wasn't due in accepting such a
salutation.

Oh, the big fieldhand could grab on to the Pastor for dear life, and show willing and strong, but he was all sweat and work, and probably a lunkhead as well.

I didn't think much of the show.

I thought to myself- "the Army has let my boy down!"

But I ask you to accept that I was in the most extreme grief of my life.

I was very wrong.

I was out of my mind with sorrow.

And now I was angry, too!

I got lofty.

I decided, in my aimless conceit, that I would rise above this cheap charade.

Somebody had to show dignity, and by God, if the Army and the Lutheran Seminary and two worthless black negro gravediggers couldn't come up to the mark in showing honour to my boy, then I would damn well show them that I was made of sterner stuff!

I had got out of the carriage determined not to display any weakness at all. I would ignore this puerile shoddiness.

I would wipe them out by my gracious affability.

Yes, I thought to myself, I will humble myself before these miscreants for the sake of my son!

So I approached these fellows, showing myself lordly, affable, humble.

Pastor Gressler made the introductions.

He indicated the cripple, and now I could see that he had what looked like a bag of black flesh hanging out from his throat, like a chicken's crop, but all on one side. And he seemed to have only one eye, cowering and closed, with the other twisted up and about as if he was trying to focus his gaze.

God, what a mess he was!

"Mr Roberts, this is Birdy. He is the man that found your son, and brought him here to rest. Birdy, this is Mr Roberts."

I gulped.
The words hit me in the heart.
It was all I could do to speak, I was so devastated.
"Hello, my good man", I heard my voice talking- unctuous, false, dissembling. "And what, may I ask, do you have to say to me"?
Birdy brought his poor twisted focus up onto my proud face, and he half whispered, half croaked- "Jesa, Jesa, Jesa".
And then he bowed his head in mute sorrow, and he looked only at the ground.
Pastor Gressler was speaking- "And this is Big Neg. He works alongside Birdy. Together, they brought your boy to sanctuary".
Big Neg reached out with two hands and clasped my hand and knelt before me and kissed my hand.
And he bowed openly, as one does to a King or Prince.
I was shocked.
I was stunned.
The tears came to my eyes and all my proud anger was blown to Kingdom Come in a second.
I wept.
God help me, but I wept, standing there proud as a peacock, and all my vanity cast down with me as lightning falling.
Dear God, forgive me, I shouted out inside my being.
Pride cometh before a fall.
From somewhere I heard a scripture- "out of the depths I cry unto thee oh Lord", and I assure you, the sentiments were real and right there, nailed into my being.
I looked around me.
The four of us were kneeling by a grave.
The grave of my child, my firstborn son.
Out of the depths I cry unto thee, oh Lord!
Pastor Gressler was crying and Birdy was crying and I was crying and Big Neg was crying.

There was but a white cross, much like to part of a picket fence.
Here was my baby, my child, my son, my boy, enclosed in this earth.
My heart broke.
I cried, I howled.
I had no dignity.
I had no anger.
I had no puffed up pride and self-righteous stupidity.
The dam burst, and all of my folly was revealed to me, in a trice, in the twinkling of an eye!
Here, here, was the fruit of my labours!
Here, here!
Here thou hast that is thine!
Your boy is dead!
You are worth NOTHING!
You have been a stupid fool!
Dear God, deliver me from this agony?
Where now is my profit?
Seize the day!
Oh what a blinded cretin was I ?
Oh, how I wept.
I was kneeling on the ground.
Pastor Gressler stood before me, on the other side of Ned's grave.
He was holding a Bible and he began to say a prayer.
I couldn't really hear him, but it was soft and suitable.
He was all of dignity, all of kindness.
Big Neg and Birdy were standing behind me, their hands resting on my shoulders.
And they were praying for me.
Big Neg was saying things like, "Yes, Lord" and "Aye-men Lord".
Birdy was wheezing, as if in great pain, "Jesa, Jesa, Jesa".

And from the hands resting on my shoulders, I began to feel a surge of strength and coolness and sweet balm for aches, spreading into all of my body and easing the dark agony in my soul.
I felt grace, for the first time in my life.
I felt peace.
I felt that I was cleaned up and wrung out, like a wet towel after washing.
In truth, I cannot really express what I felt, kneeling there at the graveside of my brave boy.
But I knew that I had three, yes three, strong men around me, and that they were comforting me in my desolation.
There would be time for shame, and time for recrimination, in all the days to come.
Oh what I blinded fool I was.
Oh, what a rogue and peasant slave am I ?
Truly, these were fine men- Birdy, however strange, and Big Neg, honest in his simplicity, and Pastor Gressler- a good man, a fine man.
He was thoroughly correct in his judgement in assembling this Honour Guard at the final resting place of my son.
These were the people who should have been present!
Not Generals and fat men in top hats with fob watches.
No!
Just a Pastor, and two black men.
Pastor Gressler was right.
He was right and I was wrong, just as Ned had been right, and I had been wrong.
I remember thinking at the time that the scales had fallen from my eyes, and that now I could see things as they really were.
I remember thinking- my eyes are wide open now, for the first time in my life my eyes can see.
But the biggest revelation was yet to come.
From somewhere, Birdy was standing in front of me.

He reached out his poor, claw-like hand, and raised me to my feet.

Then he gestured away, away off to the side.

"Jesa", he said abruptly.

"Jesa, Jesa".

He pointed with his twisted hand toward a different part of the field, up above the newest graves.

Pastor Gressler didn't even blink. He glanced sharply, like an eagle rousing.

"What is it, Birdy? What is it?".

"Excuse me sah", said Big Neg. "I think he gonna show you somethin' over thah, sah. Yassuh, I think so."

Oh, I thought. It must be the place where Ned fell. I turned.

"Pastor Gressler, might that be the site where they recovered the body of my son?".

"No sir. The field indicated is used for burning rubbish. It's fairly new. It has only been set up since these graves were placed here, some weeks ago. But our young friend definitely wants us to follow him to that locale."

He paused, but only briefly, "I know not why, but I may say that I have discovered Birdy's instincts to be sound, very sound".

Birdy led the way, and Big Neg hustled after him holding a shovel, God knoweth why.

My earlier conviction that Birdy was some kind of afflicted defective had not quite dissipated. I walked alongside Pastor Gressler as we mounted the slight incline.

There was a fence serving as a prop for clods of earth, piled up away out of the sight of the graves.

There were brief stumps of bushes, probably uprooted to clear the ground. There were bags of, presumably, garden refuse, laid out in a neat row.

It was a garbage dump, a disposal site.

A lone black man was burning leaves beside a newdug trench, stretching off further into the waste area.
Here and there were dotted larger clumps and mounds of earth, where stuff had been buried to keep all in some semblance of order.
Birdy advanced with determination to one of these, and he turned and looked up at Big Neg, close in attendance.
Birdy pointed dramatically at the ground, and said "Jesa, Jesa, Jesa".
Big Neg set to with his shovel. In no time at all he was throwing out soil and stones, working hard at a fearsome rate of progress.
I stood nearby with the Pastor. I admit that I was wondering just what was going on.
We hadn't been there for more than two minutes, and already Big Neg was standing in a hole three or so feet deep. He was now shovelling out what looked like bits of paper.
Birdy started and pointed.
Big Neg nodded and this time threw his shovel-load of debris in my direction. It landed at my feet.
I bent to examine it with Pastor Gressler.
It was a sheaf of papers, dirtied with the soil, and the edges muddied away.
There were perhaps thirty or so sheets of paper, printed paper, all packed together, rounded into a ball with the wetness.
I was intrigued.
I picked it up and I could see at once that these papers were all a sort of "pro forma", all the same size, with numbers in the top corners- almost like a sheaf of invoices tossed in the rubbish tip.
I touched lightly at the edges to separate them out, and then first one and then another came clear and I could read the writing thereon.
It WAS a sheaf of invoices!
Tossed in the rubbish tip?

Yes, and buried three or more feet underground in what was effectively a grave!
And I could now read the writing.
" The Morgan Bank of New York- invoice and receipt".
My Bank!
MY Bank!
Big Neg was throwing up more clumps of paper- more invoices!
More receipts!
Paperwork for and from MY Bank!
Buried, here, in a grave in Gettysburg!
How could this be so?
How in the name of God could this be so?
And how had Birdy unearthed it?
As I turned to demand an explanation, the paper sheaf which I was holding broke apart and scattered in the random gust of wind, blowing away.
I was left holding a single "Invoice and Receipt".
I looked at it wildly, as though this sheet of paper could explain this lunatic circumstance.
Most unexpectedly, it did precisely that.
The paper had writing across it, in good black ink, and in a fine round hand, the following words-

"PAID TO CORPORAL NED ROBERTS THE SUM OF $20.00 FOR ADMINISTRATIVE SERVICES RENDERED.LSG/EX 03.
17TH AUGUST 1863."

Then there were the initials "NR", and a squiggle that might have been anything.
Corporal Ned Roberts?
Signed by my son?
No, that could not be so. Ned always used the initials "NBR". I had taught him that. "Ned Bowes Roberts".
On the seventeenth of August?
Ned died on the third of July.
How was this possible?

And why was this document buried in a waste grave
in the new Military Cemetery?
How could this happen?
The answer was plain.
This was a forgery.
This was a fraud.
All around me was the hard, documented evidence of
fraud and theft, blowing over the ground in the
breeze.
And none of it more damning, at least to me, than the
sheet of paper held in my hand.
Pastor Gressler was perplexed.
All matters relating to my Bank, he explained, were
handled by the Army Administrative Officers and
the Staff of my Bank, which was, of course, operating
from the Lutheran Seminary.
He could not account for this circumstance.
How had this come about, where the precious name
of my child was credited with receiving payment of
money several weeks after burial?
We must consult Mr Ince, he said- Liason Officer
from the Bank. He will know.
I said that I knew of no such Employee as a Mister
Ince.
Oh, he said, but surely he works for the Army?
If that is so, I asked, why is he overseeing Invoices
and Receipts for my Bank?
He could not answer.
And so we returned at once to the Seminary.
I gave orders that Birdy and Big Neg should be fed
and retained nearby to assist if called upon to do so.
Who, what, and where was Mr Septimus Ince?
Of course, once criminality comes to light, it runs like
an old sock.
My Staff were puzzled.
But Mr Septimus Ince has an Office right here with
us, they said.
We see him every day.
He works for the Army, and for the Seminary.

His services are indispensable, they said. Surely he will explain this unfortunate confusion?
The Army Administrative Office was just down the corridor.
But, they said, Mr Ince works for the Seminary and the Bank. He is a fine man. Nobody works harder.
Where, I asked, is Mr Septimus Ince?
Nobody seemed to know.
He seemed to have placed himself at the centre of a perfect triangle.
The Seminary thought that he worked for the Bank and the Army.
The Bank thought that he worked for the Seminary and the Army.
The Army thought that he worked for the Seminary and the Bank.
Who DID he work for?
Nobody seemed to know.
Who had appointed him?
Nobody seemed to know.
Pastor Gressler remembered that Mr Ince (a fine man, a good man) had approached him offering to liase for the Seminary between the Bank and the Army.
Matters continued to unfold thus.
The Bank Staff (MY Bank Staff) thought that he had greeted them, welcomed them, when they arrived in town, and he seemed to know everything, and that he was the link with Pastor Gressler, who was very busy.
He had asked Mr Benedict and Mr Clement, my senior Managers, to meet with him to fully outline Morgan Bank procedures.
He agreed with them as to exactly what he should do to save them any trouble at all.
And yes, he would talk to the Army administrators, because they were snowed under, and he could guarantee their cooperation. He would make sure that everything would go smoothly.

The Army were certain that he was Pastor Gressler's right hand man, and he had an Office actually IN the Bank!

When he met the Army Paymaster sent from Washington, he informed THEM, the Army, of all of the procedures up and running between the Bank and the Lutheran Seminary.

So he worked for everybody, and nobody.

Each of the three Offices believed that he worked for the other two.

And he never handled cash.

Oh no.

He only organised notes of hand between the Bank and the Army and the Seminary.

No cash money was ever paid by him.

In fact, he used three separate Accounts to ease the flow of payment between Army, Bank, and Seminary.

The Bank controlled these.

He "administered them", for the Seminary, the Army, the Bank.

I examined the Records for the three accounts.

The First was a straightforward Trading Account set up to accept and expend sums of money on behalf of the Lutheran Seminary. There were two signatories for cheques- Pastor Gressler and Mr Septimus Ince.

No cheques had been issued.

There had only been large amounts transferred in from two other Accounts, and virtually every penny paid in had been transferred out to other accounts (of which more in due course).

But as to the two additional accounts which Mr Septimus Ince had opened in my Bank, with my staff hurrying to assist;

The first of these was a "comfort fund".

This had been set up to redeem invoices for external goods and services, drawn on the Seminary. So, for example, the Seminary would pay cash for thirty hogs- nine hundred dollars. They would present an Invoice (all signed by Mr Septimus Ince).

This would all seem to be right and proper. This seemed to be as it should be.
Of course we had no knowledge of the transactions resulting in the Invoices delivered to us.
Neither did we have any responsibility therein. We weren't there to ask questions and demand answers.
We were there to expedite progress, put a small charge on top, and collect on the bill that we would subsequently present. So we couldn't lose.
Each of these was a simple transaction.
My Bank would pay cash to the Seminary Trading account and apply to Washington for remuneration- effectively funding the entire enterprise.
The third account accepted large sums paid by the Army to fund wages for the Labourers. My bank would basically cash the cheque and transfer the money into the Seminary Trading Account.
Naturally, Morgan Bank charged a small fee, a proper charge, to administer these accounts, which handled all of the money spent by anybody for any purpose since inception.
I will not tell you (at this time) the amounts of money involved because I don't want to shock you.
Suffice to say that Mr Septimus Ince had stolen every penny paid to re-build Gettysburg.
All of the cash was gone out of the Seminary Trading account- all of it transferred to three accounts in the Morgan Bank of Astoria, New York.
All business accounts controlled exclusively by Mr Septimus Ince.
Everybody knew him.
Everybody liked him, and praised his enterprise.
A good man.
A fine man.
More importantly, how did my son's name come to appear on a receipt detailing payment of twenty dollars for work done weeks after his death?
Mr Clement looked at the receipt in my hand, and provided an explanation.

The account number- LSG03, referred directly to the payment of Army wages.
Mr Septimus Ince, it seemed, had got the list of Army personel involved in administration of the reburials.
But Ned's name was not on that list.
His name was on the list of the fallen.
My son was to be re-interred.
That is where his name appeared.
So Mr Septimus Ince had chalked up various monies to be paid to a Clerk, a name on the list, who was actually a dead soldier.
Nobody would come searching for that paycheck.
And of course all of the lists and payments were dealt with in the Seminary. Mr Ince had simply organised the list for payment, sharing necessary information with colleagues. And they paid it to his order. And to his controlled account. And on into his own pocket.
It was the perfect fraud.
The invoices and receipts were the evidence- just thrown out with the garbage and buried in a grave.
So, I wondered, how many more of the fallen had been paid cash for services rendered after their burial, all paid into the open hand of Mr Septimus Ince?
Again, I will not weary you with the answer to this question, lest your righteous anger come onto a par with mine own, and we both explode in fury.
Enough from me, you are just beginning to comprehend the extent of this perfidious malfeasance. I have nursed my shock by channelling my anger into action.
This man had suborned all of our communal efforts to his will.
He stole everything and left nothing.
Not content with robbing the living, he appropriated the names of the dead to further his felonious purposes.
Where were the safeguards, where the checks and balances?

Everything flowed through Mr Septimus Ince, and ultimately, everything flowed into his pocket.
In the name of God I ask whether a major Bank and the Army of these United States of America had ever heard of the word "security"?
When I enquired, I found that he had set up meetings with the Army to ascertain their procedures in finance, just as he had done with my staff.
Pastor Gressler valued his incredible energy and diligence. Mr Ince came out of nowhere and volunteered his expertise, which was considerable.
Pastor Gressler was completely taken in. He had attended meetings with the Bank and the Army, Mr Septimus Ince chairing the proceedings!
I could look at Pastor Gressler with a practiced eye and observe that he has no experience of fraud and theft; I could well imagine how a man of the cloth could become so totally befooled by a rogue- perhaps it's not so strange after all?
But I have no such excuse to apply to my own Banking procedures, my own ineptitude.
As for the Army, I will leave you to judge yourself as you see fit.
However, I believe that you will be outraged, and justifiably so.
This man has run rings around us.
I don't care about the theft.
I care about the fact that he used the name of my dead boy to increase his ill gotten gains.
I do not forgive him.
I want vengeance.
But all in good time.
All in good time.

So there I was, standing amidst befuddled colleagues.
Where, oh where was Mr Septimus Ince?
Everybody knew him, liked him, praised him, relied on him.
He was ever present, in all trials.

So where was he now?
To be brief (not before time), he was eventually arrested in New York.
I have recovered every penny which he stole from the people of Gettysburg, the Army, the Bank, the workers who buried the dead and all in attendance, and also from those who paid the ultimate price, like my son, Corporal Ned Roberts.
It is said that there is no fury in Hell greater than a woman scorned, but I am setting out to exceed that assessment with a new contention- a Banker demanding redress for the dishonouring of his fallen child.
I shall let my actions speak for me in this regard, and Mr Septimus Ince shall answer my wrath, preferably with a broken neck and an unmarked grave.
But only after a good long wait.
When I consider that this whole business unfolded because of Birdy, that strange, disabled negro, I reflect and conclude that I know nothing about life.
In truth, I know nothing about black people.
Birdy shall be rewarded.
His race shall be rewarded, and I will bend my energies thereto.
Out of the darkness of my grief, I pluck this flower of hope, that I will pursue the benefit of those who performed that sacred act of mercy for my child- feed the hungry, heal the afflicted, bury the dead.
Yours Faithfully,
Bowes Roberts

COINS AND BISCUITS

Washington DC
17th November 1863

The beard, Dutch rather than Belgian, would go away forever after this morning, and they could seek the bearded Porter where they would.
He, of course, would be adrift in the barque of the Fisherman, and none would ever find him.
The big prize, this damned Saxon Seal, awaited on the train, as did this Lincoln the Antichrist. But first things first. Appetite is but a signpost to the soul. All in it's time, and in it's place. All things come to him who waits.

The bearded man, Jean Lestrange, a Jesuit Priest, noticed the pretty girl selling biscuits as soon as he entered the Park.
Not because she was pretty, which she certainly was (although anything to do with her prettiness did not interest him).
Not because she was a girl (for exactly the same reason).
Least of all because she was selling biscuits.
He cared not for food of any kind, and surely not these vile American sweetbreads, full of sugar and nuts to stick in his teeth.
She held no interest for him whatsoever.
Nor did the biscuits.
But the boy standing beside her, there, there in the red shirt, obviously her younger brother, really was remarkably beautiful.
Ma fille! Ooohh!
Yes, he was well dressed, and he paid close attention to her, yes that's a sister, as she doled out biscuits at a few cents a bag.
Yum, yum.
And what of this little chicken?

Yes, he held their stock in a bigger bag, there, there behind the bench.
So, he is the storeman, she the purveyor!
Hmmm, what a dish! Move for me, delice!
The boy bent over slightly to reach for something and Lestrange saw his legs and mentally licked them even as he wet his own lips.
This lamb shall certainly roll on the spit, ha ha!
And so he strolled over easily to buy a packet of biscuits, just as a traveller out for a walk in the Park would.
Oh, the biscuits tempt me onward, eh bien?
But at the recognition of the manifested motivation, he mentally checked himself, for always there was danger.
Danger, everywhere.
Danger from the enemies of Christ.
Danger from the enemies of France.
And so he checked.
He checked the ground fore and aft.
There was a fat sailorman coming in fast from the right. Yes, a sailorman, francais? No, Channel Islands surely? Yes. Jersey, Gueurnsey. But those culottes are French cut, n'est ce pas?
Now what was his interest?
Girl?
Boy?
Biscuits?
Eh, bien, he already had his nickel out and his mouth open.
Slavering for the sweet, not even noticing the boy, or the girl for that matter!
Idiot!
Enfant!
Slave to his lusts!
No self control!
No mastery of events!
The fool, the fool.

Yes, he will get there before me but that is good because I shall take my time to watch and see and taste the boy, lick him in my mind, while this Punchinello aches for the biscuits and tenders his coin and waits for his change and the female dithers and this true vision of loveliness unfolds as a feast for me.
Where is the sun?
What the hour?
All's good.
Lincoln comes not for a time. He will be on time.
I am here. I shall be at the train on time. The blackamoor has arranged everything. The Saxon Seal shall be mine. Lincoln will be dead and the Porter to blame and I shall be gone ere the train decamp in the west.
All's good.
Madonna guide, and the godless giant? Oh no, he shall not escape me this day.
Rest in him. Amen.
All I need is about ten seconds in the carriage.
He will be with Seward and the two secretaries.
I shall kill them all.
And then onward they will go to a richly deserved seat in Hell.
Not hot enough for him, if justice spoke in deeds.
Oh, there will be many soldiers and Police, but not one bodyguard nearby.
He has no cover, no craft.
His entrails hang a'dangle in the wind. Such fools as these Americans I have never seen.
They have mistaken silence for security.
The only assassin they anticipate is the one who will obligingly identify himself loudly and most publicly as an assassin prior to the attack. The plot must be served! He will cry out, in passion, I shall murder you. I hereby alert you! Look now upon my vengeance! These are the rules by which all assassins must play.

Observe me, I am an assassin! And I was, until just now, a secret assassin! But now is Act three and all must be made manifest to the adoring, or horrified crowds.
They should be impressed.
All should be clearly understood by the neutral critics.
So that they, in their turn, may demonstrate in detail just how all unfolded.
Should Lincoln practise shouting "Et tu, Brute"?
Must the response be then, "Death to tyrants"?
Drama. Yes, drama is all to these cretins! It is the Theatre, yes? The Theatre in their minds.
All's a stage to them, and all shall speak only the lines they state. There is no security, none. So, he is easy meat, and I shall feed well. Gone, I shall be gone before the train departs. Perhaps they shall bring him coffee as the train arrives in Gettysburg. So.
Seek ye the Lord while he may be found, thou fool!
Here come I, and ye shall not deny. He is mine.
Yea, I shall show him the Theatre. Dream, thou fool! Dream on the event!
And I, well, I shall tarry here in this town for a time. This sweet vision will please me. The obvious is the most obscure. A good priest shall wrestle a sinner toward the altar of repentance. Bend before me, chicken! Introibo ad altare Dei. Ad Deum qui laetificat juventutem meam. Oh, and you'll bring joy indeed, ma fille! Wrestle you will, sweet one.
Shall there be confusion?
Oh yes.
The boy will be my little consolation after the confusion.
Thou'lt not muzzle the ox.
Sweet, sweet as calf's flesh.
The fat sailorman, le feu, is proffering his coin. He sees not the cliff's edge.
Now he's noticed the boy, yes, a second glance but his mouth is all for the food.

And he sees the young girl. Ah, he's caught! Sees her, does he? Eh? Ah ha! He looks again. Ho, ho. His lust is evident. But he first wanted the biscuits! Plaything, toy! If you so much as turn your head.....
Knows he not?
Eyes down, mon frère!
Eyes down, dog!
But his glance away, there, there?
Ah.
There is a Policeman.
He strolls, there, there.
He sees nothing, oh, now the Policeman notices the girl.
Hah, he twirls his stick and walks away.
He does nothing.
The fat sailorman yet lusts.
Le feu, le feu!
Madonna, but the boy is lithe!
Yes, ma fille, bend for the biscuits!
Oh! I shall tickle you well, I promise. You shall wrestle hard, oh hard.
The fat sailorman had already opened the newbought bag to munch on a biscuit, turning slightly to the side. The girl fumbled the money at her belt, glancing up against the sunshine, and the gorgeous boy looked full at Lestrange and opened his lovely lips and then, distracted for some reason or other, let go his hands and dropped the bag of biscuits, emptying onto the ground.
He looked down and up, back at the Priest, blinking. Smitten! Yes! Smitten! And the biscuits are nothing to his little gaze, eh?
Mon dieu! His pretty fingers failed him! Ho ho! Why, it was almost as if he'd done it deliberately? The biscuits went everywhere and it was so funny, so funny and he was really going to enjoy this. And so amusing for, well, certainement la petite fleur, jouet.
Hmmm! Laugh, chicken! Ho ho. So funny.
The boy was laughing carelessly.

The girl was not.
The biscuits went everywhere.
The attention of the fat sailorman was at once drawn downwards, and he gaped openly, following the progress of a rolling biscuit, there, there.
Bending stupidly! Gazing, head inclining to the biscuits spinning away! Thou fool!
Ho ho!
Le feu!
The boy smiled.
Such a smile!
Lestrange quickly dropped to one knee to help retrieve the biscuits, yum yum, the girl clucking away, the fat man yawing to and fro, picking at biscuits, mouth open.
Come, little fish.
The boy smiled, oh yes, such a smile, and the girl squeaked her stupidity and the boy bent down to join him.
Oh, come.
Oh, do bend for the biscuits!
For me!
Ma fille!
Now they were met on the grass here in this park.
Oh, delicious!
The boy half bent forward but looked full up into this new face, light and joy and yes, yes, desire in his eyes, that's desire, yes, yes, in his eyes and surely that was his tongue right out.
Oh joy, joy as he looked at that young wet tongue.
There was joy and desire in that face.
The Priest was too old a hand not to know the very real signals freely extended here and oh yes they will be requited yum yum oh joy.
Oh, such joy as shall be in my grasp, little one, look on.
I shall lick those legs!
Huh! That is open desire in his face.

I shall tickle you my sweet thing, see where I come here to enfold you?
Oh, soft hair and bright eyes I see and I shall touch all lightly.
The tableau is set and all is well.
Security is close in the barque of the Fisherman whence I scour land and sea.
Oh, I shall tickle this little fish, and none shall know.
See, see, where this fat fool scrabbles for his food, gets his gut full and the pretty little girl weeps for her toys.
Oh ye fools you'll not even know when the moment comes upon ye, no, ye'll not and the fat sailorman whipped around smoothly and jammed the corking needle all the way into the Priest's ear, killing him instantly as the dull point penetrated right into his brain and he pulled it out with a piercing twist and turned and walked away into the Park and the crowd.
The boy turned on the instant and vanished. The pretty girl was gone as quickly.
Oh, look, somebody dropped some money? That's a dime, okay. Yeah! Hey! Finders keepers, eh? And hey. Lemme help ya, yeah! I've got, but oh the biscuits never mind them in the dirty ground leave them.
Thank you.
Yeah, yeah, oh look this guy with a funny beard has fallen over.
Oh look, he might have fainted in the heat.
No I don't think he's drunk.
He's probably okay.
He's on his back go call for that cop over there.
Martha, yeah it's very hot I'm sorry but he must be very sick.
I don't know. He fell down I think. I don't think he's drunk.

He's gonna be okay. I guess? Sure, sure. Maybe, oh yeah but no I don't know him he just fell down I guess? He just fell over. Just now, I guess?
Yeah, and he dropped some things and the money is he alright no hang on.
Martha wait what happened? There, yeah, hi.
Yeah, hi, buddy, just look buddy, over there it's okay, yeah, it's gotta be okay I guess?
Yeah, I guess? But anyhow, gee, I mean, is that guy dead?

A LETTER IN CODE
17th November 1863
FAO MR BENNELL
SALES VERY MUCH ENGAGED ON OUR BEHALF. NO BOARD MEETING TODAY.
JENKINS

BOOK THREE

CONSOLATION

LINCOLN ON THE TRAIN

On a bright November in 1863, somewhat delayed, a train pulls out of Washington D.C. to make an energetic burst across the miles. They will go on over to Baltimore, and then, after a watering stop, briefly west and turning on to the town of Gettysburg, in Pennsylvania. In fact this train is the second one of three, all chugging closely together, for security reasons. Rather like to a newborn eaglet, Baby Eagle, sheltered between Daddy and Mummy Eagle's fierce talons and powerful wings, this chick is well protected and looked out for.
The first, leading train, Daddy Eagle, is armed against any Confederate troops who might loiter along the way. There might be thousands of them Rebs, leaning easy on the guns. The defenders onboard are scanning the terrain, uphill and down valley, searching for anybody gonna fire a gun. Might be Rebs? Might be just bushwhackers who would take a pot shot at anyone, anywhere, on a train or not. They could be anywhere.
They could be few or promiscuous. They might shoot just for spite and cussedness.
To oppose such as these, there are fifty strong soldiers in each of five cars, selected for their prowess with the latest, and finest, Henry rifles.
Bought for the Army at great expense, these are pointed outward at all times.
They are accurate, shiny oiled, and up and ready for instant use.

This being a time of war, the bearers are alert, well fed, looking for trouble, and loaded for bear. Should they have to fight, these men can be deployed onto the ground, fast.

So Daddy Eagle is certainly up and ready. Could be a solo sniper, a sudden skirmish, or a brute-sized battle. Bristling with menace and intent, Daddy Eagle leads the way, armed to the beak and claws. The third train, Mummy Eagle, has more cars.

It carries more soldiers, more armaments, some necessary dignitaries, and a smattering of approved civilians- newspaper writers and the like.

The soldiers are solid. Cometh the hour, cometh the chance 'fer a fight 'n 'ter kill Johnny Reb. They really can't wait.

Their collective motto might be "Bring it on, dear Lord".

The non-combatants are both less numerous and less certain.

All of them are trusted and tested and tried- up to a point, but none of them have been briefed as to what to expect. The concept of "need to know" is in it's infancy. The idea that "ignorance is bliss" is alive and strong and prospering.

Such is government efficiency in eighteen hundred and sixty three.

Doubtless, there is a man with a plan, somewhere? A man with a clipboard? Surely all is ordered, calculated, surveyed in the corridors of power?

However, since only Pinkertons Detective Agency actually knows who is who, and even who is where on all three trains, and nobody from Pinkertons is on any of the three trains, nobody knows nothin' and everybody thinks that somebody else knows everything. Maybe the armed soldiers will cover all bases?

Hopefully, they will prevail in providing care and protection, mostly utilising naked force backed by bullets, for everybody in whichever car of the three.

A soldier will do what he's told. That's his job. But the truth is simple.
We know not what we do.
Nobody said nothin'.
Nobody knows nothin'.
Confusion reigns, and that's a fact.
So the three trains embark, amidst some ignorance.
But the true subject of all of this ignorance and confusion travels in the fourth car of five on the middle train.
He is not ignorant, and he's not confused.
The train might be Baby Eagle, but this passenger is the most famous and the most fierce (in true power) of all Eagles anywhere on the planet.
He is Abraham Lincoln, President of these United States of America.
Sadly, the States are anything but united, except in name, and even that moniker, "United" is hotly disputed.
The great war is being waged some miles and tens of miles and hundreds of miles to the south- starting just there across the river; wherefore the need to take visible and effective precautions.
People are dying by the dozen, (sometimes by the thousand) on a daily basis, and the Father of the Nation, and of the war, is Abraham Lincoln.
He must have protection, and lots of it.
At any given time on any day of the week, a significant enemy force might be as close as only twenty miles away, or less.
They might be within the range of a single pistol shot, and that would be calamitous.
If these insurrectionists could end his life, they would account it a great victory for their cause.
Military intelligence must therefore protect the President; but as he says himself, smiling, the phrase "military intelligence" could be construed as a contradiction in terms.

He seldom smiles these days, the weight of the war
crushing him in his high office, but he is smiling now.
Yes, he's a mite off, a bit hot and unsteady, but he's
safe and happy in this company.
John Nicolay (Nick), his Personal Secretary, John
Hay (Hick), his Assistant Personal Secretary, and the
majestic William Seward, Secretary of State, make
merry in perfectly good taste.
Everybody is talking.
Good fellowship is in the air.
But there are conventions to be respected!
Darkies in the distant fields have their set practices,
soldiers and freight Engineers adhere to a code, and
these four men have their modes of address and
gradations of good manners.
For there are at least three classes of American
Society present and correct in the carriage.
No caste system is more rigid.
Protocol is bred hard in the bone: the economist, the
lawyer, and the secretaries, simple clerks, gathered in
this one space.
Lincoln is in a class of his own-he is the President. He
is very good at speaking. He always plays by the
rules, even though he can say what he likes.
However, when he says what he likes, his words being
unfailingly positive and complimentary, just about
everybody likes what he says.
He never scolds, never accuses.
He practices the curious art of blessing people with
his words. He openly dispenses love to people in his
speech. He does love them. He does. He admits it to
himself more and more as the days pass.
And so he works at it, speaking the truth in love. He
is cultivating reciprocal respect in every syllable he
utters. His is a free, high-spirited convention to class.
The two Johns, Hick and Nick, are more constricted,
and have to be more careful.

They will only ever dare, in most congenial moments, to speak to their President as "Sir", even amidst informal settings such as this; if anyone else is nearby, it will always be "Mr President". They will keep their heads down, metaphorically, with most of the people they encounter.
Doesn't matter high or low- mind your manners!
Certainly the fourth man present is one of the high.
He is their superior, and he knows it.
The United States Secretary of State William Seward will always, to them, be a resoundingly respectful "Mr Seward, Sir".
This is not least because Hick and Nick, in personal and unspoken unity, hate his guts and dislike and fear him most amazingly.
If they did speak about it, which they do not, they would say that they'd rather, if called upon to sup with the devil, brandish a long spoon.
They would trust Mr Seward Sir just about as far as they could throw him, which ain't too far, considerin'.
Of course they conceal these feelings- mind your manners!
Secretary Seward seemingly knows nothing of this, and would not reveal his innermost convictions if he did; which, in Nick and Hick's eyes, makes him the more dangerous.
All present are aware that he was inclined in earlier, pre-Presidential days, to call Lincoln "Abe".
He now calls him "Sir" or "Mr President".
Only if Lincoln is very happy indeed in his presence would Seward now say "Abe".
It's not beyond probability.
He COULD call him "Abe".
It might, just might happen.
But this man is a master communicator; he treads softly though sunshine, and through snow.
Most likely he will adhere to the code, unspoken but thoroughly understood.

So Seward is at his ease.
He can swim and fly and dive in this atmosphere.
Seward will promote gentleness and harmony, so that the President will be happy and content.
So he probably will stick to the honorific.
Business IS business.
When he relaxes, which he is doing now, Abe, Honest Abe, Mister President, Sir, addresses Seward, ordinarily "Mr Secretary Seward" as "Bill", and this preserves the democratic and friendly decencies all around the carriage.
They can do this.
It's all in the code.
The seats are comfortable, and "Bill" is holding forth on a humorous tale.
He speaks in a clipped, pleasant voice, surprisingly clear amidst the smoke.
These folksy, rounded tones have always been one of Seward's most attractive characteristics, and he knows it.
He is very self-aware.
He knows the range of his own weaponry, and exactly who he can hit, who he can befool with smoke and mirrors and with a nice ring to his cultivated blarney.
He can reach out to those of high and low station, smart, sharp, shrewd individuals.
And he can mesmerize the stupid people.
There are lots of them all over, and just about everywhere you look.
Seward is very good at getting his message across to such as these.
No need for that today.
Everybody present is very smart.
Seward doesn't want to fool Abe or the two Johns.
But he knows for certain that you can, if you put your mind to it, fool all the people all the time.
He gets quite enough practice in that direction, and so he smiles.

As he might say of himself or anybody, "a man may smile and smile and be a villain".
He's smiling now.
Whatever the truth behind the mask, Seward knows that he can put folk at their ease.
people really do like to listen to him.
Folk relax, and they listen.
His present audience of Abe, Nick, and Hick, are visibly relaxing, and so he proceeds with his tale....

"So anyway, Thaddeus Stevens and Andy Jackson both wind up in the same barbershop for a shave and a haircut, depending on their relevant requirements.
Now the poor barber is nervous, knowing these two firebrands for what they are.
He's trying to duck between them without offending one or the other.
And both of them, in a spirit of charity, are wont to reassure the barber that he's okay and at the same time take a pop at each other should the chance prevail.
So the barber finishes up cutting Jackson's hair first, which doesn't take long, him being the less needy aged of the two, and then deftly skips over to baldy Stevens, who only wants a shave, and applies the razor and hot wet towels. Honour's satisfied, fair enough. The barber's still on his mettle, though.
He speaks up- "would you gents like me to apply some pomade (he pronounces it "poe-made") it being the latest thing for the man of distinction?
"Lemme smell it?" says Jackson, and he takes a good whiff up his nose.
"Lord, no! If you put that stuff onto me, my wife's gonna think that I've been taiglin' inside a French whorehouse!".
The barber's crushed. He turns to Thaddeus- "and for you, Sir?"

Thaddeus smiles at him- "yes please! Lay it on! I don't hafta worry. My wife don't know what the inside of a French whorehouse smells like!"

Seward laughs aloud at his own joke.
Lincoln slaps his thigh and guffaws, choking slightly.
Nick and Hick laugh happily, but carefully.
Observing this, Lincoln chuckles again.
He knows that his two Johns worship the ground he walks on.
He knows that in like manner they fear Seward for so many reasons, all of them sound and sensible.
He fears Seward himself, equally sensibly, and cherishes the homespun wisdom of Kentucky- "keep a close eye on your friends, and you'll never need to worry about your enemies".
But now Abe decides to tell his own little tale.
The listeners hush at once, for the great Father is nodding while clearing his throat and patiently rising and lowering his right hand as though stroking a puppy or softly counting to five or ten- his invariable precursor to speaking intimately.
He repeats this process until his audience is attentive, his gaze narrowing, the long fingers on his left hand tenderly cupping his chin. And the hand beats time, strokes the imaginary puppy again, gradually ceasing as he sits forward.
It is a performance worthy of a great orchestra conductor, commanding attention in a respectful hush.
Those privileged to witness sometimes wonder the extent to which this is rehearsed. Or is it all just normal, natural?
Nick and Hick have discussed these seemingly casual mannerisms, and concluded that the President is wholly unaware of them.
They may in fact be quite correct, but they both realise that with Lincoln, as with all front line politicians, you never can tell.

Seward himself cherishes Abe's homilies, and he's heard lots of them- never, incidentally, the same one twice.
But he recognizes this power of golden rhetoric in his Boss.
He approves, knowingly, the soft spoken words, the gentle hesitations, the forceful observations vigorously, even lovingly expressed.
Lincoln's abilities as a communicator are wonderful to behold; Seward's powers of observation are equally formidable, and he values what he regards as natural, God-given skill.
Lincoln, more than anybody he knows, is capable of fooling all of the people all of the time- well at least those this side of Mason-Dixon, but he is also the man least interested in doing so.
Seward is both fascinated and amazed at just how Honest Abe can spin a web of deepest wisdom mingled freely with shrewd blarney- he's very good at it, and it all rests on "personal touch".
Seward accurately observes, weighs, and quantifies, yea he quantifies, that great virtue- "personal touch".
Oh yes, that personal touch is a rare and precious jewel of great price, and Seward tries to cultivate it for himself as much as he can.
Above all, he knows that Honest Abe has it in spades.
Partly, this is because Honest Abe really is honest, and it shows clearly, and cannot be dissembled.
He is one of the people.
He nurtures commonality, simplicity, humility. And this is all of the personal touch.
Once heard, Lincoln is never forgotten.
Not for nothing is he known as "Honest Abe".
Truth pours from his lips as thirst quenching cool water in a desert of mendacity and finely weighted lies.
Now he signals that the healing fountain is poised to gush forth.

Truth will out.
The two Johns perk up, like good children before bedtime, with Daddy commencing to bespeak "Once upon a time".
But it is not of three bears and good fairies and beautiful Princesses that Abe will speak.
He will declaim on human nature, always pertaining to the unity of mankind; for this is his Holy Grail in his own lifetime.
He is completely aware of the many forms that human division will take, that greed and cruelty will adopt and overwhelm, and it is as though he has accepted these realities deep, deep in his heart.
He strives never to wound, never to denounce, but only to enlighten.
Above all, he is a purveyor, a sower, a distributor of seeds; seeds of wisdom, seeds of kindness, seeds of warm experience.
He will never punish, but only nourish.
He knows that few are granted the vision gifted unto him, and so he will share this benefice.
My friends, he begins (and Seward delightedly pounces on the Biblical allusion- "I have called you friends", and mentally marks it for his own use in the future), thinkin' on that barber shop.
Hmmm, yes.
And apropos of the insight of wives vis-à-vis their husband's possible misbehaviour-
I recall a similar episode, pertaining to the fair sex.
(And now, internally, Seward leaps like a trout to the bait. He's going to talk about women! Who'd 'a thought it? Gadzooks!)
And of course, Lincoln does just that.
Myself when young did often admire several, if not many, well, no, many is the more honest word, fine examples of the female form.
Oh, I admit it.

Now I'm older, probably stupider rather than wiser,
I admit that I warn't truly interested in their grasp of
the Latin and Greek languages.
But it was a starting point.
And I didn't really care about the Sermon they heard
that good minister preached last Sunday. Warn't it
on piety?
And I'd nod at their holiness, but kept my view up on
them gorgeous eyes and other features of interest;
and that hair, so soft in the lamplight. Why, I even,
on occasion, fell so far as to enquire after their
comfort settin' down.
Are you quite comfortable, my dear Millie?
And I'd put a look of deep concern on me, suitable
for sympathising.
Oh, and might I extend a cushion to your back,
restin' on that there fine sofa? Please, Margarite,
allow me? It's no trouble! There now!
'Twas my experience that other avenues for further
surveillance developed! Oh, Lord, forgive me my sin.
Seward chuckles, and the two Johns nudge each
other and wink. What a card!
Lincoln nods in mellow reflection. He knows that he's
pitching perfect spitballs, and he idles forward,
developing his theme.
Turn my head to look after many a comely lady I did.
Frequent I discovered myself to be without the least
impediment prevailin' so to be sneakin' in a second
or third glance, if opportunity served.
And it did!
It's a wonder my head didn't come unscrewed, my
neck and chin rotatin' like a rooster, and all to
worship at beauty's shrine.
To speak true, I was just agog, dandlin' like a
drunkard after brandy.
And I warn't the least bit bothered by this weakness.
Fact is, I loved and admired women.
I don't think I'd ever trust the man who said he
warn't similar inclined, one time or other. (Seward

grunts a great "HUH" of agreement, and bobs his head, nodding and shaking it at the same time).
Truth to tell, I looked my fill, and certain sure had no regrets particular, leastways not when the husband warn't in attendance!
Seward now laughs openly, the two Johns shaking with mirth contained.
Honest Abe ploughs onward.
But, and it is a big "but", I always cherished the guilty assumption that this failin' was particular to just me!
Oh, I was a hog, a filthy hog, swillin' husks in the mire, wallowin' in the ordure!
Forgive me, Lord, I'd mutter, but always with one eye askance at the Parson's daughter.
Even, Lord bless me, the Postman's wife!
Give me chastity, Lord.
Just not this next week!
I'm seein' Rebecca at the County Fair!
Seward is now nodding in enthusiastic glee.
Abe, he hoots, breathless, how come we both had the same Parson and the same Postman?
And all four men join in the total shout of laughter that hails and rewards a good punchline, well-delivered. He has actually enhanced Lincoln's musings, and set the seal of humorous approval on the proceedings.
Lincoln twinkles in acknowledgement.
But now comes the meat in the platter he is serving up for supper-
As I say, 'twas all MY wrongdoin'. I was a hog, and a greedy one. But I had two revelations comin' to me. Both regardin' my sinfulness in lustin' after the womenfolk.
One, the first, was extended by my friendship with a Lutheran Minister I met with in New York. Pastor Philip Grunfeld.
He was dyin' with the shakes.

Never drunk nor smoked 'baccy, didn't chaw, his whole life.
The most truly humble man I ever encountered.
Probably the only one.
He said to me that he wanted to confess in my hearin'.
Before he died, mind?
Prior to departure fer' Elysian fields?
He said that he wanted to talk to an honest man.
Wanted to confess.
To me, if you please.
To me.
Such was his opinion.
Well, I'm no clergyman, but he was God-fearin' to a degree I'd never witnessed before, or since, and I agreed; as much for my conscience as for his.
He commenced confessin', his breath longdrawn and tortured.
I was hit hard by this evident holiness, I tell you.
Racked with unholy guilt.
And dang me if'n he didn't admit of the very sins that had dogged me from the age of fourteen or so years?
It was Mary this and Grunhilde that.
Lookin' at women!
That's what he did!
Every woman, not discriminatin'!
Just oglin' at them!
Why, he'd even seen another Parson's wife that he said wrung him out like a dishcloth after washin'.
I tell you, it set me back considerable.
It shook me, I admit.
If anything, HE was the only honest man in the room.
I warn't fit for purpose, nohow.
I'd never have had the sand to speak out like he did, dyin' or not!
Seward notices here that Lincoln has, in fact, done this very thing.

He has confessed openly, here and now, with three men present and attentive.
He has, with great skill and humour, admitted to lustful thoughts.
Therefore he accuses himself of cowardice whilst demonstrating the finest bravery.
His emphatic denial of virtue only manifests his truthful honesty the more.
It's a neat trick, and Seward envies Lincoln tremendously, and wishes that he could pull off this gift of the gab.
This is a serious subject, so why are we all set just so, convivial and comfortable?
Honest Abe's got us in the palm of his hand.
Contrition and sorrow has never been funnier.
But the great sinner mushes on.
So I knew I warn't alone in my paths of temptation.
Other gentlemen confirmed that same fact to me since, and I reckon it's a common condition, and so the good book says.
All have sinned, and fallen short of the glory of God.
Yes, I reckon it's so.
But I was set for two revelations, not just this one!
And the bigger of them was second in line, and it come off just earlier this last year, in the springtime.
That really hard-tacked my gumption, wrung me out, and pegged me up to dry.
Lincoln leaned forward earnestly, and as he did so, Seward inwardly resolved that, if Lincoln now announced that the sun rose in the west, and set in the east, he'd believe him, such was his conviction.
Bill (pause), John (pause again), John (meaningful glance at the two Johns, encompassing both) he began, and now they were all bonded as dearest kinfolk, and Honest Abe breathed out sorrowfully, poised to lower the boom-
I never knew a woman more Godly and religious than my sweet wife, Mary.
Yes, our First Lady of our nation.

If there's a saint walkin', it's her.
I am as dirt and ordure in comparison.
Her thoughts and her ways are higher, and better than mine, to paraphrase but a little.
And I don't reckon I'm denyin' the good Lord any praises due, by sayin' so!
The two Johns nodded in synchronicity and waggled their heads at the same time; in full agreement and accord, full of propriety and devout reflection.
Seward gathered up any possible slack and persevered in his role of anointing elder by breathing out slowly through open lips before concluding, with reverence, Give me the good woman, for her price is above rubies.
And now it was Lincoln who could joyfully trump this theological ace, and bring them all back to happy humour-
I never said Ruby warn't a good woman, but I ain't enquirin' as to her charges for services rendered, and I'm surely not invitin' comparisons with Mary, on any basis!
There was a universal whoop of laughter, and Lincoln joined in the fun, shoulders heaving.
Seward slapped his thigh and choked a good bit on his cheroot, wheezing, and the two Johns shook hands and slapped each other on the back, and complimented each other on their rare good luck to hear such a good 'un, and tole by the President himself!
When all had finished, and the relaxed quiet had resumed, Lincoln came in again, timing perfect, like a trouper on the stage who knows his audience down all the way to the ten cent stalls, and performs accordingly.
You were there, Bill!
And you boys!
We were all there.
Bill, you were the man in charge.

The time we met British Ambassador Lyons in
Washington?
Not so long ago, as I recall?
The two Johns nodded in unison.
Oh yes, they recalled British Ambassador Lyons.
They all did, with good reason.
Seward narrowed his gaze, as if perceiving that very
man, Ambassador Lyons, in the mid-distance just in
front of him, right there in the carriage, and pursed
his lips, the floor his own.
I do remember him, Mr President.
Yes, sir, I do.
He was Lord Lyons, if memory serves.
Hmmm. Lord indeed.
Only man who was a foot smaller'n me that
managed, glintin' up'ards, to look right down on me
as if I were trash.
It was competently done, I admit.
I doubt but that he practised in the mirror.
Yes.
Not quite two year…January of '62, that's when it
was.
Just a small matter of whether Great Britain
declared war on us or not, over the Trent. Lyons,
hmmm, Lord Lyons, was all for teaching us a lesson.
Bad cess to him.
A Diplomat who hated Diplomats.
Not a gentleman.
Sniffy, he was!
Sniffy!
Would look down his nose at you, mostly by lifting
his chin.
And he'd twitch his nostrils.
I well recall his nostrils, mousey hair inside,
perpetually sniffing as if you were a dead fish or
something sticking to his shoe.
I'd have liked to have punched him soundly on his
lordly nose, or his uppity chin!
Lord Lyons!

What of him, Sir?
Ah, said Lincoln, not him in particular, but one of his entourage accompanying.
Mr David Walker!
Just plain Mister.
Warn't no Lord, neither, not that he lacked any nobility for the absence of labelling.
But, for my money, he was ten times the man that Lyons was not and never could have been.
And I concur in your estimation of LORD Lyons, Bill!
Lyons was sniffy!
Affronted!
Lookin' for a fight.
So, nothing of him.
No, this was a humble plenipotentiary, a lawyer. Mind, they call them Solicitors in England. I've never understood why. Solicitin'? Sounds like something harlots get up to outside a theatre! But I ain't tarrin' him with that bush. Oh no, I speak well of him, no man moreso. Anyway. This jolly good chap answered to the name of plain Mister David Walker. One of the gang. Makin' up the numbers. Do you remember him, boys?
Nick was the first to answer.
I do, sir. A man of good height, florid complexion, softly spoken. Why, he alone of the British delegates made shift to shake my hand and introduce himself. Very well mannered, I do declare. And as Mr Seward rightly says, I couldn't say the same for most of the rest of 'em.
Hick now echoed the sentiments.
Yes. I agree. About him and them. I do recall him very well. Why, I noticed him from the first, and for this reason- he had his pants ends tucked into his socks.
And that meant that you could see the shine of his shoes kinda' sparkling against the white of his socks.

I initially thought it comical, but then I realized that what it did was make him look smart without bein' superior. Why, he most definitely did not look down his nose at me, even if he was head and shoulders tall 'a me. He appeared interested and genuinely friendly. Shook my hand too, grasping both hands dearly, and looked me full in the eye, like he was the Minister welcoming a long lost pal to dinner.

Yes, said Abe. Notice that if a man strikes you as comical or nicely religious, like you say, Hick, that he poses no threat?

I think you've hit the nail on the head, Sir, Seward interjects. But there was more to him than met the eye.

Seward purses his lips again, for emphasis, nods emphatically, and continues.

He alone of the Delegation had good knowledge of Maritime Law, British and American.

He alone had the gumption to talk about the money side of things.

And for what reason? Because he had no personal interest in the matter. I mean he had no money ridin'. He wanted to serve his country for the best. I say- good for him! That's his job! God bless him.

Thing is, there warn't no side to him. He wasn't looking for a cut of the pie. Just fair dealing all around. The rest of the whole passel of them were mill owners, or somesuch, or traded in King Cotton- not that they'd ever admit it!

No, it was all our sacred honour this and our gracious Queen that, and the freedom of mankind upon the seven seas. And Lord This and Sir So and So Smellynose That, all affecting not to care a fig about the cash in hand. Perish the thought, old boy! But Mr Walker hit the nail right on the head. Talkin' to him was instructive, and it was direct. I recall his very words, excellent words they were. I recall them exactly.

We are met here in the midst of a great conflict, he said, to test whether any nation constructed as yours can long endure. Eleven score years ago, we had our test, as you are doing now. We had Cavalry and push of pike in those far off days.
You use far more sophisticated weaponry, reliant on gunpowder.
And you must prevail, or your nation shall be subsumed.
To do that, you need guns and bullets and cannonballs spewing fire relentlessly, when the chips are down.
His words.
That same gunpowder, he said, in your soldiers Remingtons and Winchesters comes straight from British owned mines in India. It is a most lucrative trade in both directions, and none of us wants to imperil that, do we?
He was right.
No, we certainly didn't want to imperil trade, and we still don't, and neither do they.
I figured right away that you could talk turkey to this man. Two things about him.
One, he was not angry, not at all. That matters when you're tryin' to juggle hot potatoes. Anger clouds your vision. He was balanced. Concerned, yes, but not angry.
None of the sniffy nostrils from him. And two, he was openly generous.
Do you know what he said to me at dinner? He said this- Mr Seward, sir, may I help you to some of these peas before they disappear? They really are quite delicious.
Now, he warn't the cook, and he hadn't brought the peas with him. We were in Adam's house, as I recall, so Walker is not the host. But he conjured up generosity from nowhere, and doled it out with a liberal hand.

I've never enjoyed any peas more than those peas, I declare. So much for aristocracy. Good breeding tells! Manners maketh man!

Mr Walker is welcome at any time in my house, should he care to visit us next crisis betwixt nations. As for Lord Lyons, to borrow a timely phrase, the more he talked of his honour, the faster we counted the spoons!

Everybody laughed heartily, and laughed again. Gradually, Lincoln took up the reins.

Yes. Behold the man. He's made a good impression on us all. But as you say, Bill, there's more.

Bill nods warmly; not only is he labelled Bill at this moment, but he's being strongly affirmed here. When Lincoln approves of you, and calls you Bill, you feel it right down to your socks.

I also noted, in my researches, that he was the only one of the whole team that knew anything, could speak with authority, on basic law. And people do tell me things.

The rest of 'em were the sons of Dukes (TITTERS FROM THE TWO JOHNS) and the sons of Earls (A SHARP GUFFAW FROM SEWARD) and the sons of this 'n that (ALL NODDING HAPPILY) and for all I know sons of bitches (LOUD AND PROLONGED LAUGHTER).

But Mr Walker was sound. Good pedigree! Not only that, but he might, conceivably, have been distant kin to my dear wife, and that put a whole new construction on matters, from numerous angles.

Not least, was he aboard for that reason?

Anyways, I'll not say that I asked our spies in London to get frisky, but I made it clear in out of the way corners that I'd appreciate any relevant smatterings of accurate gossip and potential scandal appertainin'. That's what happened, and I felt fairly well informed as to his bona fides.

I don't have to tell you that his bona fides were a sight more respectable than his fellows, not that I'd break a confidence or six! (LOUD LAUGHS)

I may say, the Right Honourable Lord So and So warn't so Right at all, and not very Honourable either; why, not so much as a contentious rooster in the barnyard (LOUD LAUGHS).

I needn't have worried about David Walker. He's a decent man, as I say. But something did turn up of particular interest, certainly to Mrs Lincoln. His forebearers had departed England getting on for sixteen fifty three or thereabouts. Hailin' if I may say so, from a place called Debenham in Suffolk County, East Anglia.

Which is exactly the jumpin' off spot of Mary's great getting' on nine or so granpaws long agone.

For that reason I prevailed on Mary to most informally make polite solicitations to Mr David Walker. Ostensibly she was just going to be wondering if their grandsires might ha' been childhood sweethearts taiglin' down the leafy lanes when King Henry the Eight frolicked with Mary Queen of Scots or somesuch under a neighbourin' bush.

Unofficially I had asked her to make some measure of the sand in this man's craw.

Was he to be trusted? Did he shape up as advertised or was he one more hound in the English pack, remarkably well concealed? I count myself a fair judge of character, I admit. But I do declare that I have to stand off in admiration when I see Mary take the scales in hand, and weigh up a body. Her powers of penetrative vision put mine to shame, and all the more reliably because she seems to know me far better than I do, and frequently demonstrates the fact. So I kinda reckoned that her intervention would give me an edge. I didn't hesitate too long about recruiting her to the Washington D.C. diplomatic corps. And just by the way, they're uniformed in homemade frocks (LOUD LAUGHS).

So we're at the Reception and I hunkered down with Lord Sniffynose (CHUCKLES) to listen, or rather not listen, while he bellowed bellicose Britishness at me.

Her Majesty's intentions, sir! National honour, sir! Not to be borne! Armed forces! The sword of truth! The Shield of Strength! A shot across the bows.

I pictured Queen Victoria cuttin' loose with a cavalry sabre in one hand whilst flingin' a cannonball from the other (GREAT HOOTS).

At least the corn liquor was most agreeable, but small enough comfort in the event.

He positively thundered at me from a short distance away, maybe two feet.

Oh, my poor ears. He perhaps thought me deficient in concentration, or hard of hearin'. Or both, even though I was nodding and giving every sign of paying greatest heed to his every word (MORE CHUCKLES). They also serve who stand and get deafened by the insensitive and sniffy-nostrilled. I can truthfully say that I've suffered for my country.

But it was as well that I did. This gave Mary a chance to nip in for a sweet word on the quiet with Mr Walker, and she chose not to dither. No, she applied her feminine wisdom to the task; her close friends runnin' interference lest one of the simpler souls tried to mosey in.

I gave her ten minutes or so, until my ears could take no more pounding abuse from this jackass, and I excused myself to attend to Mrs Lincoln, who requires my immediate assistance, Lord Lyon! He couldn't argue with that. He was stumped, and not able to offer any opinion. Presumably he'd experienced Queen Victoria like to blistering his hearing if'n womenfolk are mentioned with concern.

So he kinda harrumphed at me and went away lookin' for a biscuit or somethin'. Leastways, I think so. Or it might have been somebody else to bellow at. Meanwhile, Mary was then over in a corner with the unbeknownst victim of our colloquial espionage, further up the room.

When I got there he was smiling happily and laughing and she was beaming all over her face. Of course he and I'd been formally introduced by now three or four times, but Mary and I had privately fixed up between us that she would re-introduce him again.

This would be after the surreptitious tete-au-tete. The terms of endearment extended would be indicative of her findings. (CHUCKLES) Such are the cunning machinations you might find on any day beneath our roof, God help us! (LAUGHTER). That the President of these United States has to stoop to this? Pray for me, gents!

So anyways, I approach with a degree of caution, ready and expectin' Mary to tip me the wink in one direction or the other. Bear in mind that I'm fairly well disposed and the initial signs seem favourable. So I reckon she's going to say something like- "oh, Mr President, sir, you remember dear Mr David Walker, of Great Britain? And we have discovered that our sires were certainly close and beloved neighbours in bygone days". That's what I imagined, anyways. Well, she did no such thing.

Didn't re-introduce him, neither, as she and I had agreed.

I reckon that makes her disobedient to her lawful wedded husband.

Well, I might-a took a stick to her then and there to impose discipline.

Spare the rod and spoil the spouse, you might'a thought.

If I brung her to heel, 'twould be a great mercy? So, did I do that?

I didn't, I admit. Not for mercy's sake, neither. But I did wish to avoid getting my head knocked off right quick, so I kinder avoided that course of action.
(CHUCKLES)
No, my goodwife, the First Lady, she beams and nods at my approach.
He sort of inclines his head in that not quite bowing movement that only the English can do when they're bein' charming, and I find him to be very charming, genuinely so.
I extend my hand to him, and he gives me a good firm grip back, setting good store by that handshake, all deepest respect, and Mary still hasn't spoken.
And then she turns right around and looks full at him, me over her back and shoulder to the left.
David, she says. First name terms if you please, and pretty warm sentiments in that one word, I assure you. Please, she says, walk to the other side of the room, in a measured stride, and make your way back to us directly. I wish to commend you to my husband, and I'd prefer you not to be in earshot when I do.
Please extend that favour, my friend?
Calls him her friend? Gadzooks! I tell you I was shook rigid. He kinda twinkles at her, full bowing this turn, kisses her hand, don't look back at me, and then off he goes.
I admit that I bit my lip and kept my mouth shut. I didn't know what to say anyway.
Not the first time I've been completely bejiggered, but certainly the first from that quarter. You could have knocked me down with a puff of wind.
Abraham, she says.
Don't think she'd called me that since our weddin' night. Abraham, that man is so dear! Let me declare this without cavil. He is everything my sainted mother ever warned me against and then some. If we had a daughter, I'd raise the national debt to guarantee her dowry this side of marriage to him, but I'd not let her near him unchaperoned!

These are her very words! Mrs Lincoln, mind? She looks at me, implorin' but dominant. She's the only person in the world that can do that look. Try it some time! Or, Bill, maybe you're already familiar, from the joy of the marital estate? (LOUD LAUGHTER)
Now, I contend that nobody can tonguelash the President, and get away with it. Or maybe tonguelash is the wrong word?
I mean, Mary didn't so much as raise her voice above a whisper. Nor there warn't no element of disagreement nor contention. So how come I come out feeling like a whipped puppy? Like I say, nobody can tonguelash the President. So there. I'd maintain that stance in the Senate House, but that ain't allowin' for her vicissitudes! (LOUD LAUGHTER)
Abraham, she says, I have never spoken this of any man, but I declare in the holiness of matrimony that this man affects me in The Lord!
I feel the good in him! I want to be his mother! I want to comfort him! I want to embrace him in love, and if I warn't married to you, I'd want to be married to him.
I like him, Abraham! And I admit that I don't understand it! There is truth in him! He is, well, he's desirable! And I say that with a careful mouth. Why, I've never seen this level of attractiveness in any man! When the Queen of England sent him as her emissary, I assure you that she swooned! She knew what she was doing.
But the rest of the party, them other high-born bodies, they aren't worth a plugged nickel. He's, just, well, he's just perfectly lovely. I like him, Abraham. He is honourable. When you come to grips with these men, this contingent, as you must, I urge you to incline to his words. He is a good man, Abraham. You can put your trust in him. And, just between you and me, Mr President, I am confident that the ladies of New York will see fit to honour him fully.

They shall do so, whether or not they're married; whether or not their menfolk are in the next room. He has that effect. He won't get much sleeping, not undisturbed, I declare. Not with those eyes and that line of courtesy. I doubt but that certain ladies shall require an urgent consultation with him as opportunity serves, and shall not be denied. That's a terrible thing to say, isn't it?
Am I casting aspersions on the purity of American womenfolk?
Perhaps I am. Not for the first time. But I know that I am right. There now.
We've both learned something, haven't we?
Then her voiced assumed normal levels, so the whole room can hear. (LAUGHTER) How do women do that? (A GREAT SHAKING OF HEADS) Do they teach it in girl's school?"
The two Johns are giggling in a heap, Seward is beating his thigh.
It calls for a dramatic leap. I haven't the capability. Wish I had! And on she ploughs.
Why here he is again! Mr Walker, sir! Welcome.
And just as dramatic she alters tone right downward, and just as easy. She speaks direct now, so's only him and me can hear her.
David, would you do us the honour of dining with The President and myself, just us, privately? Will you, David?
I declare, I choked on my whiskey. I'd near enough heard it from the horses mouth, not that I'd dare to call Mary a horse, ever, but that women do actually look at the menfolk and feel similar stirrin's as us befuddled unfortunates. 'Course, she wouldn't use that terminology. And she would only look askance at these OTHER women, but I tell you, it got my dander up. I determined to keep a close eye on young Walker.

But, truth to tell, he was so danged nice that even if'n he HAD offended someways, I'd have been Counsel for the Defence pro bono! Not that he ever did, mind?

Well, our private supper happened about three days later. Bill, I believe you'd spoken with him in the interval? Anyhow, your position on the Trent was set by then, with mine all but settled. So now I seat Mary to table, Mr Walker bowin' as only he can. Mary's grinnin' with what I would call great delight. But tonight she's holdin' her cards very close to the…., well, under the table. All present know that it's him and me that are here for the hagglin', so Mary's playin' her part, keepin' mum.

But she is so happy! And he's all grace and elegance. She's lookin' him over like he was one of our boys announcin' he's takin' the pledge, or somesuch. She's so happy. I've never seen her so content. And this yere gentleman the cause and origin of it. It bodes well for the negotiations to come. I declare, the way to win a President's heart, or an international argument, is by pleasing his wife.

Well, I was fairly relaxed. I'm hopin' to learn somewhat, with my red lines on the matter pretty well drawn. But, dang me, Mr Walker, over the soup, laid out my entire strategy, hopes and fears, in about two shakes. He just cut through all the highfalutin' nonsense. His words, and here he goes- Mr President, permit me to be direct?

We, the British, have got ourselves into hot water. That much is certain. It's a tangle, and no mistake. We desperately need you to give us a way out; but of course we will only admit to the fact that YOU need a way out. We have decided to base our outrage on the insult to Britain's honour, whilst in truth it is the sniff of money that attracts us.

When did our Royal Navy hesitate, from the time of Good Queen Bess up to this very day today, to board a foreign vessel anywhere in the world? Hypocrites we!
And so we howl in righteous anguish! But we are at a cleft stick. Only money can assuage our hurt, we cry, affronted. We've hung our hats on that. But if we demand thousands in punitive damages, we lose millions in trade. We don't want to achieve that. So we won't mention money. And we'll hope to God (forgive me, Mrs Lincoln) that you won't mention it either. If you suggest plain dealing, and say this is a money matter, set a price, John Bull, and offer as much as a million pounds, I tell you, that will not be enough. No amount offered will ever be enough, and then we will declare War!
If we demand a dollar, that will be too high a price for you to pay, and you will declare War. Take this as a given. If filthy lucre emerges from it's cistern, there will be War.
So, how to defuse the situation?
Forgive my temerity, Mr President, but I love my country and my Queen.
I don't want the stupidity of our Envoys to destroy our friendship.
Four score and several years ago, our two nations parted in enmity and sundered our house.
It was all of our dwelling, and we destroyed it, brother fighting against brother.
Blood was spilled, but harmony prevailed. And so your land came to be as it is now, sovereign. So we proceeded, learning how to contend whilst in the way, in the path, as we must do, if difficulties such as this are to be avoided.
Two score and ten years gone, we again quarrelled, but we've patched that up.
I don't want us, our two nations, to ever repeat that journey of foolish agony.

Please allow me to offer a solution. Permit me to be honest and direct. Forgive my temerity, but may I speak from the heart?

This should be your stance.

Blame the whole thing on the Captain of the American ship. He acted without orders. Exceeded his brief. Outrageous misconduct! Upset our dearest friends and neighbours.

He will be dealt with most severely!

But there was no intention, now, or at any time, to upset the United Kingdom of Great Britain. We will hold this man to account, make no mistake! He shall be punished. We admit that his actions were very wrong, very wrong indeed. And we shall offer a most suitable apology in good time, ere long, post haste, and without delay.

And having said that, be still and quiet.

Not a word about compensation, not a farthing or a pennyweight piece. Nobody will ever ask to see the apology. Nobody will want to do so. And we'll all go quietly home to bed.

He beamed at Mary. This bread is delicious, Mam. (Here he said "Mam", as in"ham".)

May I ask, would you favour me with the recipe for my dear Mama? (And now it's "muh-mah".)

She would truly love this meal, and I am so blessed, so privileged to enjoy this time.

I declare, Mister Walker said all the right things. I doubt I've ever seen my wife so happy. She was like a well behaved schoolgirl at a speechnight ceremony.

Mr Walker distinguished himself with his good manners and his joie de vivre. She was right. All the women loved him. They wanted him. They desired him. Lucky fellow, but it's not luck, is it? Good breedin' tells! Manners maketh man!

And his turn of phrase, "four score and several years ago", or "we sundered our house", that's horse sense, vigorously expressed.

And of course, he was completely right about everything, about how the land lay. His side were in a cleft stick and so were we. Both sides needed a way out. I had been calculating how to bring that very thing to pass. He anticipated my position, our position I may say, to the cross of a "t" on the word "troubled".

Bill, you'd already come to that very same course of action which he suggested.

When you put it in writing, upstairs, formally, I could but agree.

I think that both you and I have Mr David Walker to thank for that.

That may be so, Mr President, but of course I reserve the secretarial and administrative responsibility of taking all the credit this side of the Atlantic!

Lincoln laughed generously, and choked, and laughed again, and slapped his thigh.

The two Johns rocked with unrestrained merriment. Seward smiled, full to the brim with good fellowship, and offered whiskey sours with an open hand.

ADDRESSING GETTYSBURG

An hour has passed. The easiness of the atmosphere has engendered a cosy splendour.
Warmed by the smooth liquid, Abraham Lincoln has at first reclined, then slouched a bit, and then mellowed off into a mild catnap.
Is he dreaming, or is Hick draining away out of a long tube of red ribbons into a field of daffodils?
It is deep down in the autumn, and the leaves are drifting, drifting across the bloodstained sheets of the hospital tent in which he stands. Yes, autumn leaves are falling on the faces of the boys, skulls burst open at the forehead from a Henry Rifle that hit the target.
That's blood on the walls and buggies. Notice the white ladder, though, leaning on a juniper bush?
Smoke?
Now he stirs, jumping, and squints at the sun low adown in the red west, and he coughs for emphasis, and to wake his fellows, and they are aroused out of their own light slumbers, upright and staring.
Sitting forward, his own head positively heaves with dizziness. He sucks in air, gasping. His breathing strains, and he is noting the saliva almost dripping out, and, panicking a little, wipes his chapped lips. He sniffles, and it occurs to him that he has caught a mild chill, and that he isn't very well.
Unbeknownst to himself and to all, he has contracted smallpox, and he is experiencing the first stages of that disease.
But he ascribes his discomfort to tiredness, and to overwork. The good Lord knows that he does enough of that.
He assembles his forces-
Mr Hay? Mr Nicolay? I propose that we demonstrate the delicate art of speech-writing to our esteemed guest. How say ye?"
Seward is stunned.

In these brief words, Lincoln has, sequentially, established his authority, called his troops to order, included all of them in the decision to get to work, laid out what the work will be, ostensibly deferred to his secretaries whilst in fact doing no such thing, and complimented him while putting him firmly into his rightful place as honoured observer.

Hick and Nick enthusiastically agree and nod and murmur approbation, and there is a great shifting of bags and extrusion of paper and pen and ink in and of and from various writing cases.

Seward leans forward, all spit and polish.

If he is to be an honoured guest and observer, then he intends to be a danged good one.

Mr President, Sir, he begins; he is bending an immediate knee to formality and high office.

I assume that you are referring to the speech you intend to deliver tomorrow. May I ask, how do you intend to proceed?

Lincoln is now sitting bolt upright, his posture mirroring his role, for in truth he might well be a judge in a Court, a Chairman of a County Municipal Authority, or even a President overseeing the composition of a speech with typical efficiency and design.

Mr Secretary, Sir, we shall feel the ground underneath, the mud below our feet. We shall survey the terrain. We will calculate the variables, consider the imponderables, and weigh the benefits against the demerits. And these good men shall strive mightily to craft a good work, and I shall seek to deliver the fruit of their, of our diligent labours, to the advantage of all.

Lincoln pauses gravely for one long second while Seward blinks, waiting.

So, we'll think it up, the boys will write it down, and I'll speak it sideways!. That's how we'll do it.

Seward grins, but does not laugh aloud.

He appreciates the humour, but doesn't want to break the spell of professionalism which is now energising the carriage.
He knows that the President will harness and harmonise these elements.
He is eager to actually see the hows and whys unfolding before him, like a fine concerto well performed.
Seward, like Lincoln, loves music; and Seward is now complimenting himself on this very apt analogy.
Lincoln half-closes his eyes, purses his lips.
His right hand softly beats the tempo in gentle motion, a conductor calling forth the violins in an adagio. All present are stilled, attentive, tranquil.
John, he says, encompassing both Johns-
John, just remind me about the main order of the thing….?
Hick at once refers to a single sheet which he holds up a little, consulting and inspecting, as though for dust, and he taps it in verification;
Mr Edward Everett shall provide the central content- I would surmise that it is implied within the terms of the invitation that your speech should be respectful of this premise, Sir.
Quite so, quite so. I concur, John. I concur. Nick, what do you think?
Nicolay fields this pop fly with his eyes closed.
Sir, he says, "You have the right of it. That is the line to take.
Good. That's what we'll do. So, short and to the point. No frills.
Nicolay interjects; Mr Watts speculates that Mr Everett will give us a good two hours worth of wisdom. From previous experience, I think that he's right. There will be more than one observer yawning, or freezing dutifully.
By the time you rise, I suggest that the levels of concentration apparent shall be, well, diminishing, Sir. Please forgive my temerity.

Lincoln laughs, nodding. I think your temerity is highly justified, Nick. If this was a horse-race, you'd be expectin' to win a dollar for a ten cents bet.
Everett is one of the most affable of men, but he prefers not to use three or four words when a couple of thousand will easily do. I believe that he will commence by describin' the cushion upon which he sits, and then he'll kinda work outwards, like butter meltin' in a skittle. If I'm alongside or behind him on the platform, I calculate that I'll have thirty minutes good sleep before he gets to praisin' my chairleg, and you'll roust me out so's I can look impressed!
The company chortle in unison, but they do so most respectfully.
Lincoln has kept hold of the reins, and Seward watches admiringly as he summons possibilities and options. Now, the speech to be delivered the next day will take shape, here in this very carriage, and he will watch the genesis of it all. Lincoln is in command, a master at work.
Hick, commands the President of these United States of America, please fly a kite, just for a curveball served up in the first inning?
Yes Sir. Thank you, Sir. That I surely will.
Now, let me see....? Ladies and Gentlemen. Our brave soldiers, who perished in this marvellous victory, sorry, this wonderful victory, no. This wondrous victory. Yes. This wondrous victory, that's it, will never be forgotten. They were sons, and brothers, fathers and good husbands, who did not flinch in the face of death.
All right-thinking men will remember them. We will remember them. The flowers on their graves will bloom forever, watered by the tears of their sweethearts, and by the weeping of their mothers.
Ah, dah dum dee dum de dah!
Lincoln actually applauds, nodding warmly.
Ever thought of runnin' for Office, Hick? You'd be a shoo-in! Well done.

I reckon I'd do some weepin' myself if I struck that tone. And when I'd done wipin' my tears away, I'd throw myself in the river to relieve the sufferin' engendered. It's altogether too near the mark for comfort. Should we set up as Undertakers you're the man I'll come to for advertising funerals. But well done. Thank you. Now. Nic? Your turn.

John Nicolay has had several vital minutes, and most of the previous night, to consider his first response in this game that the three have played so often.

He knew that this was coming. He is ready now. He knows the drill. He must put forward cannon fodder to be blasted away. Whatever he offers will be dismissed, rejected, disposed of, and that out of hand.

Any suggestion is doomed, by definition, to be regarded as a dollop of fodder. Now, at this juncture!

But presently, after four or five dollops of fodder have been obliterated, some words, some elements, served up despairingly a while ago, will re-emerge and will make it all the way into the final draft of the speech.

Yes Sir, he begins.

In seventeen seventy six, the men who fought our enemies died so that their posterity might survive. That same posterity died here at Gettysburg so that we might survive. Our brothers died here, in this fertile soil, no, this fertile field, no, this field, so that we can survive. The good Lord willing, we will prevail in this fight. We will survive.

I stand before you today because of their sacrifice, the sacrifice of all of our brothers and fathers who suffered to survive. And so we survive, and we shall continue the struggle, and we shall honour their sacrifice for our children, and the children yet to come. Something like that, sir?

And now it is Seward who applauds, perching upright. And there is great sincerity as he speaks, complimenting Nick.

Mr Nicolay, sir, that was most impressive. Should our President ever have the foolishness to dispense with your services, which I doubt heartily that he will, (dispense with your services I mean, he'll never get shot of his foolishness) then I shall come knocking on your door to be MY secretary. That was very good. Very good indeed!

Lincoln nods, assuming command again, easily.

It is good, John. It is. Now tell the Secretary of State why it's not good enough. In your own opinion, that is?

Thank you sir. Mr Secretary, it is not rounded enough. It does not possess a central theme which is both positive and rewarding. And the overall language is not sufficiently Biblical. It should be more Biblical.

Well, it IS Biblical enough in morbidity, I would say, Lincoln intones. But the repetition of the idea of survival is not warming, does not stir the heart. It sounds like our boys just about dragged themselves off the battlefield, nary the spring in their step. Sounds like they just crawled in the door, one eye lookin' for the sawbones. I think you gave us at least five "survives", in perhaps twelve sentences. That's too much survival and not enough victory. But one thing I do like about that offering, John, is the brevity. I say that you were right on the danged money there. And, my friends, I think we're going to build up using that very model. I believe that Nick has struck the keynote. We'll keep it short and to the point. Very good, John, very good indeed!

Thank you, sir. Thank you, says Nick, and Hick softly applauds, and pats his friend on the shoulder, and they shake hands. When Honest Abe affirms you, you stay affirmed, and no mistake. Even though the President of the United States has torn his offering limb from bloody limb, John Nicolay knows that what he really said was "well done, thou good and faithful servant".

Something you observed in your self-critique, John? I think we might gainfully focus on that, boys? A "central theme", which is, how'd you put it, Nick, "both positive and rewarding"? That's the ticket. That's what we need. Might we consider central themes, boys?

Forgive me, Mr President, Sir, says Seward. Just before you do that, may I please enquire regarding what, by implication, all three of you seem to hold as common ground- that it should be "Biblical"? Please explain that, if you would?

With pleasure, says Lincoln.

Hick, you have the floor.

Feel free to show off all our devices for the danged Seck-er-tary here, and then he'll likely compass it hisself, 'n the whole consarned kit 'n caboodle's done fer!

Everybody laughs, and spirits are high.

John Hay reaches into his briefcase and, after a short search, brings out a thick piece of paper with two scrawled messages written in ink on the top and bottom of the page.

Mr Secretary, Sir, this is an exercise we devised some time ago to illustrate the purpose of the task.

President Lincoln showed us this memorandum, and the subsequent translation into what he called "Feedstore Bible".

We use this idea, this model if you like, in the background, like music in a play.

It's behind all speeches and public matters, all pronouncements.

So that's everything that's to be printed and circulated.

The first extract is the example. A mother sent her son to the feedstore. We pretend that this is the speech to be delivered. Here it comes-

"JIMMY, DON'T FERGIT YER PAW LIKES APPLES. GIT SOME. AND WHILE YER AT IT, GIT GRANDMAW A NEW BROOM. LEVON BURNED THE OLD ONE, LEF' IT IN THE COAL PAN AND SHE MAKES DO. PUT IT RIGHT, GOD BLESS HER AND YOU."

So here's the Feedstore Bible Translation-

"LET US NOT FORGET THOSE WHO TOILED TO GIVE US GREEN PASTURES. THEY BROKE THE WILDERNESS TO THE SHARP PLOUGH, THAT WE SHOULD INHERIT RICH SOIL, AND GOOD FRUIT THEREFROM. BUT WE, CHILDLIKE, RAN WILD AS YOUNG COLTS IN SPRINGTIME, HEEDLESS OF OUR MOTHER'S CALL. YET WE PRAY, MAY THE LORD BLESS US ALL, EVERY ONE."

Lincoln looks to Seward, eyes raised. Seward brightens.
I don't expect that Jimmy came home with the apples? Not when he got THAT message?
Everybody laughs. Seward is shrewd enough to know that Lincoln has gifted him the punchline. But the point is well made. Seward leans forward, yet holding the floor.
I have two questions. One, does it work? Now, I admit that, probably, it does. It sounds like it works. And so to my second question. If it does work, why does it work?
Lincoln remains silent, tugging slightly at his chin. An upward glance is sufficient to delegate responsibility, and Hay takes the reins.

To be direct, Sir, yes, it does work. This is an extreme example, admittedly. The question as to the success of the speech is measured not by the words used, but by the message folk hear. Does a fieldhand recognize the voice inside the message? Does a muleskinner? I say yes. May I show you what I mean?

Please do.

Okay. Let's suppose that some Senator gets up in New York to speak about money. He's at a big dinner and there's lots of mashed potatoes and gravy. The Chairman of the Board is at his ease, smokin' nicely.

Anyway, Senator Moneybags rises up from his comfortable chair. He smiles and nods, and he mentions every single person that matters in that room and a few more who don't. He sips some wine with but a thimble of water, waits just the right amount of time for silence and three distinct coughs that somebody always makes just before a speech starts, and he leans forward earnestly.

He says somethin' like this- "the fiduciary benefits, local and national, inherent in this measure before us, may not necessarily be fully comprehended, or indeed, appreciated, in a continuum of concurrent fiscal probity dictated by appropriate application in a rapidly changing environment. However, in time, when our underlying stategy commences to prevail, when the soi disant Cassandra siren voices withdraw, we will count our triumphant victories in cold hard cash!"

He sits down to applause. The Reporters scribble busily. Likely his speech is widely reported, word for word, not forgetting everyone mentioned. Let's allow that the speech has been circulated everywhere.

That don't bake no bread. Why? Because nobody reads it in Kentucky or even in Maine or Massachusetts, even if it's in the papers. Maybe the Banking officials chaw on it, and they're happy. But the ordinary folk don't understand one word of it.

It ain't their lingo! And it does nothing for them. Some fat man said something. So what?
Even if they can read, which very many cannot, they ain't gonna stick with that. Nobody's gonna read it out to them. If they did, folk won't listen. Why should they? Point is, they can't hear it, nohow. They hear no message.

Now the Feedstore Bible ain't their lingo, their spoken speech, either. They don't speak like that. Nobody talks like that, leastways in the town or the street. But that lingo is precisely what folk hear! Where do they hear it? In the church services, that's where! Suppose some preacher has an announcement he has to make to the Baptist meeting one Sunday, and pretty urgent too? He doesn't say "Lizzie Smith has run off and took up with some cowpoke in the next county", now does he? No, he says " a dear daughter, a holy friend, has fallen, and we are bereft. The ways of the Lord are not our ways, and there is no help in us", Amen, doesn't he? No names are mentioned, no particulars are mentioned. Lizzie Smith might've died of smallpox or Yellow Jack Fever.

Bob Johnson could have broken his leg under the plough, we don't know yet. The details are all going to come out anyway at the cornroast come Saturday, but the real message has been understood. You betcha they're gonna talk about it. Something bad happened, let us now repent. Keep your eyes and ears open, and shut your mouth and you won't go far wrong! That's what we're aimin' for.

Nodding softly, Abe Lincoln takes up the slack; Thank you John. That was well expounded. And you are very right. It is the message which people hear that matters. The King James Bible is a wonderful model. It covers everything if you look in the right place. And that's the trick. Lookin' in the right place. That's what we're aimin' fer, hopin' to achieve.

Changing political jargon into Bible speech, makin' it Biblical.

That's our task with the tools we've got, which starts with the King James Bible. Our adapted copy, what we call the Feedstore Bible, is derivative. But it works. It surely does. Folk hear the message because of the style of speech. That's all that we hope to achieve. Do you reckon we've answered your question, Bill?

Subtly, and gradually, Honest Abe has eased into a folksy style of speech himself. He might be sitting in a log shack, puffing on a corncob pipe, and he crowns this eloquent segue with the first-name touch, and everybody is very comfortable.

Seward has again been gifted the punchline-

Oh, most eloquently, Mr President, Sir!

Everybody laughs at the mock formality, and the result is a delighted concordance in resuming the process of composing this Address.

Lincoln again takes command, delegates direction, compliments, approves, and energises his fellows with a few brief words.

I think we were looking fer' major themes afore the Secker'tree gived ya yer exams, boys? Well, ya got a "A". Let's crack on.

Seward laughs happily, very much one of the gang. As he does so, he realises that, in laughing in just that way, he has accepted the yoke of authority, admitted his "observer" status, and complied with the ongoing seminar on speech-writing.

Hay speaks up.

Sir, I have a suggestion.

Yes John.

Sir, I have a conviction that the major theme of this speech should be equality. I well recall you pronouncin' on Euclid. I don't pretend to fully understand those principles, it isn't my field. But you were talking about equality. That Euclid had put forward equality as a mathematical proposition.

You said that the ideas were many hundred years old, and that equality was the major theme of the founding fathers in composing our Declaration of Independence. So I suggest that, somehow, equality should be our major theme.
Lincoln is nodding.
I concur, John. I concur. I go further. I contend that any speech grounded on the concept of equality cannot go far wrong. There was a famous English naval Captain, or Admiral, or somesuch, Nelson. He came out with a good solid epithet that all of our soldiers should take to heart- "if you put your ship alongside the enemy and open fire, you can't go far wrong." Words to that effect, anyway. In battle, strike first and ask questions later. That's roughly what he meant. It is the soldier's lot to wield the sword, or the cannon ball. Those are the tools of his trade. And I would give full weight to a similar premise in the politicians armoury. If you're fightin' for equality, and by that I mean union of the States, all of us together, then you urge equality before all. Well done, John, well done. I think that you're right on the money. Well done.
There are nods and coughs of assent around the carriage, in varying degrees.
Seward leans forward, eager to contribute, as ever. Young man, he begins. Are you perhaps alluding to the words spoken by the President earlier this year? When he mentioned Jefferson and Adams, and Monroe? When he echoed the phrase, "all men are created equal", in that speech?" In July, was it not, if memory serves?
Not intentionally, no sir. But now that you mention it, I think that our purpose would be very well served by hearkening to that speech, to the thematic conclusion inherent.
Lincoln almost snorts with amusement.
The thematic conclusion inherent, indeed! There is nothing of the feedstore about this interaction.

No corncob pipes are being emptied into the log fire. Seward has shown off his excellent memory and powers of application. There was more than a declaration of seniority in his query, because everybody knows that Nic and Hick wrote that excellent speech. Hick has given as good as he got, and done it most respectfully.
This could be a debate in Yale or Harvard. And everybody has broad shoulders and good manners. So now ideas begin to flow. The keynote has been struck. And then both Nic and Seward join forces in a gleeful alliance, echoing the phraseology of that paragon of romantic virtue, Mr David Walker, the Englishman from England.
What did he say to the President? No, it wasn't "in seventeen seventy six," oh no! It was "four score and several years ago"!
I like that!
So do I, young man!
And that is direct Feedstore Bible!
It is, it is!
They beam at each other, full of heartfelt cooperation, cheering onward, eager to extend all credit to the other.
But what was the other thing he said to you, the words you first remarked upon?
Why, he said, "We are met in the midst of a great conflict to test whether any nation constructed as yours can long endure".
I like that too! I want that for this speech! In fact, I shall insist on it!
Yes, indeed, young man. You are absolutely correct. I shall extend my support!
But you were actually there, Sir, were you not? You most certainly heard him use those words?
I did, I did! Now I recall it most clearly. Well done!
Yippee!
By jinks!

Ain't we copying somebody's ideas? Can we do that? Is that allowed?
Well, in response, I've heard tell that Ben Franklin hisself said- "poor writers plagiarise. Great writers steal!"
Ha ha ha! That does crown it, yessir!
Warm grins and handshakes abound. Ideas are swapped, glanced at, some adopted at once, others mildly returned to the ether of invention whence they came, and no offence taken by anybody.
It is a smorgasbord of origin, exegesis, and composition.
And there is plenty of feast to be shared, as Hick scribbles busily and Nicolay reaches for documents in his bottomless valise. Seward laughs and laughs again, and slaps his thigh. Lincoln twinkles and approves, nods and gestures agreement, and the fun is at its height.
The President is above it all, mainly dispensing blessing and encouragement like an affectionate Professor. And this is very suitable, for his colleagues are behaving like three excited schoolboys, chattering away at each other, almost shouting into each others faces.
The lordly Seward has discovered his new best friend in Nicolay. If there were marbles to be propelled against a dirt wall, both would be down there, dressed in short trousers, kneeling keenly and shouting triumphant joy and cussing empty fate.
Good fellowship abounds.
Lincoln has accepted a single sheet of paper from Hay. This is significant. He has already decided what the opening line of his address will be. He has fixed on his theme, and, yes, it is the same theme as that of the speech he delivered in July- Equality. He has fully accepted the lyrical style of the attractive and enigmatic Englishman, David Walker, and yes, he overheard those exchanges regarding him.

In keeping with the good American frontier spirit of Benjamin Franklin, he has no qualms about stealing ideas, even from a Brit.

The Feedstore Bible has been applied, in all of it's folksy fullness, to impart the spirit of veneration, and to eliminate political jargon.

Seward, in a burst of righteous generosity, has contributed an intriguing sub-theme, that of birth, death, and resurrection. It's been woven into the text.

And in addition, the President has fixed with determination on the fact that all of this is going to fit onto but one side of that single sheet of paper.

Simplicity, brevity, clarity.

Lincoln writes. As a good lawyer, he is an old hand in his own element.

Practice makes perfect and he has been practicing for many years.

He knows that he is very good at this business of speech-writing, and that he has been practicing for many months to this end- to just such a speech as this. Despite his earlier invitation and declaration to his fellows, Honest Abe has been working on this speech since word came through that Lee was gone from Gettysburg and Meade was dithering.

It's important, and at one time might have been a speech announcing total victory, had events been timely. Sadly, they were not. But these sentiments remain, even if the War is uncompleted. This speech was coming, as sure as Christmas. So it's important.

Lincoln knows that it has to be very good, so he'll give it his best. And he knows that his best, at his best, is very good indeed.

He's been experimenting with brevity, and honing his delivery.

Sometimes he speaks to the mirror, sometimes to his dear wife, snoring lightly of a nighttime. Sometimes he pictures a jury in a Courtroom. Practice makes perfect.

He closes his eyes and imagines the podium, the dignitaries, the urgent, anxious faces and the bleak stares. This speech must bake bread, as they say in Kentuck. Don't tell Hoosiers or whores anything about cash on the barrel, they know it from the back. Talk is cheap, liquor costs money. This has to count for lots. He envisages how it will be, how he will pause for gravity here and appeal for empathy there. He weighs the formality against the simplicity, always inclining to the latter.
Keep it simple.
Make it Biblical, but echoing, not quoting.
Use simple words for simple folk.
Be brief and to the point.
Be direct but not bombastic.
Leave enough room for folk to colour the paper in their minds.
May their colours flow.
Yes, this is THE speech. This is the one. This must scour, as they say on the ploughing fields.
He has written, carefully. He ponders each word before committing it to paper, avoiding messy scratchings out and deletions and insertions.
When he finishes, he is quietly pleased. He is tired, and there is that slight queasiness again in his head, somewhere on the fringes of his consciousness.
His fingers are aching, almost tingling. The back of his neck is a bit hot, but it could be the whiskey.
He knows that he could sleep now, most beneficially. Normally, he would put a finished speech into his hat.
However, he does not do that now.
He knows that the two Johns would recognise that move as a sign of finality, that his speech was all done, without their joyful input.
In consequence, they might possibly feel diminished in their delegated task.
He doesn't want that as the fruit of their good labours. So he will fold the single sheet of paper and place it in the old Lutheran Bible, inside the neat box,

the Saxon Seal, which the Queen of England has asked him to deliver to the Lutheran Seminary at Gettysburg.
That way, nobody will be offended.
He'll look at it again later, alongside whatever the two Johns come up with.
But he knows that his mind is made up.
This is the text.
This is his speech.
He is sure of it.
This is his Gettysburg address, here, under his hand.

"Four score and seven years ago our fathers brought forth on this continent, a new nation, conceived in Liberty, and dedicated to the proposition that all men are created equal.

Now we are engaged in a great civil war, testing whether that nation, or any nation so conceived and so dedicated, can long endure. We are met on a great battle-field of that war. We have come to dedicate a portion of that field, as a final resting place for those who here gave their lives that that nation might live. It is altogether fitting and proper that we should do this.

But, in a larger sense, we can not dedicate -- we can not consecrate -- we can not hallow -- this ground. The brave men, living and dead, who struggled here, have consecrated it, far above our poor power to add or detract. The world will little note, nor long remember what we say here, but it can never forget what they did here. It is for us the living, rather, to be dedicated here to the unfinished work which they who fought here have thus far so nobly advanced. It is rather for us to be here dedicated to the great task remaining before us -- that from these honored dead we take increased devotion to that cause for which they gave the last full measure of devotion -- that we here highly resolve that these dead shall not have died in vain -- that this nation, under God, shall have a new birth of freedom -- and that government of the people, by the people, for the people, shall not perish from the earth."

He glances at the opening phrase, and weighs it in the scales of the Feedstore Bible.
Yes, it is very much of the Bible.
And the closing clincher, that nails the whole thing to the ground?
Yes, yes.
That last phrase?
It surely works.
Pure Feedstore.
He recalls that dusty old tome out in Kansas somewhere, a one-horse town with but one book slung in an old cupboard.
A tentmaker drew it forth so that Lincoln could pass an hour, waiting for a cart.
Funny thing at the time, there wasn't even a Bible in that town, just this book pertaining.
It was about an English Christian, four hundred odd years ago, who translated the old Latin Bible into English, one John Wycliffe.
That man had a fine mind, and one of his utterances from this book had impressed itself on Lincoln forever.
The phrase had jumped up and smacked young Abe soundly in his heart, and he had never forgotten it-

"This Bible is for the government of the people, by the people and for the people."

Indeed.
Just so.
Just so.

LUCIFER AND RHODE

Whilst these intentions and determinations are growing in the mind of President Lincoln, he is gradually slipping into a nagging doze.
It is a kind of foggy haze that overcomes his clear vision, leaving him squinting into the dim landscape of confusion that is descending like a cloud into his valley of perception.
So he discerns only shadowing crags and remote precipices, unfathomed, off the path.
He imagines that this is tiredness catching up with him, but he has not ever tasted such a peculiar brand of tiredness before.
He is commencing to see events BEFORE they happen. And THEN they happen.
Nicolay, sitting opposite him, says that he will just get a particular paper.
He arises and takes two steps forward to retrieve a valise from the luggage rack above, but impossibly remains in his seat at the same time.
How can this be?
Lincoln's head swims in delirium, and he blinks rapidly to clear his mind.
And now, only too quickly, Nic is announcing that, yes, he will just get that very paper, and he arises and takes two steps forward to reach above for the valise.
But this time he does not remain seated, and the scenario unfolds like an inverted déjà vu. This process begins to multiply, event piling on event prior to it's actual happening- a paper is passed before it is drawn from a file, then out comes the file, and the paper passes again, this time for real. Somebody looks out the window, and makes a remark, and laughs. And then he does it again, in exactly the same way.
The realisation is like a soft blow to Lincoln's head, repeated and repeated.

Words are spoken while somebody is smoking or sipping, and they could not possibly do so- but then the cheroot or cup is placed aside, and the conversation takes that very turn, with the very words in the exact tone now manifest.

Seward is scratching his ear in that quizzical gesture of his, but lo, both of his hands are twisting at a pen. And now the pen is set aside, and he is scratching his ear, and uttering the same words.

Lincoln is beginning to realise that he is very sick, very sick indeed.

This is not a chill. This is not simple tiredness.

He remembers, thirty years agone, vomiting on rotgut whiskey, and yes, this is a similar sensation. But there is no bad liquor in this carriage, and the weird visions are getting longer and longer, clearing and befogged at the same time.

Here is the party departing the carriage, which they will not do for some time yet.

The platform at Gettysburg is splattered with ruin, and a roof dangles down, upright joist busted off by a shell.

Here is an Alderman or something introducing Colonel so and so, and he turns to Nicolay consulting his timepiece, marking the hour and the day, or is it the night?

Nothing is settled. Events move in and out of consciousness. Nicolay comments on the hills just yonder. Surely that is real? Or is it imagined?

Here is Mary, placing her hands to her brow, those troublesome headaches assailing her comfort, and here she sleeps, laughing a little. But she is at home, back home in Washington. She is not on this train!

How can this be?

Surely we'll be pulling into Gettysburg?

Not very far away, now, is it?

Can it be? How so?

Here is Seward addressing a packed assembly, waving a book overhead, and pointing skyward with an imperious finger.
And there, addressing John Hays, he looks longingly at the cheroot in his hand, as though inviting an explanation of the inexplicable.
And now Lincoln sees a whole scene, nay, a playwrighted drama, unfold before his gaze.
He is very much part of it. He himself is not the author, or even the Director. But he is an important actor, and he must now play his part.
Yes, he shall set the scene and prefer the props.
As though to announce the prologue, he steps up in his mind and makes certain necessary movements, all of which are germane to the approaching production.
He sees it all, in perfect detail.
Carefully, yea, with reverence, he lifts the Lutheran Bible, yes, Queen Victoria's gift to the Gettysburg Seminary, containing that single sheet with his fully composed speech handwritten, and he opens at the flyleaf.
There is writing here.
Gothic text. Old ink, fading. Square letters.
A signature.
Martin Luther.
No, two signatures.
Below the first, a more recent and elaborate scriptum.
His gaze is woozy and he cannot discern the fine lettering.
A rounded hand.
Victoria R.
And it hits him with a great wallop of urgency that he must witness this passing.
Normally he would never even think of writing in, inscribing a book with his signature.
But now he is an actor in a play, following his lines, doing as he's told, and he is very certain that this is his role and this action his prescribed part.

He is being instructed, yea, even from on high, to write his signature close to and beneath the other two above on the fine white paper, not yellowed at all. And so he does so.

He signs it.

He writes "Abraham Lincoln" carefully, quizzically. His speech, his completed speech, is yet within the thin pages, here, here, apart and as yet one with this treasure in earthen vessel.
There, there.
His task is done, over and complete.
Amen.
He closes the Bible and then, almost reverently, lays it gently onto the seat beside.
He packs his papers, puts on his hat.
He sees the script.
Okay, actors, go to it!
A previewed scenario presents itself to his addled perception.
The déjà preceding the vu.
A little black boy will come to the carriage with his shoeshine box.
He will knock the door loudly, louder than he needs to, provoking hilarity.
The Porter, obviously his proud father, shall stand behind him in the corridor, beaming.
Yea, though he is beckoned forward, the youngster shall continue to knock loudly at the door.
The boy grins brightly.
He will offer to brush everybody's shoes, starting, of course, with the President.
There will be mirth, and laughter, and approval.
Seward will proffer a silver dollar.
The child will graciously decline payment.
Daddy will respectfully depart.

President Lincoln will accept the honour, first among scuffy boots unpolished, and will place his big feet up on the box.
He shall bow his head, interested in the whole thing, the entire scenario, the play.
At this point, he does not have a line to speak.
No, President Abraham Lincoln has got nothing to say or do…..
Then…. Well, then events will take their course.
But Honest Abe knows with the conviction of all of his substantial life experience that he MUST perform these actions.
He MUST put the Lutheran Bible, the Saxon Seal, now signed by himself, onto the seat hard beside, with his Gettysburg Address inside, folded, abandoning it there.
It is an essential prop, and this is the correct place for it.
Here, on the seat beside.
He MUST welcome the little shoeshine boy.
He MUST put his big feet in his good leathern boots up on that tiny stand, and await the outcome.
All of this has not yet happened.
But Lincoln knows that it will happen. In utter certainty, he sees the future.
He cannot see beyond the point at which he will bow his head in acceptance to deference and honour, interested. But up to there…..
It occurs to him, in a sudden whiff of clarity, that he is like unto weaving a tapestry in a tower. What is this? Is it madness? What wild fancies are these?
And there is a curse, yes, a curse, and a way not his own, and he may not look out beyond. Words come tumbling out of the ether….he looked away, away beyond….?
A loud knock sounded at the door of the carriage.
It was louder than need be, and provoked hilarity.
It jolted him upright into the here and now of his dream.

Curtain up.
Enter, stage left.
Actors, go to it!
A little black boy was standing at the carriage door, continuing to knock, even when all four occupants were regarding him with interested humour.
He was knocking loudly, hammering on the wood, louder than he needed to do.
The Porter, obviously his proud father, was behind in the corridor, beaming.
Places?
Actors, go to it!
Lincoln checked that the Lutheran Bible, the signed Saxon Seal, was beside him on the seat, his Gettysburg Address folded safely inside, and he hearkened to the actors delivering their lines as agreed and directed.
The little black boy stands at the door.
The Curtain has been raised.
Yassuh, I'se come to give you all a shoeshine,
(LAUGHTER, whoever heard of a shoeshine? How absolutely funny?)
Seward, as always, takes commond.
How much do you charge, son?
Why, nossuh, they ain't no charge, seein' as you's one of ya the President hisself.
Oh, no, that must not be!
This is the land of opportunity! And you are free to tender your application!
But if we choose to retain your erstwhile services, you MUST be remunerated, don't you think?
You MUST be paid!
Nossuh, that's mah perv-ih-lege, like mah Daddy say so, yes. Yessir!
Well I never.
Oah yassuh. My daddy says!
And nossuh, they ain't no charge, thank you suh. Are you the President hisself, suh?
No, this gentleman is the President!

(SMILES AND GESTURES AND LINCOLN BOWS HIS BARE HEAD IN MOCK ACKNOWLEDGEMENT)
Ha ha ha, and ha ha ha, and we all laugh on cue, ah ha ha ha, and you are?
(GREAT ANTICIPATION)
Rhode, suh. Rhode. Mah name is Rhode. Fum the state, suh? Rhode Island? But I'se Rhode.
Oh yes, my boy I've heard of it, I assure you.
Mr President, sir, may I present to you Mr Rhode, named eponymously for the state?
And this fine young man is without doubt the most efficient and shoeshine proficient in these United States of America!
Mr Rhodes will now demonstrate his ineffable skills. In short, he'll be tidying up the mess that you have engendered on your good leathern boots!
(GREAT LAUGHTER)
While you have been traversing the highways and railway carriages of these same United States of America, this young man has been eager to serve!
Now have you ever been in Rhode Island Mr President?
Yes I have and hope to return to Providence (LOUD LAUGHTER) but I have also been in Massachusetts and even Connecticut but Rhode Island is very fine indeed and all rock with laughter.
Daddy the Porter salutes happily and somewhat nervously and properly respectably and moves to depart, proud as a god-fearing parent can be.
His is the subservience of kindly humility. His stance, posture, and delivery are all of perfection. He says his lines just right.
But Lincoln rises easily and extends his hand and the proud Father looks amazed at this display of humility and familiarity before bowing in true thanks, honored and affirmed, and he turns and makes his way from the carriage while everybody grins with the success of the move.

The President has shaken the hand of this Railroad Porter!
Such perfection on all sides.
Such regal condescension?
Rhode the Shoeshine proficient grins at the President and kneels before him in obeisance; kin' ah shine yo' shoes, suh?
Oh yes that would be most kind and Seward is proffering his silver dollar again and saying that he must extend it anyway for the sake of the honour of these United States of America.
Everybody laughs even Lincoln in weary resignation for the ultimately unknown moment fast approaches and he knows not what the curse may be or what the moment brings or shall bring and he drops his eyes and bows his head before the axe.
Beyond these facts and these actions, he cannot see.
He has done his bit.
Curiously, he registers, with cool equanimity, that he really does not care.
Is this death?
The genuine article?
Will he die here, in a train in Pennsylvania?
As though in immediate answer, he feels a sharp stabbing at the back of his skull, a flash of light and intensity, but brief, so brief, and all his colours turn to black.
But only briefly, oh so briefly and then death wings it's way away, his answer answerless.
The stage is disported before him.
Rhode spits on a cloth and spits onto Lincoln's good leathern boots, and commences to rub his small fingers together as though in great satisfaction.
He spits again into the cloth, this time with great confidence in his ability.
He knows that he can clean these fine leathern boots.
Lincoln looks down with interest.
His head is clear.
He can see everything.

He's got a box seat for the first time.
He is smiling, smiling as he seldom has in so long, so
many months, other than in the brief drama
accorded this fellowship in this carriage.
He is smiling. He is ready.
This is it.
The moment has come.
What, he wonders, is going to happen next?

WHAT IS TRUTH?

Aloof and aloft, God sees the scene.
The Author of All Things is at it again!
All is not as it seems.
At the very centre of all of this, kneeling as though in
worship before President Abraham Lincoln, is the
little black boy.
He does not kneel in adoration, everybody knows
that.
He's just a little shoeshine boy.
But all is not as it seems.
Rhode is surely a shoeshine boy, but he is also a well
trained ringer and spotter.
He is a magnificent thief.
He is a professional thief, and he works very hard at
his trade, an astonishing aptitude bent to this unusual
determination in one so young.
At the present time he is exactly where he wants to be
for his true purposes; and he is making a good job, a
very good job, of doing the real job with which he has
been entrusted- robbing the carriage.
No matter the ring of steel and soldiers and guns and
bullets and Secretary's and even a Secretary of State
deployed to protect Honest Abe - Rhode has
penetrated these with the greatest of ease.
He is in position, in time, on time, first time! And
every time! But most definitely THIS time! Top
marks!

His job, in his usual circumstances, is to pinpoint the likely spots where billfolds and wallets may be concealed about the persons of all four of the inhabitants of the carriage.

He is here, where he should be, suited up and ready to go.

And he has a special brief extended on this day of days- to steal the box, the one with the curious flower motif upon the top.

Pinpoint it, good.

Steal it, even better, but are you kiddin' Carlo? Steal from a President?

This President?

The man gonna free up the niggers?

Steal from him?

Nonetheless this is his task which he may attempt if circumstances cohere.

Or maybe he can aspire to identify exactly where it is placed.

His father, the proud Porter, will run interference as necessary, once he re-enters the carriage; putting a question here as to personal comfort, offering to move this bag or that valise, and pouring smoke and mirrors over the proceedings of convivial theft which is his stock in trade on this train of trains.

Father and son work closely together in a most productive partnership.

They look out for each other, and cover each other.

Rhode will "spot" opportunities.

If he can, he will take these opportunities to steal anything which can be reasonably and safely stolen himself.

But he will only do this if he is completely certain that the elephant is in the room and nobody can see it.

It takes time and patience and practice to bring the elephant into the room.

But if everything is in place, and he can "hook" the target, then he will.

More likely, most likely, he will signal where the valuables are, and set things up for Daddy the Porter a little later on.
Or he might produce a little smoke and mirrors himself so that daddy can hook the loot once he is appraised of it's whereabouts.
These little tricks are so easy, so easy.
He can accidentally tip over his box of brushes and polish, and then convincingly burst into tears.
Or he can "get something in his eye", and draw the attention of any numbers of spectators exclusively toward him, waving his hands and crying piteously.
He can look wildly at two persons, and four persons will follow his gaze.
Or, more crudely, he can suddenly observe something shocking outside the window;- was that a man with a gun he will demand, and point over there, or there, jes' beyond you, suh, oh yes, ah'm sho' ah saw it! Quick boys! Git 'de soldiers! Help, help! Kin' yo see whut I kin' see?
All of these scenarios are open to him, once Daddy comes back into the carriage.
The Porter and the sunny shoeshine boy have worked together well and often.
Rhode could tell you a thing or two about that.
But he won't.
He is too experienced a hand, at nine years of age, to tell anything to anybody outside the family, which is very much his business, his stock in trade.
But he could tell you, he could. He could boast, in truth, and it would be no idle or empty boast. But he ain't gonna say nuffin'!
Oh yes, oh yes, he could tell ya jes' nuffn'', cos' ain't nobody gotta know nuffn', an' 'dat de troof!
Bizarrely, he is more aware of the "need to know" principle than his Government.
Also, he could tell ya his daddy is the top hook man in America!
He is! He can steal anythin' fum anybody!

And he wouldn't be speaking a word of a lie, oh no.
Daddy the Porter is not only the best thief in America, he is also the great master of legerdemain, not that he knows that name for the sleight of hand manoeuvres which he practices so effortlessly and so wonderfully.
Among the Railway Porters, Daddy is known as Lucifer.
Such a perfect name!
Such a man, even if'n he IS a darkie.
But Lucifer objects to this epithet, this watered down babies milk.
He knows himself for what he expects himself to be- a hardworkin' nigger!
The other Porters, and assorted Railway employees involved in this generalised theft (skilled thieves all, or approving contributors within their precise degree) admire and respect him as top dog.
Lucifer accepts this accolade as his due.
It is only right and fitting that he be accorded this title.
He attributes his success to a rigorous practice of two applied principles-misdirection and observation.
Observation is a basic.
Keep yo' mouf' shut n' yo' eyes n' ears open!
Yo' sees, yo' hears, n' yo' learns!
Dat's why you's gots two eyes an' two ears an' jes' one mouf!
Misdirection is the delicate art of bringing an elephant onstage to shit in somebody's hat without anybody noticing, least of all the elephant.
He is very, very good at misdirection.
He has brought the amazing elephant into many a carriage, where it has obligingly shat into somebody's hat.
Not only have the victims not noticed the shit in the hat, but they have tipped him most handsomely for his trouble.

And then there is his beloved son, in whom he is well pleased, Rhode.
He is aware of the value of Rhode- after all, he has taught the boy everything he knows, every detail, and he is thoroughly satisfied with the lad's progress and aptitude.
Other Porters greatly envy his blessing with Rhode- it's as if he gets all the luck!
Lucifer sho' is 'de man! Yassuh!
An' 'dat boy sho' is sumfn' special, yassuh!

Meanwhile, this master thief, colloquially known as "Lucifer", is untroubled by conscience. He is good at his job! An' he dam-well should be!
Cos' any nigger who ain't gonna bend his ass an' make a buck ain't worth nuffn'.
In his parlance, any nigger that 'kin steal anythin' 'fum a white man cain't do nuff'n wrong! No suh!!
The white man buys and sells the nigger.
It is the sacred duty and the RIGHT of a decent nigger to steal all he can!
If Lucifer cannot, indeed cannot, steal from THIS man, THE PRESIDENT, then he is worthless as a thief, a father, a nigger and a man.
But Lucifer is confused.
He has been paid two hundred and fifty dollars, TWO HUNDRED AND FIFTY DOLLARS!!!.
This to hook the white box with the seal on top, like a flower.
This from the bearded man who was going to be aboard the train.
Now the target, that is to say, approachin'the hook, as it turned out, ain't no problem!
Gittin' Rhode into the carriage weren't no problem.
He just had to knock harder and louder and longer than anybody with any horse sense would, and they beckoned him on in, yessir!
And they laughed! Jes' a l'il boy, come on in. No problem!

The problem is that the bearded man is NOT on the train!
He shoulda been here!
He was right on time on two previous occasions, and the money was right on time, upfront and fair an'square on 'de barrel! Nothing' like to this amount, fer' a fack', but good cornbread dough paid out. As to the bearded white man, where is he?
He knew the times of arrival and where to go and where to be at what time, oh yes!
Even though Lucifer procured the uniform and organised the work rota, and was right on time in the right place (no easy task wif' all these danged soldiers about) the bearded wonder just did not show! To be fair, in both previous cases, the target "hooks" were pretty easy. Surely Lucifer's methodology was being explored and considered?
Ways and means? Could he cut the mustard? Could he deliver?
The answer to all of these questions was an unequivocal "yes".
Lucifer knows that his own capabilities were being tested, and he takes a great pride in his work, and in the knowledge that he delivered, both times, on time, as requested!
He, Lucifer, was in place, in perfect position, on time, each time.
But we are right here, right now, in perfect position, this time!
We are suited and booted, all spruced up and ready to go, and the white man with the beard DID NOT SHOW!
And we've got the hook in!
Not only has Rhode spotted and located it, this very box with the seal, but it lies open to the naked gaze of all (but most importantly Rhode's gaze) right there on the seat beside the President!

Why, if the President had not unaccountably risen to shake Lucifer by the hand, Rhode or he would have hooked it on the instant, there and then.
And now Lucifer comforts himself a bit.
Mebbe things ain't too bad, eh? Perhaps Rhode has already got it, and just needs a tiny bit of misdirection to hand it over in full view of all the carriage, because they will only see what you show them!
But Lucifer is confused as to his immediate objectives. Should he go for the box? Or should he try to pick a pocket or two? All of his instincts warn him to stick to the main ticket- get the box! Get the box! The bearded man will come around again. He will show.
The money is good and is already in Lucifer's pocket. Nobody's gonna pay that much money and just walk away! The bearded wonder gonna show up, yessir! And Lucifer will be waiting with the box. Rhode will deliver. Oh yay! Time to go back 'n see how Rhode's getting' on! Yessir! Bend yer ass and make a buck!
Or in this case, two hundred and fifty!

Back in the carriage, Rhode has hooked the target.
Oh yes.
Rhode has stolen the Saxon Seal.
Rhode has done his job.
Seizing the perfect moment, he now has the little box with the bright picture "like a flower" in his possession.
It is concealed from the gaze of all.
Only he knows that he has it.
The rest of the people concerned- Lincoln, Hay, Nicolay, Seward, are all unaware of the existence of the target, never mind the fact that it has been hooked.
They don't even know that theft has occurred.
It was a full meal eaten in full view.
There was a well-earned burp to finish things off.

Toothpicks shall not be required.
And they didn't even notice the little shoeshine boy exercising his skills.
Rhode is 'de man, yassuh!
Dat li'l boy, yassuh, he gone 'n done a mansize job, yassuh!
He has done the job, first time, on time, every time!
And certainly THIS time.
Lucifer will be delighted.
But it is Rhode who has done the business.
He has adhered to protocol in the most minute detail.
All conditions were completely filled, all boxes ticked.
He envisages the imaginary dialogue with Lucifer, post mortem to a successful operation-
Nobody was lookin'?
Nossuh.
Nobody could see?
Nossuh.
You made yo' move in full sight?
Yessuh.
'Dey was distraction?
Yassuh.
Did you make 'de distraction happen?
Nossuh.
Whut was 'de distraction whereby yo' knows yo' ain't suspected?
De President fainted. Fell over, sick n' unconshuns'.
He did?
Yassuh.
An' 'dey don't know about 'de hook?
Nossuh.
Do 'dey even 'speck 'de target gone?
Nossuh.
An elephant appeared in the carriage and shat into the hat of President Abraham Lincoln, and nobody, least of all Lincoln, saw that elephant. Nor did they see it shit!
Rhode is pleased with himself.

He is certain that he has done the right thing in stealing the Saxon Seal and he is confident that his Daddy, Lucifer, shall approve his actions.
He is correct.
At his ultimate moment of revelation, Lincoln's sight fails and all of his colours turn to grey. His lips become white like unto chalk, and he utters a great groan of broken breath.
He falls over onto his side, away from the Saxon Seal.
Now, unbidden, an elephant enters the carriage, unseen by all except Rhode, who watches in delight as the huge beast shits all over the place, not forgetting to fill Lincoln's hat to the very brim.
Seward is all of a flutter, a great help in times of trouble such as these. His beaurocratic obsession now not only aids and abets, but positively greases the wheels for the little shoeshine boy.
Oh, Lord, what is it, Abe?
Quick!
John?
Out of the way, boy.
This is no place for you.
Quick, boys.
What's happened?
Is he all right?
Are you all right, Mr President, sir?
Are you all right?
Hurry, now.
Good Lord.
(Rhode reaches down and takes the little box with the flowered picture and transfers it first under his bootblack cloth for interim cover and then on into his shoeshine bag for secure storage until he can pass it on to his Daddy. He steps back, not getting under anybody's feet. He is being obedient and good. He is behaving very well in a difficult situation, not getting in anybody's way.)
All three adults in the Railway Car are attending to the President.

The authoritive Seward gives orders now.
"Out of the way, boy. This is no place for you".
Rhode could do a tap dance on the table and nobody would notice.
And then the room is descending into farce and furore and confusion and Lucifer fills the doorway and Rhode gives him the sign and gives him the sign again and gives him the sign again that he HAS HOOKED THE TARGET, and Lucifer takes control with smooth ease.
Lucifer exudes calm and authority and actually enjoys using the words he now uses, pardon me, suh, but we must all keep our bearin's at 'dis time.
Jes' move ovah a little bit, suh, and yes, ah 'kin see 'dat de' President seem to be unwell.
Ah shall personally fetch 'de doctor on 'de train, gennulmen.
Bettuh still, I'll sen 'de boy!
May ah suh-jes' 'dat yo' loosen his necktie 'n give him some air?
Rhode, run to 'de nex' carriage and bang on 'de do'.
Ah shall be 'dere direckly, yassuh!
Off'n' yo' go, boy.
'Dis ain't no place fo' yo'.

Seward notes that on the one hand the Porter is being admirably authoritative, and therefore must be rewarded when all of this mess is at an end, and, simultaneously, that Lincoln is turning blue about the gills.
He holds his nerve, maintains order.
Somebody has to do it.
Somebody has got to stay in control!
Assuming command, as is his due, he surveys his new Kingdom. The two Johns are attending to Honest Abe. The little shoeshine boy has run off to do his father's bidding. Good boy, that! Seward briefly curses himself that he did not give the child a silver dollar earlier on.

This might never have happened if he had.
He knows that this idea is irrational nonsense but his thoughts are crowding in and flying out and he is not too hard on himself. This is a time of crisis. He must take the helm!
All hands on deck!
The Porter and the little shoeshine boy have been first class, good American citizens! Black they might be, loyal, good, and true they certainly are! They, of all people, salt of the earth, have given the lead on how to behave in these times of trouble!
These are the real Americans!
God bless 'em!
They, humble souls, nevertheless shine as bright beacons!
Now it is his turn to show what he is made of!
Is he up to the job?
More than at any time, he must serve his nation now, here, when it really matters.
Many are called, but few are chosen!
William Seward, Secretary of State, raises his chin to soldier onward, and face the future.

BANKING THE LOOT

Lincoln continued to swoon sideways, gasping wetly with a thin trickle of spittle dripping onto his collar. John Nicolay hastened to ease the simple necktie away from his throat, and was rewarded for his pains with an immediate gulping up of air into the President's mouth and nose and lungs.

Hick proceeded to remove the good leathern boots from off Abe's feet, and it seemed that Lincoln brightened somewhat, and shook his head a little, and murmured.

Seward stood above it all, convinced that he and he alone now held the rudder on the ship of state, steering the nation forward. An entire drama unfolded for him; a typhoon of imagination engulfed him. The storm broke about his ears, the wind howled. Onward, America, onward 'twixt shot and shell, he commanded, and his invisible myrmidons complied.

Rule, Seward, rule these wayward elements!
All that oppose shall bend unto your will!
Away with doubt and dread!

Yes, he thought to himself, this is how it must have been in all of the great battles fought on these, our precious shores.

These were the trials of the worthy and the good, faithful unto death on the watchtower, leading from the front.

Yes, these very doubts and fears had ravaged the hearts of General Grant and General Meade, and their efforts were crowned in victory.

And yea, yea, Lee and Longstreet also struggled in their time. They too had wrestled with dark chaos, oh yea, hear ye. But the Lord is righteous above all the works and ways and manners of men! Those gentlemen did not prevail, for lo, their cause was not just in the eyes of the Almighty!

Seward wryly observed that he was getting pretty good at declaiming in Feedstore Bible fashion, and he mentally patted himself on the back for the splendid job he was doing in the midst of this terrible crisis. Others, he thought, might have staggered under the load. He would not. His knees would not buckle. He would stand. Whenever in the entire tale of mankind had any mere being, thrust of a sudden into the fray, been so assailed, and yet so assured, so competent? Yes, he thought, cometh the hour, cometh the man. Ecce homo. Behold the man. And he was very satisfied indeed, coping with the crisis, as Lincoln lay there in a faint, grey cheeked and gravely ill.

In the meantime, Lucifer hovered, which is what he did best.
Whilst ostensibly offering support, assistance, and help, he was in fact covering Rhode's tracks.
And he was busily forging and constructing a new version of the truth of events, just for additional cover.
All would cohere to his direction.
This is what everybody would remember.
This would be truth.
Truth is, in Lucifer's parlance, exactly what you make it!
Or, to be more precise, exactly what HE made it!
Everybody in the room would testify that this was exactly what had happened and ya can't get more truth-fuller than that!
Here ah goes, swingin' low, sweet chariot!

Yassuh, he seem to be respondin'. Yo' is kine, yo' sho' is kine!
(WHATEVER YOU'RE DOIN' IT'S OKAY BY ME. ME N' MINE AIN'T DONE NUFFN'!)

De Doctor be here direckly, mah boy long gone fo' him.
(NOTICE THAT THE BOY HAS BEEN GONE A LONG TIME? HOW COULD HE HAVE STOLEN IT, IF YOU EVER DO NOTICE SUMFN' MISSIN'?)

Bes' if'n ah don't come near, suh. You understand me?
(NONE OF US POOR BLACK PEOPLE HAS EVER COME ANYWHERE NEAR THE PRESIDENT. WE ARE NOT WORTHY TO TOUCH HIM, AND WE NEVER DID. SO DON'T BLAME US.)

Yo' seem to have de' mattah in han', suh.
(OH, HOW WISE AND GOOD YOU ARE. I, BUT A LOWLY PORTER, KNOW AND UNDERSTAN' PRECISELY NUFFN'!)

Yo' knows bes', yo' knows bes'!
(OH, HOW WISE YO' ARE!. LUCKY ME TO EVEN BE HERE!)

Ah'll jes' see what's goin' on.
(AH'M OUTTA HERE N' AH NEVAH WAS HERE IN DE' FURS' PLACE.)

Lucifer moved easily to the corridor, closing the door behind him. He was now freed to stash the loot. This process was known as "Banking". If Rhode was in the right place, then that objective would be fulfilled within seconds.
And of course Rhode was exactly where he should have been, awaiting by the connecting doors between the carriages.
He was clutching his shoeshine box, making himself small against the bellwall.

As Lucifer approached, Rhode signaled that he had the loot available.
Lucifer observed that Rhode had placed the dirtied rag over the shoeshine box, bunched up and retained by Rhode's left hand.
This was the loot which Rhode had hooked.
This was the prize.
Just beyond where Rhode sat at the bellwall, there was a key cupboard placed at eye level by the carriage window.
Lucifer would open that cupboard, retrieve the loot, and stash it within behind the false bottom, placed there for this very purpose.
Only he could retrieve it.
Only he knew it was there.
A legion of investigators might search for years and never find the hook, whatever it was.
He could even leave the cupboard openly unlocked.
The carriage window was down, a chill wind blowing into the train.
This was all to the good for Lucifer's purposes. Any passengers who did venture out while the process of Banking was going on would quickly go back inside the warmer carriages.
The cold wind helped.
They would see nothing.
The overall trick which Lucifer and Rhode must now accomplish was to stash the hook in as short a time as possible.
It would only be in view for about two seconds, as Rhode transferred the Saxon Seal from under the dirtied shoeshine cloth on into the concealed cache.
Although all seemed to be clear and safe to proceed, both of these competent and professional thieves understood the absolute importance of protocol.
Do it by the book!
Or don't do it at all.
The deviant is an over-conformer to uniformity.

Lucifer opened the key cupboard, and removed the sliding back wall to reveal the little cave within.
He looked up and down the carriage.
All clear.

He nodded, everything proceeding perfectly, on time, first time, every time.
Rhode stood up by the bellwall and turned toward his father, so that even his tiny frame was now blocking and concealing the view of the hook from any unexpected interloper, even at this late stage.
The train whistle blew.
They were coming in to Gettysburg.
Nothing could stop them now.
The Banking process was virtually complete.
All boxes were ticked, all bases covered.
Now the loot must be stashed, fast.
This was Banking at it's best!
On time, first time, every time!
Lucifer reached for the Saxon Seal.
Rhode removed the dirtied rag and presented it to him.
Almost, almost, into Gettysburg, hear the whistle of the train?
Lucifer grasped the bright box in his hands, and moved it toward the cupboard cache.
As he turned it in his hands, he noticed the beautiful pattern of the letters "ML" on the top.
And it was so delicate, such fine workmanship?
Lucifer had paused.
Standing in the corridor of the carriage, the cache yawning, Rhode onlooking, Lucifer paused.
He had never once paused in his life.
Not at this stage.
Not at any stage.
But now, he paused.
He held the little box in his hands, and wondered at it.
So pretty, so pretty.

He looked closely at the Saxon Seal.
Something caused him to hesitate.
The train whistle blew aloft, whoo, whoo.
Lucifer stopped.
Rhode stared at him, stunned.
The train lurched sideways.
Seward stepped into the corridor.
In a rush, Lucifer panicked.
He swung round, away from the cupboard and toward the window.
He slipped and his momentum carried him onward and the Saxon Seal flew out of his grasp and right out of the open window and on into the darkness.
The loot was gone!
Rhode shouted.
Appalled, Lucifer looked up at Seward, rapidly approaching.
Seward was saying something.
Rhode was saying something.
Suddenly, strangely, and with calm detachment, Lucifer thought of the fineness and the beauty of that pretty little box.
On the instant, he faltered.
His eyes blinked once, startled.
Everything fell away and all of his colours turned to black, and he thought no more.
All of his colours dissipated into darkness.
His mouth stopped.
Taste and smell ceased.
His eyes closed.
He was dead, even as his fingers failed him.
Reeling forward, he toppled headlong into the corridor, and seemed to stretch himself in abasement before Seward's feet.
Rhode gaped.
Seward pursed his lips in grim satisfaction. Another crisis!
Right here, right now.
More to deal with!

The Porter had collapsed!
This was additional grist to his busily churning inward mill.
Oh, but the work was hard, the labourers few (just himself!).
Undismayed, he admired his powers of adaptation again.
Such coolness!
Such balance!
Go on, Seward, be a King!
Yea, yea, and thrice yea, he responded, imagination blowing him upward in his own estimation.
Fling at him what you would, he was going to weather this storm, come what may.
So now even the poor Porter was sick?
Seward's mind raced furiously on into fantasy. Now he was the Cup Bearer, now the Prophet.
I am here, Lord. I am here. Send me your burdens, for you are with me.
Together, he thought, we shall prevail.
Yes, we are coming into Gettysburg.
Hear the whistle of the train!
Our vessel, tempest tossed, comes safe to shore.
Onward, onward!
Onward to Gettysburg!

Rhode, meanwhile, sat with his shoeshine box on the floor.
The loot was gone!
Lucifer was lying on the floor!
What had happened?
Sick with fright and disbelief, he tried desperately to make sense of this bucket of donkey shit that they had somehow constructed from a beautiful, shining, masterpiece.
Leaning back against the bellwall, he put his thumb into his mouth, and sucked on it.

GOLD IN THE GROUND

On one evening, when Mrs Robinson had yet again failed to find her poor dead boy, she asked Pastor Gressler for prayer and poured her heart out to him.
Wilfred was a good boy, a truthful boy, an honest boy and had always done what his Pa told him, she explained tearfully.
But his Pa had gone to glory four year since, and Wilfred had got wild, as boys will do, not always heeding his crying mother, distracted in her lonely grief.
This was away off up and over in Canada and again a ways North up to near Owen Sound.
So young Wilfred was not even an American, not that the fact didn't cut no ice with the recruitment officers.
The Robinsons had come over from England fifty year or more since and the farm, worked hard, presented the whole family with gradual prosperity and growing plenty as cows fattened and crops burst forth. Wilfred wasn't more than taken with his books, and had grown extremely restless, now that his father had not the strength to extend a restraining hand. It was mayhap that he needed to prove himself worthy as a man, she didn't know, with Pa dead and gone.
But anyway he headed South to join the Army off in America, and went for a soldier at barely fifteen year, she knew.
That was more than comin' up to a year agone.
He had turned up in Buffalo, she had heard off a churchgoing woman in that town when she herself came South out of Ontario by way of Buffalo to find him, praying as ever for his safety and deliverance.
The woman knew because her own boy had done the same thing, running off like that.

And there was recruiting in the town for a Company
going out soon to the war but her boy would have
had to show his permission to sign up and so he went
off trying to get to New York City.
He had met with Wilfred in the town and they run off
down to Kingston in Ulster and joined up where it
was easier to lie about his age, she said.
She had found out that much.
Traipsin' down to Kingston brought as much
knowledge as the fact that Wilfred did indeed join up
there with that militia.
There was his name as signed and printed correctly,
for he could read and write very well, and not just
make his mark like some did.
Here in the Town Hall, such as it was but not the
main office, Wilfred had signed his name.
So she went for the true facts to the real and main
Army Office at the Town Hall in New York.
An Officer there had said that he had most likely
marched off with the 80th Militia, and if he did, then
he had done well.
She could be proud of him for a brave boy, and many
a growed man skulkin' in bed and leavin' the young-
uns to do the fightin'.
It was a sin and a shame, but she had nothing to
regret in her boy, who for a fact had joined up
willin'.
As to where he was now, the man couldn't say.
The best he could do was point her further west,
where the whole Army had gone, and not just that
one company of volunteers, but by this time to a town
in Pennsylvania called Gettysburg. If he was
anywhere, he was there.
There had been one hell of a fight there.
Most likely Wilfred had fought there with the rest of
the militias.
That's where she must go to find him.

And he had tried to comfort her when she told him that her Wilfred was but fifteen year, and must of told a lie to join up.
No, the man said, he wouldn't of needed to tell a lie.
No, he didn't do that.
Many's the boy was welcome to join up, even at fourteen or more if they could shoot a gun.
So she was not to concern herself, he wouldn't of told no lies.
He sounded like a brave boy, a truthful boy, and willin' to do what was right.
And Mrs Robinson was to be proud of him, for he was a credit to his family, and not many can say that these days.
And he didn't tell a lie about being but fifteen years old.
He was a truthful boy.
He was a brave boy.
He was a good boy.
This was of some comfort.
So she had winded up in Gettysburg, here, seeking her boys whereabouts.
And now she had looked and looked to no avail.
So she poured out her heart in prayer.
The best that Pastor Gressler could do was promise to see the Army here in the town, and that's what he did.
Somebody would probably know if a whole Regiment had been here, wouldn't they?
Surely they would.
And the Officer now come to the town to help supervise the burial of the dead and keep good records as best he could said that the 80th Militia out of Kingston was definitely in the line of battle on all three days.
Most surely they fought in the Seminary grounds on the first day.
80th Militia out of New York went into the line at the very first, in the first battle on the first day.

And he didn't know what on the Thursday, the second day, and the second of July.
Everybody was in the line that day.
The militias, all of 'em, could have been anywhere.
But he had a written order from a Colonel Stuart Hill on that second day dated in the late evening and squaring things up.
This Officer outta Ulster County he was told to coordinate the militias before the Southrons came on the next day, which they did, in a last big charge.
80th Militia was ordered into first reserve line midway in the centre line.
Line of battle.
Retrospective and confirmation.
Yes sir!
Here it was, certain sure, right here.
And this is the written and factual account such as we have.
So we know that they moved to the center ground that second day, or at the evening anyway. That's what they did. The rest we know.
That's where the rebs hit the hardest.
That would be afternoon. Pretty much late afternoon, they came on.
Straight on centre, that's where they came on.
That's where the real fight was. Yes sir. That's where the Rebs came on.
That's where they was broke.
The militias stood up tall and did good.
The 80th men outta New York got commended, it said so right here.
They had done very brave and orderly fightin' and had winded up on Cemetery Hill in the town. They had went on into the battle line with all of the reserves on that day.
That was as far as could be told.
Thing is, the Officer had said, thing is, most all of our boys that fell on Cemetery Hill was the first in line to be cared for, and laid to rest first up afterwards.

I mean, they were the first to be interred, of all the good men we put into the ground.
It is a work of mercy.
That we bury the fallen.
It may be…..
They were as brave and good, and Mrs Robinson ought to be proud of her boy.
And now those same brave soldiers were being reinterred out at the new Cemetery lines, a ways south and east of the town.
So, may the good Lord bless him, if her boy had fallen in the fight, then he might be anywhere.
He might be near up to the Seminary on the far side of the town.
He might be on Cemetery Hill.
He might be out in the new field, honoured and glorious.
She must be proud of him.
For he was a brave boy, and full of truth.
A good boy.
And there's not many that can say that these days.

Pastor Gressler wondered and prayed.
Eventually he spoke again to Mrs Robinson, and attempted to define the task, not sharing his inner convictions with her, not speaking his thoughts.
First, find the boy.
That much she knew, and concurred in hope.
Was he alive?
He didn't ask her this, knowing that her belief was similar to his, but not to rub salt into her wounds.
But he wondered. Was Wilfred alive? Probably not.
Was he dead? Almost certainly.
Again, this must not be spoken aloud, but it lay before any considerations like an open wound, bleeding fully back and down into the black earth.
So, do not ask the question, but hint in a gentle and oblique manner toward the purpose.
Was he dead? Almost certainly.

The words must not be spoken.
Their silence shook the very ground on which they stood in great rumblings of volume.
If dead, where lay his remains?
He seemed to have fought most everywhere, might have fallen at any time over three days.
So what was the answer?
Anywhere from the Lutheran Seminary to Big Round Top, if unburied.
A distance of about twelve square miles, if not more.
And if buried?
Anywhere from Seminary Ridge to the new graves outside the town.
Lots of the boys were buried there, in the first inspired burst of digging, and after the four hundred darkies had arrived to do the job.
More and more had been laid there since.
Some had been dug up out of the ground and planted in more orderly rows, with names of men on wooden crosses where known.
Pastor Gressler knew that Wilfred was not among these last few, because he was not named in any records.
And there were others, other graves, mass graves, for want of a better word. These of necessity remained unmarked where the good soil covered pieces of men and sometimes small pieces of men, and no decent and considerate man could mention this possibility to a grieving mother.
So his choice of words was very limited and very constrained and very gentle and very tactful. He managed at length, amidst many prayers, to squeeze out his sad question to Mrs Robinson. Did Wilfred have on or about him any mark or possession or picture or ring or trinket? Pastor Gressler was rewarded immediately with gold, a sudden revelation of gold in the gloom of desolation. Yes, said the weeping mother, her boy had something made of gold.

Strange to relate, this was true, and might the lord bless the worthy Pastor for reminding her, oh how could she have forgot?
Wilfred had carried a gold artefact, got from his poor dead father, and passed on down from his grandfather before him, and from his, ever since the original family had come to Canada over one hundred years before.
It was a Hebrew "Mezuzah".
He called it the Moose.
Wilfred was given this at his fathers deathbed, and it was his to keep forever and pass on after his father had gone to glory. It was a little gold casement, very fine, about one inch long, maybe an eighth of an inch thick, about a quarter inch wide.
It was made of gold, and housed a Bible text from Deuteronomy, written on a tiny scroll inside.
But yes, it was gold.
She had seen it first when she was young, and got married.
And her man had give it to the boy as he lay a' dyin'.
And she saw it then.
She would know it anywhere.
Wilfred had took it with him to America, and to the war.
Gold.
He had gold with him, in his dyin' and in his burial.
If he was dead, if he was buried, then the Mezuzah was buried with him.
Did this help, Mrs Robinson wondered?
Would this make it easier, if it was even possible, to find her boy?
Pastor Gressler prayed out his thanks.
Somewhere, he knew not where, a tiny window had opened in the light of heaven's grace.
For the first time in this pall of sadness and sorrow, somehow, somewhere, the light was shining.

Somehow, the word got out.
Somebody, and nobody ever did know just who said what to who, but within hours and maybe days the word got out.
Maybe somebody or other overheard a conversation and stretched it somewhat and then the word got out.
The word was that there was gold in them thar graves, and it got out.
Like a puppy dog wrigglin' out under a wire fence, the word escaped it's safe and enjoyable captivity and set up it's own store, purveyin' rumour and gossip at knockdown prices and then growin' bigger and bigger and fatter and faster than a bristlin' hound dog with a whiff of bitch in it's twitchin' wet nose until it had not only a store of it's own but a free life and a merry one.
The dog was off the porch, the word was out, and an aching leg was lifted to piss on the grass, and on the roadside, and in the highways and byways.
Credence and credibility, fuelled by wild imagination, positively burst forth from it's burgeoning loins, spouting out as streams in the wilderness or the residue and liquid remnants of loaves and fishes at a picnic in Galilee.
The word was out.
There was gold, and lots of it, buried somewhere in Gettysburg.
And the word was full of grace and truth and full with promises of undeniable and unmeasurable wealth for anybody with a willing shovel and a good old American spirit of "can do!".
Gold!
Gold!
Gold!
When Pastor Gressler spoke with Mrs Robinson, it was a private matter told in confidence, in his small office and no record was set down in writing and there wasn't anybody else even in the building, let alone within graduated earshot.

Pastor Gressler couldn't have recollected, even if he'd tried to (which he didn't) some weeks afterwards, just whom he might necessarily have shared the extremely sensitive and confidential Pastoral Ministry Task with, other than his very close-mouthed and secretive Leadership team, and they certainly didn't tell anybody.

Well, they didn't tell almost anybody.

Apart from the proper people who they were instructed to inform.

And those of whom they must enquire!

Folk like the Army Quartermaster of Stores and Ordinance, and the Clerk of Records for Dead and Wounded Servicemen.

Admittedly, there might have been the personage of the Town Clerk?

He was charged with knowing who was buried where and when in the different Cemeteries.

He had records of the burial places in the whole town.

Yes he did.

But only up to and including the thirtieth day of June eighteen hundred and sixty three.

There were no deaths recorded on that day.

And that's where the records ended.

But he had no information about anybody killed in the battle.

Still, he had to be told.

Apart from these few, Pastor Gressler told nobody.

To be fair, everybody who WAS told repeated this tale to very few.

And all of THOSE folks spoke only in earnest secrecy to everybody who NEEDED to be told.

So it was of course directly as a consequence of that fact that all of the other clergymen and elders and the like were eventually made aware of the gold in the grave.

And probably as well various husbands and wives and brothers and sisters and sweethearts had their ears opened.
All were discreet.
Vergers and wagon-wheel repairers and horse traders huntin' up feed at a competitive rate, everybody the soul of discretion.
Of course the finer points of the matter that must have been of necessity shared out were quickly altered, distorted, twisted, and exaggerated in no time, and in no small sense.
This was understandable, if unregretful to nobody because nobody knew about the confusion.
The resulting witches brew of hearsay, gossip, rumour and innuendo was itself both refined and elongated.
This was all latterly embellished and expanded to impossible proportions, each re-telling of the myth akin to the blowing up of a balloon or the scum and grease overflowing from a too-long boiled pot of pigs bones.
Gold!
Gold!
Gold!
A tiny Hebrew casement, smaller than the first joint on a woman's little finger, and devised to retain a scripture scrawled on papyrus, became, after a thousand gossips or ten, a gold bar.
Gold!
A gold bar, this same emerging gold bar, then dropped off a wagon or howsomever, somehow or other, it was lost, misplaced or discarded.
As gold bars will, it then turned into ten gold bars, and then a hundred.
So it was a hundred gold bars up for grabs.
No more, no less.
For some reason, the limit was attained, and nobody knew why, or argued.
Stands to reason, some murmured, and that was that.

One hundred gold bars.
Not ninety-nine!
Gold!
One hundred gold bars!
No, the size of the cache of gold bars didn't rise above one hundred.
This was a reasonably credible amount of gold bars likely to be secretly buried inside a coffin and grave somewhere in Gettysburg.
Gold!
Whether one hundred gold bars would have ever fitted inside a coffin was not discussed.
Nobody asked why in the name of Sam Hill would anyone in their right mind want to put one hundred gold bars into an unmarked grave in the middle of a still blood-wet battlefield. So when somebody or other casually recounted to Pastor Gressler the curious notion doin' the rounds that there was a mighty hoard of by this time Mexican gold bars buried in a coffin the worthy clergyman didn't even recognise that this nonsense had come from his own mouth.
Oh, yes, there was gold up on Seminary Hill or it might have been up by Cemetery Road yearning to be unearthed by any lucky guy with the gumption to go out and get it,
Pastor Gressler heard the rumours. God moves in mysterious ways, he mused.
Bein' a firm believer in the expository dictum that "the Lord Helps Them That Helps Theirselves",
Pastor Gressler coupled this determination with another enigmatic metaphor "carpe diem"- "seize the day".
He at once announced that there was shovels and jobs a'plenty for diggin' graves at five cents a corpse and to spare.
His word went out, flyin' on the wings of the story of one hundred gold bars.

The Pastor needs men to dig, and he knows about the gold.

In no time, he had another hundred-odd eager beavers marchin' into town, some of them enquirin', not too delicately, if they were allowed to use the shovels in their spare time?

Pastor Gressler assured them that they most assuredly might do this, always bearin' in mind that there were plenty of necessary holes in the ground that needed diggin' anyway, and lots of overtime for them that was willin', at five good cents per corpse, or grave dug here n' there, dependin' on your deployment under the overseers.

But yes, they could use the shovels after a reasonable shift. Please don't break 'em or try to gouge out stone in the fields, of which there was much.

Also, they must respect the Army organisin' the layout of the graveyards, and must not dig up anybody, anywhere, on a whim or impulse, unless they were asked to do so.

They must ask permission, which would not be unreasonably refused, but, yes, they could do that.

There were indeed buried soldiers, even now, and there'd be more that needed diggin' up and reburying in properly consecrated soil.

So this might well chime in with their more private ambitions and interests, and they were welcome.

Let's face it, went the official line- if you care to dig holes in the ground, you've come to the right place.

Sign here, and pick yourself up a shovel.

That will be your shovel, Mister, and nobody else is gonna take it off you.

You can say to yourself- "This is MY shovel. There are many others like it but this is MY shovel"!

And God bless ya, brother!

All round, Pastor Gressler judged the incredible stories of buried gold to have given his sacred task a darned good shot in the arm, with strength to his back and power to his elbow. He now had a good, well motivated workforce, with more pourin' in and arrivin' daily, askin' for shovels and diggin' for gold.
For a while, holes in the ground appeared in most unlikely places all over Gettysburg, and with most if not all of them filled in after a quick and fruitless quizzical excavation.
For the most part nobody minded.
In fairness, nobody cared, long as it wasn't in the plots as marked up and laid out in the new foundations. Thousands of bodies were bein' dug up and re-buried.
All of 'em had been buried in horse blankets, not coffins.
Time went by, and the tall stories waned. There sure warn't no mention of a hundred bars of gold buried in a horse blanket!
Probably this gold in a coffin story was jes' horseshit. But the job of diggin' graves was real!
Most men decided that their current life, liberty, and pursuit of happiness would be best served if they bent their backs to diggin' as directed, never mind any gold. This they enacted. Having done so, they then noted and observed the attendant hundreds of like-minded gold-hunters and searchers alongside of them and everywhere in sight.
This reinforced their conviction that horseshit was horseshit, and no mistake.
They concluded that five cents per corpse in the hand was worth much more than as many as a hundred imaginary gold bars somewhere underfoot, and the treasure probably wasn't there anyway, not when you come down to things anyways.
Why would it be?
What fool buries his gold in a meadow littered with corpses?

Gold? A hunnerd gold bars in a coffin? Where would you look?

What was this fertile crop, seekin' harvest?

Here was a human leg-bone, thigh joint, knee and foot, all five toes visible, under a bush, and not the only one neither, not by a long chalk.

Wonder how much gold that was made up of?

Here's a head, half-eaten by rats and birds? That's a hairline and a bald scalp, so probably weren't no spry young'un. God bless him.

How much gold does that fetch?

Or mebbe carry that pore skull and the picked bones on by yonder to the overseers.

Mark up five cents, which is the goin' rate for such significant discoveries, if you're allocated to search and scavengin', as known.

Who sticks gold in the ground anyway?

Five cents a corpse meant upwards of a dollar and a bit more in a day, and the grub threw in, regular, generous, and right tasty.

Hundred bars of gold! Huh! In a pigs ear!

The Minister surveyed his vineyard, and saw that it was good.

Schedules of planning progress, impossibly difficult at first, were becoming attainable.

Decent folk were coming to the town, with gifts of bread and milk and produce abounding for the labourers toiling in the fields.

Plenty of workers were here, more of late with the interestin' gold rush fever.

Black men dug and lifted and made up the task-gangs side by side with whites, no preference or discrimination, and all were served up good hot grub by ladies of both persuasions.

The work proceeded, and the business of buryin' the dead at Gettysburg moved onward at a rapid pace.

BIRDY BREAKS

Birdy was sick.
He didn't moan and he didn't cry.
Birdy sought out a comfort from the wind, a tent in the lee of a great stone on or near to Devil's Dyke, and lay down, shakin', over on a horse blanket flung between tremblin' flesh and the cold stone ground.
He turned his face to the darkness and closed his eyes, curling up like an old cat that sleeps most day and night, blinkin' betimes.
Big Neg fetched Mama Caliba and Mama Bear and Cassie and they were very afraid for him.
The women said a prayer and sung lowly over him as he got up first a ragged coughin' in fits and starts and then into a hot fever nothin' less than ragin'.
Cassie stroked his poor head and Mama Caliba offered him good fire-warmed and flour-thick broth mixed with lamb boiled soft in saffron and water.
Birdy didn't but lap at it, spoon fed by Cassie.
His brow got hotter and hotter and he coughed helplessly, sleep denied him by the illness.
Mama Bear sent Big Neg to fetch Pastor Gressler.
Up toward the town, Pastor Gressler was prayin' with a troop of soldiers late come to Gettysburg to join in the layout of the new Cemetery, with upward of ten thousand men to be buried or to be reinterred there in the new fields.
Pastor Gressler knew Big Neg for his hardest workin' darkie, coupled as he was with Birdy, and like to clean out as many as ten full graves in a single hour, not breakin' sweat.
Alone of all the labourers in Gettysburg, Big Neg commanded ten cents a grave, and nothin' was more deserved.
The wages thus accrued were mountin' on his account.

And Pastor Gressler had often looked in wonder at Birdy, the most lowly and twisted cripple of all the darkies with a dogs vomit of black flesh at his throat and chin, weak and lookin' miserable with one eye starin' up and mouth twisted as if cryin' out in pain. But what Birdy only cried out in true holiness was "Jesa, Jesa, Jesa".
Blessed is he that cometh in the name of the Lord. Workin' as he did along with and beside and in the company of Big Neg, Birdy got five cents credit for every full grave dug, dug that is by Big Neg, not but that he never broke sweat, or put a spade into the ground. He didn't have to.
Birdy was amazin' and inspiring.
More graves were dug, more bodies found and transported and shifted, more soldiers laid to rest, in the near proximity to Birdy than in any other arena of the great enterprise, a thousand bein's strong, that now constituted the Federal Government funded enterprise dominating the life of the town and all environs.
Birdy, in short, was worth it.
As Pastor Gressler understood it, one may judge a vine only by the fruit thereof.
Now Big Neg told him that Birdy lay on point of death and swelterin' on the ground and that the women had sent for him, please sir, most swiftly, mos' quick, suh?
Pastor Gressler veritably come runnin' and leaned over Birdy in the dark of the tent as the women kept up prayers and singin' soft hymns from the Bible classes held on our day of rest before everybody got up to go out and off to work under kindly dispensation 'til dark, the good Lord permittin'. He looked down at Birdy and put his hand on his brow and touched his face and felt the heat and the pulse of fever ragin' under and on the tormented black skin.

He prayed the most solemn prayer of his life, touchin' Birdy's poor head the while.
Birdy turned his lips out, pursing them in pain, and a thin spittle trickled out of his mouth and dribbled over the Minister's fingers.
Pastor Gressler did not remove his hand, but prayed the more.
As he did so, he felt and saw Birdy jolting like a startled gundog, twitching visibly under his hand, the whole body writhing in juddering alarm.
A plethora of scriptural images burst into his mind.
He saw two men in a field, the one left, the other taken.
He saw a maiden scrabbling for a coin in a corner of an ill-lit dwelling.
He saw a man selling all of his possession for the purchase of a single field.
He saw Elijah feeding the Widow from a pot of grain unending.
And something jarred in him, resonated in his mind when he thought of and felt the bleak sorrow of the Widow, and he thought of Mrs Robinson and her poor dead boy, lying somewhere out in that field, far off or nearby, with a tiny sliver of gold grasped in his clutching fingers.
And here was Birdy, of the soil, sick on the horse blanket, stirring in a tent amidst the stones of the field. Birdy stirred and sniffed a bit, and coughed.
He turned his face up toward Pastor Gressler, and opened his eyes.
The Clergyman stroked the weary brow, softly, gently, lovingly.
Birdy jolted again under his hand, lurching violently, and cried out "Jesa, Jesa, Jesa"!
Mama Bear grabbed at her stomach and felt the sudden explosion of pain and sorrow that she had only ever known before in nine tortuous births.

Mama Bear gave a great whine of agony, her cries ascending up the scale into a falsetto shriek, gasping out into nothing at the top.
Cassie wept.
Big Neg started, useless and unable.
Birdy jolted again.
For a very bad two seconds of real time Pastor Gressler thought that Birdy had died under his hand. Then, in an utter instant, he felt the boiling flesh beneath his wettened fingers stiffen, shake itself dry, and go cool as a good cream pie at a picnic.
Birdy opened his mouth, hawked deep into his throat, and spat out a thrum of white spittle.
He smiled, crying a little at his eyes, but his tiny jolts were now the rumblings of laughter.
"Ahuh, ahuh, ahuh", he gurgled.
"Ahuh, ahuh, ahuh".
He opened his lips and spat out more white phlegm, knowin' it was okay to do so, that nobody minded his seekin' comfort in the dark.
"Jesa", he croaked, weakly.
"Jesa, Jesa, Jesa"!
The women bowed their heads, sobbing.
Pastor Gressler felt the garment of an Apostle placed upon his shoulders, covering him with authority and power, warming him and strengthening him to the purpose.
More clearly than he had ever expressed the thought in his entire life, he said- "Amen".

SEYTON CALLS

The walls have ears.
Even the walls of a thin tent on the ground near to or on Devil's Dyke have ears.
These walls, everywhere alert, with their ultra-sensitive ears that can hear anything ever spoke anywhere by anybody to anybody else, no matter how softly whispered, extend to both the inside and outside of all buildings, large or small.
They also have voices.
For the walls not only assimilate information, they also transmit it.
They hear secret things, whispered in silence, and they broadcast these same over loudspeakers of cunning design, which hide in open sunshine, nor bear corporeal form, and you can't stop them.
How this process occurs nobody knows, or is even wondering.
But it is alive and well in the realms of gossip and jungle drums and scandalous talk and even divine and sacred revelation.
Mayhap the same Author of all things that leaned down and whispered gently into Pastor Gressler's compliant ear that he should acquaint Birdy with the gold mezuzah buried some'eres in Gettysburg let dribble the resultant determination into everybody's collective ear. Birdy would do his level best to search for the missing artefact and thus locate the bones of the boy holding it.
But the spirit of scandal kicked right in, and it's big brothers rumour and falsehood went straight to work.
Pastor Gressler had intimated to Birdy that Mrs Robinson would give a reward of one hundred dollars, Yankee dollars that is, to whoever brought her the tiny gold mezuzah, and the location of her son's grave. He might agree to look for it, might he not?

He had nodded weakly, understanding her sad pain.
Furthermore, she would offer a home to the needy person who brought her such consolation, if wanted. She would take them back up to Canada and look after them, up near the Sydenham River, clear to Owen Sound on Georgian Bay, if wanted.
Such was the word.
That word was spoken quietly, in a tiny tent to a young darkie faint with fever, nodding with eyes closed.
But the walls have ears, and the walls have voices.
Tentflaps have ears.
The song of the sirens rose amidst the waves of euphony.
The walls positively thundered their message out from the mountains, or certainly from the rounded crests of Big Round Top and Little Round Top.
The unholy trio of scandal, rumours and falsehood put out another version of the pure and unvarnished truth- that Mrs Robinson would give ten thousand Yankee dollars for the return of the one hundred gold bars buried in a coffin, and (she bein' a droll widow) would marry the man who done it.
So the word went forth, was refined and relayed and related and expanded in the telling.
Word was that twenty scientific men with dousin' machines that were unstoppable was already in Gettysburg, already on the trail of the gold, fresh arrived from as far as New York City!
Mrs Robinson would take her pick of the bachelors among them.
She would marry them up in Canada, and make them wealthy men beyond their wildest dreams.
Why, she had a farm bigger than the county!
She had five hundred horses and two thousand cows and seven bulls to increase the stock!
She was owner of a gold mine up beyond Hudson Bay.

She was partial to tomatoes, and wouldn't never eat apples, fer she was God-fearin' to a degree unspecified.
She owned two hotels in Montreal, and three in New York.
Why, her castle in London over in England was bought off the Queen of England herself, and paid in cash, right on the barrel!
Such were the tales that were flying abroad.
Nearer to home, more sober and better informed stories danced about.
Birdy, the amazing Soilman, was known to many.
He had located several graves at need.
His only word was the name of Christ, such as he could speak. No man had ever heard him bespeak aught else.
And if God had put his hand onto him, and afflicted him with a limpin' leg and but one eye and a black skin, well, who can tell the mind of The Lord?
His trappings were Big Neg, always grinning, always wielding a shovel, always thanking the women for the generous portions of stew which they ladled onto his plate; Mama Bear and Mama Caliba, good Christian coloured women recently freed from bein' slaves, and they joined in prayer and worked their piece and done their bit uncomplainin' and every body knew it; Cassie, sweet child of Jesus, always smilin' like to the very sunshine, always listening intently to prayer and truth, eyes only on her crippled friend.
Such was the man and his works- by his fruit ye shall know him, and Birdy brought but inspiration, edification, and consolation to many.
Mrs Robinson had been feeding the workers for several months, living in their midst.
Broken- hearted at the loss of her husband four year agone, and her son that laid down his life, she was no Merry Widow, seekin' after the flesh.

Yes, some heard she had spoke of a modest farm up in Canada, but all the rest was fanny may and fanny might and confusion.

A gold mine?

A hotel?

Stuff and nonsense.

She wanted to weep at the grave of her son, and nothin' else.

Blessed are them that shall mourn, for they shall be comforted.

Of her small store, she had offered a hundred dollars, and a home if wanted.

As for these men with machines, dousin' and malingerin', nobody had seen nobody of that description and the story was a doggone lie.

Folk labouring in the fields of the dead could make up their own minds as to which story was nearer to the truth.

For Luke Seyton, there was a third option, not allied to either modest reward or fabulous wealth.

He called it "reading 'twixt the lines".

Partly this perception was born of adherence to what the poet says- "a man hears what he wants to hear and disregards the rest".

Not that Seyton was a poet, but he believed in making a balanced decision based on a sound judgement informed by factual experience.

His personal decisions tended toward the darker elements in his being, with his self-interest well to the fore.

Having travelled from New York, where he had first heard the legend of the Gettysburg gold in a coffin, he had now heard just about every variation of the tale.

When he arrived in town, he heard it all.

He could map out the whole fairy tale, and discern clearly what was likely and what was horseshit.

This time, as before, there was gold, and a coffin, but there was also some other matters pertainin'.

To these he turned his attention.
They had not featured in the earlier disclosures.
One was a cash money reward, varyin' in value
dependin' on just who was doin' the talkin', and
another was the matter of a new home in Canada.
The most important thing was the very attractive
body of the woman walkin' around Gettysburg this
very minute.
Mrs Robinson was very tasty, and she warn't no
notion slung from a whiskey bottle.
She was real, and real flesh on her frame.
Ten thousand dollars and a goldmine was probably
horseshit.
Now read betwixt the lines!
Marriage 'n title to even a small farm up North in
another country was desirable, even if debateable.
Readin' betwixt the lines, it MIGHT be arrived at.
But a new home in a faraway land, with THAT
woman there, opened up prospects that made him
water at the mouth.
He could put his hands on her.
And not just his hands!
If luck served, maybe he could unpack an awful lot
more.
Even a small farm with but seventy acres and a mule
would fetch upwards of a thousand dollars.
Or what the hell?
Keep it.
Live in it.
On yer' own, once ye've wore her out in comfort, her
views to the contrary!
Maybe taigle with other ladies in the privacy of
Canada?
And still more of them?
Somewhere way out in the pine trees.
Yes sir.
Just him and her.

That would make for a most enjoyable situation, if only for a few weeks before he got full rid of her, eat by a bear mostlike, way off in the woods.
When he was good and done!
Amazin' how these things happened?
Yes, grievin', sad, who knew what women wanted?
Gone off.
Or mebbe dead?
But who'd be askin'?
And where there was one woman gone off, why not two or three?
Why not several?
Who, when all was done, would be countin?
Not him!
Not by a long chalk.
Moseyin' around the town, he fell in with the Preacher that confirmed the essentials.
Yes, the poor woman was a widow.
Good.
Searchin' fer her child, thought killed by the Rebs some months agone.
Very sad indeed.
Yes, comed down here from Canada, a good n' Godly woman!
May the Lord bless her, Pastor!
Thank you most kindly fer them good words, Sir.
And you are…Mister….Mister..and what might I call you?
Jes' call me Luke, Pastor.
Thank you Luke. And may I hope to greet you at Services come the Sabbath, Luke?
Most certainly, Pastor. But tell me this, how fares the quest to discover the grave of her child?
We have good hopes.
One of the darkies here has particular gifts in excavating the soil.
If anyone can locate the boy, wherever he lies, then Birdy is the man to do it.
Birdy?

Yes. That is his name. But you will know him by his gait, for he is lamed. And he stays with his family, the other darkies who bear him hither and yon if he is pained, for he is betimes sickly.

Forgive my curiosity, Pastor, but what are your expectations?

My hopes, rather? I, we, all of us, hope that Birdy shall find the grave of Wilfred and bear the proof to his weeping mother, thence consolation and comfort to her in this, her desolate loss.

My fervent hopes are with you, Pastor, and for the sure accomplishment of your endeavours.

Why, thank you, son Luke, and do be pleased to join us in breaking bread in the house of prayer, betimes and often. May God bless you.

And you, Pastor, and all of your flock.

Seyton moved on into the town.

In one hour he had established where the Seminary was, and where the labourers, dark-skinned and white, ate alongside each other on trestle tables served by women, young and old, of both races.

SHE was here, and he easily introduced himself, and took a good stern measure of her worth even as he imagined her helpless in his grasp.

This was easy meat, and juicy.

This woman sought no marriage- but her obvious compassion for the niggers made his task that much easier.

Yes, Birdy would find the grave, and whatever was in it.

Birdy would find the proof.

He, Seyton, would be there.

And if the other big nigger was there, Seyton would put him in the grave with a bullet in his eye.

That close!

That close!

Then he'd kill the limpin' nigger and go off with the loot to the woman.

No need to mention the niggers.

They'd be deep in the ground, and nobody would
ever find them.
Plant them in an empty grave.
Who'd come lookin' fer niggers?
She would marry him in gratitude fer' his reward.
The fun would start when he got her on her own, far
away, in a farm up in Canada.

BIRDY AT THE GRAVE

November 17th 1863

For the next several days Luke Seyton bided his time,
watching and waiting.
There was no hurry.
Birdy was goin' nowhere.
He looked like to be recoverin' from fever, to his
mind and way of thinkin'.
Weak, dandlin', more indoors than out.
Tired and coughin' when he was out, and soon
headed home with the big nigger.
So much fer' him!
Patience is a virtue.
Seyton knew that he had it in spades.
He also knew that it was not really patience.
Rather it was cunning.
The cunning of the fox, the wiles of the snake in the
grass, most subtle beast of the field.
That he was, that he was.
And his sin and his nature was always before him.
He acknowledged it freely, admitted it totally.
It was the cunning of the snake that waits fer' the
rabbit.
Then, a single strike!
Death walks with me, in my pocket.
That would do fer' him!
Mrs Robinson, or "the white bitch", as he dubbed
her, was on constant show.
His thirst for her increased, in inverse proportion to
his opportunities to foster cordial relations, which
were limited, to put it mildly. He would not startle
the game.
He was too old a hand to awaken an early epiphany
in her.
No, let that be.
All things come to him as waits.
Preparation- preparation is everything!

He was patient in pursuit of flesh, and this prize was worth the patience and the preparation.
He knew just how it would be.
She would be grateful, he would be gracious.
Oh, come on in here to my den, woman.
You'll get to know me soon enough.
Oh yes.
I know!
He knew to a fine degree just how he would break her before puttin' out her lights altogether.
Smarmy woman!
Impudent bitch!
Time was on his side, and he knew it.
All of these niggers, and the white bitch, have no idea.
They know nothin' of what's comin' their way, and wouldn't credit it if'n you told 'em.
And why should they know?
He, for a fact, sure wasn't gonna tell 'em, was he?
Yes, he knew just how he'd break the bitch. Let me get at you with the lash, and then we'll see, won't we?
Birdy he had identified early on, and he was nothin' special, not so much as a crazy nigger with but one eye and a trailin' leg behind and a thick mess of what looked like black dogshit at his throat.
On all sides Birdy garnered smiles and handshakes and Seyton couldn't credit it.
All this stuff about bein' a Soilman or some such bilge he took no stock in.
Readin' betwixt the lines he was an uppity nigger with a limp and a piteous aspect.
Pity was for fools, and you couldn't throw a nigger three foot in Gettysburg without hittin' another fool broadside on, and another three hidin' behind that one, not to mention the one you threw!
And all of them up to their watery eyeballs in croakin' pity!

Seyton considered more deeply the fact that Birdy had a significant entourage accompanying him about the place at most or all times.
These individuals, each one a useless nigger (more or less) were easily categorised.
Big Neg, and he wasn't called that fer' nothin', oftentimes would be seen carrying the cripple.
More pity!
The only pity that Seyton foresaw was the fact that he'd have to kill Big Neg, and couldn't enjoy the sellin' of him.
Maybe that was a brother, devoted to his charge.
If this nigger was on hand when the body of the boy showed up, then Seyton would put his lights out, there n' then.
No talk, no paybill.
Just a bullet in the eye.
There were graves in plenty to chuck him inwards.
No, he wouldn't choose to flirt with the notion of fittin' up Big Neg fer' the murder of Birdy- too risky, and it might not scour!
Birdy, of course, would be easy meat.
He'd just put his hand over the nigger's mouth and nose.
Choke the bastard!
No marks, no packdrill!
The three nigger women didn't ever come out when Birdy went diggin', not that Birdy did!
Big Neg did all the diggin'.
Seyton had observed and learned.
And the three nigger women were clearly his mother, her sister, and his little sister, in whatever proportions they mixed it.
Readin' betwixt the lines, here was a whole passel of inbred niggers, hangin' together like wild dogs in the desert.
Some said they'd all got religion, and was pious to a degree!
Seyton didn't hold with lettin' niggers get religion!

Look at these uppity fools?
Every one of 'em from below Mason-Dixon, and, good dogshit in a bucket help us, there was a war on!
Slaves, all of 'em!
Runaways, every one, and no denial!
Open, brazen to the air, defiant!
Niggers run off from their legal masters and owners, and folk like this white bitch disinclined to even admit the fact!
Shameful!
Filthy goddam niggers!
Well, he would learn her.
He smiled tightly at the thought of it.
Oh yes, he was goin' ter' enjoy this event.
And he would play it out so fine!
Kill the niggers.
Get the treasure, or proof, or whatever. He would get it. Go off in a buggy with the white bitch. Smiles and winks and congratulations.
Flowers! Consolation and encouragement.
Canada, here we come.

On the third day, Birdy come out at sundown nigh on to dark, and with Big Neg in tow.
Seyton had been keeping a close eye on his movements.
Mostly, these were confined to in and about the Seminary.
There was so many people comin' and goin' that it was perceptibly easy to tail anybody, let alone Birdy, who stood out like a Priest in a whorehouse.
Birdy was limpin' along just fine, and commendably quick. He was gabblin' endlessly at Big Neg, jaw twitchin'.
Seyton moved closer to hear what was bein' said between the two, and this was real easy to compass, real easy.
Full dark was comin' on fast, and he could linger just some feet away, and hear every word undetected.

But it didn't cut no ice or burn no bread because all the one nigger said to the other was "Jesa, Jesa, Jesa" over and over.

Big Neg only replied "amen", again and again.

To Seyton, it seemed a particularly pointless conversation.

Birdy and Big Neg sorta lollopped away outta the town.

They commenced to headin, not south to the Round Tops, but north and west up to Barlows Knoll.

From there they skirted around and back toward Gettysburg to make their way, most indirectly and gradually, to where the track ran on the Hanover Railroad line.

When the track hove in view, Birdy followed the line of it on the southernmost side, and hard up to the very rails.

It was now full dark, but the moonglow glinted on the shining rails, stretchin' off away there to the eastward.

It was moonbright curtained by clouds.

Like to a light in a theatre, goin' on and off, the scene moved between shadow and clear visibility.

Presently, Seyton observed that the two weirdly hoppin' figures had stopped.

They had paused near to the railroad track aways by a cluster of three great stones ten feet or more tall that pointed up outta the ground.

It was for all the world like the twisted roots of a giant back tooth all rotten and pulled outta the gums of Goliath, but that Goliath would of had to be over two hundred or so feet long in length to open his big mouth and snaffle candy with it.

Birdy knelt on the rough ground in the darkness and bowed his head.

Big Neg joined him, and for a while Seyton could see clear that the only thing they were doin' was probably prayin', Big Neg mutterin' the most of it, as such folk do.

Outlined against the big jagged tooth of stones, they presented as two harpies or goblins brewin' up a curse agin' the trees and crops of the field.
Seyton couldn't but state to himself that he approved, metaphorically.
After a time, Birdy stood up, not leanin' on his trailin' crippled leg, and it seemed that he pointed to a slimy depression on the ground, hard up by the railtrack, and it looked to be filled with oil or muck or black vomit.
Seyton couldn't judge from this distance, even moon bright, but noted that the hole, or whatever it was, commenced in a rude trough this side of the track, nearer to his concealed position.
Big Neg sorta shimmied around, getting secure footing, wieldin' a shovel, Birdy pointin' down, just aways off of from the steel rail maybe six or so foot there near the track.
Big Neg commenced to not so much dig a hole like to a grave, but clear out a muck filled trench, wet and sodden and vile and stinkin'.
Big Neg choked and gagged at the smell, spat out and vomited excresence or somesuch.
But then he bent to the work with a will, and the evil soil positively flew out from the diggin'.
Soon he was standin' in a hole four foot deep, churnin' up stones from the railway line, and dry earth piled from the perimeter.
Birdy just kept on pointin' and singin' out "Jesa, Jesa, Jesa", propped aloft over Big Neg weird and strange in the night-time.
The fieldhand shifted ground at an astoundin' rate.
By and by he commenced to reachin' down and liftin' out at first pieces of wood and then a whole human leg, rotting tangibly, and he retched and vomited. Another nameless hunk of what might be flesh and bone and carcass come up shapeless and mangled, and Seyton construed that this must or might be the body of the missing boy.

What was most evident was that this trough in the ground looked to be some kinda garbage pit. There was as much wet muck stinkin' high of shit and decay that reached out all over everywhere, like to choke Seyton right where he stood a ways off in the shadows, as there was bits of stick or wood or even sick soil.

By and by Big Neg flung out a shovelful of vileness and Birdy positively larrupped out "Jesa, Jesa, Jesa", jumpin' up and down on the spot.

Big Neg clambered out of the pit, and give a whoop and shouted that's it?

We found it?

Birdy was dancin' like a mad thing on the edge of the railway track in the dark, noddin' and bobbin' and holdin' up whatever it was that constituted the treasure.

Seyton suddenly noticed that the deep rumble that was burstin' up through the edge of his mind was a train comin' on in fast to Gettysburg.

At the same moment he realized with a flash of revelation that has no place in time as we ordinarily experience it that now was the time and the moment to shoot the big nigger and steal the treasure off the little crippled nigger before killin' him under cover of the noise of the train and he stood up out of the blackness and moved on up to the track, the approachin' train now but fifty or so feet away on the bend and comin' on fast.

The whistle blew.

Train approachin'.

Seyton stepped forward in the blackness, placing himself between the open pit and the two leapin' niggers, and raised his gun and pointed it at Big Neg. "Hand it over, nigger!", he shouted, conscious that he had at one stroke taken total control and command of the situation.

Both of them could see the gun and the rapidly arrivin' train was gonna cover any noise or scream when he shot the nigger in the eye.

He checked his footing carefully to see that he wasn't too close to the line, no, the train would pass him comfortably but he would feel the wind of it.

In a sudden burst of enlightenment the train was right there on top of the three of them and then was just as quick gone by.

Blow me to blazes, he thought, I'll be damned, and then he reckoned in another very fast flash of realization that there was a SECOND train right there, right on top of them, and he fetched a clear bead on the right eye of Big Neg and levelled the pistol to kill the bastard on the instant.

At the same time, takin' his time and checkin' every step before he made it, he looked down at Birdy.

Birdy took a sudden step to his left and sung out "Jesa, Jesa, Jesa" and Seyton hesitated fer' just one second but made a compensatin' decision, instant in thought as in action, that possibly fer' reasons yet unclear Birdy was the more dangerous of the two.

Let that be his final utterance, he thought darkly. I'll send this bastard home to Jesus in the twinklin' of an eye.

He raised the gun and pointed it straight at Birdy's head.

There, nigger! How does Jesus look to you now he shouted.

His finger tightened on the trigger even as he felt the waft of the wind from the train right behind him.

No hesitation now, he would blow this little black bastards brains out.

Unbeknownst to him, the fourth car of five rattled by, the window open, and the Saxon Seal came spinning down out of the blackness and hit Luke Seyton hard at the top and back of his skull, killing him in about one second.

All of Seyton's colours turned to black.

His final thought in his lifetime was the question he had seemingly asked of himself- "how does Jesus look to you now?".
He toppled forward into the emptied pit, the gun not fired.
Birdy's finger came up to point downward in command, traversing a graceful circle in the motion, indicatin' the grave or shithole.
Big Neg took his shovel, and set to with a will, buryin' the thing that had reared up out of the blackness and died in the doin'.
In five minutes, it was done.
The garbage pit was full.
Birdy bent over and picked up the Saxon Seal, puttin' it into his shirt.
The Mezuzah rested in his palm.
When Big Neg was done, Birdy pointed to the three big rocks, and said "Jesa, Jesa, Jesa".
He looked at the Mezuzah in the moonlight.
He looked back over his shoulder at the trees away off on the edge.
Now was not the time.
He signalled to Big Neg, and they headed back to the town, Birdy strollin' along most graceful and without conspicuous assistance.

THE MOOSE

Subsequently, and on the next mornin', Birdy selected both Big Neg and Cassie to go with him when he went to see Mrs Robinson.
He found her prayin' with Pastor Gressler, and she stood up tall and flinchin' bravely as she anticipated the worst when he seemed to come in the doorway almost in a formal capacity.
Her lips tremblin' with fought back tears she prepared to face the discovery of the death of her beloved child in the only way she knew- noddin' to the Lord in the direct face of his wisdom over all.
She had never believed in her heart that Wilfred was dead but now she knew, or thought she knew to the full that her greatest fear was now gonna be told to her, always makin' the assumption that Birdy might have found the body.
Birdy looked up at her with a bright smile and happy, and Mrs Robinson dared just for one second to hope that maybe the death of all of her cherished and prayed for dreams would not come to pass.
Birdy smiled direct at her, and she felt the beginnings of something very like to fresh air blowin' into a hot and smoky room in her weary mind.
Birdy smiled and moved up forward to her and then he seemed to turn and looked full at and toward Cassie, blinkin' in her nervousness before these great white folk, and Mrs Robinson knew that he was definitely bringin' Cassie to her attention.
Birdy looked Mrs Robinson full in the eyes with a look made all of sweet accord in fastness and then he bowed his head and lifted up his right hand.
He extended it to her, opening his twisted fingers as he wept and the tears springin' and startin' up in her eyes too.
The mezuzah lay on his palm.

Mrs Robinson felt a sort of whirling greyness in her eyes and all of her colours spun around in a dervish dance and she would have collapsed but some ways or other Big Neg had seemed to anticipate the moment and she was sittin' upright in a chair swiftly provided and all present showin' their concern except Birdy, who was grinnin' wide, one eye dancin' with joy, gurglin' a bit as if he was burping out laughter.
Questions surged up and up and into her mind and mouth but she couldn't and didn't speak.
All of her instincts inclined her to shut up and keep mum and just say nothing at all because when you really don't know what to say, this is a very good time to be silent.
She looked down at the mezuzah, she now holding it in her hand, and it appeared to be pumping power and healing and energy and holiness throbbing into every tiny bit of her mind and divinity.
She had first seen it some twenty-five years before, when George took and nailed it up on the doorpost, they bein' new married and they had almost nothin' but this one thing come down from his family.
George placed it inward on the doorpost, just inside about her eye level and canted across in an angle like the hour hand on a clock pointin' to half past seven.
He had told her it was a promise that everybody goin' in that door was to be blessed and that everybody goin' out that door was to be blessed in their comin' in and goin' out and everything they did would be good and have in it that blessedness and holiness.
Years later she had found mention of it in the Bible and she knew it was so.
But now Birdy was smilin' at her with a warmth and goodness that would have lit up the sunshine, and against all the bubbles of fear and death that she was blowin' out of her mind, peace and order was bein' re-established.

She was beginning to understand something, and it was growing in her mind.
The discernible features of hope were clearing in the mist of thought.
She was beginning to understand that maybe, just maybe, but why might it be maybe at all for the Lord is not yea and nay but yea only and if that was the case then it wasn't maybe at all but really and truly Wilfred was not dead, but alive.
Here was the mezuzah, which is what her blessed child had always called the Moose, and had taken it with him when he went off down to the War, as boys will.
Really and truly in her heart she knew that the Lord doesn't fool about with likely coincidences, open to question and discussion, but will of a sudden make the sun stand still in the sky or raise the dead while the whole earth shakes and vomits up corpses and confusion.
And Birdy was grinnin' and lookin' over at Cassie and what that portended Mrs Robinson didn't know or yet understand but this was the genuine mezuzah safe in her hand and she was able to think the unthinkable as Pastor Gressler covered them all with prayer and the uppermost question in her mind and in her heart and now comin' up out of her mouth was but where was Wilfred?

There was a positive spring in the step of Birdy as he led the group out of the town and into the fields on the north and east where the railway line runs from Hanover Junction.
He was positively glidin' along on the ground, seeming to almost float most gracefully and with no trouble at all from his bad leg, or conspicuous assistance from Big Neg or anybody.
Mrs Robinson walked with Cassie, holding her hand tightly, not just because the day was gettin' up cold.

Cassie leaned in to the warmth of her breast, comforted.

All traffic in the persons of the townsfolk walkin' and now and then a buggy or a wagon was headed in the opposite direction where the President of the United States of America would later that day be addressing the people of Gettysburg and the nation.

Pastor Gressler had met the President himself the previous evening when he had stayed at the Lutheran Seminary by arrangement, Mr Lincoln confessin' to a dizziness that precluded much of the extension of civilities.

The formalities would come later on, and the Pastor's role and portion was assured in the order of procedure not surprisingly, him having led the efforts to bury the dead.

Just for now, Mrs Robinson's urgent business took priority.

Birdy led the way to above the railway line and up to where a great three stone boulder jagged up out of the ground like a giant tooth.

Lookin' back toward the treeline on the edge of the land rollin' upward, Birdy pointed with one finger upraised and said "Jesa, Jesa, Jesa" and Big Neg said "Amen", much to the shock of Pastor Gressler, who usually expected himself to intone the words as and when it was fittin', him bein' the acknowledged leader of the flock.

Birdy was pointing to a break or clearing in the trees and when they got there Pastor Gressler remembered that there was always talk of the old deaf woman that lived up in these parts and never came into the town of Gettysburg and some said she was a witch and this must be her spread.

In fact it was no better or worse than a woodshed buried under moss in the cool of the forest trees.

Standin' outside, as if waitin' on them, was a poor old woman who looked most amazin' like to an injun or a gypsy or somethin' all brown and weathered.

Right beside her, holdin' her hand as if to make sure she wasn't gonna blow away, was a young man or big boy with a tangle of hair cut and sheared off roughly.
His eyes were round and dark and starin' with no recognition of time or place or seasons or what was the arrival of these puzzlin' strangers but he never reacted in any manner, simply grasping onto the hand of his lonely benefactor.
Mrs Robinson knew him at once.
It was Wilfred, her boy, looking back at her with full confusion and bewildered.
Mrs Robinson started forward, and let go Cassie's hand.
Cassie had never seen anything as thoroughly beautiful as this young man in all of her days.

Pastor Gressler raised his hands to pray with holy hands uplifted as Birdy sang out "Jesa, Jesa, Jesa" and Big Neg echoed "amen" right on cue and this somewhat discomfited the Minister, himself determined to proceed in perfect order, with anointed Apostolic authority in good repair.
Most likely as not but perched atop a white fluffy cloud some few yards away, possessed of vision that could penetrate through walls and trees and the roof, God oversees and approves of the resulting disentanglement of the particular details.
The old deaf woman, who isn't really very old at all, and who has an active and sharp mind that would beat all of them into a pulp, not leavin' out the Lutheran Pastor, can read and write, which the three black members of this new comminglin' cannot do, not that it matters.
She makes like to funny squeaks and whistles with her speech, unpractised for years after years of solitude and only recently revived as such.

Thus and thus she thereby acquaints Pastor Gressler and Mrs Robinson with the fact that she had found Wilfred unconscious on the ground some four months previously on the very day that the battle commenced.
He has not spoken to her, not that she would have ever heard him anyway, and the deaf woman shall never discover the fact that another boy took and hit him over the top and back of the head with a shovel, thus rendering him not only silent but devoid of memory and experience.
She has been feeding him on herb soup flavoured with wild onions, which ingredients grow a'plenty in these parts. He is well. He is back on his feet somewhat, but he doesn't know enough to come in out of the rain, figuratively speakin'.
He just doesn't say a word, or do anything. He can walk okay, but he won't leave the shelter of the trees, which tends to show that he's got something in there in that there head of his somewhere.
She would have shielded him from the war, to keep him from the danger of death and destruction, but nobody has ever come near the place anyway, so there is and has been no need.
Birdy didn't hesitate, his directions clear, and he gave the Saxon Seal to Cassie, and made his goodbyes with gestures and his head bowed.
He went off not so long after that with Big Neg, calling out, as he did so, "Jesa, Jesa, Jesa", his job done.
Mama Caliba and Mama Bear tagged along.
Mrs Robinson took Wilfred home to Canada with her.
Cassie came too, by particular invitation, a valued and honoured guest and friend, and cared for Wilfred.
She adored him from the first.

Getting as far as Owen Sound meant that she had completed her run, and in style, and in no great shakes of a hurry.

In time Wilfred began to recover.

In time his memory and his experience came back, at first fleeting and dribbling but then, especially when he held the mezuzah, more quickly.

In time he began to understand that he really did like and enjoy this precious child, Cassie, who looked at him with eyes of wonder, and who listened when he spoke, however haltingly.

Speak he did, as words returned, and his speech to Cassie was all of kindness and approval.

Marriages are made in heaven and here was a prime example, two beautiful children saved and preserved to find each other and come together as one as boy and girl do oftentimes and again.

Mrs Robinson knew from the start that it would be so, and cauterised the wound in her soul of her dead prejudice.

She just looked at Wilfred, and knew that God is goodness and love and mercy and redemption. She looked at Cassie and gave open thanks that it was so.

Cassie loved Wilfred and tended to his every need, and the two youngsters came together as one and got married quietly up to near Eugenia Falls in Ontario and lived out their long lives in harmony and the new life in their love for each other.

Mrs Robinson thanked the Lord for this deliverance and miracle on every day of her life, her child called back from the fields of the departed, from the very fields of the dead, the corpses disported promiscuous in the hope of a glorious resurrection which Wilfred had indeed experienced.

Wilfred and Cassie put the mezuzah on the doorpost of their home, so that everybody going in and coming out would be blessed in everything that they did, in or out.

Cassie never learned how to read the scroll within, not that anybody did, but she clutched the Saxon Seal close to her for all of her days, precious to the memories of Birdy.

She told Wilfred all about Birdy, and they passed the Saxon Seal on down in the family amongst their several children to finally go back to the Seminary in Gettysburg, when circumstances dictated, when time permitted, when God allowed.

POSTSCRIPT

THE WHITE HOUSE
WASHINGTON D.C.
1st-3rd JULY 2013

The Central Post Office of Washington, District of Columbia, receives, on every day of the year, hundreds of packages and thousands of letters addressed to the President of the United States of America at his place of residence, The White House, 1600 Pennsylvania Avenue.
On most days, these numbers vary only a little, with an increased number of items mainly arriving on birthdays of a member of the First Family, especially the First Lady. Michelle Obama is very popular right across America.
Christmas Day always heralds the greatest number of posted items for The White House, with the Fourth of July, America's Day of Independence, running a good second.
On July First, 2013, a small package arrived for the attention of President Obama; the Sender clearly named, Recorded Delivery employed to trace the progress of this gift thus presented on this day of days, all details displayed openly for easy verification and efficient despatch.
No postal item is ever delivered directly to The White House.
All packages and letters and missives of any kind, addressed to anybody who is anybody at 1600 Pennsylvania Avenue, are carefully filtered by an undisclosed number of security units and sections and departments prior to being forwarded further on up the line.
This, of course, is exactly as it should be.
All letters, parcels, and packets receive equal treatment.

Some of these, a small number, may eventually make it all the way to the very desk of President Obama inside the Oval Office.

Most do not.

But this item was marked out as a winner almost from the start.

The initial assessment of the package, once it had been scanned and tested and pronounced good and clean and pure and snow white, was that it contained a brief covering letter and two constituent parts- a single sheet of paper and a small book.

There was a flurry of excited interest from the more expert personnel who were lucky enough to be on duty at the time, and they summoned their fellows and colleagues and eventually dozens of highly qualified people were strolling to and fro and giving opinions. Nobody involved was backward in coming forward.

It was the sheet of paper which initially excited comment. But then the book was glanced at, and bore impressive fruit.

Presently, the two "constituent parts", or CPs, were sent off to the Smithsonian Institute, and the Research Department of that Museum consulted. A meeting, urgently convened, swiftly arranged a further meeting to consider all of the important matters which now required examination, and the relevant experts were alerted and brought up to speed. Somebody particular arrived from Baltimore. Academic heads pondered, and theories were rehearsed, polished, practiced, and delivered.

Everybody wanted in on this one.

Everybody had a view, and everybody also believed that their own personal opinion was correct.

Everybody was happy about that fact, and even happier to say that "their" ideas were deserving of the greatest praise, all free from prejudice and pork barrel.

If these "CPs" held up under scrutiny, held water, baked bread, cohered, added up, and just generally was all right every which way you looked at it, then it was "their" baby.

"They" would have to be given the privilege and the honour of pronouncing any pronouncement that was likely to be pronounced.

Happily, the ten points of the Law, concerning possession, were not in the least troubled, let alone disputed.

Ownership was not in question.

The package was addressed to the President, Mr Barack H. Obama, and that fact settled all controversy.

If these things were genuine, and even if that "if" was a big "if", then the President would be looking at them on his private desk come sunup, come sunup, come sunup, tomorrow or the day after that, and yes, that sounded just about right!

On the Fourth of July!

When all of the panel of distinguished magnificos had been consulted (ranging abroad so as to encompass certain individuals as far afield as Erfurt in Germany, London in England, and not very far away at all, at Gettysburg in Pennsylvania) and when all of the "if's" had been fulfilled in positivity, the venerable Trustees and Management of the Smithsonian Institute put all of their metaphorical eggs into one basket in the person of a modest gentleman rejoicing in the title of Sir Daniel Baker, of Deptford, in London, in England.

Astoundingly, he was a Brit, afloat in a sea of Americans, and he had reached the top of a very tall tree, distinguished (and dominated) by hundreds and hundred of academics, most of whom hailed from Yale and Harvard and Berkeley.

However, he unquestionably (and indisputably) held pre-eminence on the matter of the writing skills, habits, and peculiarities of Queen Alexandrina Victoria of the United Kingdom- 1819 to 1901, and he could state with absolute authority that this was her most royal autograph, right there, right there, right there.

Putting this, their best (albeit British) foot, forward, Sir Daniel Baker was selected to attend The White House on the Fourth of July 2013 to lay certain information before The President of the United States of America.

All of this was certified as good and pure and truthful, right down to the venerable socks worn by this emissary of Academia.

The first fact presented by Sir Daniel Baker was that President Obama, on behalf of these great United States of America, would undoubtedly be pleased to acknowledge his and their heartfelt appreciations, inasmuch that a Mrs Tara Costello of Owen Sound, Ontario, Canada, had shown great kindness in returning one small book and a single page of handwritten prose to The White House.

In so doing, she was discharging a family debt which had begun almost one hundred and fifty years before.

And it was right here, right here, right here, in the Oval Office and in the hands and in the lawful possession of President Obama himself, and well in time for some festivities upcoming in the November approaching. All details had been verified by the most learned authorities in the world; the pedigree of these treasures was factually established, and nobody could decry them as false. The tiny book was of German, in fact, Saxon origin. It had been personally signed by three persons.

The book was indeed the very first copy, the very, very first copy, of the Bible translated into the German tongue.

Signed, sealed, delivered- Martin Luther, of Erfurt, Saxony, Germany.
Also, it had been graced with another name- Victoria Regina of the United Kingdom, and with the simple words "in Piety".
Below, last but by no means least, a simple scrawl- "Abraham Lincoln".
The single sheet of paper was a handcrafted original, word perfect, of the Gettysburg Address, in the handwriting of, and signed by, President Abraham Lincoln.
It was all genuine, verifiably so.
These treasures were now presented in grateful memory of those good people, known and unknown, who had accomplished this amazing achievement- the coherence of truth, justice, mercy, and freedom, wrought over five centuries of time as measured on the clock. As the enormity of the epiphany unfolded, President Barack Obama heard a snatch of song in his mind. It had been sung to him first in childhood, an old Negro Spiritual. Elvis Presley had sung it, he remembered. Doctor Maya Angelou had leaned across the buttered toast and sung it to him above the breakfast table, four and a bit years previously when he had been sworn in as President.
Now, with these written proofs before him, it resonated again, on this day of days-

"When Israel was in Egypt's land
Let my people go
Oppressed so hard they could not stand
Let my people go.
Go down, Moses
Way down in Egypts land
Tell ole' Pharaoh
Let my people go."

Printed in Poland
by Amazon Fulfillment
Poland Sp. z o.o., Wrocław